nickelodeon

THE LOUD HOUSE

3 IN 1 #2

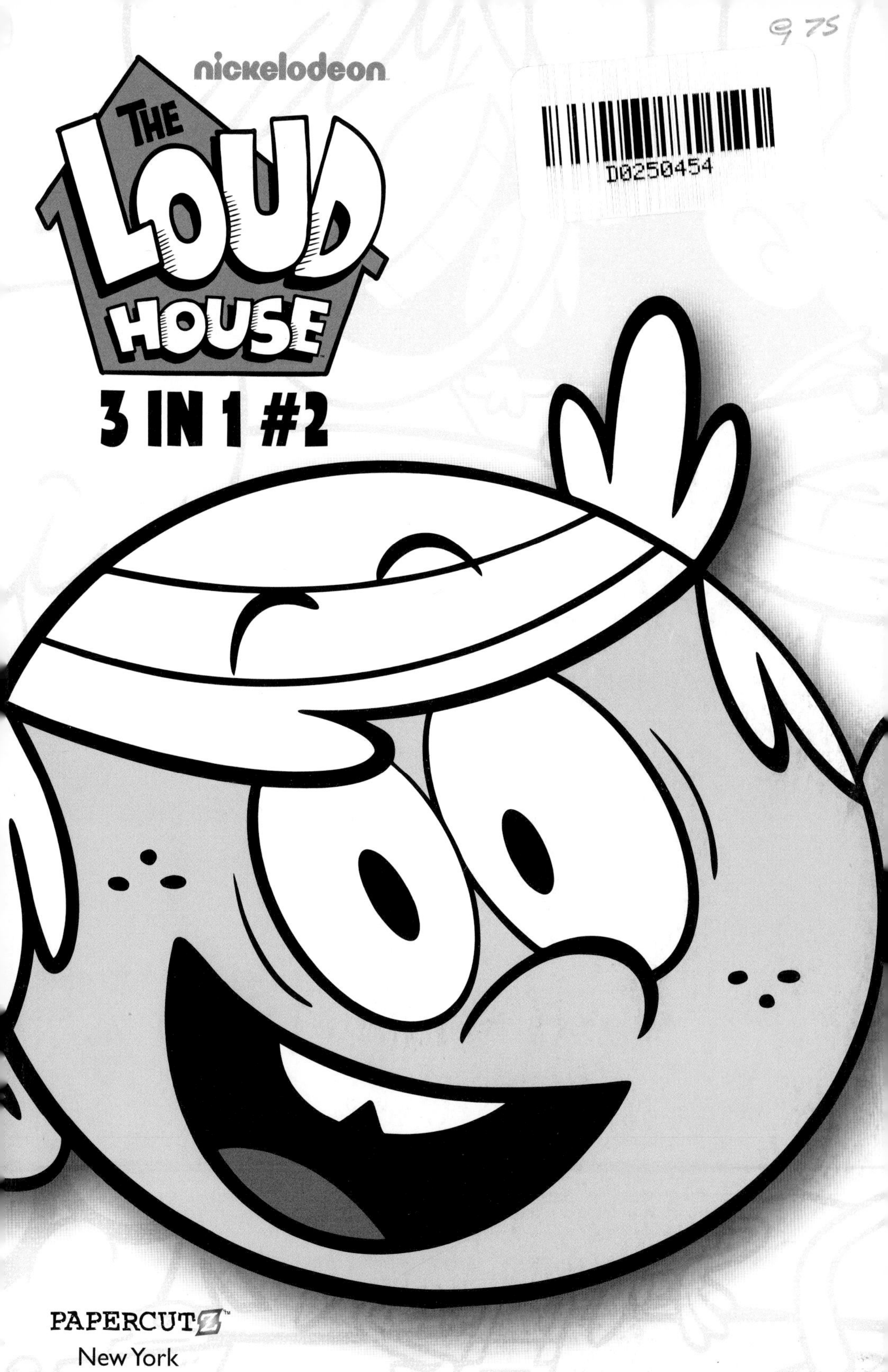

PAPERCUTZ
New York

nickelodeon GRAPHIC NOVELS AVAILABLE FROM PAPERCUTZ

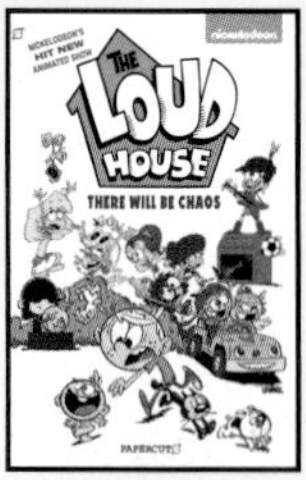
THE LOUD HOUSE
THERE WILL BE CHAOS

THE LOUD HOUSE #1 "There Will Be Chaos"

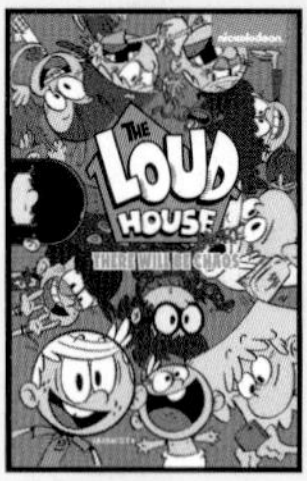
THE LOUD HOUSE

THE LOUD HOUSE #2 "There Will Be More Chaos"

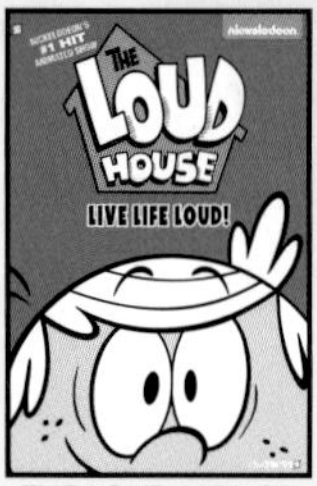
THE LOUD HOUSE
LIVE LIFE LOUD!

THE LOUD HOUSE #3 "Live Life Loud!"

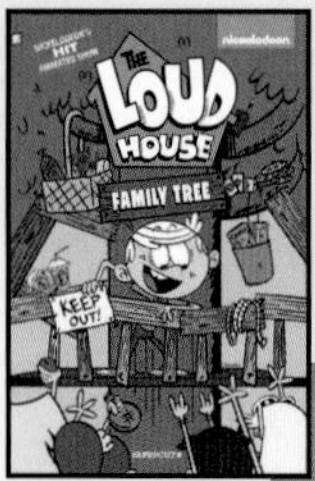
THE LOUD HOUSE
FAMILY TREE
KEEP OUT!

THE LOUD HOUSE #4 "Family Tree"

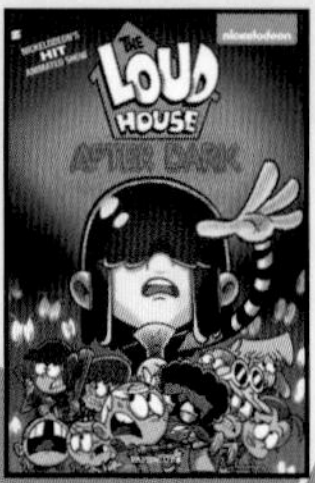
THE LOUD HOUSE
AFTER DARK

THE LOUD HOUSE #5 "After Dark"

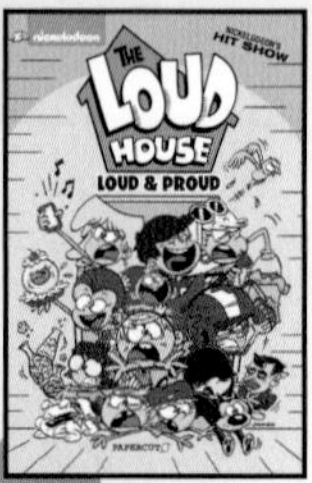
THE LOUD HOUSE
LOUD & PROUD

THE LOUD HOUSE #6 "Loud and Proud"

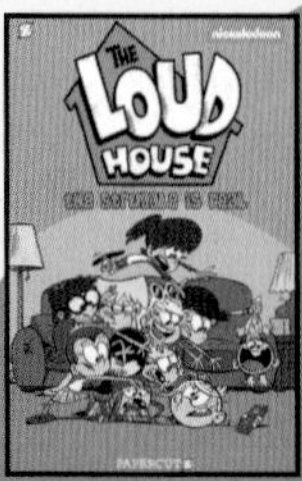
THE LOUD HOUSE

THE LOUD HOUSE #7 "The Struggle is Real"

COMING SOON

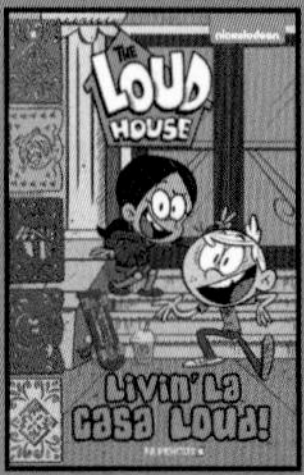
THE LOUD HOUSE
Livin' La Casa Loud!

THE LOUD HOUSE #8 "Livin' La Casa Loud"

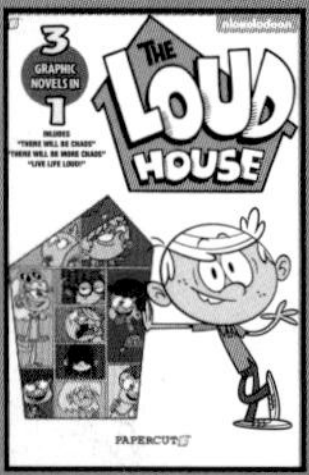
3 GRAPHIC NOVELS IN 1
THE LOUD HOUSE

THE LOUD HOUSE 3 IN 1 #1

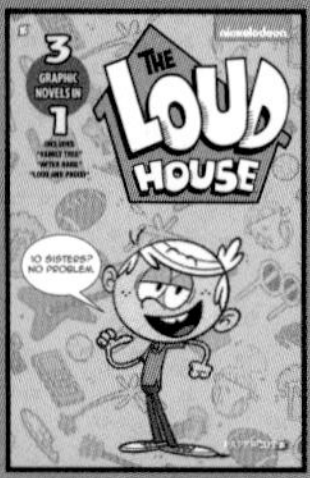
3 GRAPHIC NOVELS IN 1
THE LOUD HOUSE
10 SISTERS? NO PROBLEM.

THE LOUD HOUSE 3 IN 1 #2

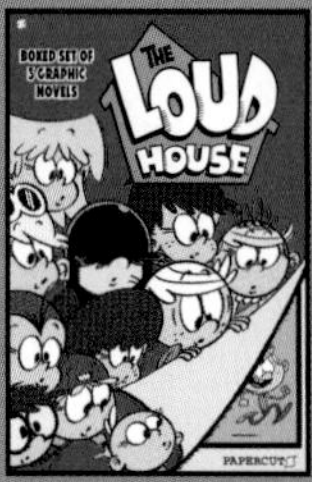
BOXED SET OF 3 GRAPHIC NOVELS
THE LOUD HOUSE

THE LOUD HOUSE BOXED SET $23.99

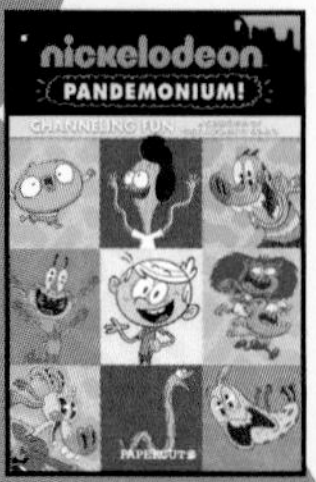
nickelodeon
PANDEMONIUM!

NICKELODEON PANDEMONIUM #1 "Channeling Fun"

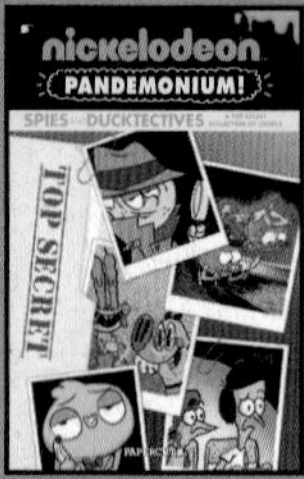
nickelodeon
PANDEMONIUM!
TOP SECRET

NICKELODEON PANDEMONIUM #2 "Spies and Ducktectives"

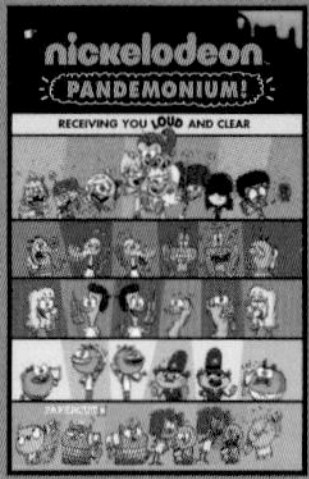
nickelodeon
PANDEMONIUM!

NICKELODEON PANDEMONIUM #3 "Receiving You Loud and Clear"

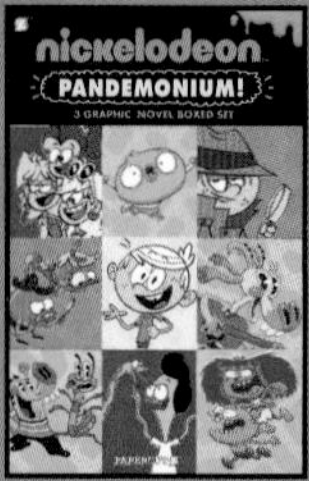
nickelodeon
PANDEMONIUM!

NICKELODEON PANDEMONIUM BOXED SET $24.99

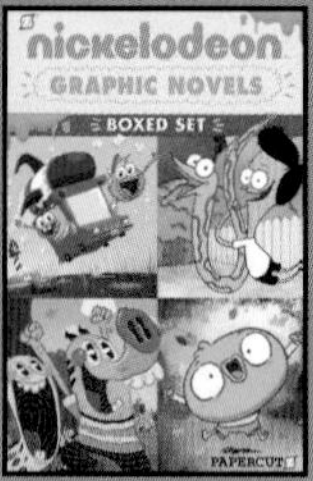
nickelodeon
GRAPHIC NOVELS
BOXED SET

NICKELODEON BOXED SET $31.99

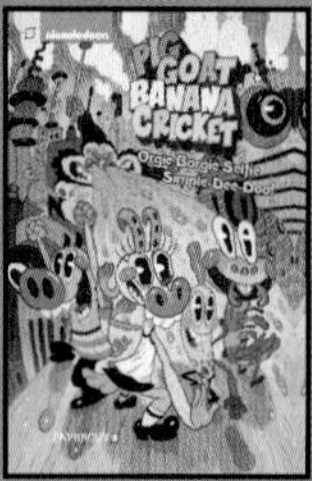
PIG GOAT BANANA CRICKET

PIG GOAT BANANA CRICKET #1 "Orgle Borgle Selfie Simple-Dee Doo!"

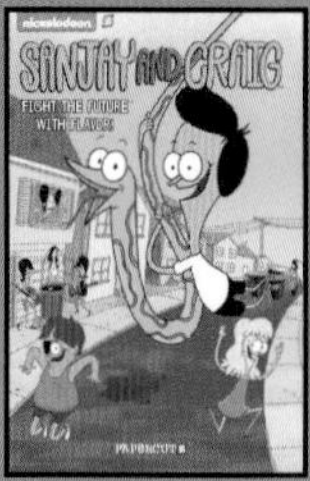
SANJAY AND CRAIG

SANJAY AND CRAIG #1 "Fight the Future with Flavor"

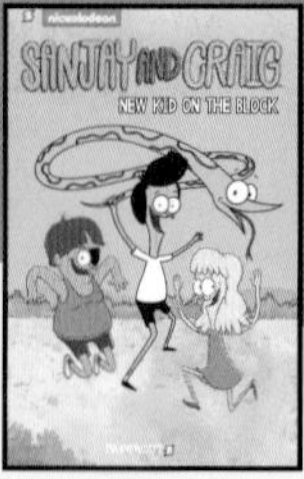
SANJAY AND CRAIG
NEW KID ON THE BLOCK

SANJAY AND CRAIG #2 "New Kid on the Block"

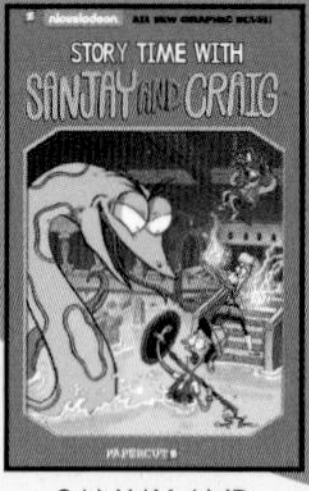
STORY TIME WITH
SANJAY AND CRAIG

SANJAY AND CRAIG #3 "Story Time with Sanjay and Craig"

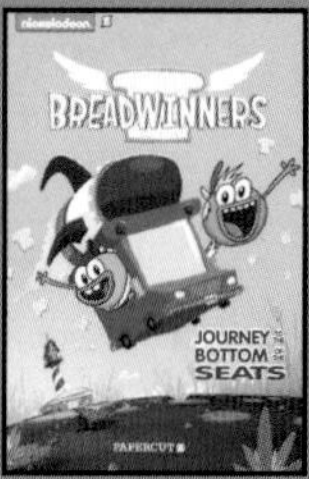
BREADWINNERS
JOURNEY TO THE BOTTOM OF THE SEATS

BREADWINNERS #1 "Journey to the Bottom of the Seats"

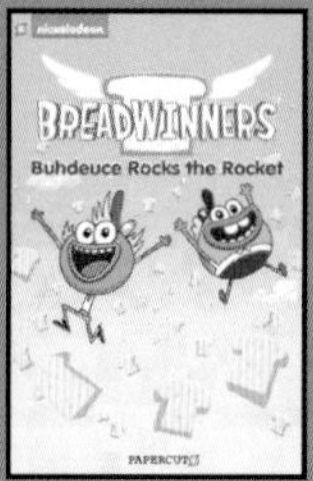
BREADWINNERS
Buhdeuce Rocks the Rocket

BREADWINNERS #2 "Buhdeuce Rocks the Rocket"

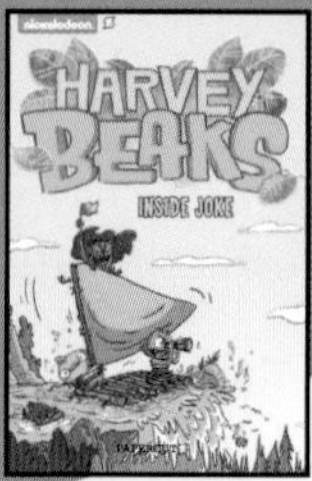
HARVEY BEAKS
INSIDE JOKE

HARVEY BEAKS #1 "Inside Joke"

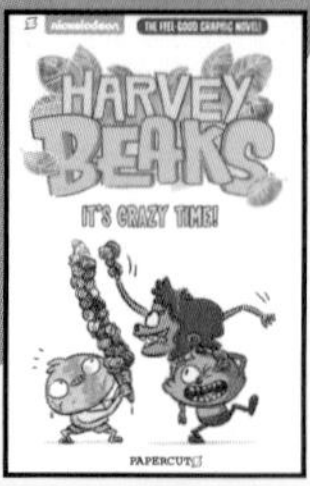
HARVEY BEAKS
IT'S CRAZY TIME!

HARVEY BEAKS #2 "It's Crazy Time"

Nickelodeon graphic novels are available for $7.99 each in paperback, $12.99 each in hardcover. NICKELODEON PANDEMONIUM #3 is $8.99 each in paperback, $13.99 each in hardcover. BOXED SETS differ in price. Available from booksellers everywhere. You can also order online from Papercutz.com, or call 1-800-886-1223, Monday through Friday, 9-5 EST. MC, Visa, and AmEx accepted. To order by mail, please add $5.00 for postage and handling for the first book ordered, $1.00 for each additional book and make check payable to NBM Publishing. Send to: Papercutz, 160 Broadway, Suite 700, East Wing, New York, NY 10038.

Nickelodeon graphic novels are also available digitally wherever e-books are sold.

"TREEHOUSE OF SOLITUDE"
Sammie Crowley—Writer
David Teas—Artist, Letterer, Colorist
7

"HAI-POO"
Jared Morgan—
Writer, Artist, Letterer, Colorist
11

"STARVING"
Whitney Wetta—Writer
Ashley Kliment—Artist, Letterer, Colorist
12

"COOKING WITH THE CASAGRANDES"
Gabrielle Dolbey—Writer, Artist, Letterer,
Colorist
14

"CODE CRISIS"
Whitney Wetta—Writer
Jordan Koch—Artist, Letterer, Colorist
17

"DISJOINT CUSTODY"
Sammie Crowley—Writer
Angela Entzminger—Artist, Letterer, Colorist
19

"THE LOUD JOURNEY"
Diem Doan—Writer, Artist, Letterer, Colorist
25

"WORKED UP"
Sammie Crowley & Whitney Wetta—Writers
Ida Hem—Artist, Letterer
Hallie Lal—Colorist
28

"MAYBE IT'S NATURAL"
JARED MORGAN—Writer, Artist, Letterer,
Colorist
33

"SWISHFUL THINKING"
Andrew Brooks—Writer
Gabrielle Dolbey—Artist, Letterer, Colorist
34

"SITUATION SOUFFLÉ"
Sammie Crowley—Writer
Ida Hem—Artist, Colorist, Letterer
Hallie Lal—Colorist
37

"TOUGH HOOKY"
Jared Morgan—Writer, Artist, Letterer,
Colorist
40

"SORE PLAYERS"
Diem Doan—Writer, Artist, Letterer
Gabrielle Dolbey—Colorist
43

"CITIZEN LOUD"
Angela Entzminger—Writer, Artist, Letterer,
Colorist
45

"BABY BREAK"
Diem Doan—Writer, Artist, Letterer
Gabrielle Dolbey—Colorist
48

"LEAVE A PENNY, TAKE A PENNY"
Jared Morgan—Writer, Artist, Letterer,
Colorist
49

"DRESSED OUT"
Andrew Brooks—Writer
Ashley Kliment—Artist, Letterer, Colorist
51

"LUCY'S ABCs OF THE LOUD HOUSE"
Karla Sakas Shropshire—Writer
Kiernan Sjursen-Lien—Artist, Letterer
Amanda Rynda—Colorist
53

JAMES SALERNO – Sr. Art Director/Nickelodeon
JAYJAY JACKSON – Design/Production
JEFF WHITMAN – Editor
JOAN HILTY – Comics Editor/Nickelodeon
DAWN GUZZO, SEAN GANTKA, DANA CLUVERIUS, MOLLIE FREILICH, and ANGELA ENTZMINGER—Special Thanks
JIM SALICRUP
Editor-in-Chief

ISBN: 978-1-5458-0334-9

Printed in Canada
August 2019

Distributed by Macmillan
First Printing

LORI LOUD
THE OLDEST (17)

LENI LOUD
THE FASHIONISTA (16)

LUNA LOUD
THE ROCK STAR (15)

LUAN LOUD
THE JOKESTER (14)

LYNN LOUD
THE ATHLETE (13)

106

"BREAKFAST IS READY!"
Kevin Sullivan—Writer
Angela Entzminger—
Artist, Colorist
Ida Hem—
Letterer

59

"GHOST OF THE TOWN"
Sammie Crowley—Writer
Ari Castleton—Artist
Gabrielle Dolbey—
Colorist
Ida Hem—Letterer

105

"BOYS
IN THE
ATTIC"
Sammie Crowley—
Writer
Ari Castleton—Artist
Gabrielle Dolbey—Colorist
Ida Hem—Letterer

65

"DRAWING
A PRANK"
Andrew Brooks—
Writer
David Teas—Artist, Colorist
Ida Hem—Letterer

99

"TUB TIME"
Kevin Sullivan—
Writer
Ashley Kliment—Artist,
Letterer
Colton Davis—Colorist
Ida Hem—Letterer

70

"MIDNIGHT
MELODY"
Hannah Watanabe-
Rocco—Writer, Artist,
Colorist
Ida Hem—Letterer

93

"THE PRINCESS AND THE
PLEA"
Hannah Watanabe-Rocco—
Writer
Isaiah Kim—Artist
Lauren Abhay—
Colorist
Ida Hem—
Letterer

75

"GOAL-ORIENTED"
Andrew Brooks—Writer
Gabrielle Dolbey—
Artist, Colorist
Ida Hem—
Letterer

"BUSTED!"
Sammie
Crowley—Writer
Ari Castleton—Artist
Gabrielle Dolbey—Colorist
Ida Hem—
Letterer

"GHOST IN THE
BASEMENT"
Sammie Crowley—Writer
Ari Castleton—Artist
Gabrielle Dolbey—
Colorist
Ida Hem—
Letterer

92

"SHIPS IN THE
NIGHT"
Sammie Crowley—
Writer
Gizelle Orbino (Lisa's
room), Marcus Velazquez
(Dream sequence)—Artists,
Colorists
Ida Hem—Letterer

"THE EARLY
BIRDS AND THE
WORMS"
Kevin Sullivan—
Writer
Ida Hem—Artist, Letterer
Hallie Lal—Colorist

80

86

81

WE'RE LOUD
EVERY
NIGHT....

LINCOLN LOUD
THE MIDDLE CHILD (11)

LUCY LOUD
THE EMO (8)

LANA LOUD
THE TOMBOY (6)

LOLA LOUD
THE BEAUTY QUEEN (6)

LISA LOUD
THE GENIUS (4)

LILY LOUD
THE BABY (15 MONTHS)

155

"BRAG RACE"
Andrew Brooks—Writer
Gizelle Orbino—Artist,
Colorist
Wilson Ramos Jr.—
Letterer

110

"BUCKLE UP"
Sammie Crowley—Writer
Angela Zhang—Artist,
Colorist
Wilson Ramos Jr.—
Letterer

152

"AN
UNEXPECTED
JOURNEY"
Sammie Crowley—Writer
Colton Davis—Artist
Emily Merl—Colorist
Wilson Ramos Jr.—
Letterer

112

"MALL
FLOP"
Andrew Brooks—
Writer
Isaiah Kim—Artist, Colorist
Wilson Ramos Jr.
—Letterer

147

"I'M
GONNA
FINE YOU"
Whitney Wetta—
Writer
Suzannah Rowntree—Artist
Lauren Abhay—Colorist
Wilson Ramos Jr.—Letterer

116

"BANDS ON
THE RUN"
Kevin Sullivan—Writer
Erin Hyde—Artist, Colorist
Wilson Ramos Jr.—Letterer

142

"HATTA BOY"
Scott Tuft—Writer
Brian Smith—Artist,
Colorist
Wilson Ramos Jr.—
Letterer

122

"THE PAGEANT TRAP"
Kevin Sullivan—Writer
Angela Zhang—
Artist, Colorist
Wilson Ramos Jr.—
Letterer

"THE
GOOD OLD
DAYS"
Sammie Crowley—Writer
Ida Hem—Artist,
Letterer
Hallie Lal—
Colorist

"HURRY UP AND
WAIT"
Sammie Crowley—Writer
Colton Davis—Artist
Emily Merl—Colorist
Wilson Ramos Jr.
—Letterer

136

"VAN GO"
Sammie Crowley—
Writer
Colton Davis—Artist
Emily Merl—Colorist
Wilson Ramos Jr.—
Letterer

127

"DOWN IN
THE DUMPS"
Angela
Entzminger—
Writer
Agny Innocente—
Artist
Gabrielle Dolbey—
Colorist
Wilson Ramos Jr.—
Letterer

"STAGE
FRIGHT"
Hannah
Watanabe-Rocco
—Writer
Melissa Kleynowski
—Artist
Karolyn Moses—Colorist
Wilson Ramos Jr.—Letterer

135

132

128

....AND EVERY
DAY!

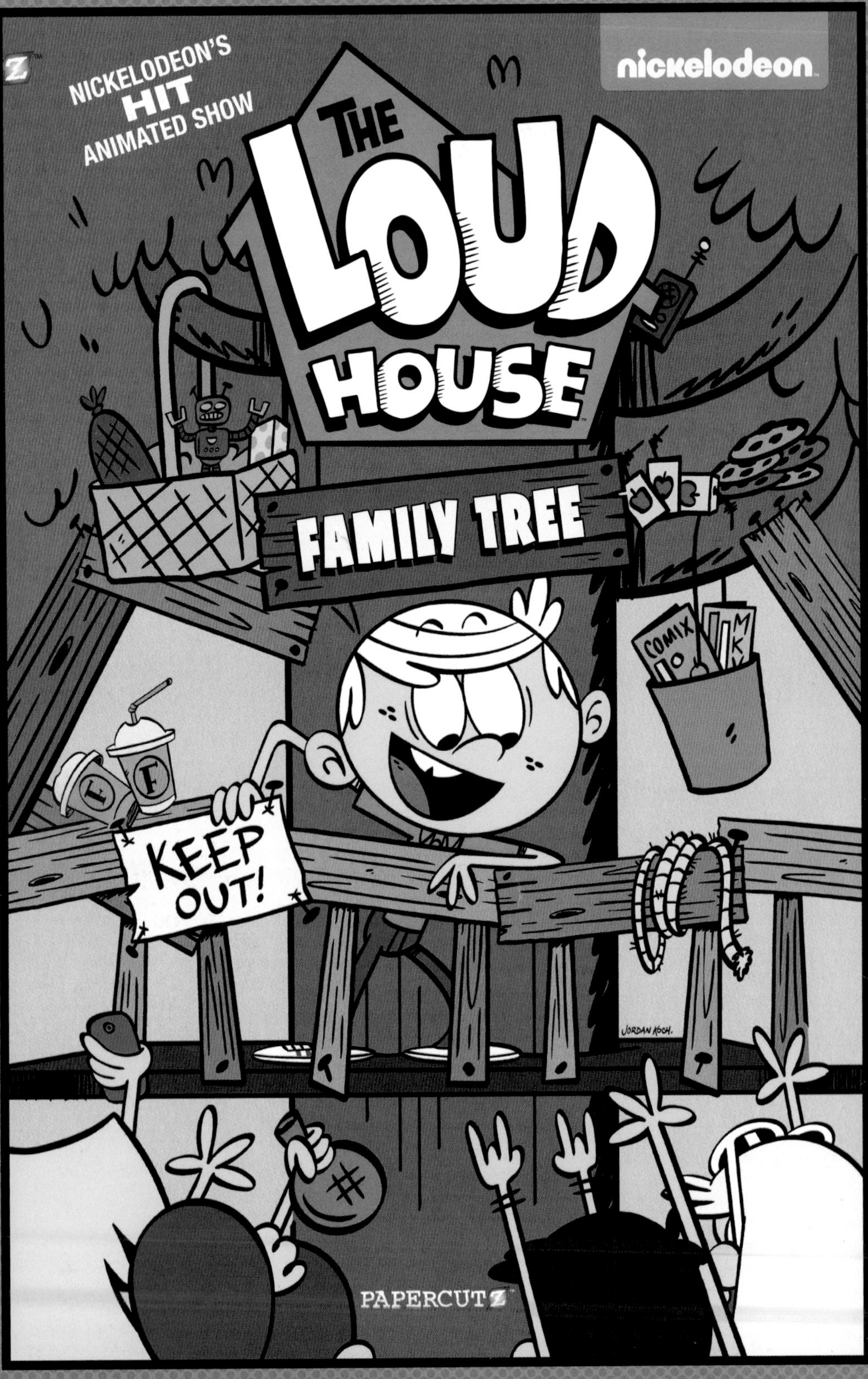
NICKELODEON'S
HIT
ANIMATED SHOW
nickelodeon
THE LOUD HOUSE
FAMILY TREE
COMIX
KEEP OUT!
JORDAN KOCH.
PAPERCUTZ

THE LOUD HOUSE #4 Cover Art by Jordan Koch

"TREEHOUSE OF SOLITUDE"

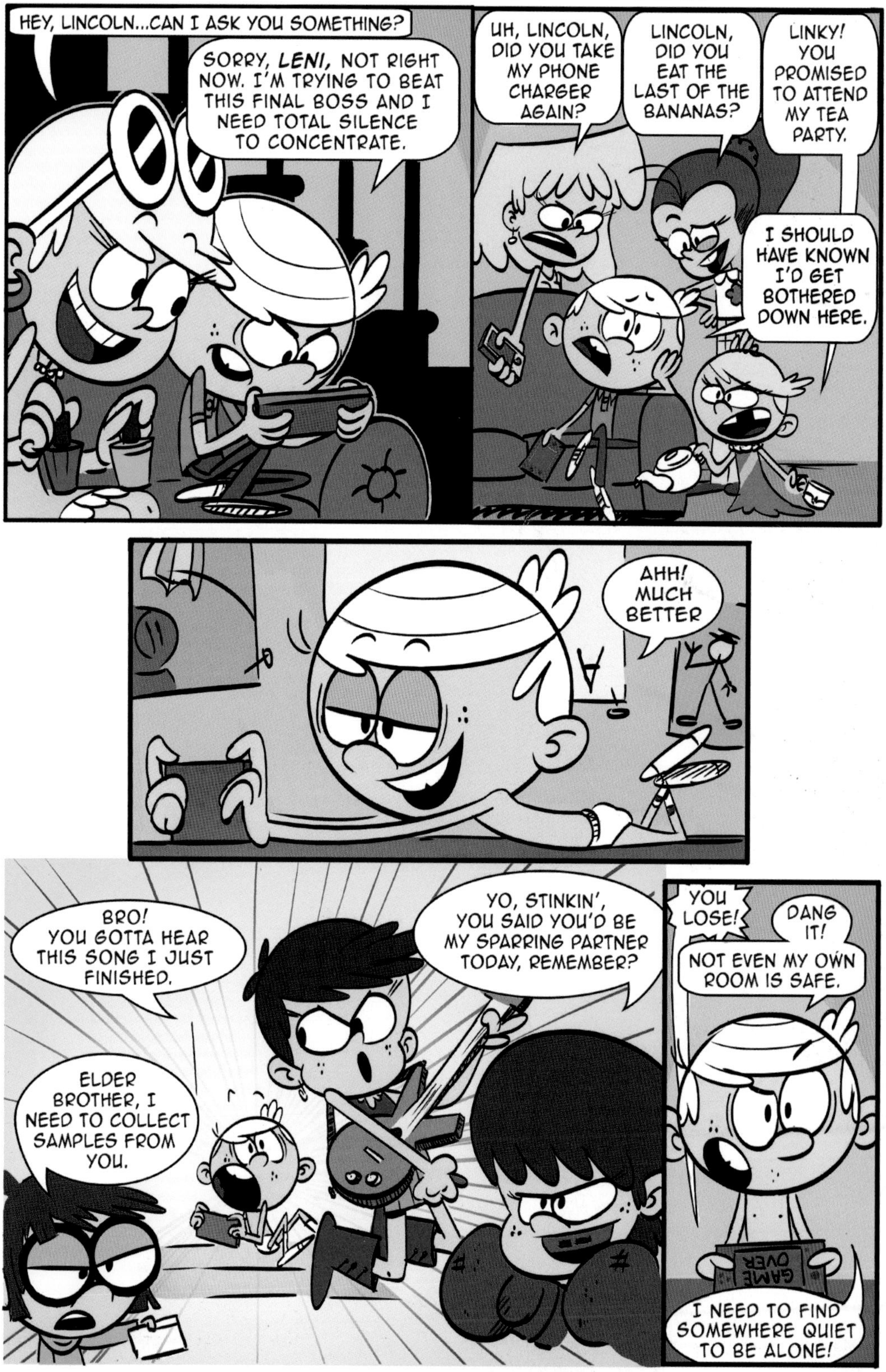

HEY, LINCOLN...CAN I ASK YOU SOMETHING?
SORRY, *LENI,* NOT RIGHT NOW. I'M TRYING TO BEAT THIS FINAL BOSS AND I NEED TOTAL SILENCE TO CONCENTRATE.
UH, LINCOLN, DID YOU TAKE MY PHONE CHARGER AGAIN?
LINCOLN, DID YOU EAT THE LAST OF THE BANANAS?
LINKY! YOU PROMISED TO ATTEND MY TEA PARTY.
I SHOULD HAVE KNOWN I'D GET BOTHERED DOWN HERE.
AHH! MUCH BETTER
BRO! YOU GOTTA HEAR THIS SONG I JUST FINISHED.
YO, STINKIN', YOU SAID YOU'D BE MY SPARRING PARTNER TODAY, REMEMBER?
ELDER BROTHER, I NEED TO COLLECT SAMPLES FROM YOU.
YOU LOSE!
DANG IT!
NOT EVEN MY OWN ROOM IS SAFE.
GAME OVER
I NEED TO FIND SOMEWHERE QUIET TO BE ALONE!

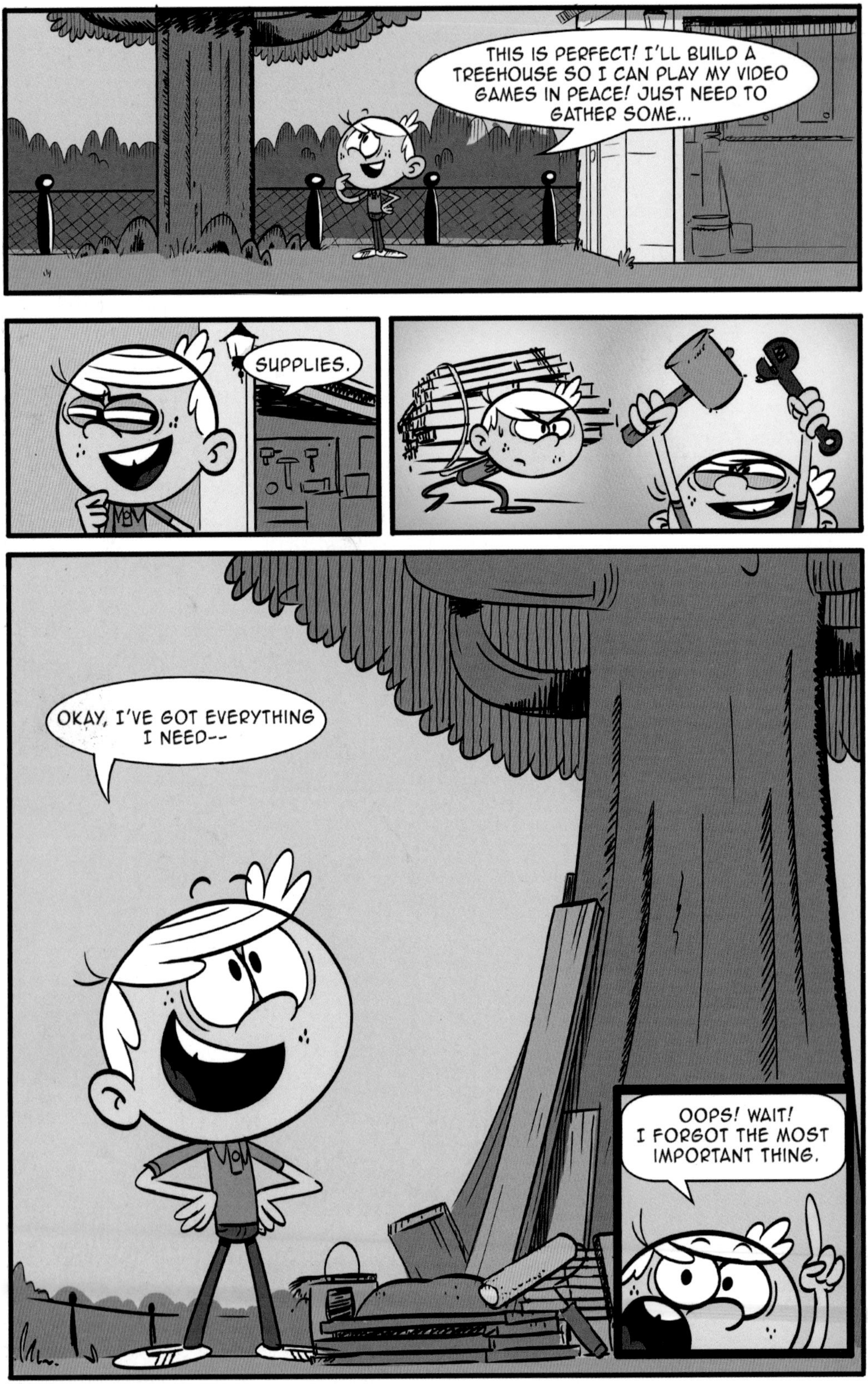
THIS IS PERFECT! I'LL BUILD A TREEHOUSE SO I CAN PLAY MY VIDEO GAMES IN PEACE! JUST NEED TO GATHER SOME...
SUPPLIES.
OKAY, I'VE GOT EVERYTHING I NEED--
OOPS! WAIT! I FORGOT THE MOST IMPORTANT THING.

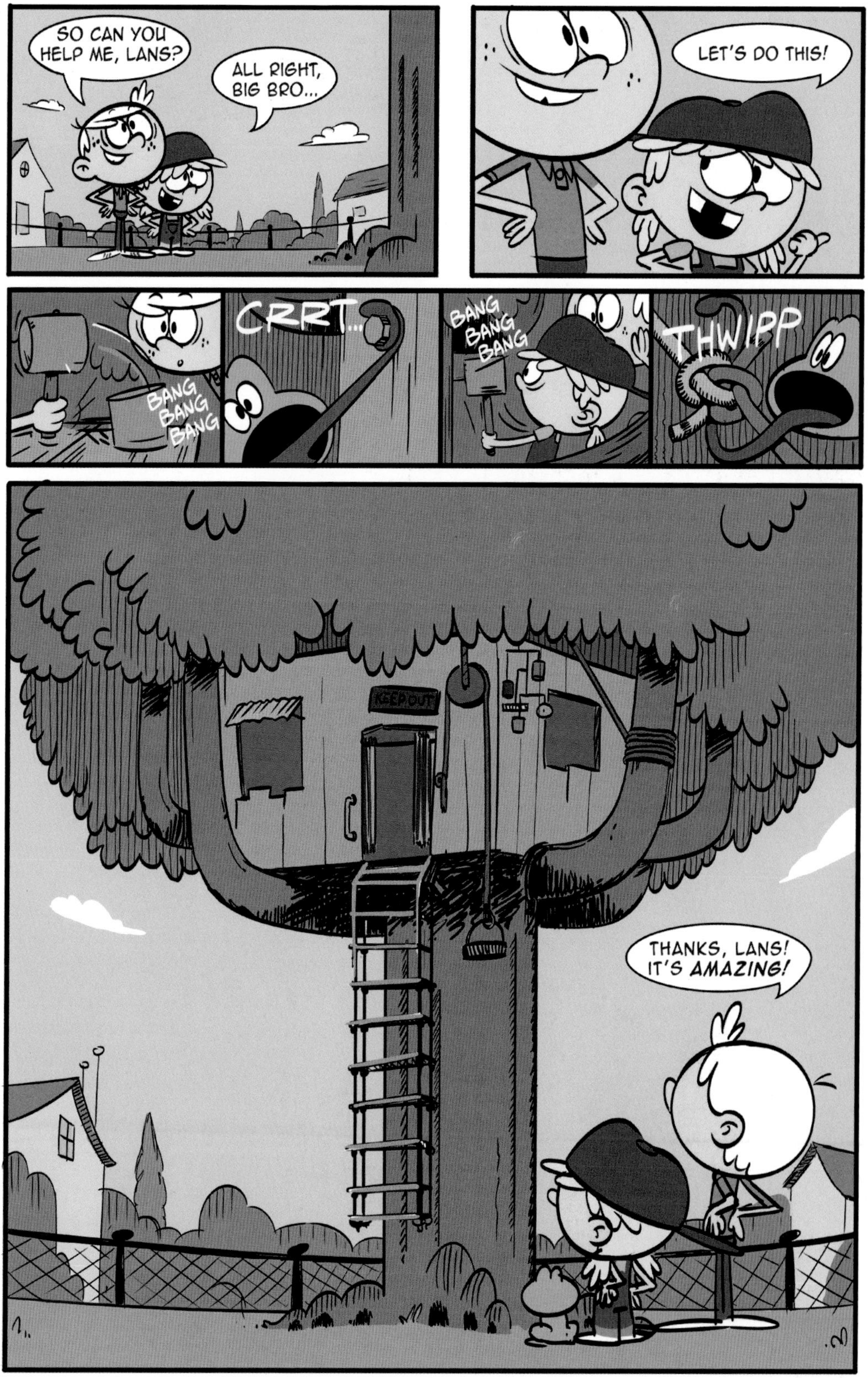
SO CAN YOU HELP ME, LANS?
ALL RIGHT, BIG BRO...
LET'S DO THIS!
BANG BANG BANG
CRRT...
BANG BANG BANG
THWIPP
KEEP OUT
THANKS, LANS! IT'S *AMAZING!*

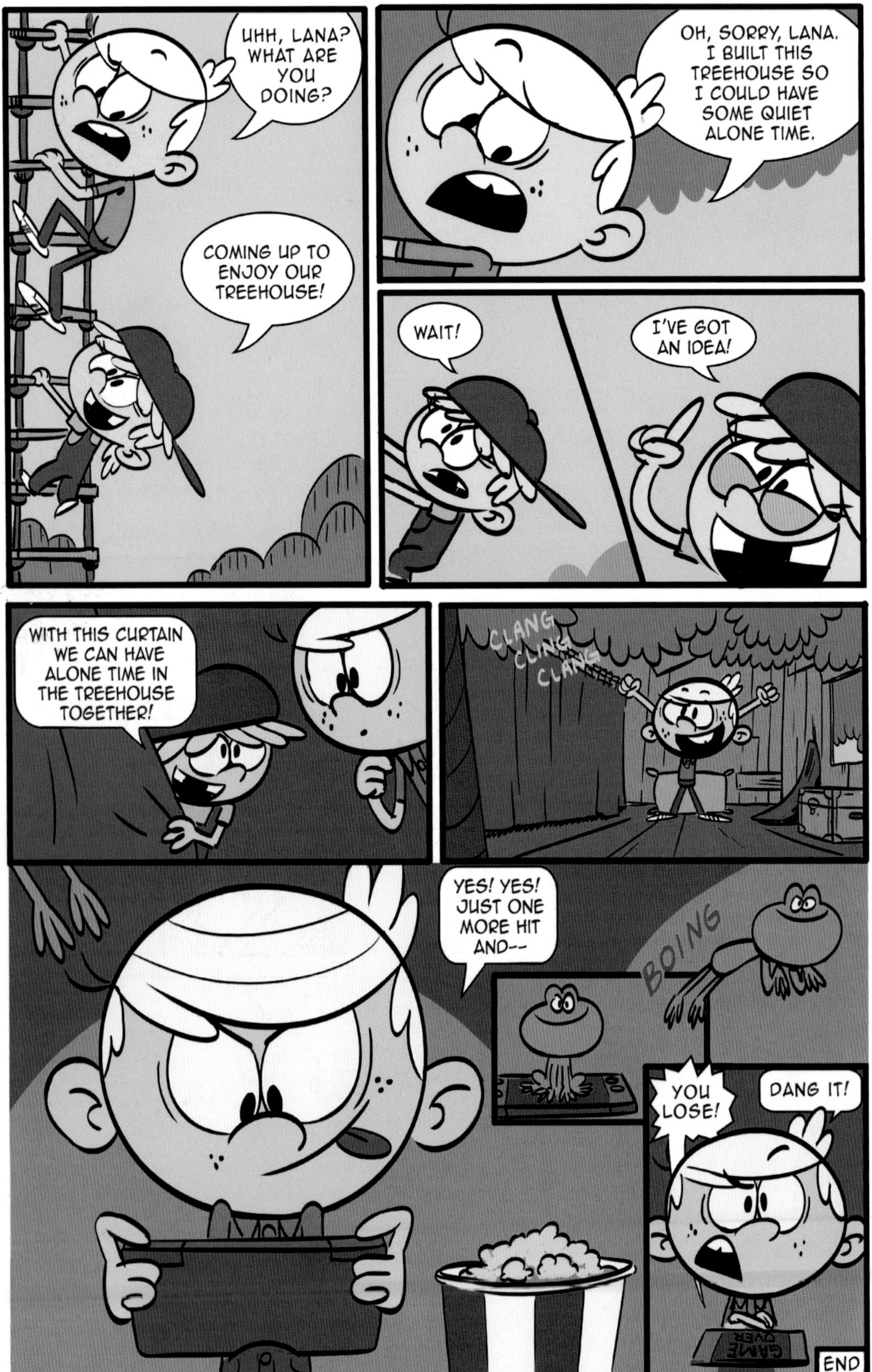
UHH, LANA? WHAT ARE YOU DOING?
COMING UP TO ENJOY OUR TREEHOUSE!
OH, SORRY, LANA. I BUILT THIS TREEHOUSE SO I COULD HAVE SOME QUIET ALONE TIME.
WAIT!
I'VE GOT AN IDEA!
WITH THIS CURTAIN WE CAN HAVE ALONE TIME IN THE TREEHOUSE TOGETHER!
CLANG
CLING
CLANG
YES! YES! JUST ONE MORE HIT AND--
BOING
YOU LOSE!
DANG IT!
GAME OVER
END

"HAI-POO"

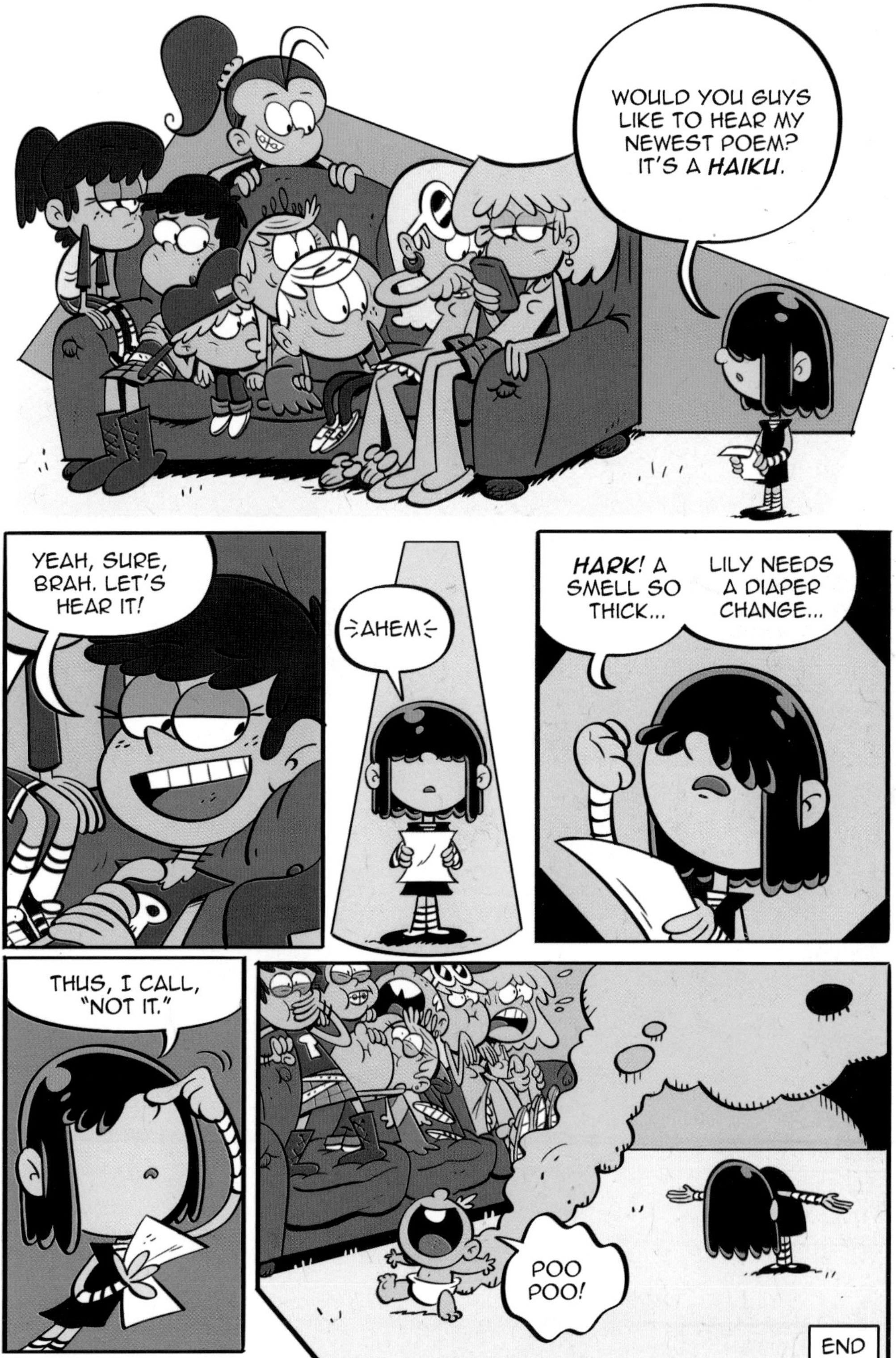
WOULD YOU GUYS LIKE TO HEAR MY NEWEST POEM? IT'S A **HAIKU**.
YEAH, SURE, BRAH. LET'S HEAR IT!
AHEM
HARK! A SMELL SO THICK...
LILY NEEDS A DIAPER CHANGE...
THUS, I CALL, "NOT IT."
POO POO!
END

"STARVING"

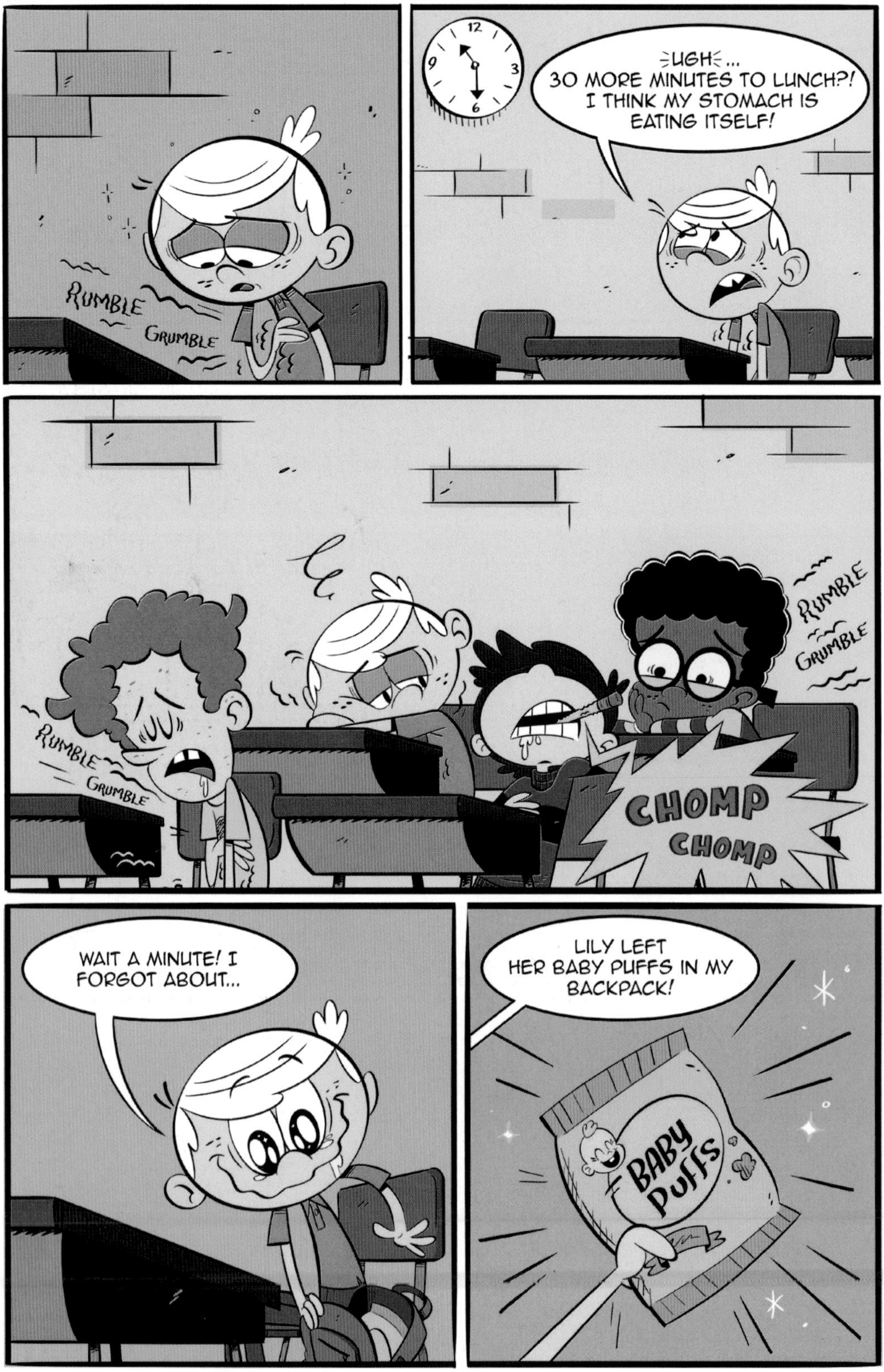
RUMBLE
GRUMBLE
UGH...
30 MORE MINUTES TO LUNCH?! I THINK MY STOMACH IS EATING ITSELF!
RUMBLE
GRUMBLE
RUMBLE
GRUMBLE
CHOMP
CHOMP
WAIT A MINUTE! I FORGOT ABOUT...
LILY LEFT HER BABY PUFFS IN MY BACKPACK!
BABY PUFFS

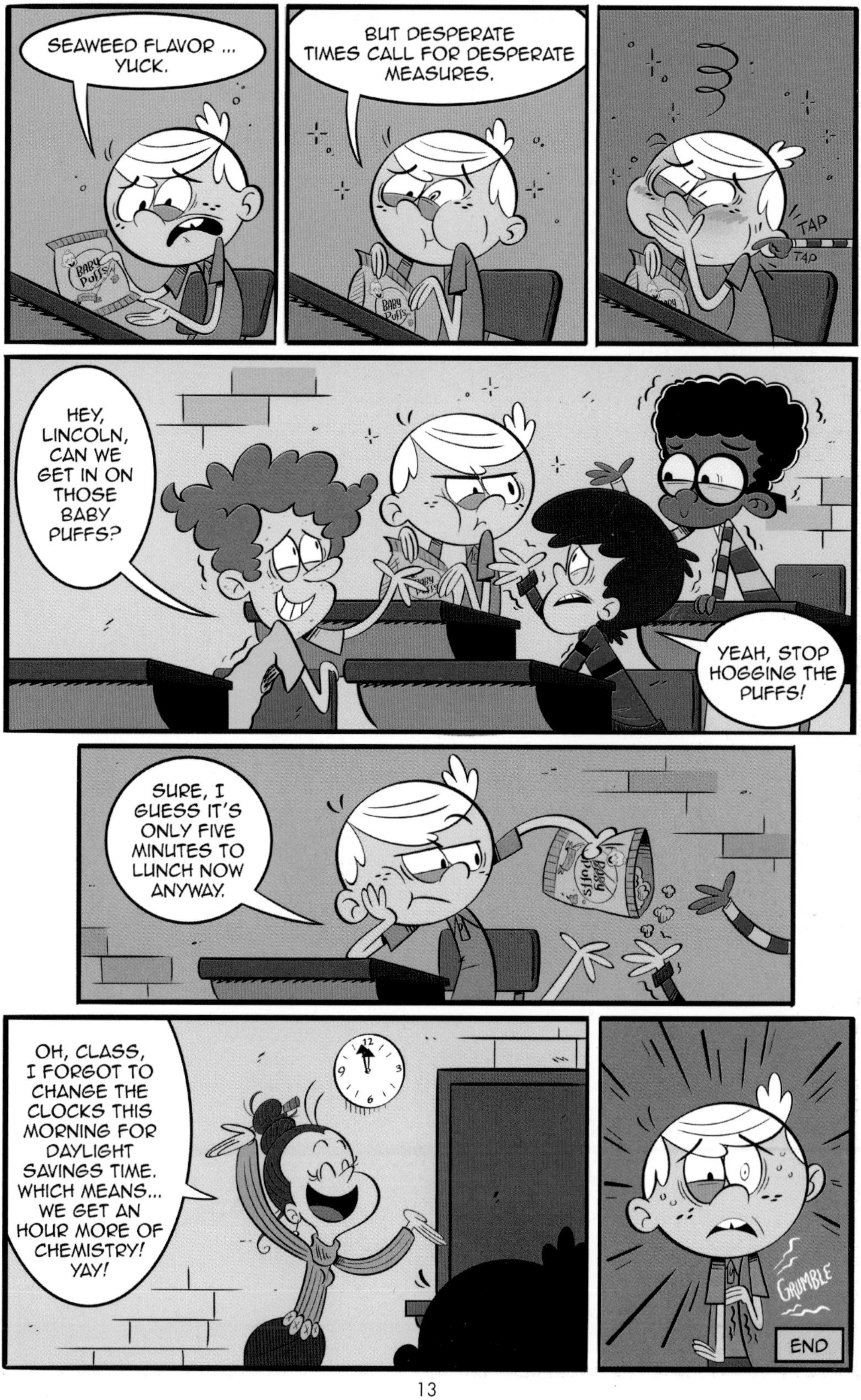
SEAWEED FLAVOR ... YUCK.
BABY PUFFS
BUT DESPERATE TIMES CALL FOR DESPERATE MEASURES.
BABY PUFFS
TAP
TAP
HEY, LINCOLN, CAN WE GET IN ON THOSE BABY PUFFS?
YEAH, STOP HOGGING THE PUFFS!
SURE, I GUESS IT'S ONLY FIVE MINUTES TO LUNCH NOW ANYWAY.
OH, CLASS, I FORGOT TO CHANGE THE CLOCKS THIS MORNING FOR DAYLIGHT SAVINGS TIME. WHICH MEANS... WE GET AN HOUR MORE OF CHEMISTRY! YAY!
GRUMBLE
END

"COOKING WITH THE CASAGRANDES"

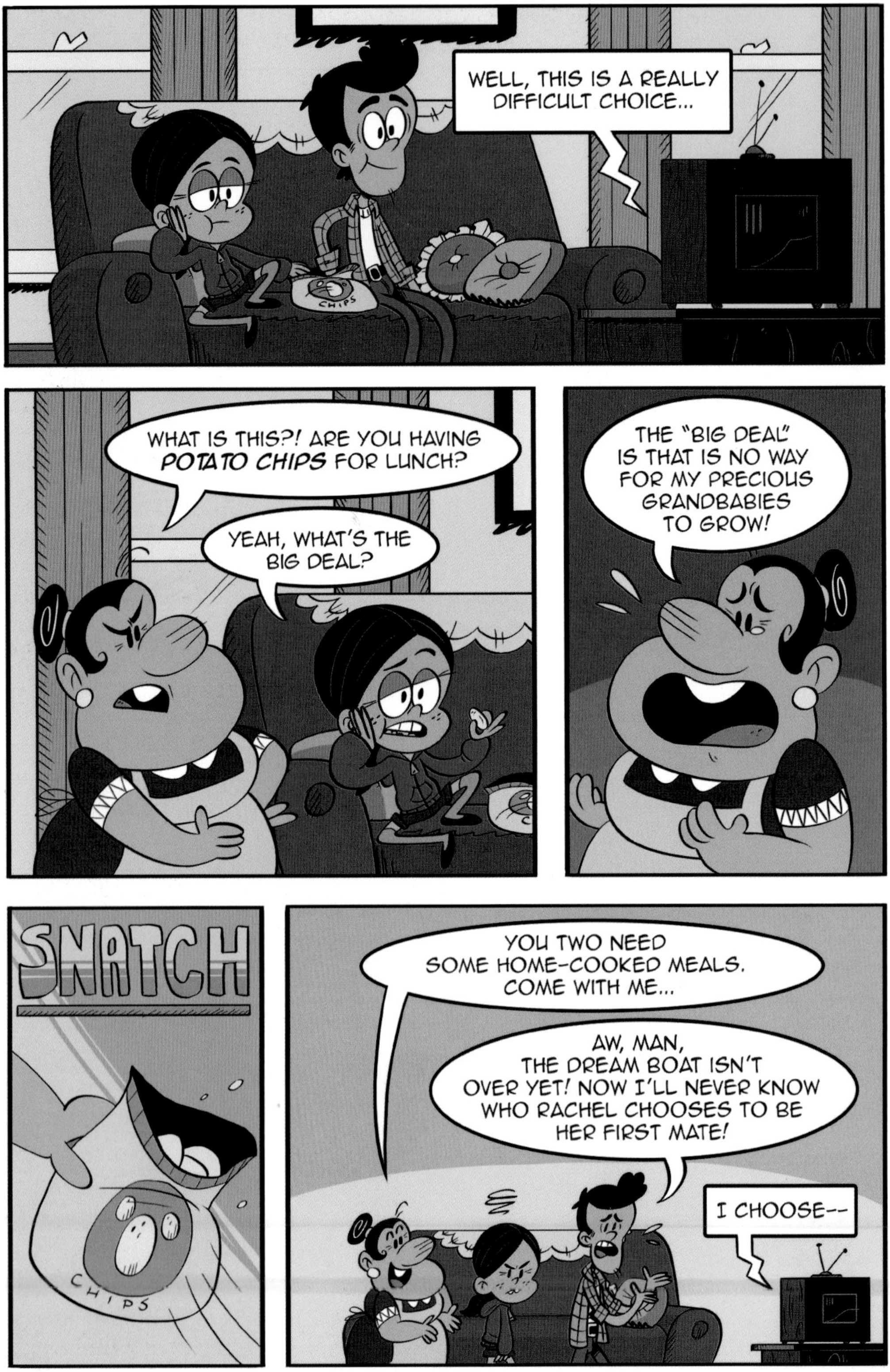
WELL, THIS IS A REALLY DIFFICULT CHOICE...
CHIPS
WHAT IS THIS?! ARE YOU HAVING *POTATO CHIPS* FOR LUNCH?
YEAH, WHAT'S THE BIG DEAL?
THE "BIG DEAL" IS THAT IS NO WAY FOR MY PRECIOUS GRANDBABIES TO GROW!
SNATCH
CHIPS
YOU TWO NEED SOME HOME-COOKED MEALS. COME WITH ME...
AW, MAN, THE DREAM BOAT ISN'T OVER YET! NOW I'LL NEVER KNOW WHO RACHEL CHOOSES TO BE HER FIRST MATE!
I CHOOSE--

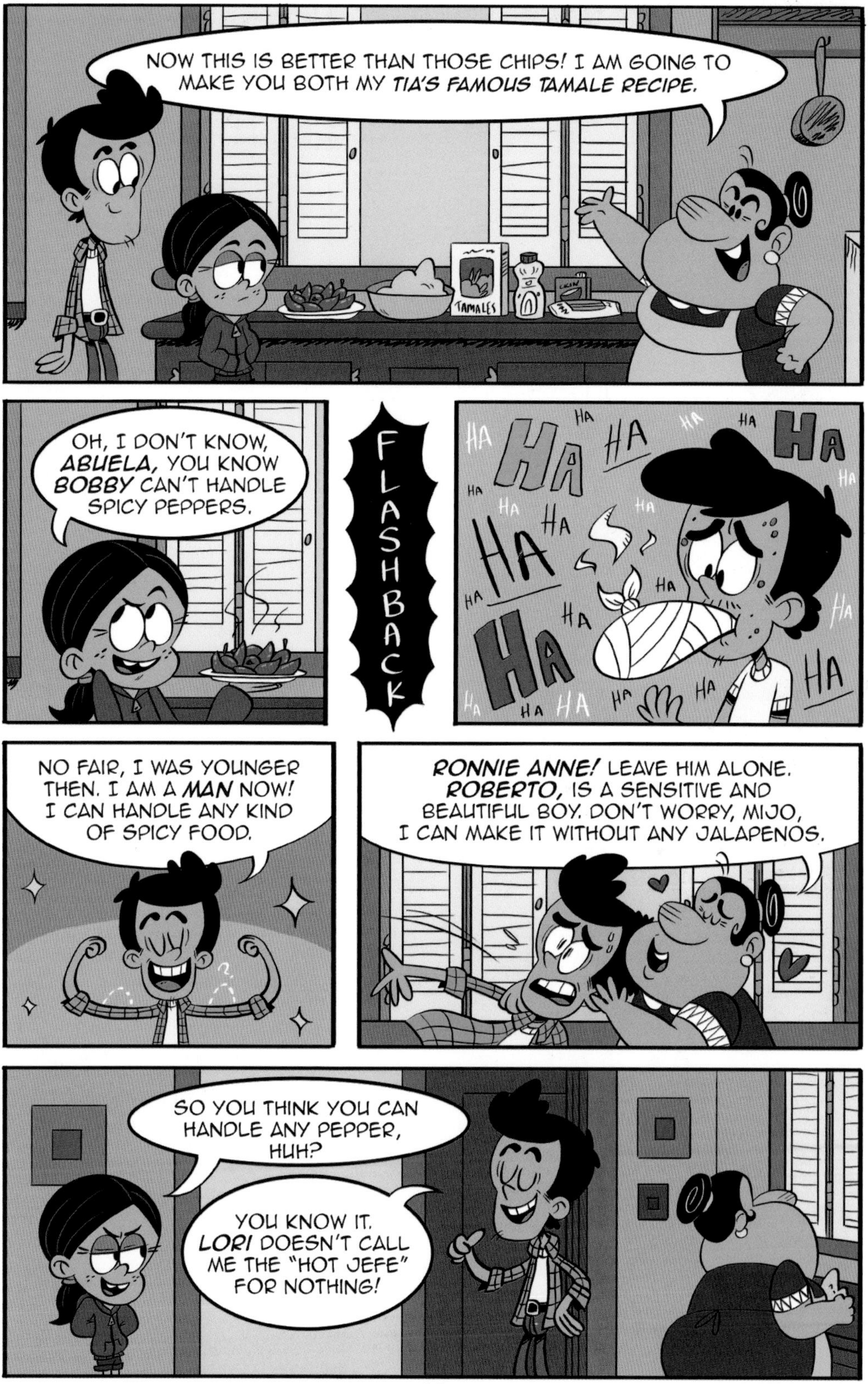
NOW THIS IS BETTER THAN THOSE CHIPS! I AM GOING TO MAKE YOU BOTH MY *TIA'S FAMOUS TAMALE RECIPE.*
TAMALES
OH, I DON'T KNOW, *ABUELA,* YOU KNOW *BOBBY* CAN'T HANDLE SPICY PEPPERS.
FLASHBACK
HA HA HA HA HA HA HA HA HA HA HA HA HA HA HA HA HA HA HA HA HA HA HA HA HA
NO FAIR, I WAS YOUNGER THEN. I AM A *MAN* NOW! I CAN HANDLE ANY KIND OF SPICY FOOD.
RONNIE ANNE! LEAVE HIM ALONE. *ROBERTO,* IS A SENSITIVE AND BEAUTIFUL BOY. DON'T WORRY, MIJO, I CAN MAKE IT WITHOUT ANY JALAPENOS.
SO YOU THINK YOU CAN HANDLE ANY PEPPER, HUH?
YOU KNOW IT. *LORI* DOESN'T CALL ME THE "HOT JEFE" FOR NOTHING!

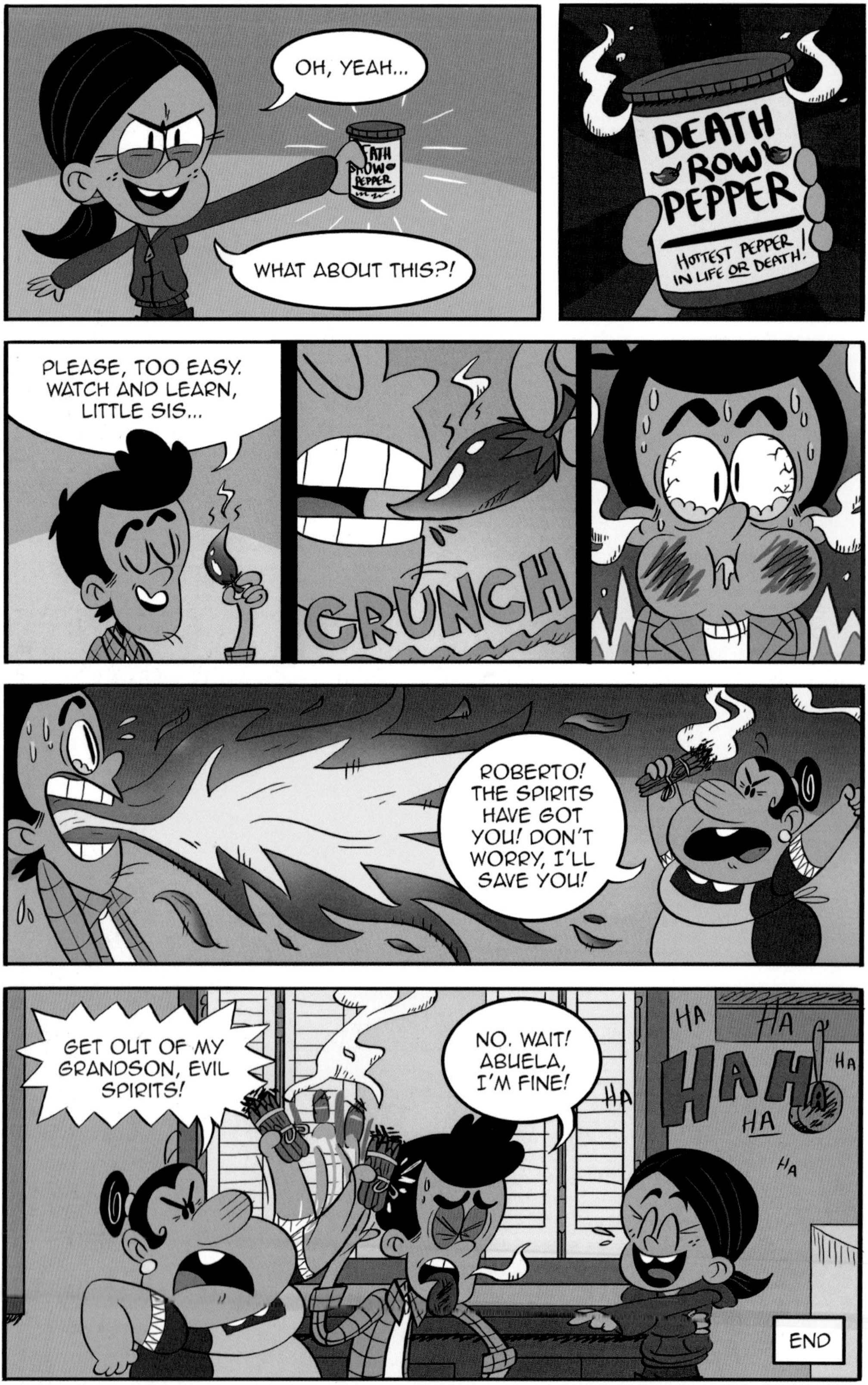
OH, YEAH...
WHAT ABOUT THIS?!
DEATH ROW PEPPER
HOTTEST PEPPER IN LIFE OR DEATH!
PLEASE, TOO EASY. WATCH AND LEARN, LITTLE SIS...
CRUNCH
ROBERTO! THE SPIRITS HAVE GOT YOU! DON'T WORRY, I'LL SAVE YOU!
GET OUT OF MY GRANDSON, EVIL SPIRITS!
NO. WAIT! ABUELA, I'M FINE!
HA HA HAH HA HA HA HA
END

"CODE CRISIS"

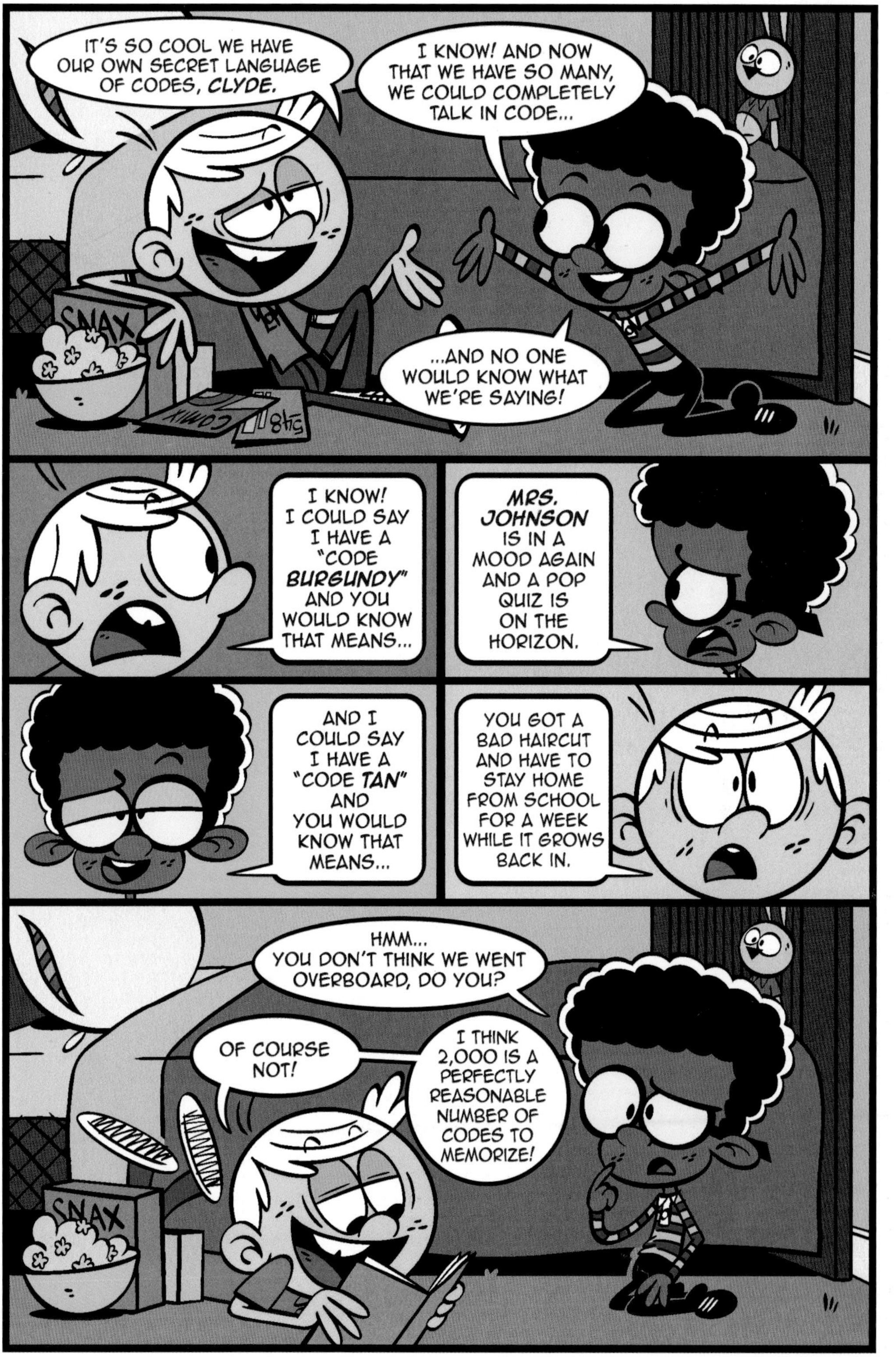

IT'S SO COOL WE HAVE OUR OWN SECRET LANGUAGE OF CODES, *CLYDE.*
I KNOW! AND NOW THAT WE HAVE SO MANY, WE COULD COMPLETELY TALK IN CODE...
SNAX
COMIX
...AND NO ONE WOULD KNOW WHAT WE'RE SAYING!
I KNOW! I COULD SAY I HAVE A "CODE *BURGUNDY*" AND YOU WOULD KNOW THAT MEANS...
MRS. JOHNSON IS IN A MOOD AGAIN AND A POP QUIZ IS ON THE HORIZON.
AND I COULD SAY I HAVE A "CODE *TAN*" AND YOU WOULD KNOW THAT MEANS...
YOU GOT A BAD HAIRCUT AND HAVE TO STAY HOME FROM SCHOOL FOR A WEEK WHILE IT GROWS BACK IN.
HMM... YOU DON'T THINK WE WENT OVERBOARD, DO YOU?
OF COURSE NOT!
I THINK 2,000 IS A PERFECTLY REASONABLE NUMBER OF CODES TO MEMORIZE!
SNAX

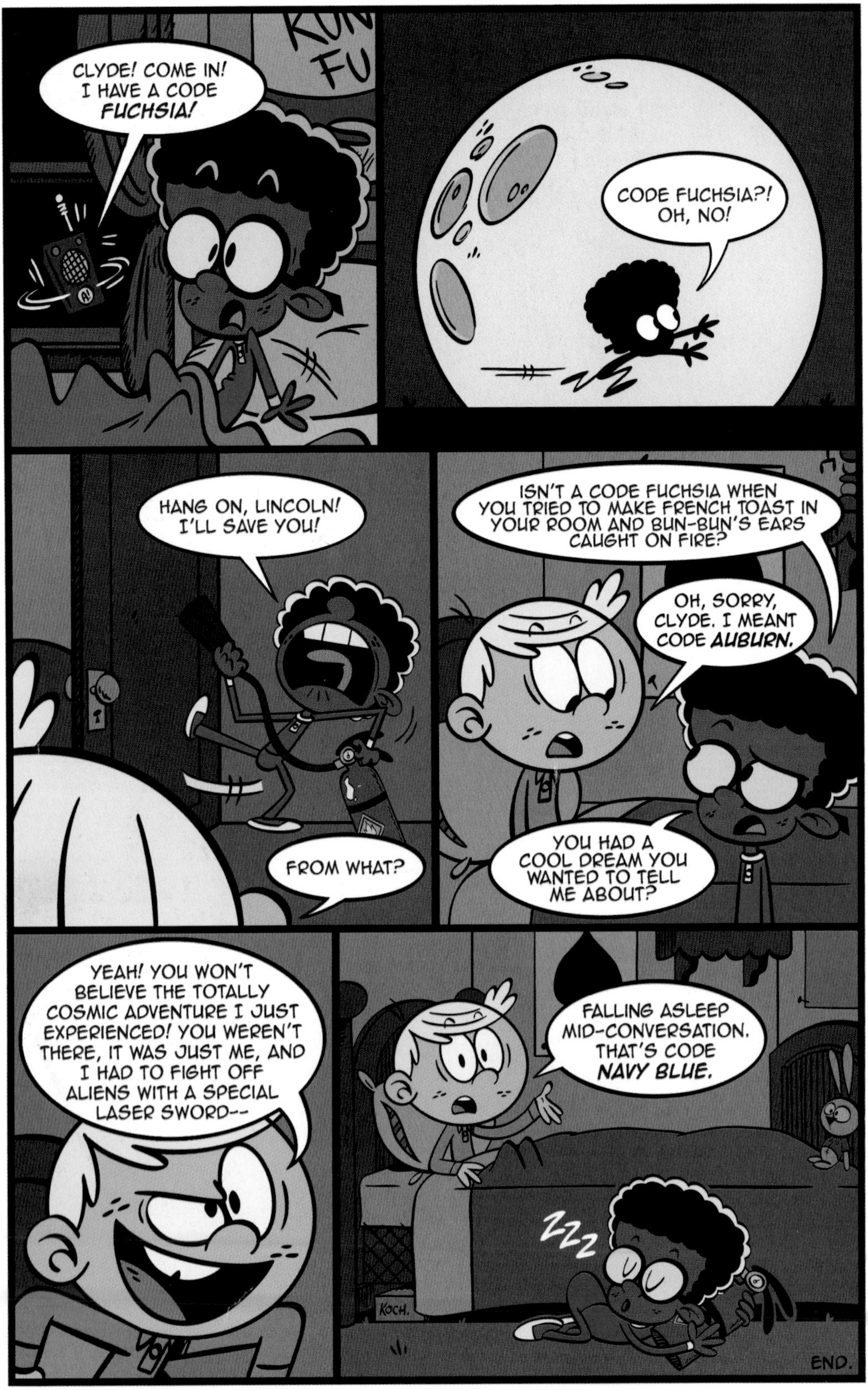
KUN FU
CLYDE! COME IN! I HAVE A CODE **FUCHSIA!**
CODE FUCHSIA?! OH, NO!
HANG ON, LINCOLN! I'LL SAVE YOU!
FROM WHAT?
ISN'T A CODE FUCHSIA WHEN YOU TRIED TO MAKE FRENCH TOAST IN YOUR ROOM AND BUN-BUN'S EARS CAUGHT ON FIRE?
OH, SORRY, CLYDE. I MEANT CODE **AUBURN.**
YOU HAD A COOL DREAM YOU WANTED TO TELL ME ABOUT?
YEAH! YOU WON'T BELIEVE THE TOTALLY COSMIC ADVENTURE I JUST EXPERIENCED! YOU WEREN'T THERE, IT WAS JUST ME, AND I HAD TO FIGHT OFF ALIENS WITH A SPECIAL LASER SWORD--
FALLING ASLEEP MID-CONVERSATION. THAT'S CODE **NAVY BLUE.**
ZZZ
KOCH.
END.

"DISJOINT CUSTODY"

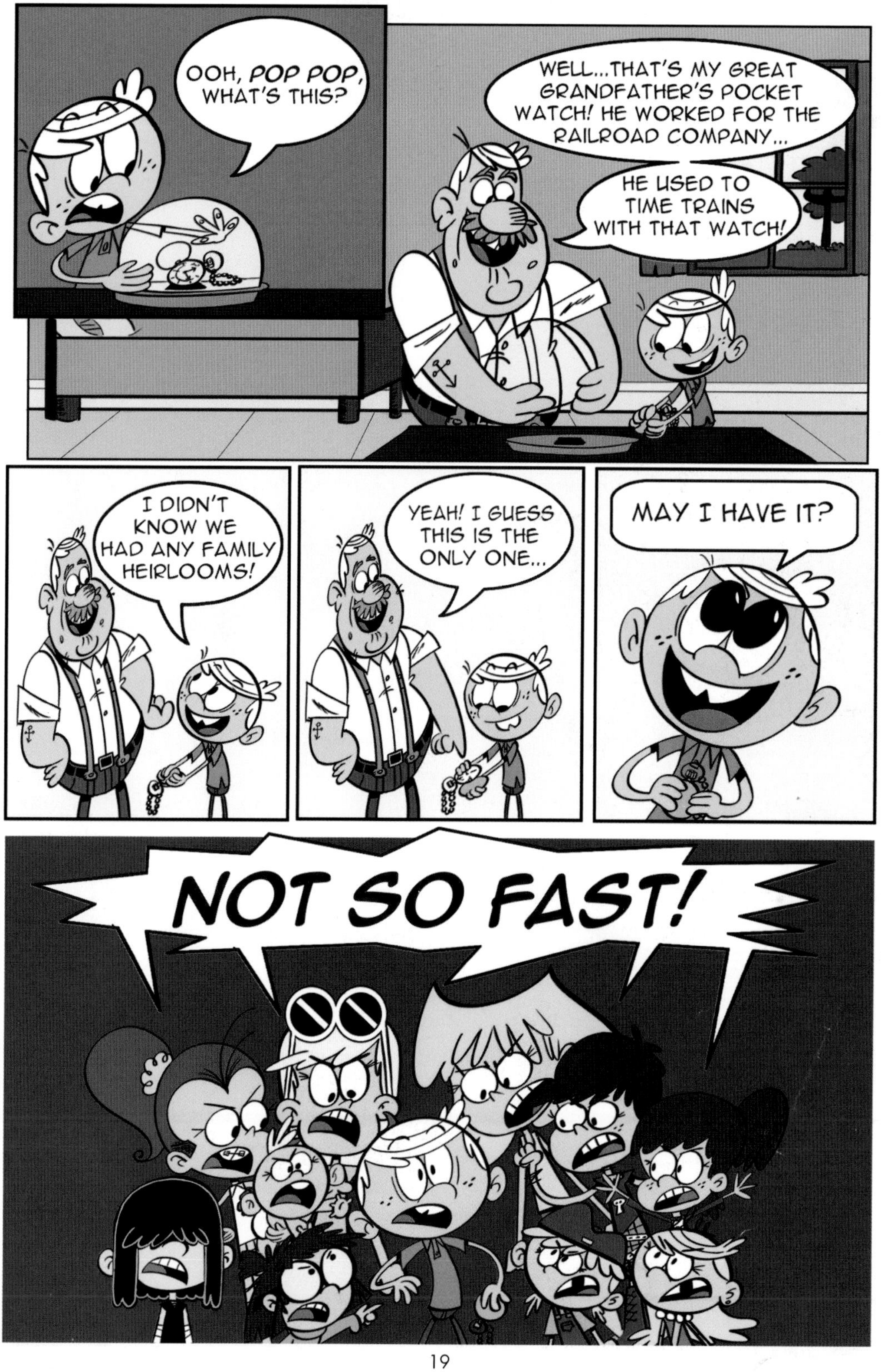

OOH, *POP POP*, WHAT'S THIS?
WELL...THAT'S MY GREAT GRANDFATHER'S POCKET WATCH! HE WORKED FOR THE RAILROAD COMPANY...
HE USED TO TIME TRAINS WITH THAT WATCH!
I DIDN'T KNOW WE HAD ANY FAMILY HEIRLOOMS!
YEAH! I GUESS THIS IS THE ONLY ONE...
MAY I HAVE IT?
NOT SO FAST!

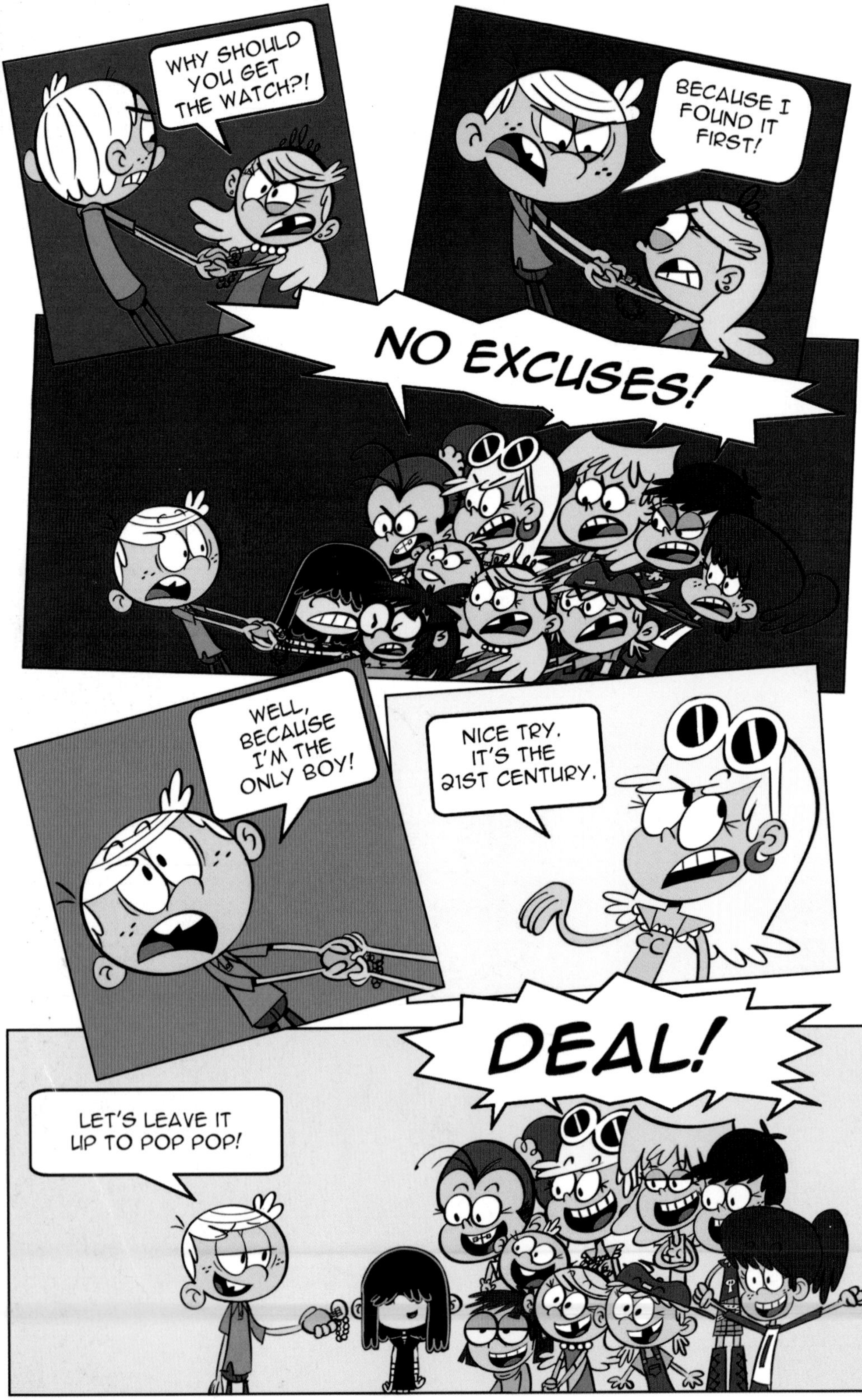
WHY SHOULD YOU GET THE WATCH?!
BECAUSE I FOUND IT FIRST!
NO EXCUSES!
WELL, BECAUSE I'M THE ONLY BOY!
NICE TRY. IT'S THE 21ST CENTURY.
DEAL!
LET'S LEAVE IT UP TO POP POP!

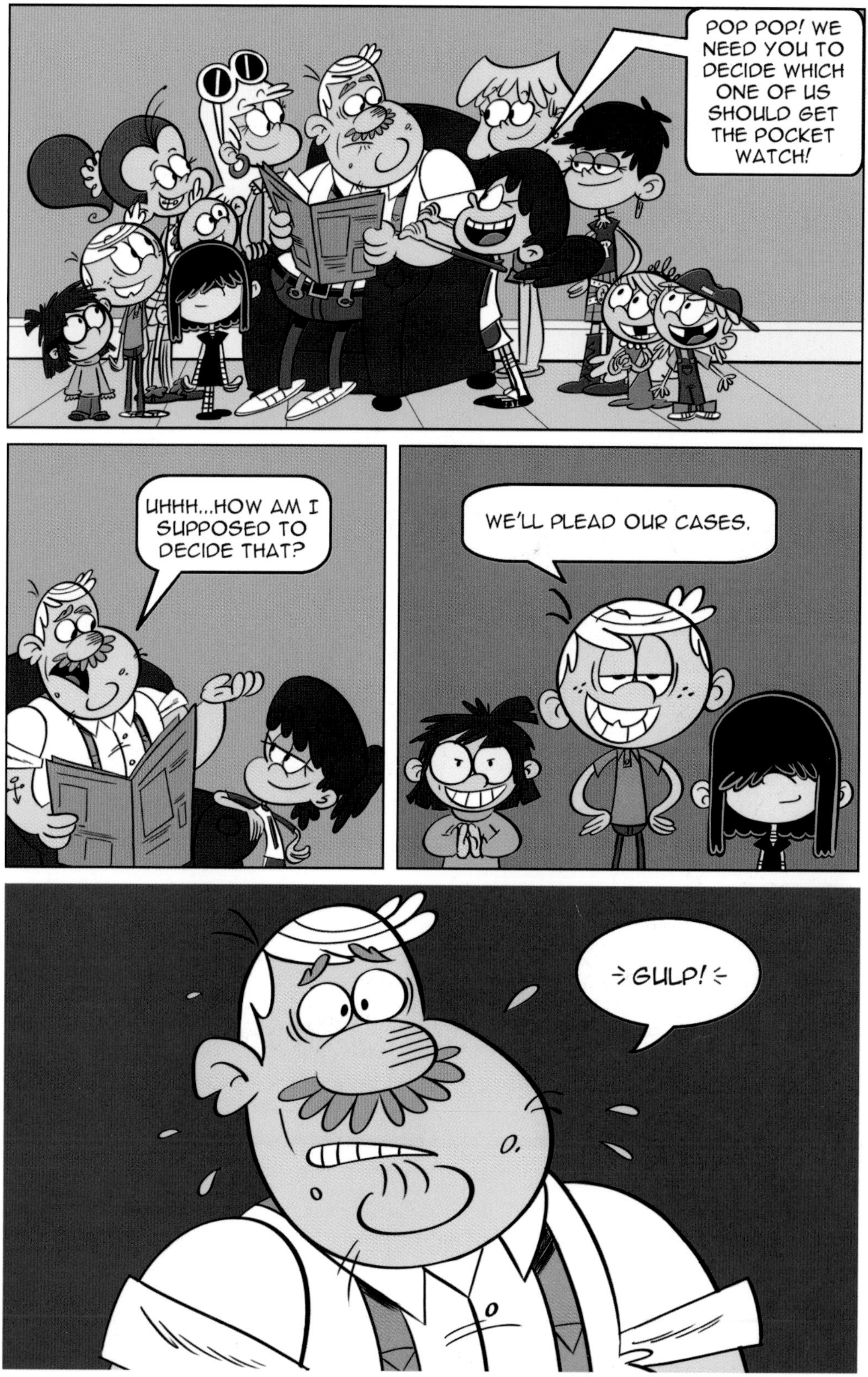
POP POP! WE NEED YOU TO DECIDE WHICH ONE OF US SHOULD GET THE POCKET WATCH!
UHHH...HOW AM I SUPPOSED TO DECIDE THAT?
WE'LL PLEAD OUR CASES.
GULP!

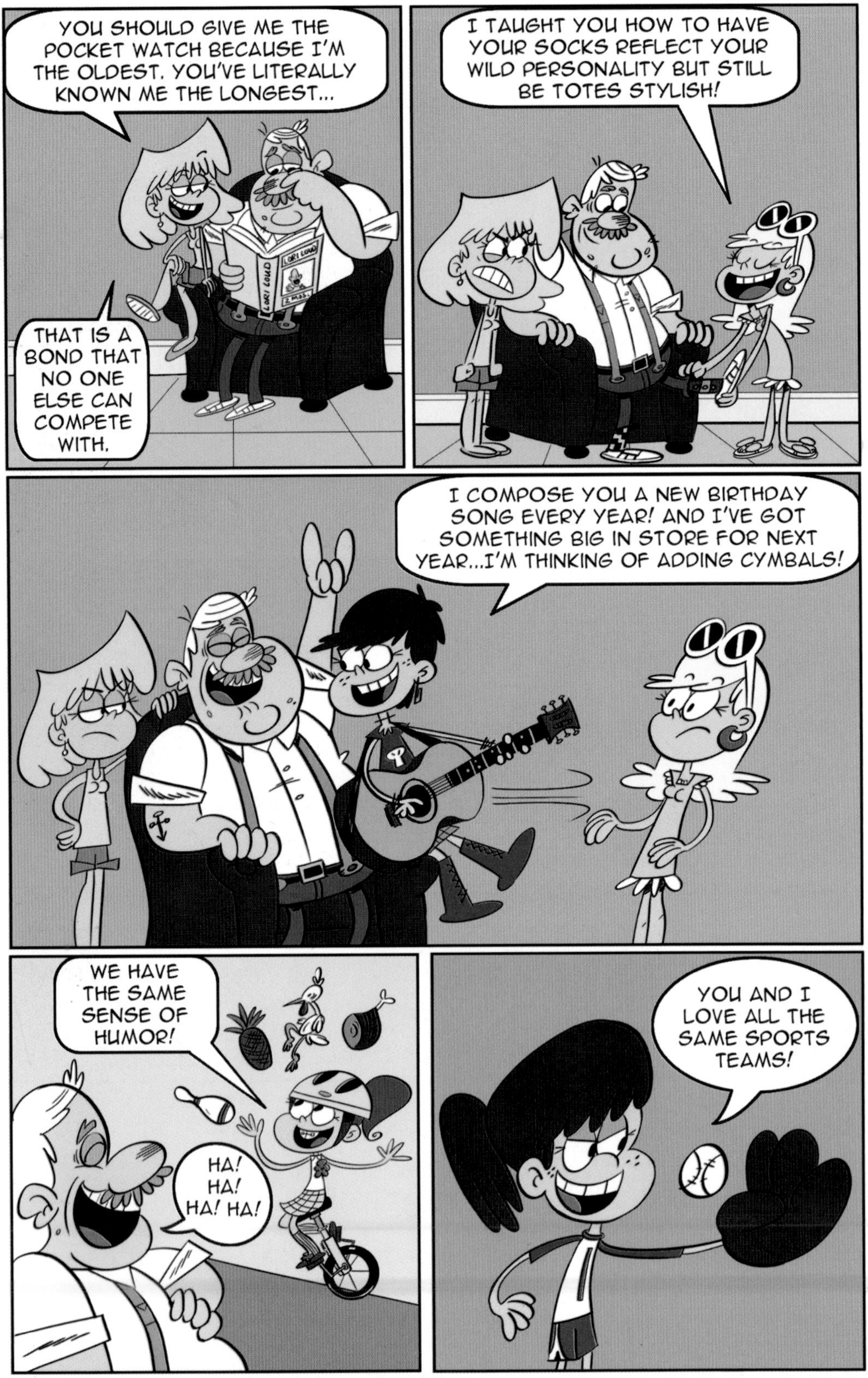
YOU SHOULD GIVE ME THE POCKET WATCH BECAUSE I'M THE OLDEST. YOU'VE LITERALLY KNOWN ME THE LONGEST...
THAT IS A BOND THAT NO ONE ELSE CAN COMPETE WITH.
LORI LOUD
I TAUGHT YOU HOW TO HAVE YOUR SOCKS REFLECT YOUR WILD PERSONALITY BUT STILL BE TOTES STYLISH!
I COMPOSE YOU A NEW BIRTHDAY SONG EVERY YEAR! AND I'VE GOT SOMETHING BIG IN STORE FOR NEXT YEAR...I'M THINKING OF ADDING CYMBALS!
WE HAVE THE SAME SENSE OF HUMOR!
HA! HA! HA! HA!
YOU AND I LOVE ALL THE SAME SPORTS TEAMS!

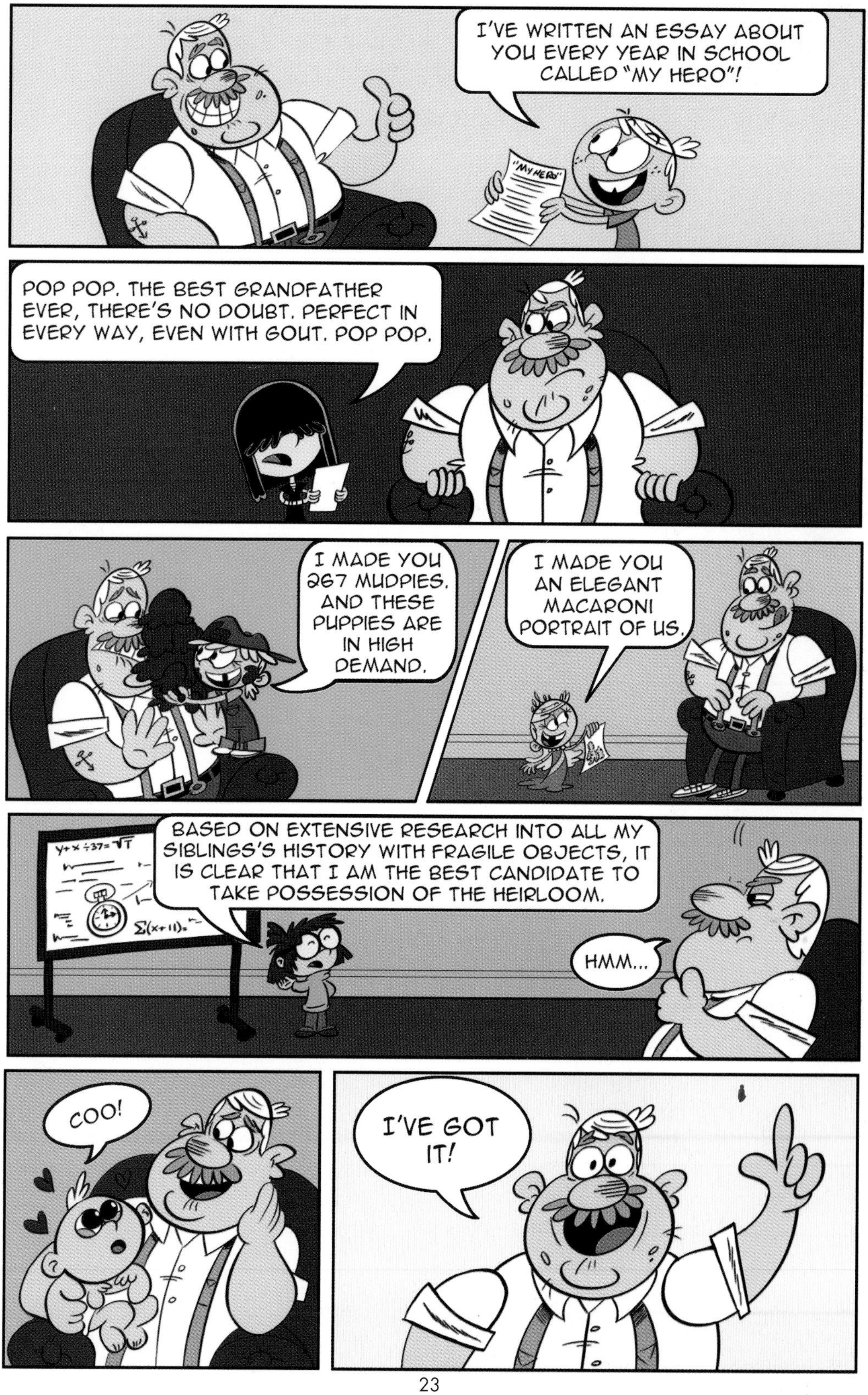
I'VE WRITTEN AN ESSAY ABOUT YOU EVERY YEAR IN SCHOOL CALLED "MY HERO"!
"MY HERO"
POP POP. THE BEST GRANDFATHER EVER, THERE'S NO DOUBT. PERFECT IN EVERY WAY, EVEN WITH GOUT. POP POP.
I MADE YOU 267 MUDPIES. AND THESE PUPPIES ARE IN HIGH DEMAND.
I MADE YOU AN ELEGANT MACARONI PORTRAIT OF US.
BASED ON EXTENSIVE RESEARCH INTO ALL MY SIBLINGS'S HISTORY WITH FRAGILE OBJECTS, IT IS CLEAR THAT I AM THE BEST CANDIDATE TO TAKE POSSESSION OF THE HEIRLOOM.
HMM...
COO!
I'VE GOT IT!

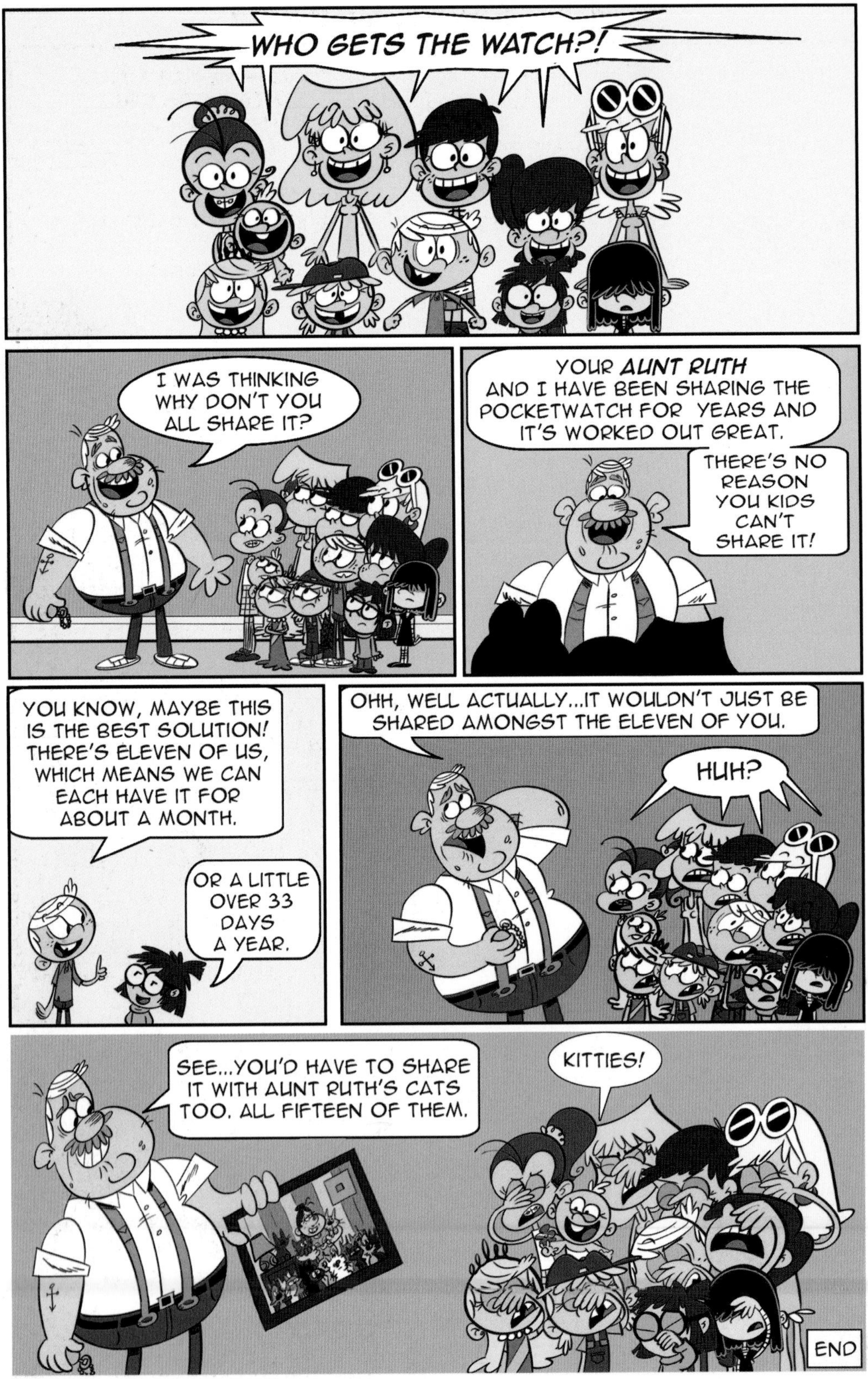
WHO GETS THE WATCH?!
I WAS THINKING WHY DON'T YOU ALL SHARE IT?
YOUR AUNT RUTH AND I HAVE BEEN SHARING THE POCKETWATCH FOR YEARS AND IT'S WORKED OUT GREAT.
THERE'S NO REASON YOU KIDS CAN'T SHARE IT!
YOU KNOW, MAYBE THIS IS THE BEST SOLUTION! THERE'S ELEVEN OF US, WHICH MEANS WE CAN EACH HAVE IT FOR ABOUT A MONTH.
OR A LITTLE OVER 33 DAYS A YEAR.
OHH, WELL ACTUALLY...IT WOULDN'T JUST BE SHARED AMONGST THE ELEVEN OF YOU.
HUH?
SEE...YOU'D HAVE TO SHARE IT WITH AUNT RUTH'S CATS TOO. ALL FIFTEEN OF THEM.
KITTIES!
END

"THE LOUD JOURNEY"

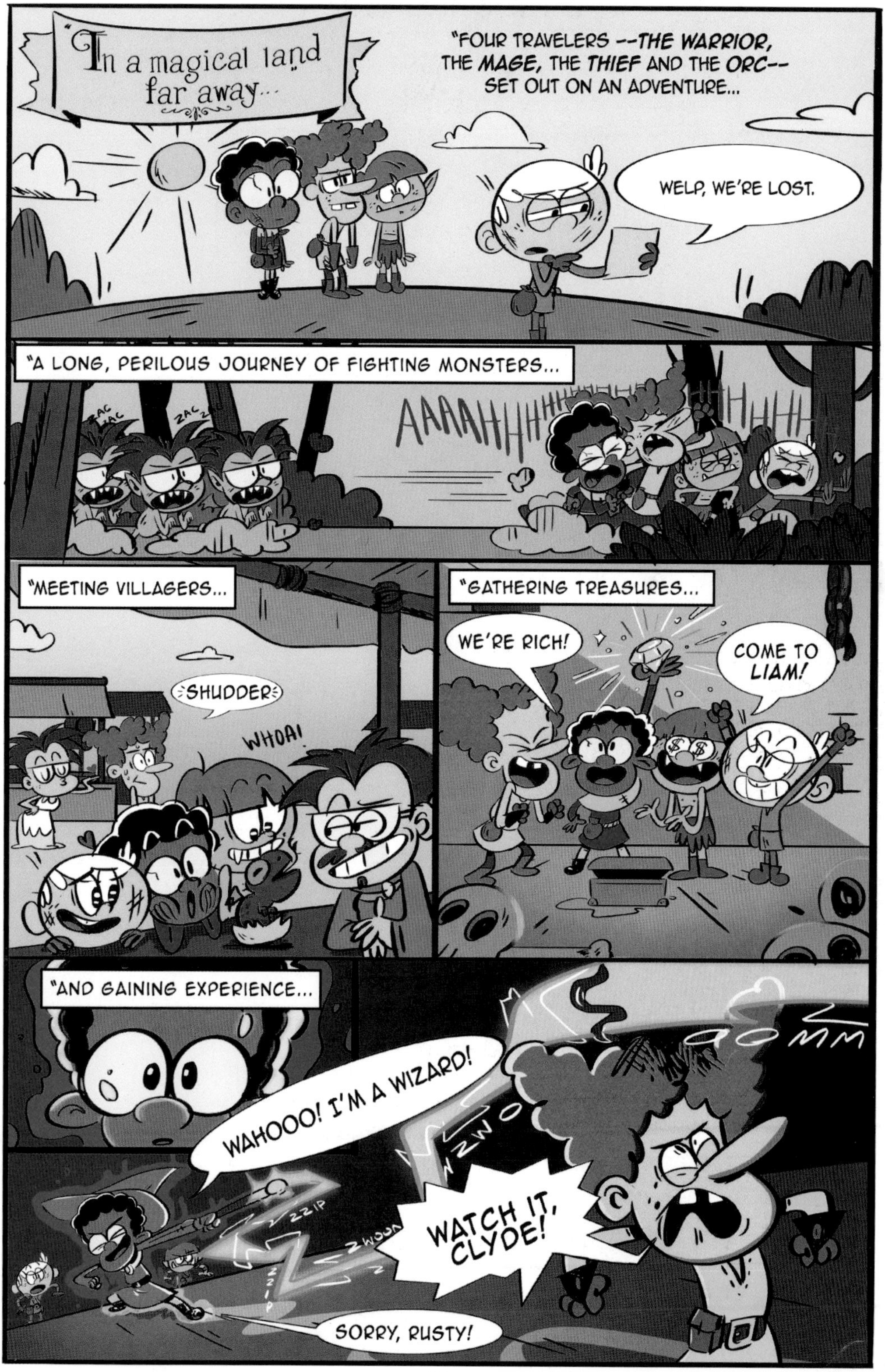

"In a magical land far away..."
"FOUR TRAVELERS --THE WARRIOR, THE MAGE, THE THIEF AND THE ORC-- SET OUT ON AN ADVENTURE...
WELP, WE'RE LOST.
"A LONG, PERILOUS JOURNEY OF FIGHTING MONSTERS...
"MEETING VILLAGERS...
SHUDDER
WHOA!
"GATHERING TREASURES...
WE'RE RICH!
COME TO LIAM!
"AND GAINING EXPERIENCE...
WAHOOO! I'M A WIZARD!
WATCH IT, CLYDE!
SORRY, RUSTY!

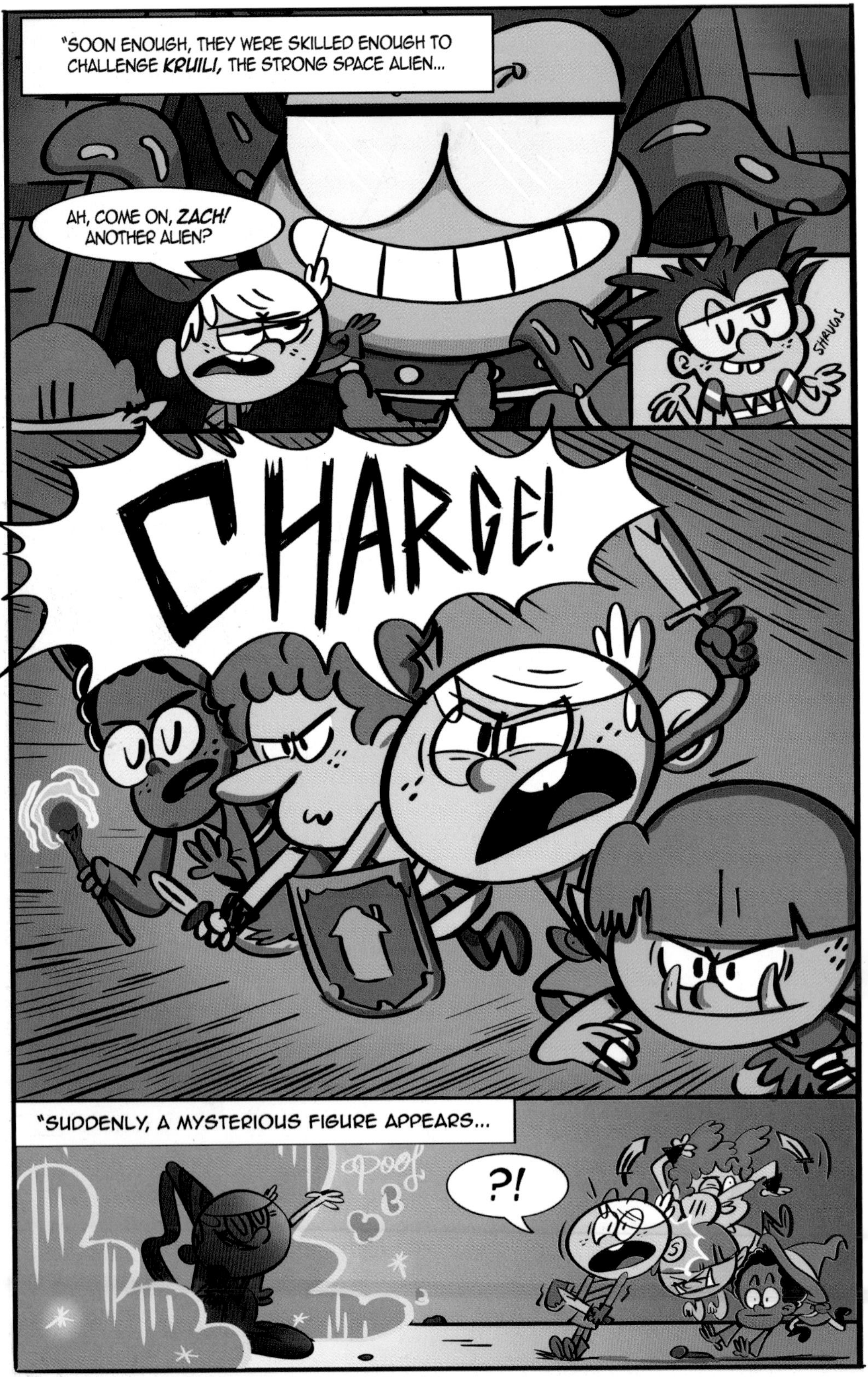
"SOON ENOUGH, THEY WERE SKILLED ENOUGH TO CHALLENGE KRUILI, THE STRONG SPACE ALIEN...
AH, COME ON, ZACH! ANOTHER ALIEN?
SHRUGS
CHARGE!
"SUDDENLY, A MYSTERIOUS FIGURE APPEARS...
poof
?!

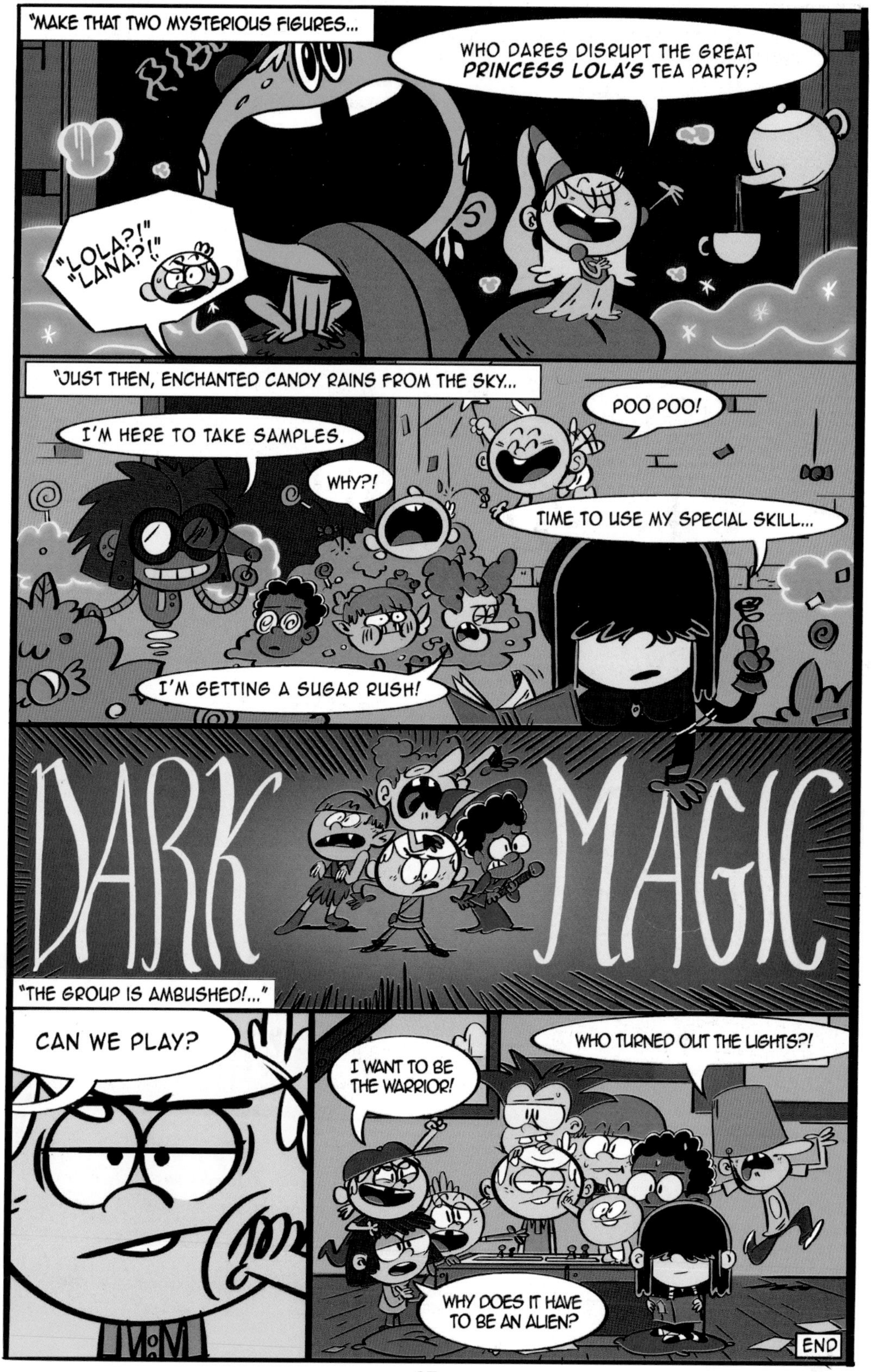
"MAKE THAT TWO MYSTERIOUS FIGURES...
WHO DARES DISRUPT THE GREAT PRINCESS LOLA'S TEA PARTY?
"LOLA?!" "LANA?!"
"JUST THEN, ENCHANTED CANDY RAINS FROM THE SKY...
I'M HERE TO TAKE SAMPLES.
POO POO!
WHY?!
TIME TO USE MY SPECIAL SKILL...
I'M GETTING A SUGAR RUSH!
DARK MAGIC
"THE GROUP IS AMBUSHED!..."
CAN WE PLAY?
I WANT TO BE THE WARRIOR!
WHO TURNED OUT THE LIGHTS?!
WHY DOES IT HAVE TO BE AN ALIEN?
END

"WORKED UP"

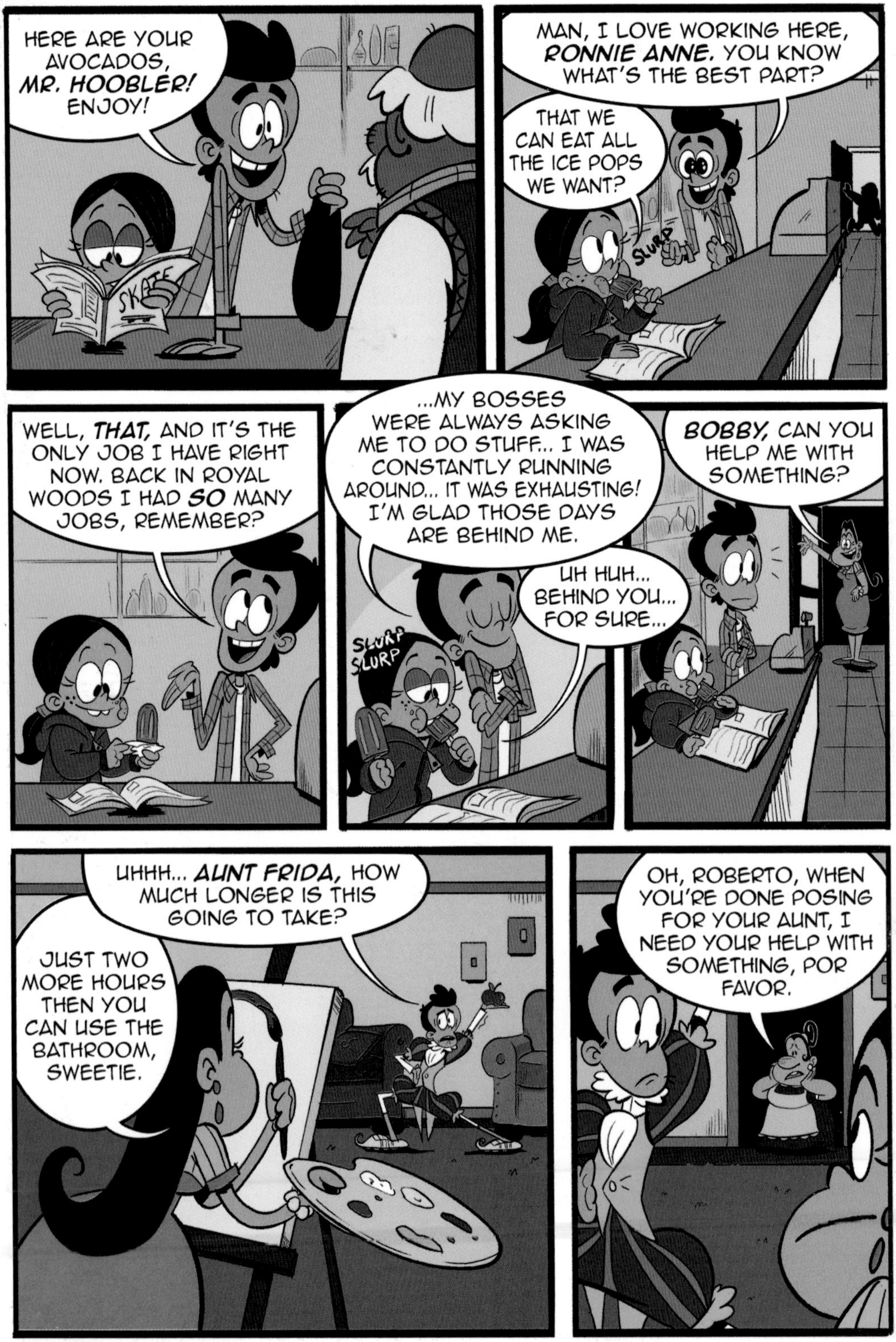
HERE ARE YOUR AVOCADOS, ***MR. HOOBLER!*** ENJOY!
SKATE
MAN, I LOVE WORKING HERE, ***RONNIE ANNE.*** YOU KNOW WHAT'S THE BEST PART?
THAT WE CAN EAT ALL THE ICE POPS WE WANT?
SLURP
WELL, ***THAT,*** AND IT'S THE ONLY JOB I HAVE RIGHT NOW. BACK IN ROYAL WOODS I HAD ***SO*** MANY JOBS, REMEMBER?
...MY BOSSES WERE ALWAYS ASKING ME TO DO STUFF... I WAS CONSTANTLY RUNNING AROUND... IT WAS EXHAUSTING! I'M GLAD THOSE DAYS ARE BEHIND ME.
SLURP SLURP
UH HUH... BEHIND YOU... FOR SURE...
BOBBY, CAN YOU HELP ME WITH SOMETHING?
UHHH... ***AUNT FRIDA,*** HOW MUCH LONGER IS THIS GOING TO TAKE?
JUST TWO MORE HOURS THEN YOU CAN USE THE BATHROOM, SWEETIE.
OH, ROBERTO, WHEN YOU'RE DONE POSING FOR YOUR AUNT, I NEED YOUR HELP WITH SOMETHING, POR FAVOR.

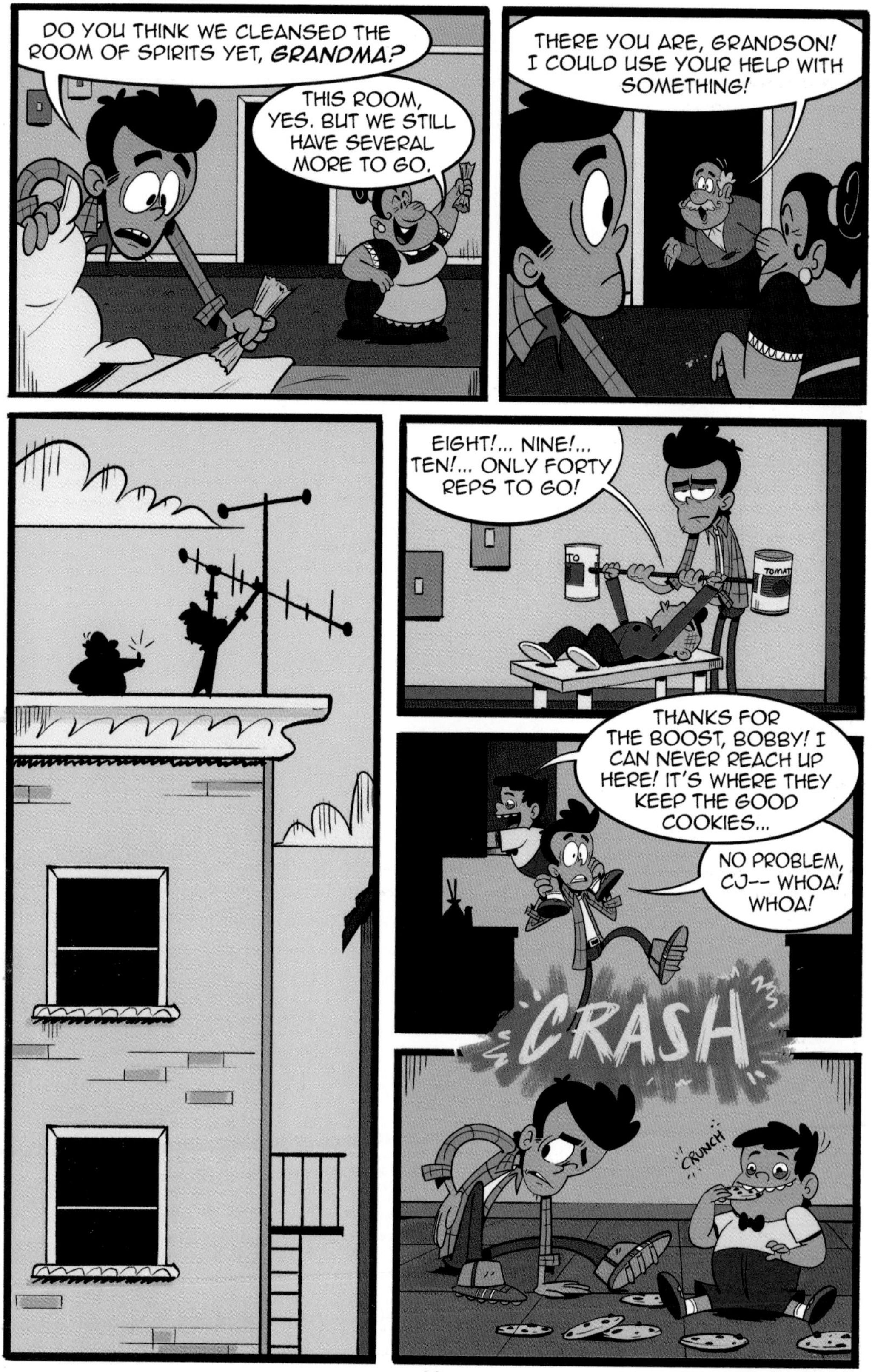
DO YOU THINK WE CLEANSED THE ROOM OF SPIRITS YET, *GRANDMA?*
THIS ROOM, YES. BUT WE STILL HAVE SEVERAL MORE TO GO.
THERE YOU ARE, GRANDSON! I COULD USE YOUR HELP WITH SOMETHING!
EIGHT!... NINE!... TEN!... ONLY FORTY REPS TO GO!
TOMAT
THANKS FOR THE BOOST, BOBBY! I CAN NEVER REACH UP HERE! IT'S WHERE THEY KEEP THE GOOD COOKIES...
NO PROBLEM, CJ-- WHOA! WHOA!
CRASH
CRUNCH

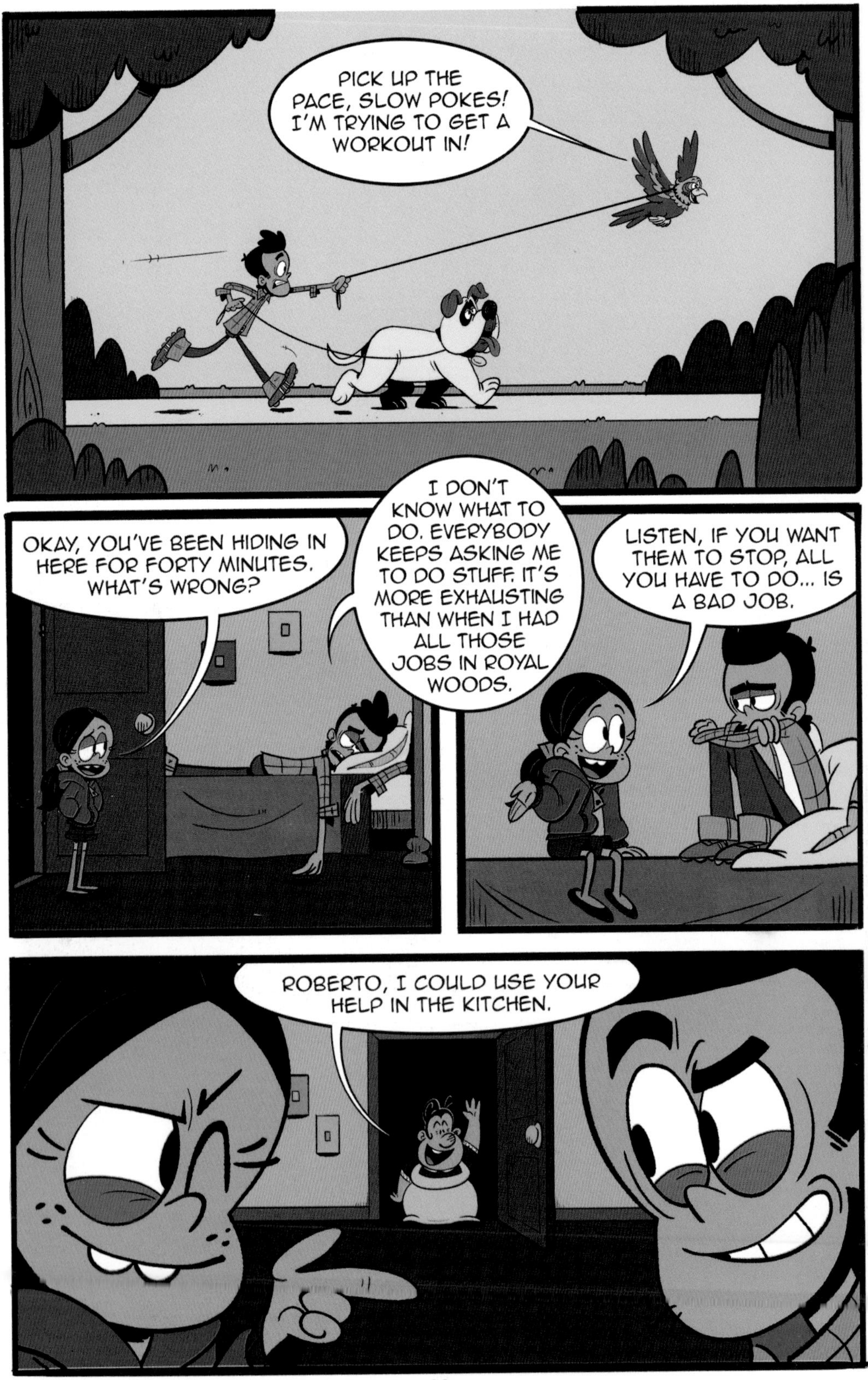
PICK UP THE PACE, SLOW POKES! I'M TRYING TO GET A WORKOUT IN!
OKAY, YOU'VE BEEN HIDING IN HERE FOR FORTY MINUTES. WHAT'S WRONG?
I DON'T KNOW WHAT TO DO. EVERYBODY KEEPS ASKING ME TO DO STUFF. IT'S MORE EXHAUSTING THAN WHEN I HAD ALL THOSE JOBS IN ROYAL WOODS.
LISTEN, IF YOU WANT THEM TO STOP, ALL YOU HAVE TO DO... IS A BAD JOB.
ROBERTO, I COULD USE YOUR HELP IN THE KITCHEN.

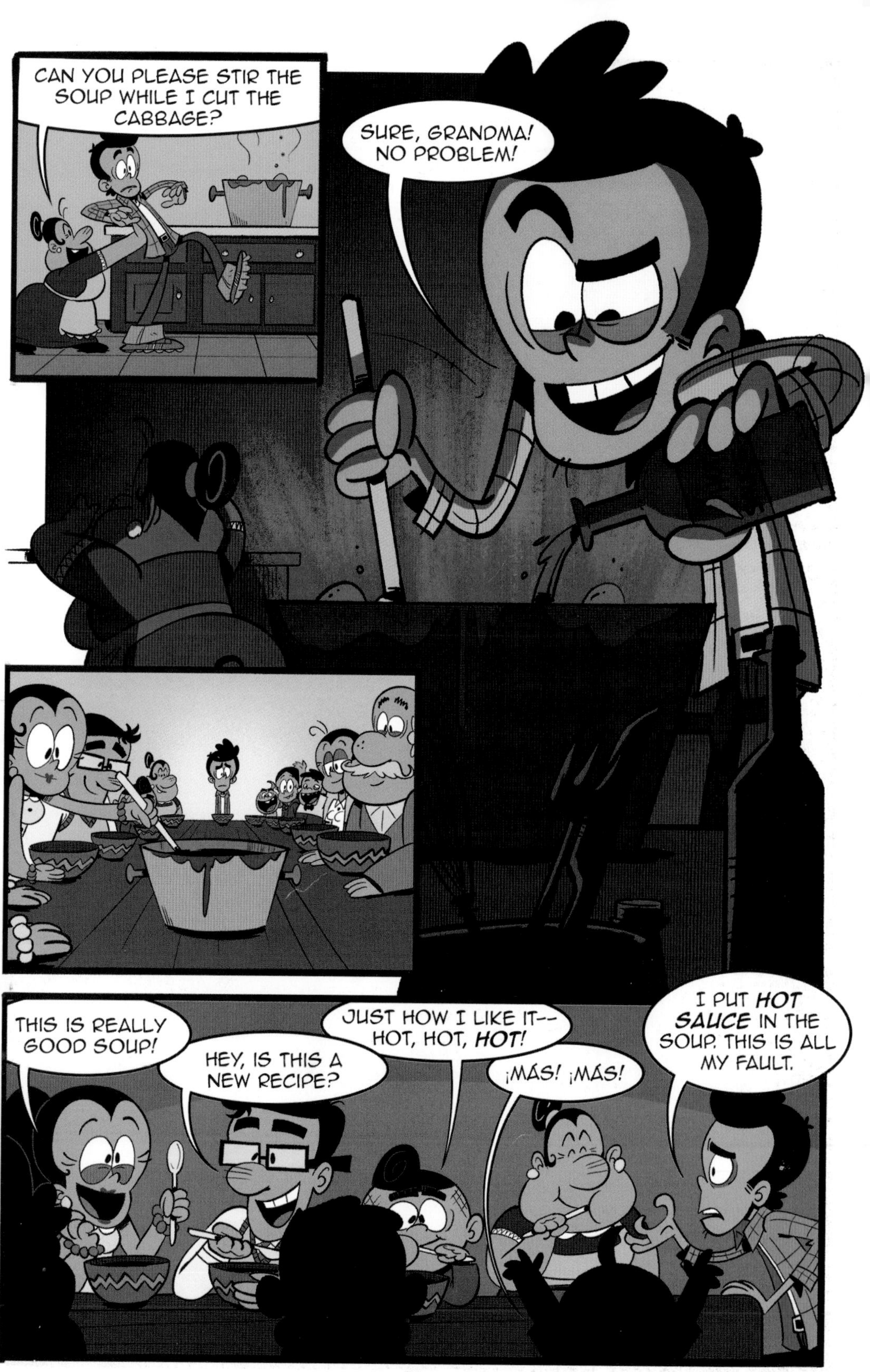
CAN YOU PLEASE STIR THE SOUP WHILE I CUT THE CABBAGE?
SURE, GRANDMA! NO PROBLEM!
THIS IS REALLY GOOD SOUP!
HEY, IS THIS A NEW RECIPE?
JUST HOW I LIKE IT-- HOT, HOT, **HOT**!
¡MÁS! ¡MÁS!
I PUT **HOT SAUCE** IN THE SOUP. THIS IS ALL MY FAULT.

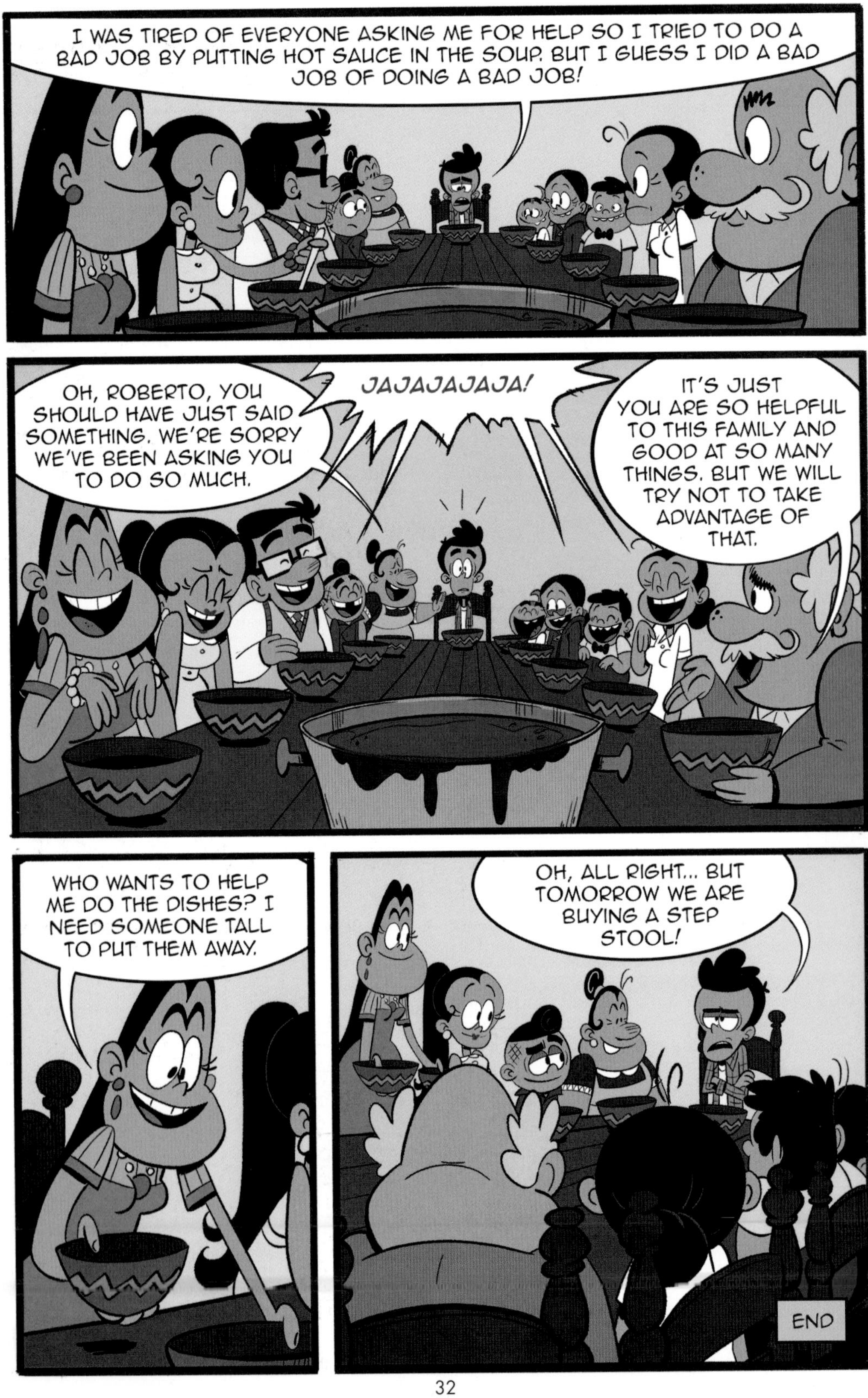
I WAS TIRED OF EVERYONE ASKING ME FOR HELP SO I TRIED TO DO A BAD JOB BY PUTTING HOT SAUCE IN THE SOUP. BUT I GUESS I DID A BAD JOB OF DOING A BAD JOB!
OH, ROBERTO, YOU SHOULD HAVE JUST SAID SOMETHING. WE'RE SORRY WE'VE BEEN ASKING YOU TO DO SO MUCH.
JAJAJAJAJA!
IT'S JUST YOU ARE SO HELPFUL TO THIS FAMILY AND GOOD AT SO MANY THINGS. BUT WE WILL TRY NOT TO TAKE ADVANTAGE OF THAT.
WHO WANTS TO HELP ME DO THE DISHES? I NEED SOMEONE TALL TO PUT THEM AWAY.
OH, ALL RIGHT... BUT TOMORROW WE ARE BUYING A STEP STOOL!
END

"MAYBE IT'S NATURAL"

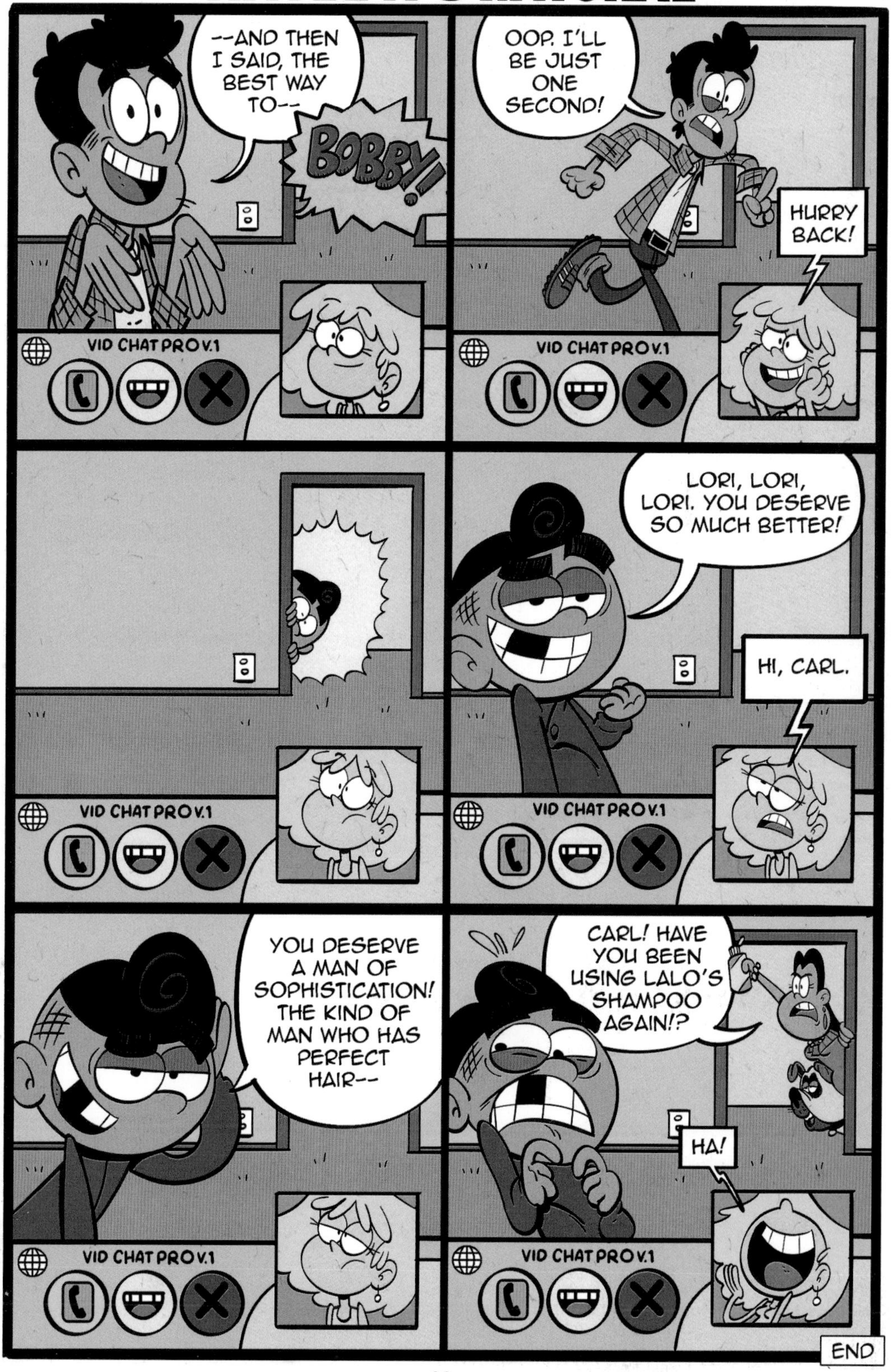
--AND THEN I SAID, THE BEST WAY TO--
BOBBY!
VID CHAT PRO V.1
OOP. I'LL BE JUST ONE SECOND!
HURRY BACK!
VID CHAT PRO V.1
VID CHAT PRO V.1
LORI, LORI, LORI. YOU DESERVE SO MUCH BETTER!
HI, CARL.
VID CHAT PRO V.1
YOU DESERVE A MAN OF SOPHISTICATION! THE KIND OF MAN WHO HAS PERFECT HAIR--
VID CHAT PRO V.1
CARL! HAVE YOU BEEN USING LALO'S SHAMPOO AGAIN!?
HA!
VID CHAT PRO V.1
END

"SWISHFUL THINKING"

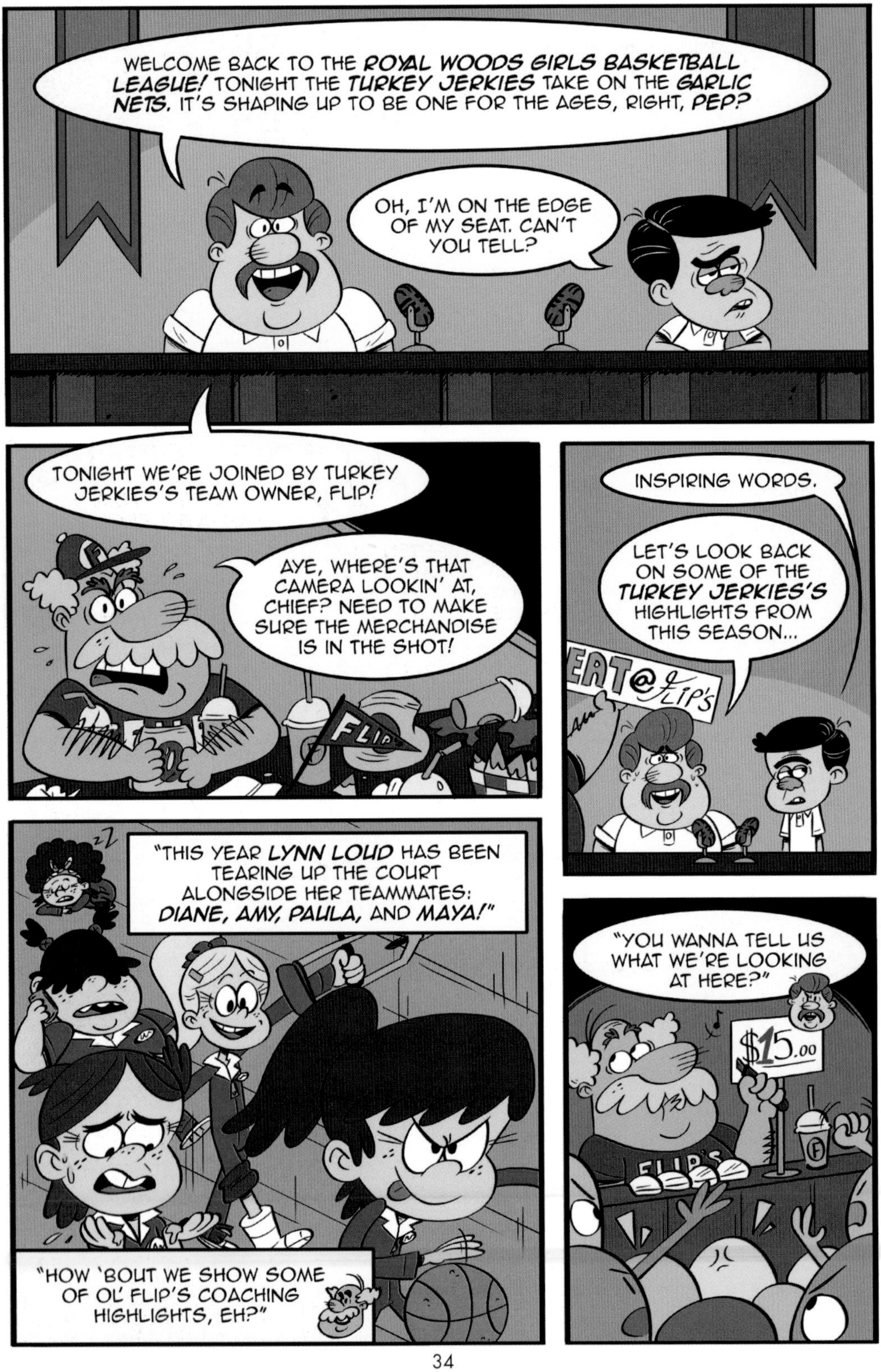
WELCOME BACK TO THE ROYAL WOODS GIRLS BASKETBALL LEAGUE! TONIGHT THE TURKEY JERKIES TAKE ON THE GARLIC NETS. IT'S SHAPING UP TO BE ONE FOR THE AGES, RIGHT, PEP?
OH, I'M ON THE EDGE OF MY SEAT. CAN'T YOU TELL?
TONIGHT WE'RE JOINED BY TURKEY JERKIES'S TEAM OWNER, FLIP!
AYE, WHERE'S THAT CAMERA LOOKIN' AT, CHIEF? NEED TO MAKE SURE THE MERCHANDISE IS IN THE SHOT!
FLIP
INSPIRING WORDS.
LET'S LOOK BACK ON SOME OF THE TURKEY JERKIES'S HIGHLIGHTS FROM THIS SEASON...
EAT @ FLIP'S
"THIS YEAR LYNN LOUD HAS BEEN TEARING UP THE COURT ALONGSIDE HER TEAMMATES: DIANE, AMY, PAULA, AND MAYA!"
"HOW 'BOUT WE SHOW SOME OF OL' FLIP'S COACHING HIGHLIGHTS, EH?"
"YOU WANNA TELL US WHAT WE'RE LOOKING AT HERE?"
$15.00
FLIP'S

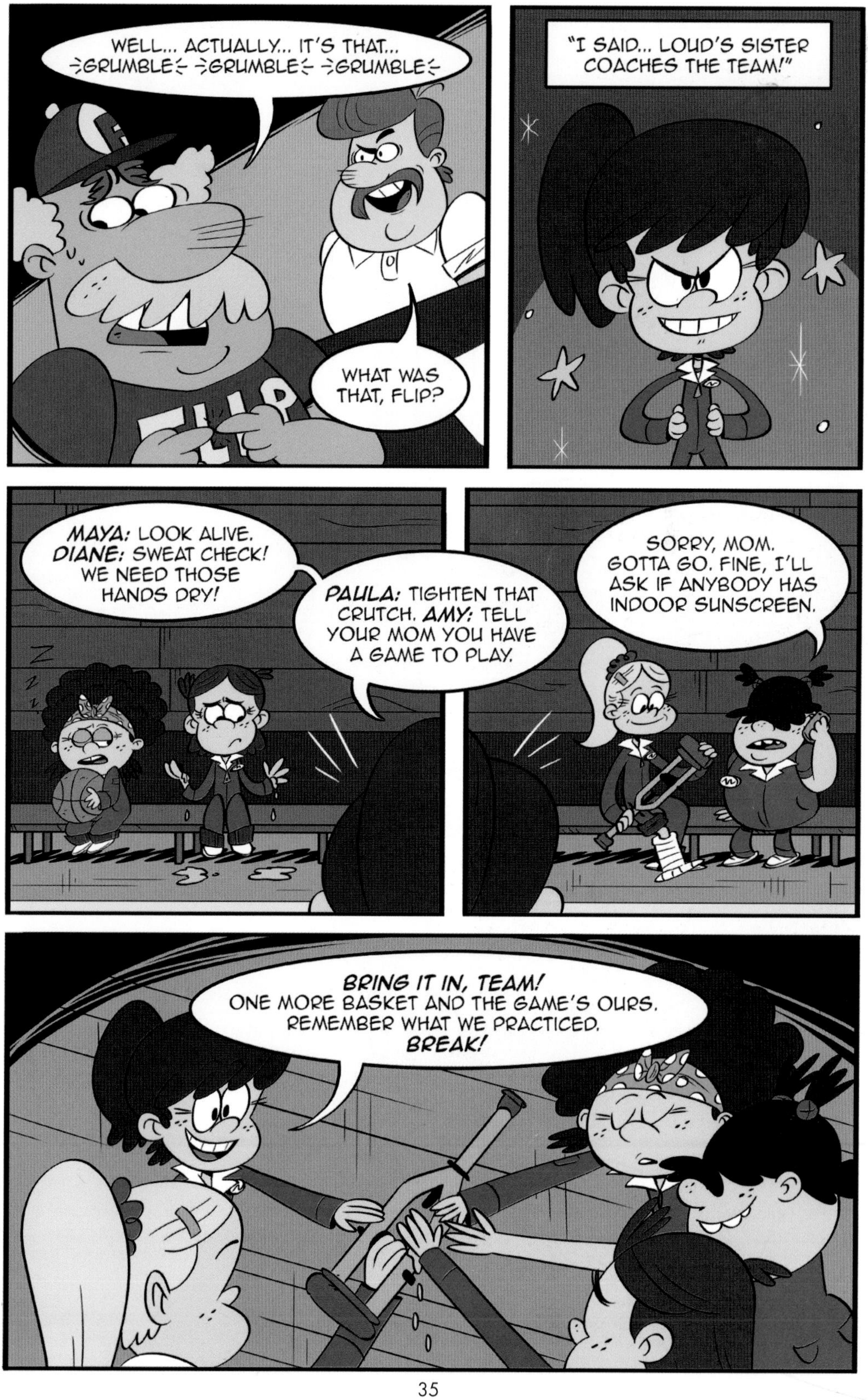
WELL... ACTUALLY... IT'S THAT... GRUMBLE GRUMBLE GRUMBLE
WHAT WAS THAT, FLIP?
"I SAID... LOUD'S SISTER COACHES THE TEAM!"
MAYA: LOOK ALIVE. DIANE: SWEAT CHECK! WE NEED THOSE HANDS DRY!
PAULA: TIGHTEN THAT CRUTCH. AMY: TELL YOUR MOM YOU HAVE A GAME TO PLAY.
SORRY, MOM. GOTTA GO. FINE, I'LL ASK IF ANYBODY HAS INDOOR SUNSCREEN.
BRING IT IN, TEAM! ONE MORE BASKET AND THE GAME'S OURS. REMEMBER WHAT WE PRACTICED. BREAK!

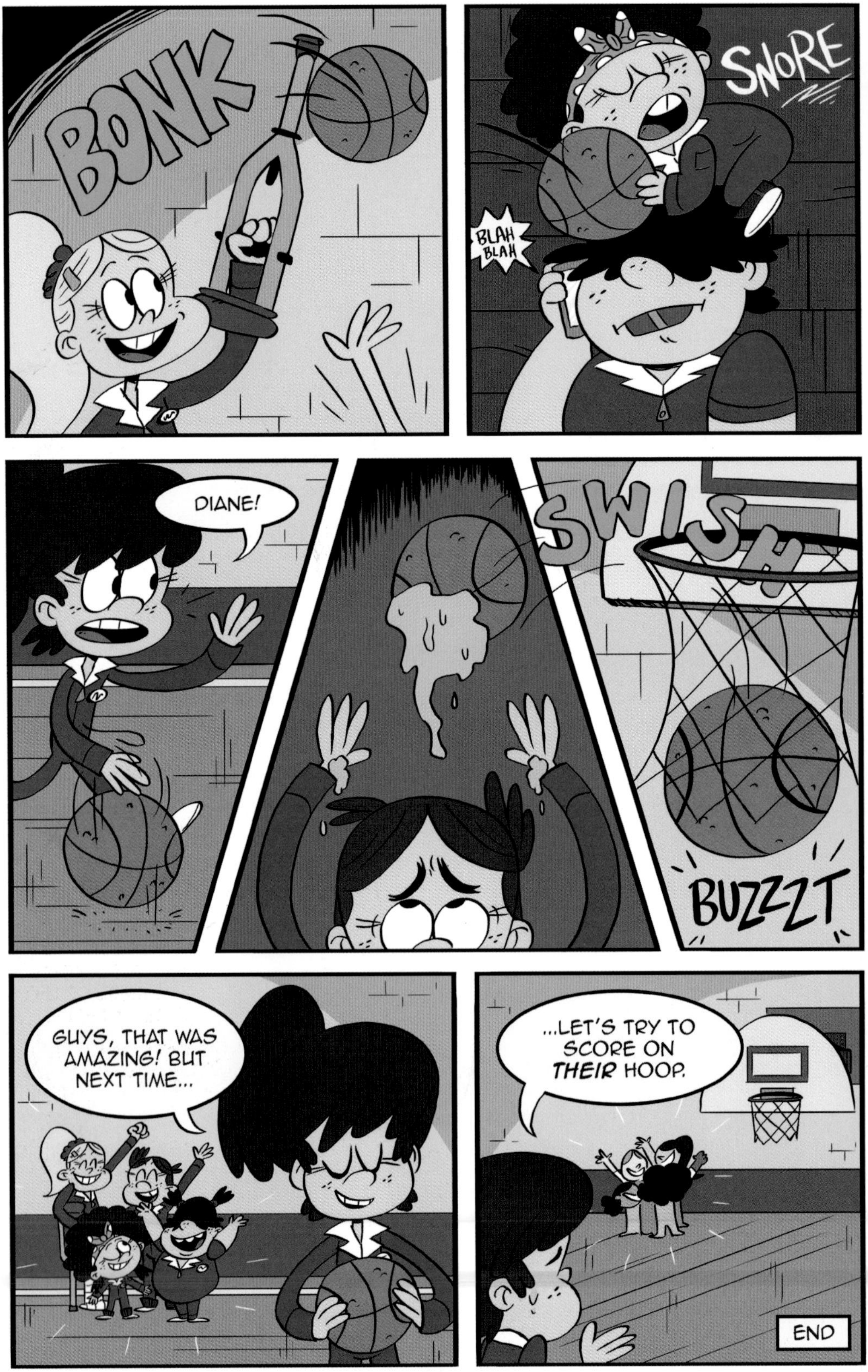
BONK
SNORE
BLAH BLAH
DIANE!
SWISH
BUZZZT
GUYS, THAT WAS AMAZING! BUT NEXT TIME...
...LET'S TRY TO SCORE ON THEIR HOOP.
END

"SITUATION SOUFFLÉ"

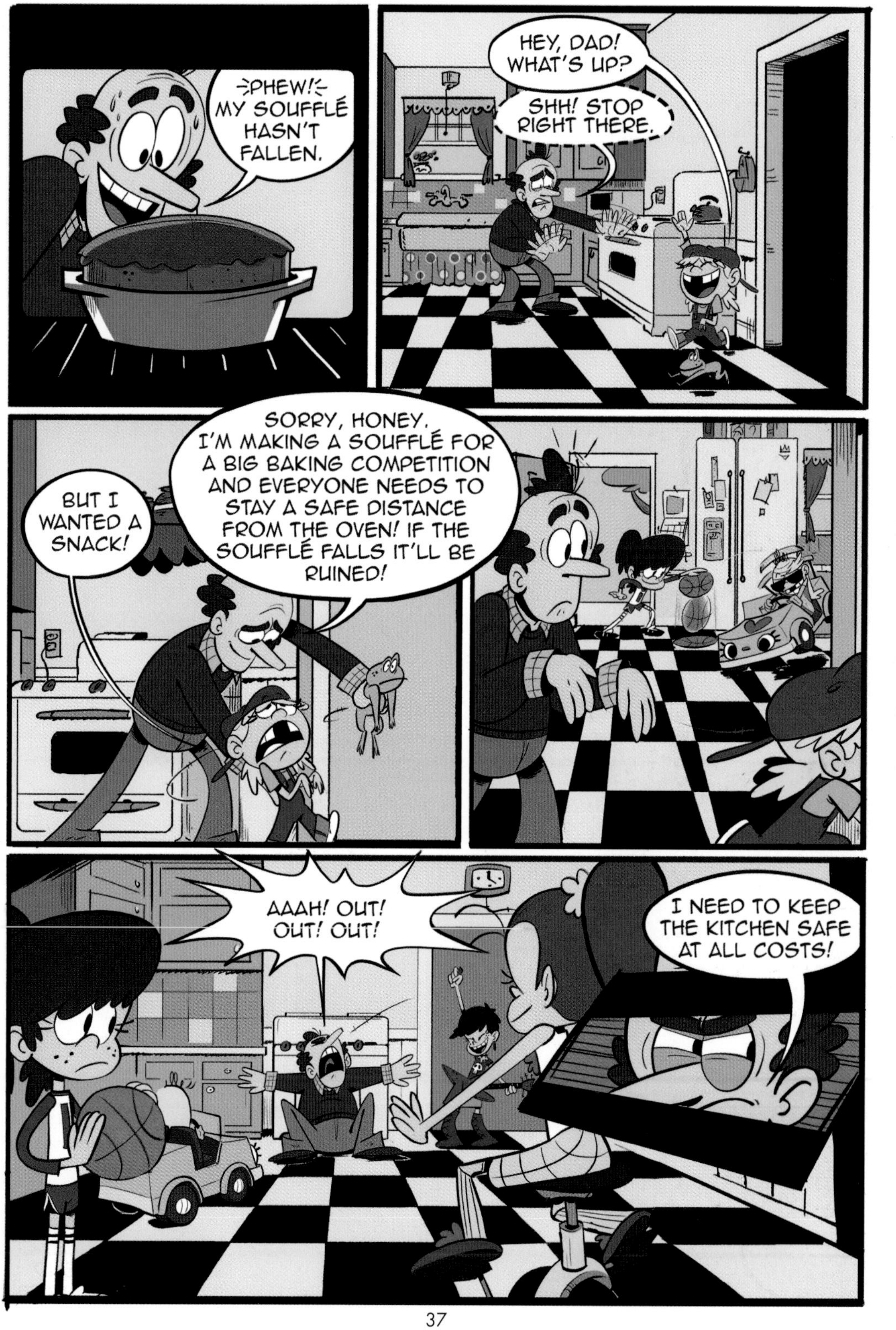

PHEW! MY SOUFFLÉ HASN'T FALLEN.
HEY, DAD! WHAT'S UP?
SHH! STOP RIGHT THERE.
BUT I WANTED A SNACK!
SORRY, HONEY. I'M MAKING A SOUFFLÉ FOR A BIG BAKING COMPETITION AND EVERYONE NEEDS TO STAY A SAFE DISTANCE FROM THE OVEN! IF THE SOUFFLÉ FALLS IT'LL BE RUINED!
AAAH! OUT! OUT! OUT!
I NEED TO KEEP THE KITCHEN SAFE AT ALL COSTS!

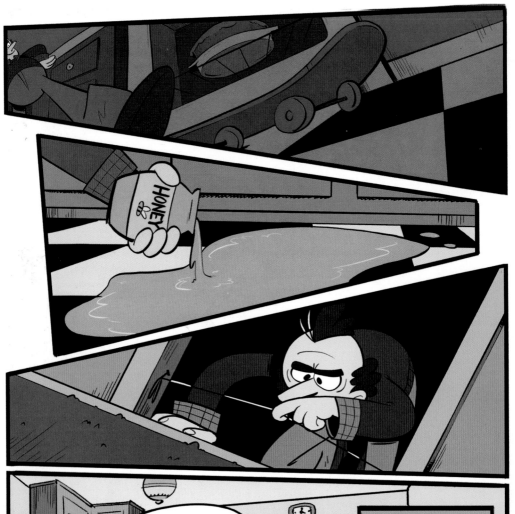

THERE!
NO ONE IS GETTING ANYWHERE NEAR THIS OVEN!

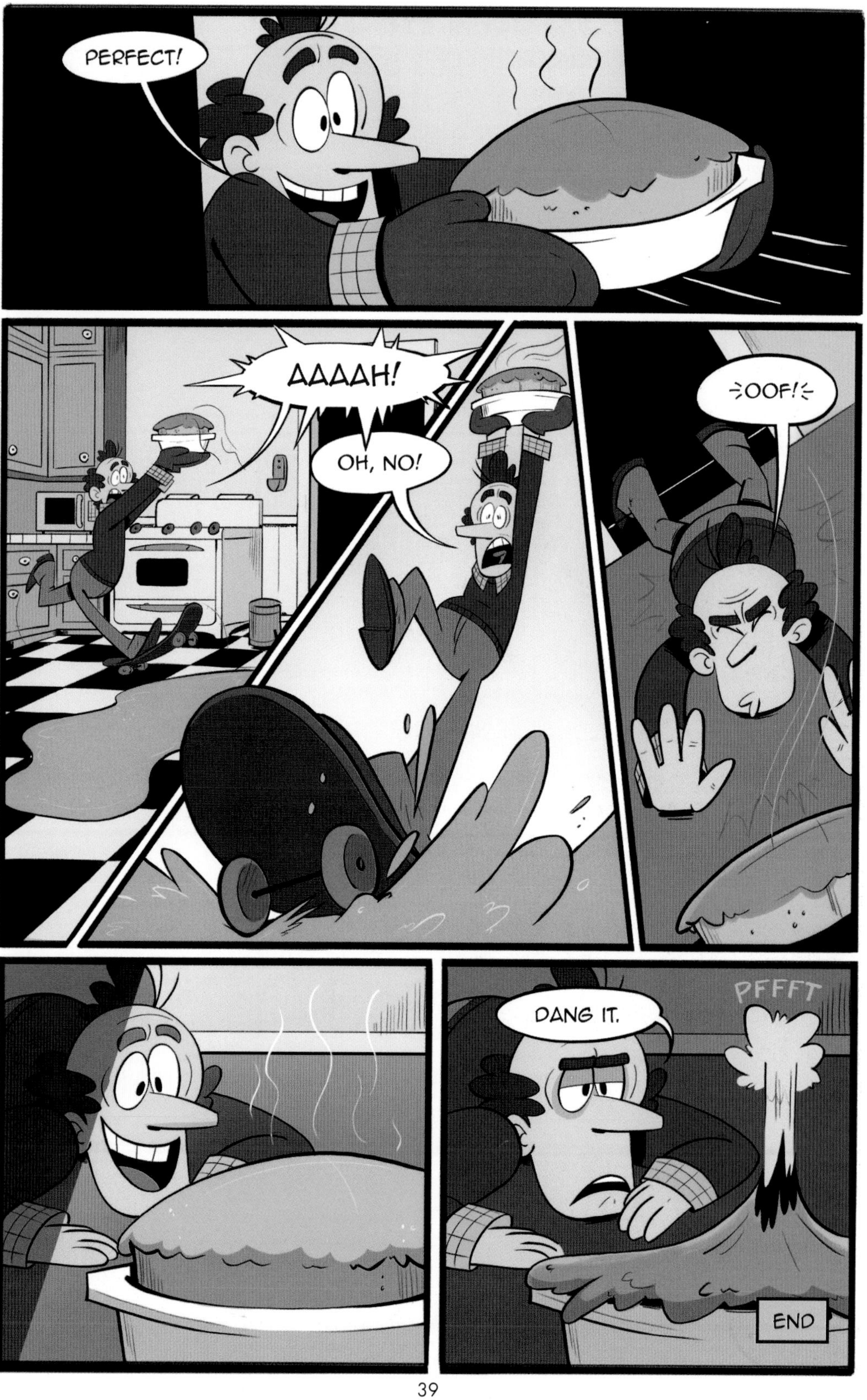
PERFECT!
AAAAH!
OH, NO!
OOF!
DANG IT.
PFFFT
END

"TOUGH HOOKY"

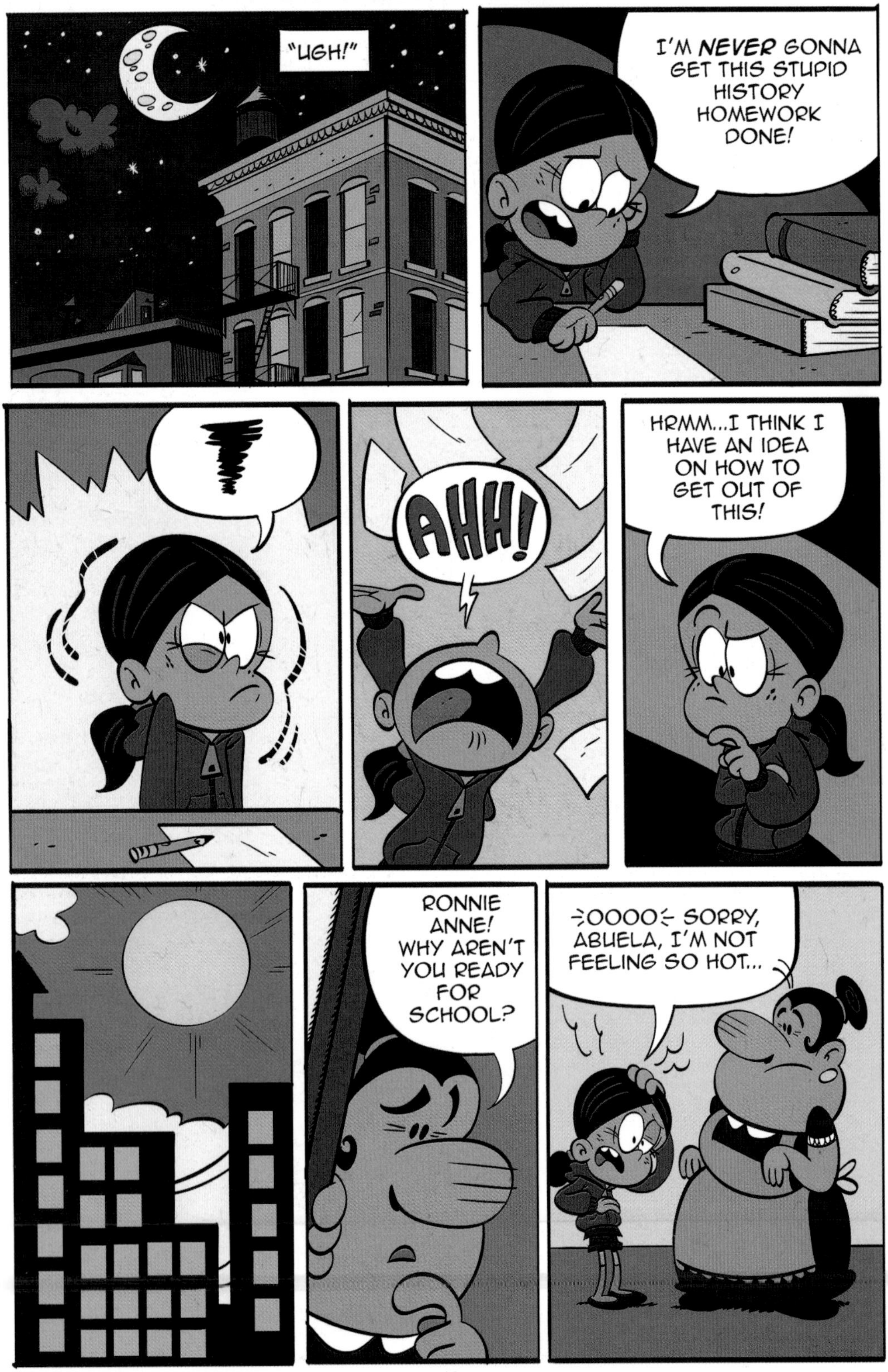
"UGH!"
I'M **NEVER** GONNA GET THIS STUPID HISTORY HOMEWORK DONE!
AHH!
HRMM...I THINK I HAVE AN IDEA ON HOW TO GET OUT OF THIS!
RONNIE ANNE! WHY AREN'T YOU READY FOR SCHOOL?
OOOO SORRY, ABUELA, I'M NOT FEELING SO HOT...

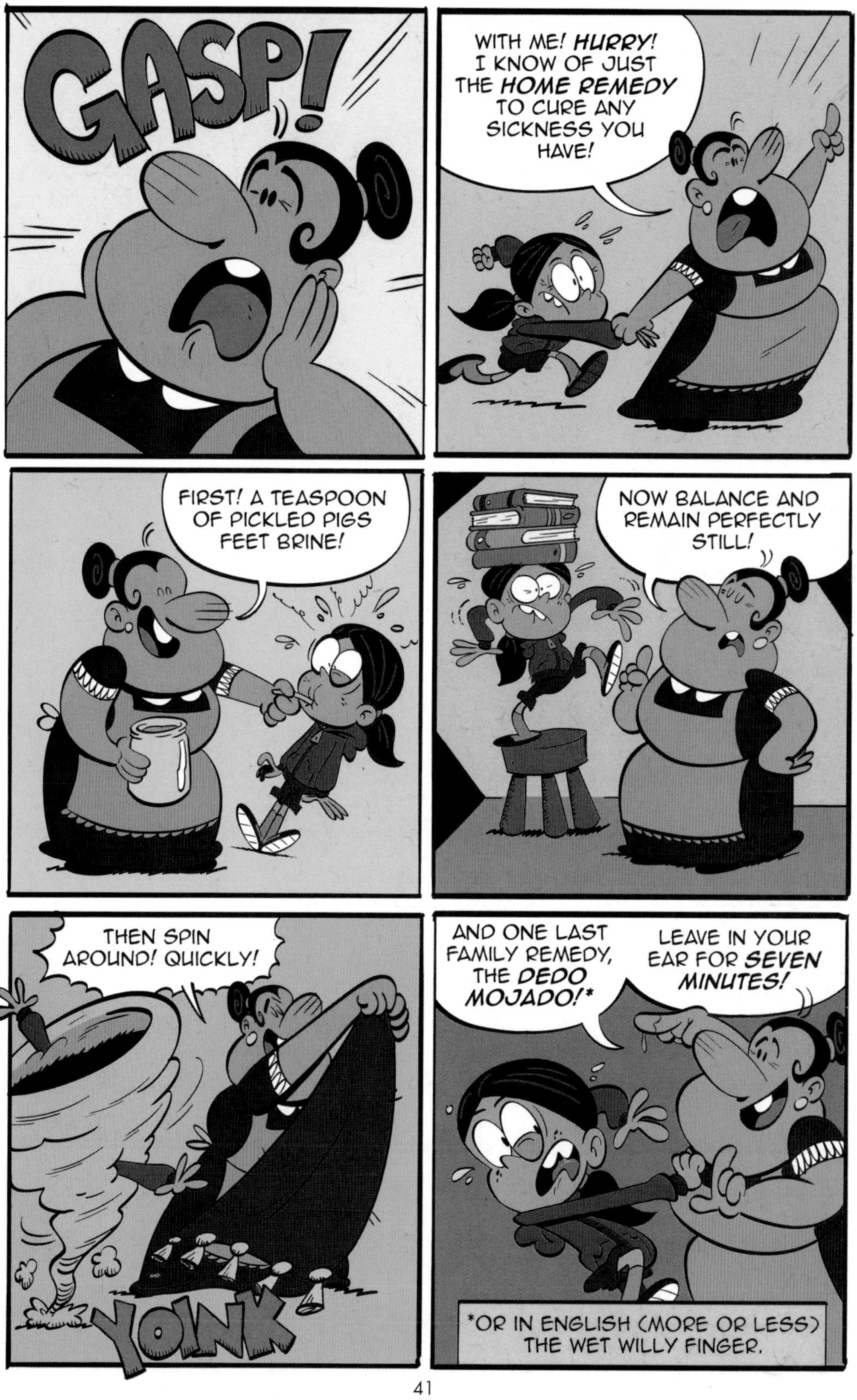
GASP!
WITH ME! HURRY! I KNOW OF JUST THE HOME REMEDY TO CURE ANY SICKNESS YOU HAVE!
FIRST! A TEASPOON OF PICKLED PIGS FEET BRINE!
NOW BALANCE AND REMAIN PERFECTLY STILL!
THEN SPIN AROUND! QUICKLY!
YOINK
AND ONE LAST FAMILY REMEDY, THE DEDO MOJADO!*
LEAVE IN YOUR EAR FOR SEVEN MINUTES!
*OR IN ENGLISH (MORE OR LESS) THE WET WILLY FINGER.

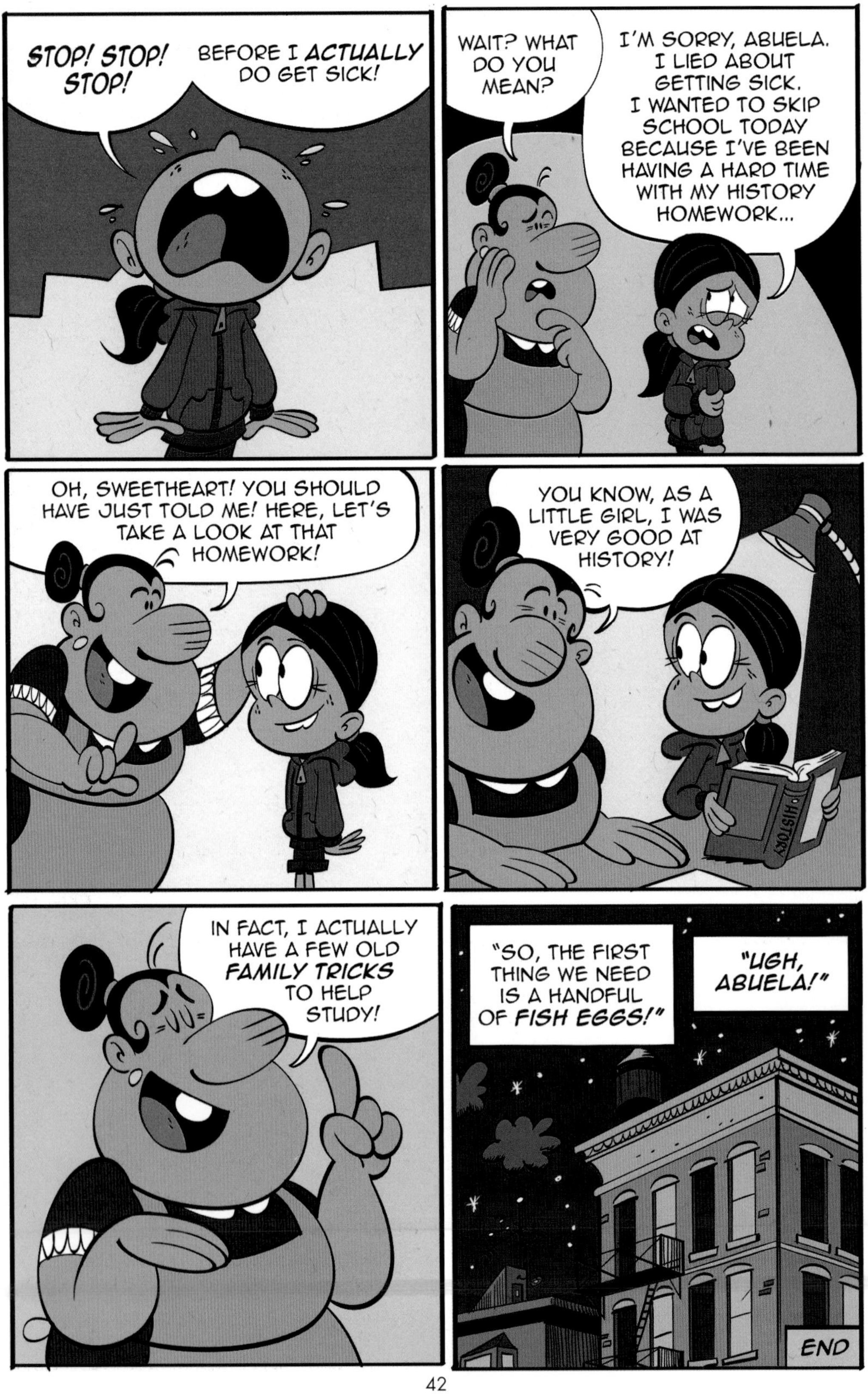
STOP! STOP! STOP!
BEFORE I ACTUALLY DO GET SICK!
WAIT? WHAT DO YOU MEAN?
I'M SORRY, ABUELA. I LIED ABOUT GETTING SICK. I WANTED TO SKIP SCHOOL TODAY BECAUSE I'VE BEEN HAVING A HARD TIME WITH MY HISTORY HOMEWORK...
OH, SWEETHEART! YOU SHOULD HAVE JUST TOLD ME! HERE, LET'S TAKE A LOOK AT THAT HOMEWORK!
YOU KNOW, AS A LITTLE GIRL, I WAS VERY GOOD AT HISTORY!
HISTORY
IN FACT, I ACTUALLY HAVE A FEW OLD FAMILY TRICKS TO HELP STUDY!
"SO, THE FIRST THING WE NEED IS A HANDFUL OF FISH EGGS!"
"UGH, ABUELA!"
END

"SORE PLAYERS"

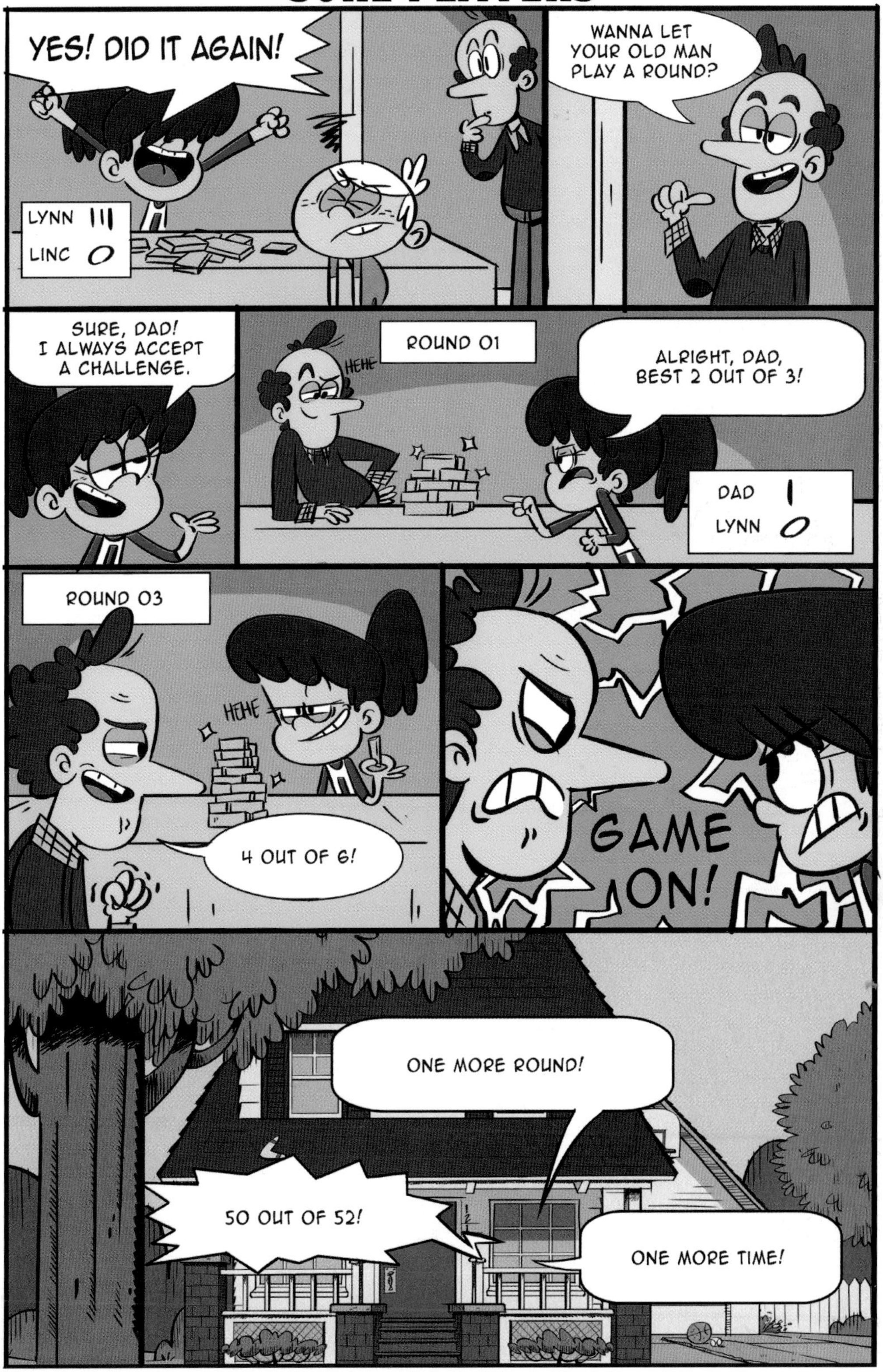
YES! DID IT AGAIN!
LYNN III
LINC 0
WANNA LET YOUR OLD MAN PLAY A ROUND?
SURE, DAD! I ALWAYS ACCEPT A CHALLENGE.
ROUND 01
HEHE
ALRIGHT, DAD, BEST 2 OUT OF 3!
DAD I
LYNN 0
ROUND 03
HEHE
4 OUT OF 6!
GAME ON!
ONE MORE ROUND!
50 OUT OF 52!
ONE MORE TIME!

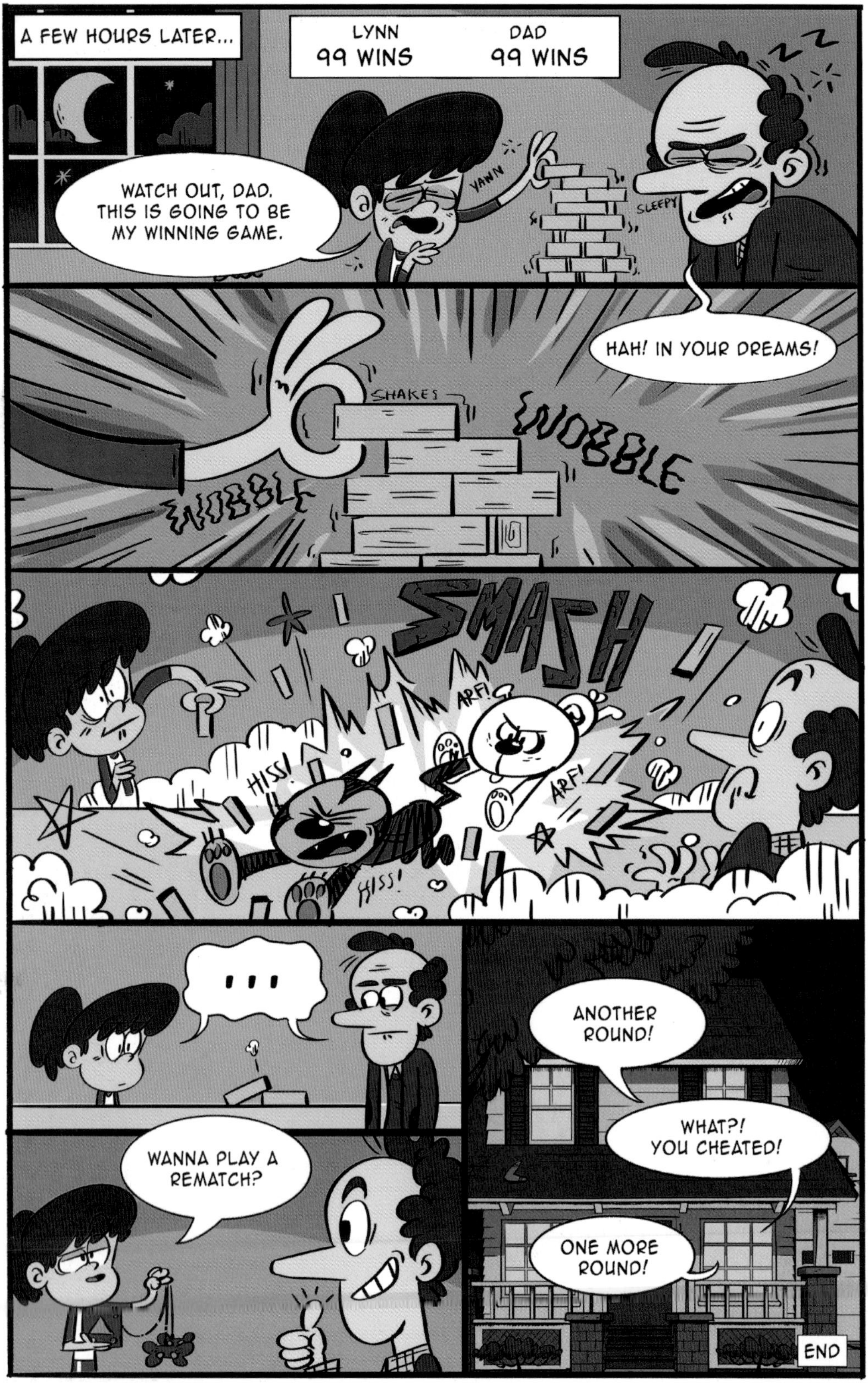
A FEW HOURS LATER...
LYNN 99 WINS
DAD 99 WINS
WATCH OUT, DAD. THIS IS GOING TO BE MY WINNING GAME.
YAWN
SLEEPY
HAH! IN YOUR DREAMS!
SHAKES
WOBBLE
WOBBLE
SMASH
ARF!
HISS!
ARF!
HISS!
...
WANNA PLAY A REMATCH?
ANOTHER ROUND!
WHAT?! YOU CHEATED!
ONE MORE ROUND!
END

"CITIZEN LOUD"

CLYDE AND I ARE ENTERING THE ANNUAL ROYAL WOODS JUNIOR FILMMAKER'S CONTEST! FIRST PLACE WINNERS WILL GET THEIR FILM SCREENED AT THE ROYAL WOODS HISTORIC THEATER!

LINCOLN, THIS MOVIE WILL BRING JOY TO THE MASSES FOR SURE!

CLINCOLN McCLOUD: THE MOVIE!

LET'S DO IT!

ACTION!

LYNN LOUD SHOOTS AND SHE SCORES!

BONK

DANG IT, LYNN! YOU RUINED OUR TAKE!

STINKIN', YOU MADE ME FOUL!

LET'S TRY THIS AGAIN.

ACTION!

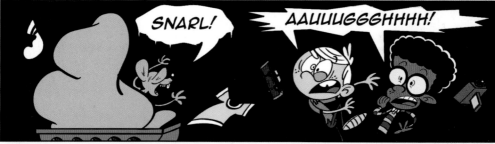

SNARL!

AAUUUGGGHHHH!

AWWW, THERE YOU ARE, BITEY! IT'S TIME FOR YOUR MUD BATH!

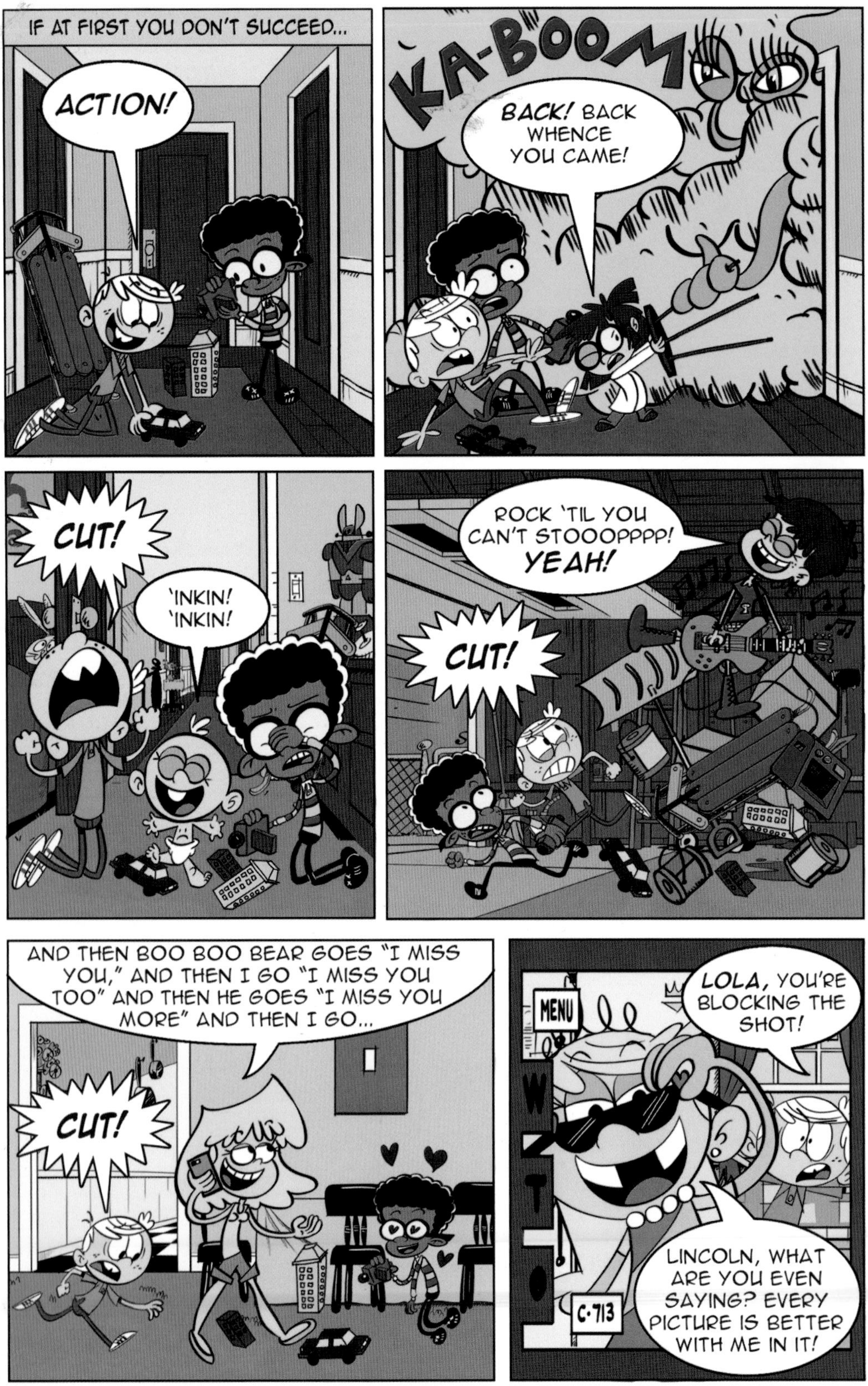
IF AT FIRST YOU DON'T SUCCEED...
ACTION!
KA-BOOM
BACK! BACK WHENCE YOU CAME!
CUT!
'INKIN! 'INKIN!
ROCK 'TIL YOU CAN'T STOOOPPPP! YEAH!
CUT!
AND THEN BOO BOO BEAR GOES "I MISS YOU," AND THEN I GO "I MISS YOU TOO" AND THEN HE GOES "I MISS YOU MORE" AND THEN I GO...
CUT!
LOLA, YOU'RE BLOCKING THE SHOT!
LINCOLN, WHAT ARE YOU EVEN SAYING? EVERY PICTURE IS BETTER WITH ME IN IT!
MENU
C-713

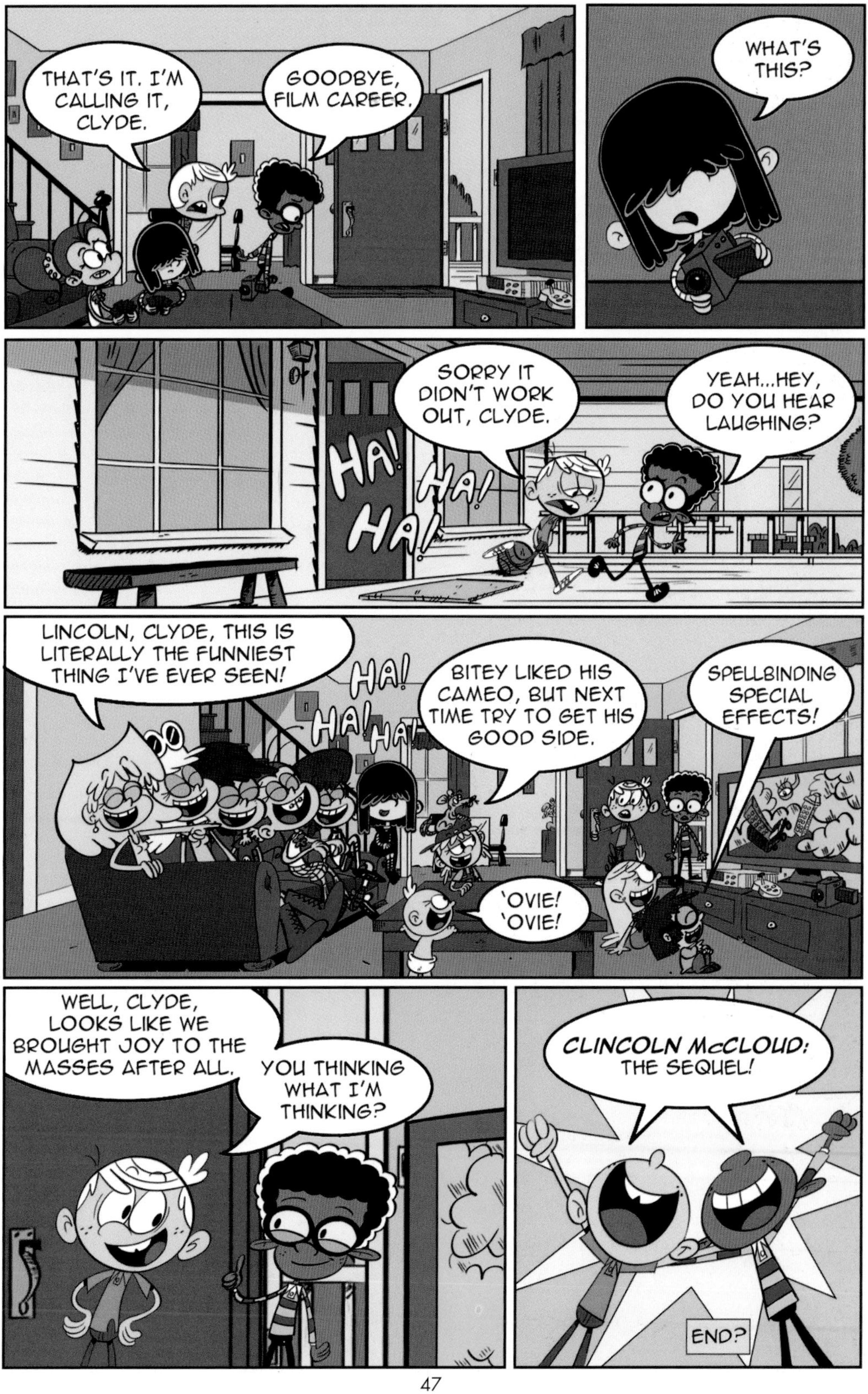
THAT'S IT. I'M CALLING IT, CLYDE.
GOODBYE, FILM CAREER.
WHAT'S THIS?
SORRY IT DIDN'T WORK OUT, CLYDE.
HA! HA! HA!
YEAH...HEY, DO YOU HEAR LAUGHING?
LINCOLN, CLYDE, THIS IS LITERALLY THE FUNNIEST THING I'VE EVER SEEN!
HA! HA! HA!
BITEY LIKED HIS CAMEO, BUT NEXT TIME TRY TO GET HIS GOOD SIDE.
SPELLBINDING SPECIAL EFFECTS!
'OVIE! 'OVIE!
WELL, CLYDE, LOOKS LIKE WE BROUGHT JOY TO THE MASSES AFTER ALL.
YOU THINKING WHAT I'M THINKING?
CLINCOLN McCLOUD: THE SEQUEL!
END?

"BABY BREAK"

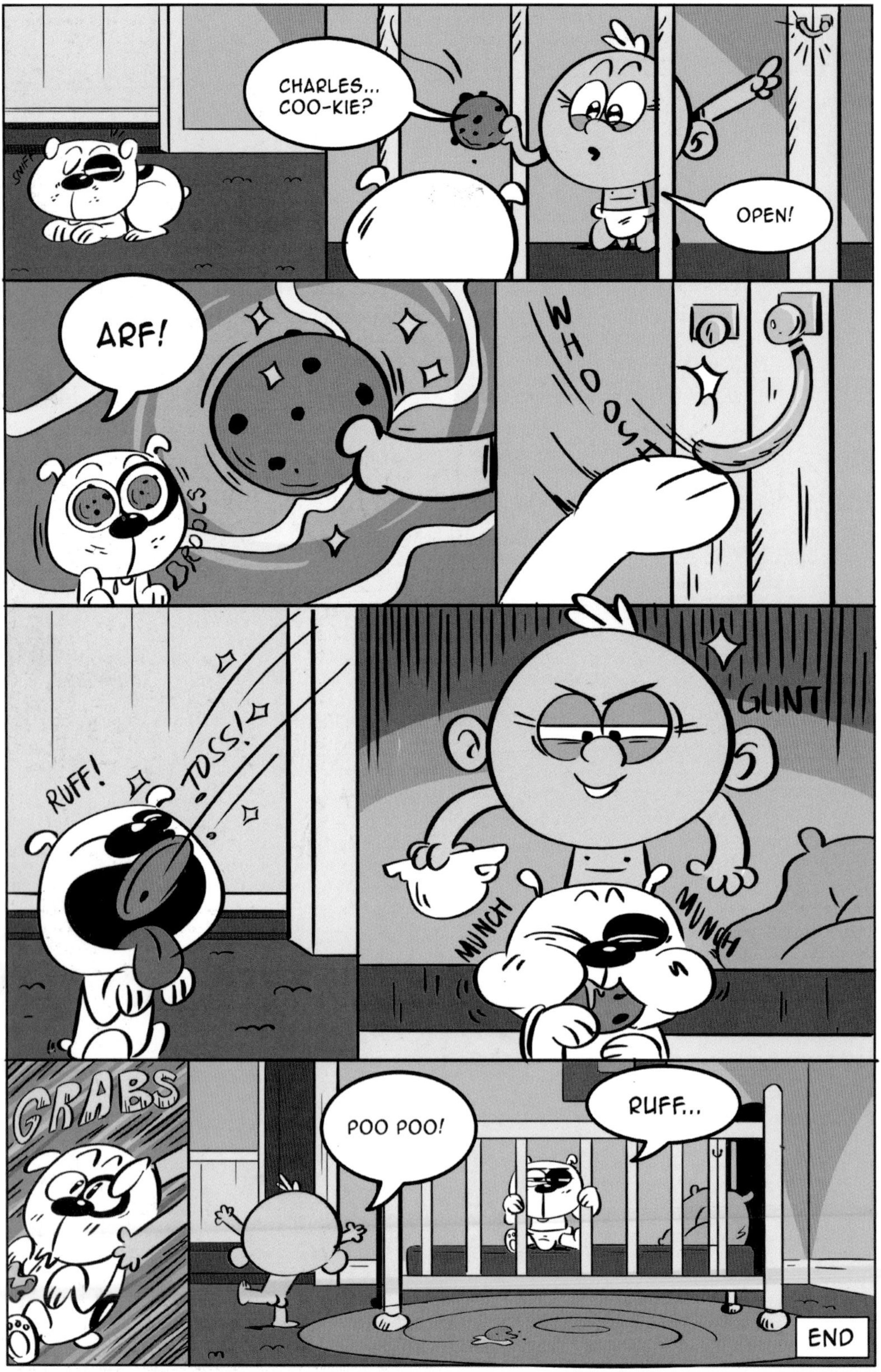
SNIFF
CHARLES... COO-KIE?
OPEN!
ARF!
DROOLS
WHOOSH
RUFF!
TOSS!
GLINT
MUNCH
MUNCH
GRABS
POO POO!
RUFF...
END

"LEAVE A PENNY, TAKE A PENNY"

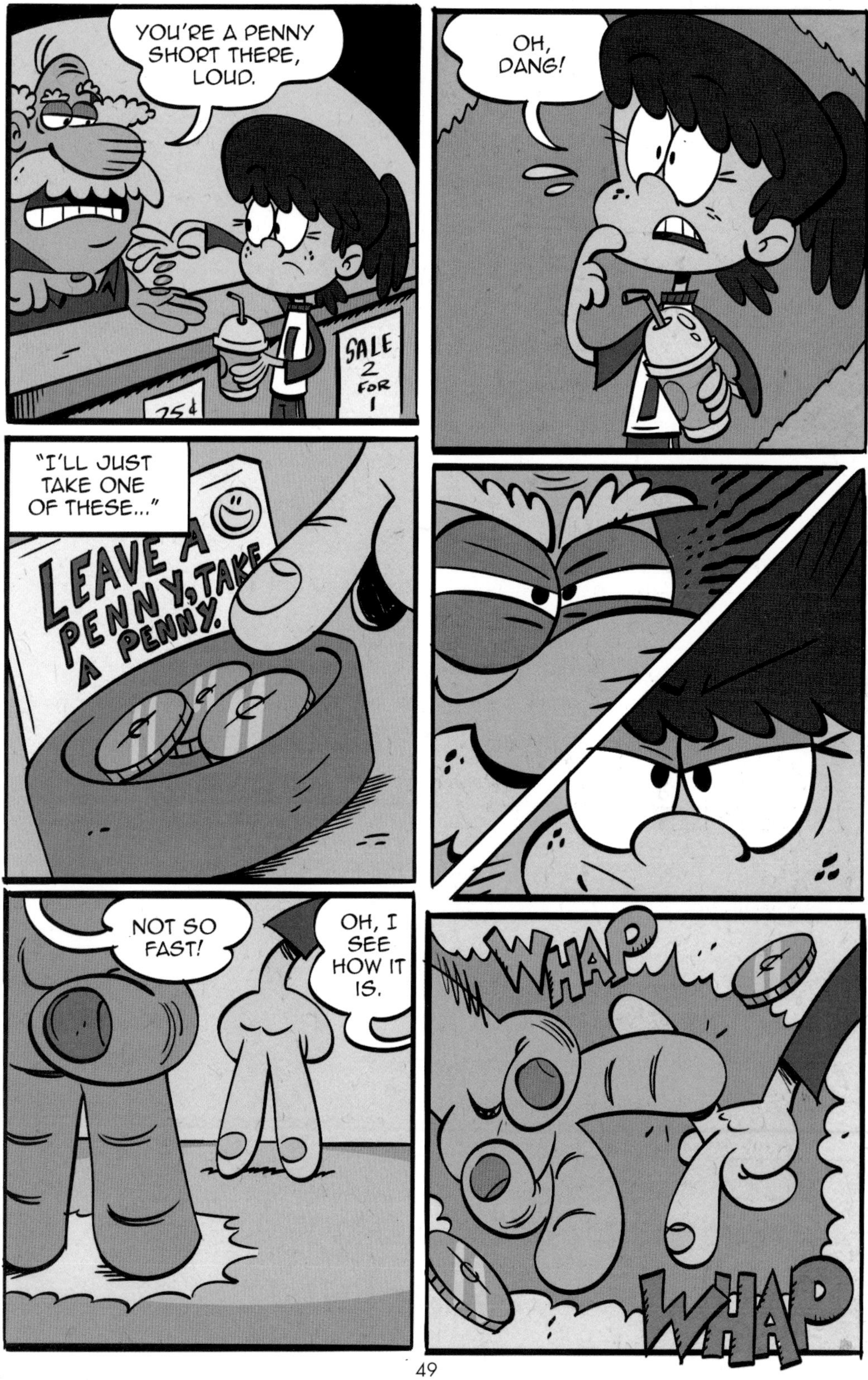
YOU'RE A PENNY SHORT THERE, LOUD.
SALE 2 FOR 1
25¢
OH, DANG!
"I'LL JUST TAKE ONE OF THESE..."
LEAVE A PENNY, TAKE A PENNY.
NOT SO FAST!
OH, I SEE HOW IT IS.
WHAP
WHAP

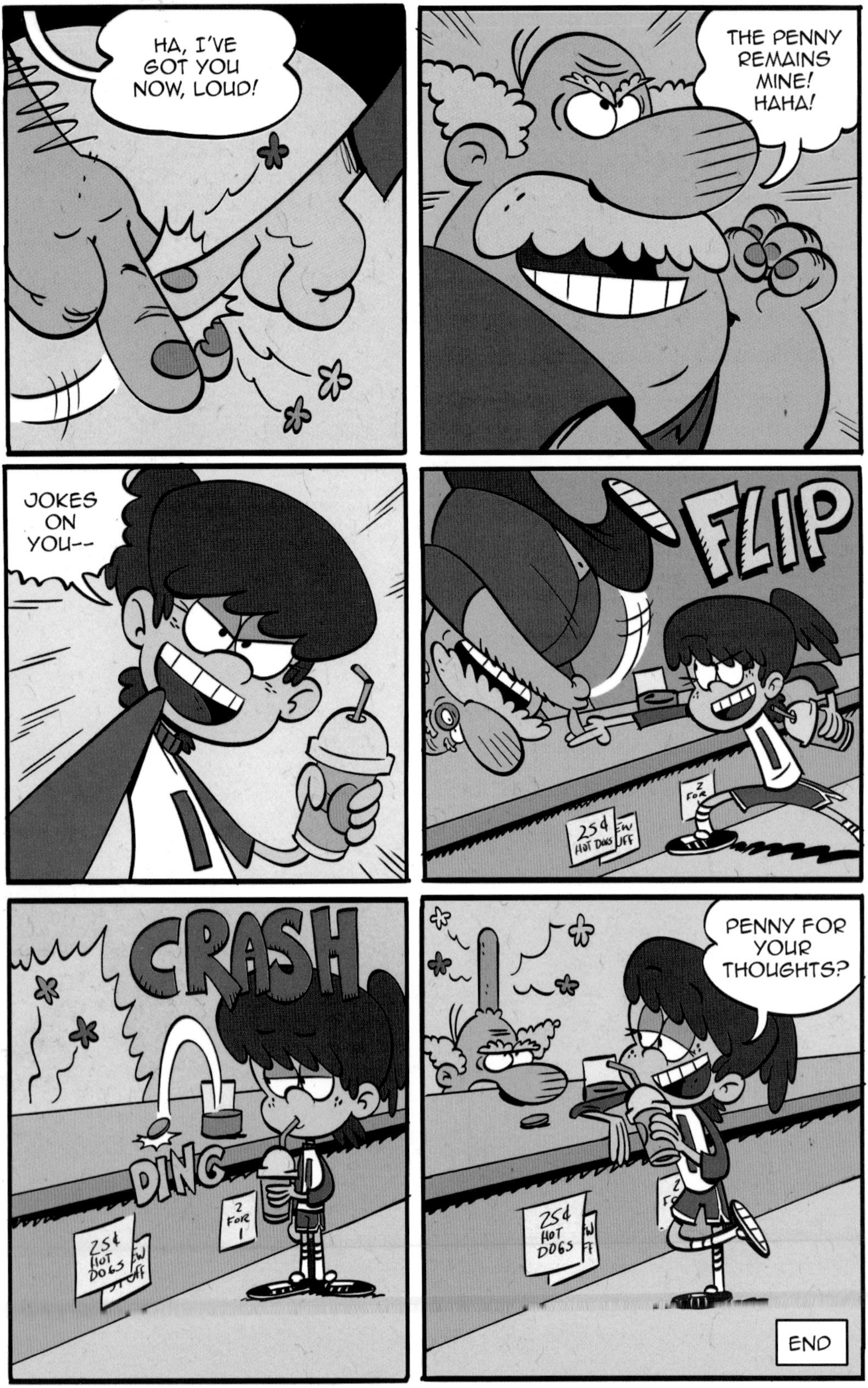
HA, I'VE GOT YOU NOW, LOUD!
THE PENNY REMAINS MINE! HAHA!
JOKES ON YOU--
FLIP
25¢ HOT DOGS
CRASH
DING
2 FOR 1
25¢ HOT DOGS
PENNY FOR YOUR THOUGHTS?
25¢ HOT DOGS
END

"DRESSED OUT"

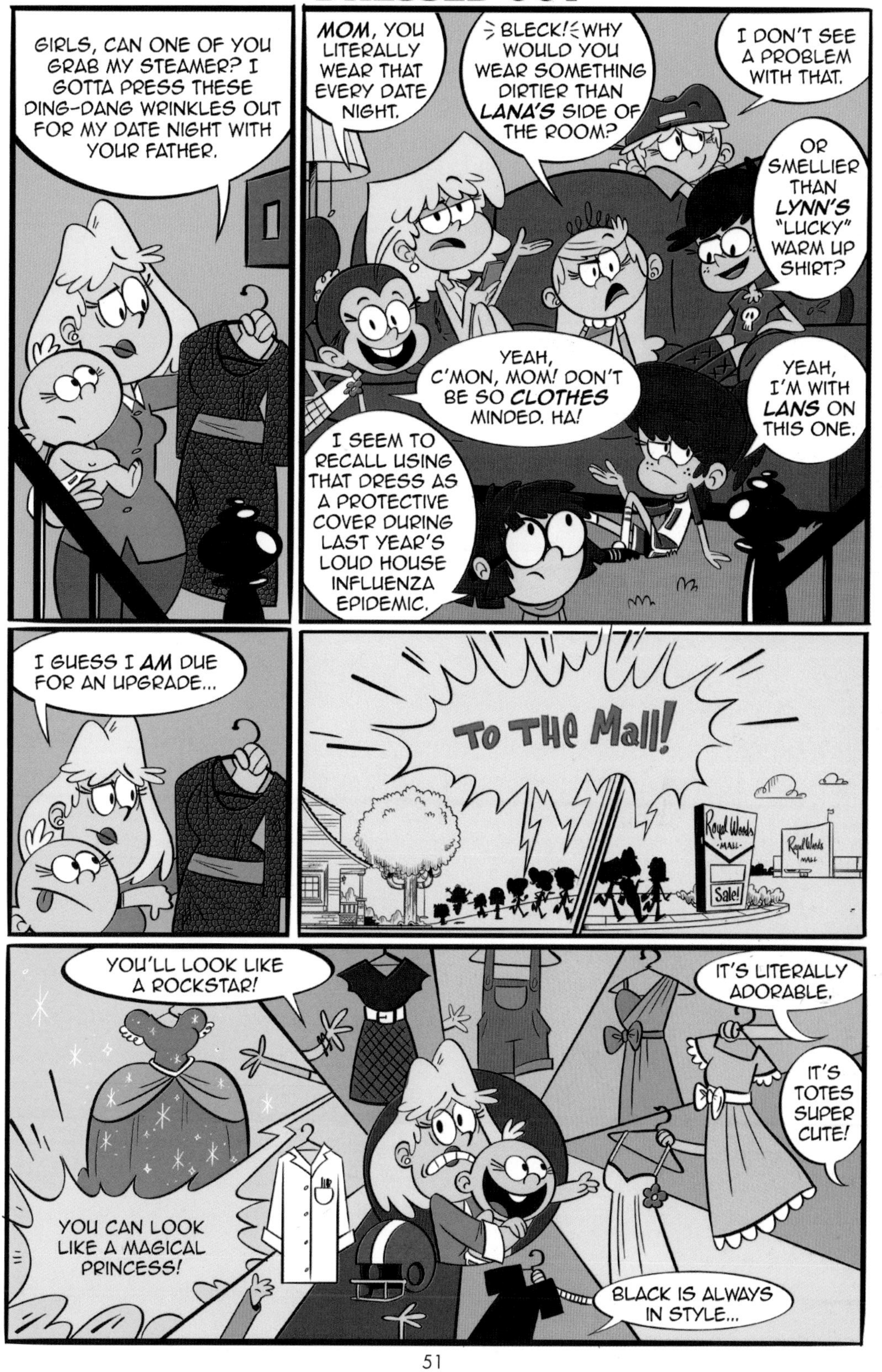
GIRLS, CAN ONE OF YOU GRAB MY STEAMER? I GOTTA PRESS THESE DING-DANG WRINKLES OUT FOR MY DATE NIGHT WITH YOUR FATHER.
MOM, YOU LITERALLY WEAR THAT EVERY DATE NIGHT.
BLECK! WHY WOULD YOU WEAR SOMETHING DIRTIER THAN LANA'S SIDE OF THE ROOM?
I DON'T SEE A PROBLEM WITH THAT.
OR SMELLIER THAN LYNN'S "LUCKY" WARM UP SHIRT?
YEAH, C'MON, MOM! DON'T BE SO CLOTHES MINDED. HA!
YEAH, I'M WITH LANS ON THIS ONE.
I SEEM TO RECALL USING THAT DRESS AS A PROTECTIVE COVER DURING LAST YEAR'S LOUD HOUSE INFLUENZA EPIDEMIC.
I GUESS I AM DUE FOR AN UPGRADE...
TO THE MALL!
Royal Woods MALL
Sale!
Royal Woods MALL
YOU'LL LOOK LIKE A ROCKSTAR!
IT'S LITERALLY ADORABLE.
IT'S TOTES SUPER CUTE!
YOU CAN LOOK LIKE A MAGICAL PRINCESS!
BLACK IS ALWAYS IN STYLE...

AW, THANKS, GIRLS, BUT I JUST DON'T THINK ANY OF THESE DRESSES ARE *MY* STYLE...

WAIT A MINUTE! I THINK I FOUND THE DRESS!

CHECK OUT

DO YOU KNOW WHAT MOM PICKED?

NOT A CLUE...

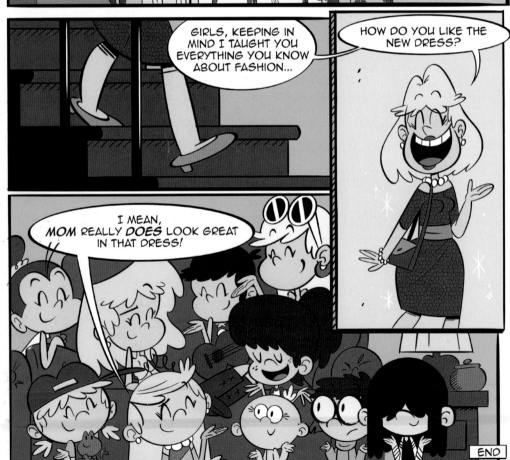

GIRLS, KEEPING IN MIND I TAUGHT YOU EVERYTHING YOU KNOW ABOUT FASHION...

HOW DO YOU LIKE THE NEW DRESS?

I MEAN, *MOM* REALLY *DOES* LOOK GREAT IN THAT DRESS!

END

"LUCY'S ABCs OF THE LOUD HOUSE"

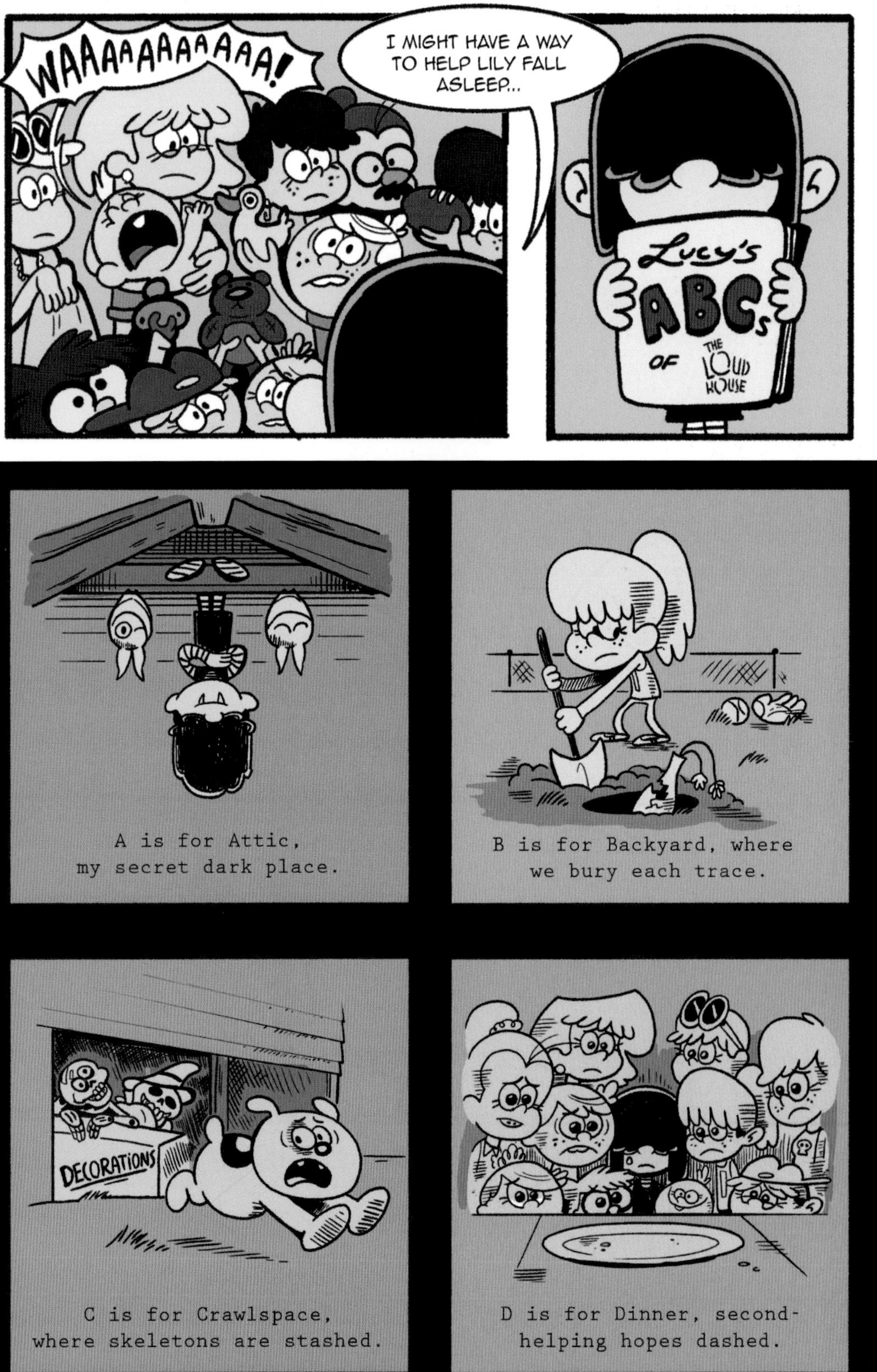
WAAAAAAAAAAA!
I MIGHT HAVE A WAY TO HELP LILY FALL ASLEEP...
Lucy's ABCs OF THE LOUD HOUSE
A is for Attic, my secret dark place.
B is for Backyard, where we bury each trace.
DECORATIONS
C is for Crawlspace, where skeletons are stashed.
D is for Dinner, second-helping hopes dashed.

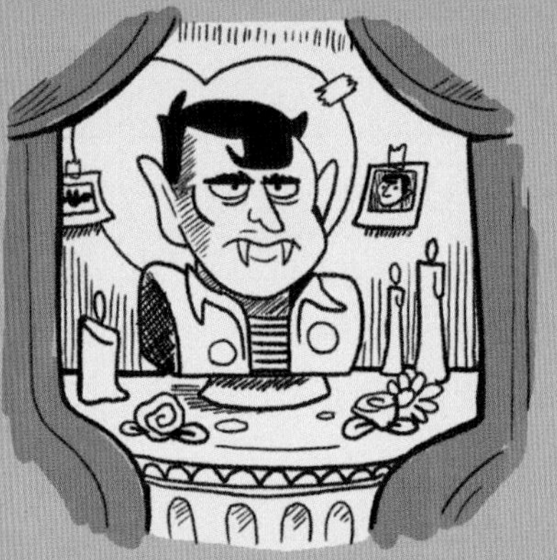

E is for Edwin shrine,
safe in my room.

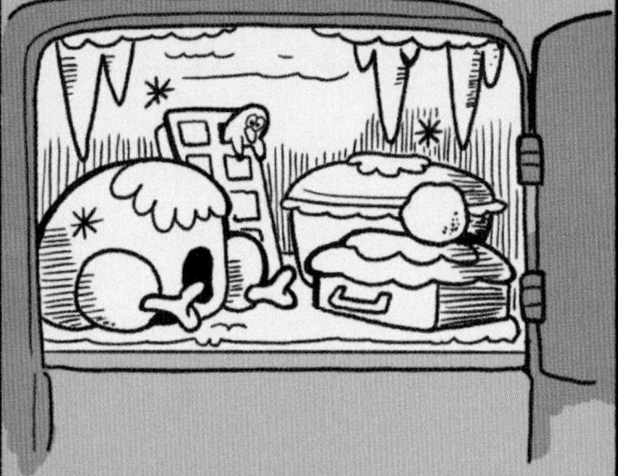

F is for Freezer, where
leftovers meet their doom.

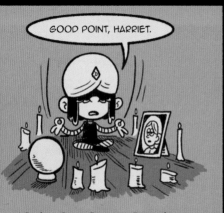

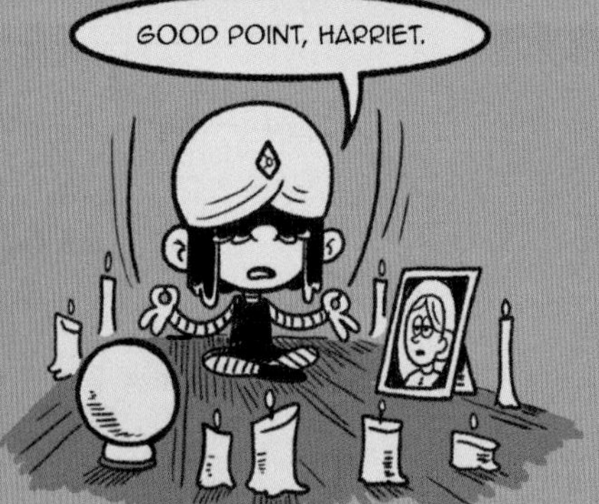
GOOD POINT, HARRIET.

G is for Great Grandma,
of whom I'm so fond.

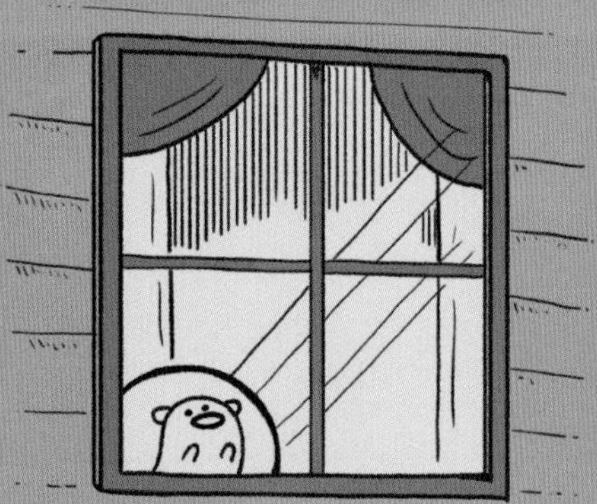

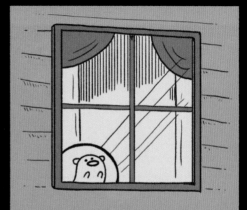

H is for Hamster ball,
Geo can't get beyond.

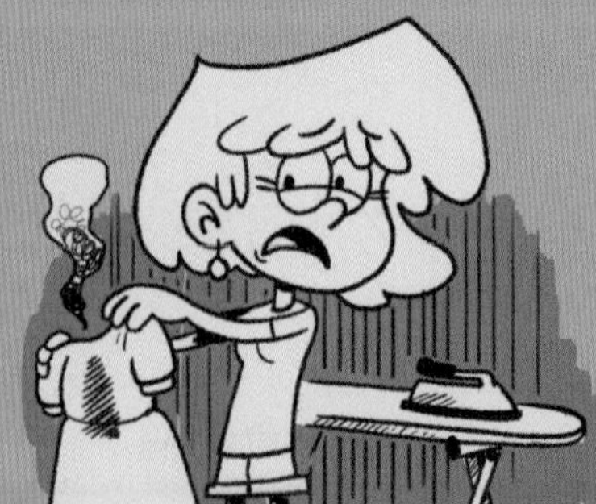

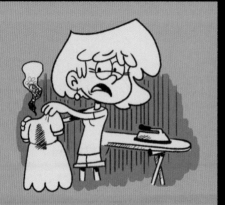

I is for Iron,
feared by our clothes.

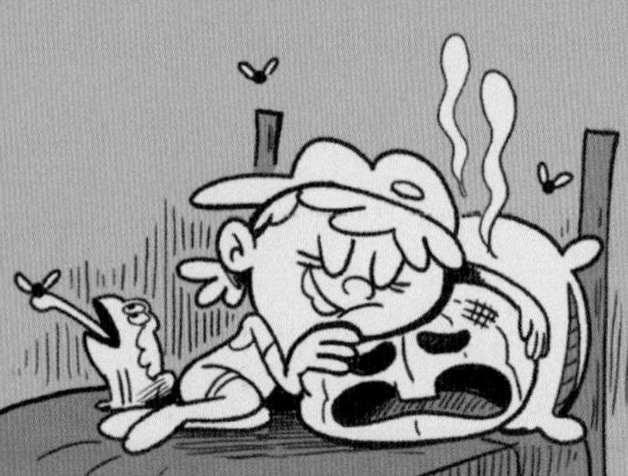

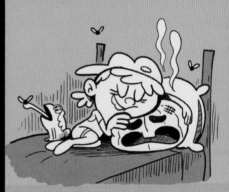

J is for Jack-O-Lantern
that got really gross.

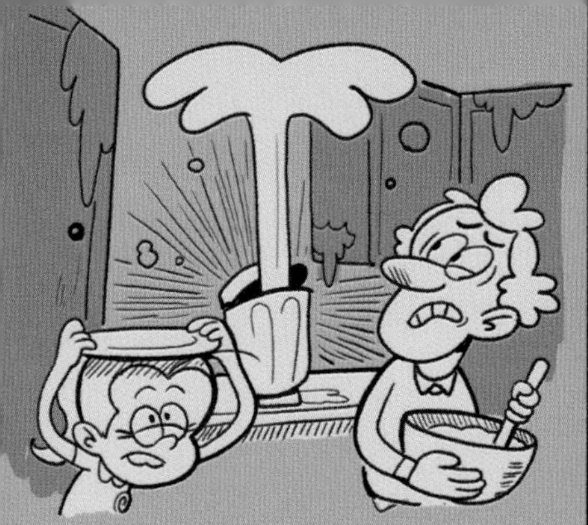

K is for Kitchen,
whose hazards are various.

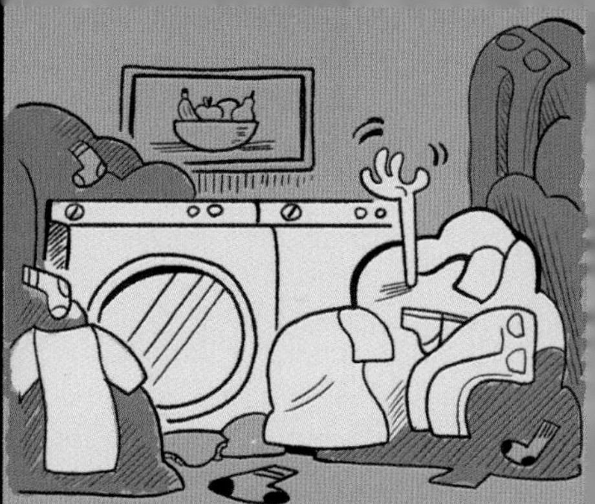

L is for Laundry that
threatens to bury us.

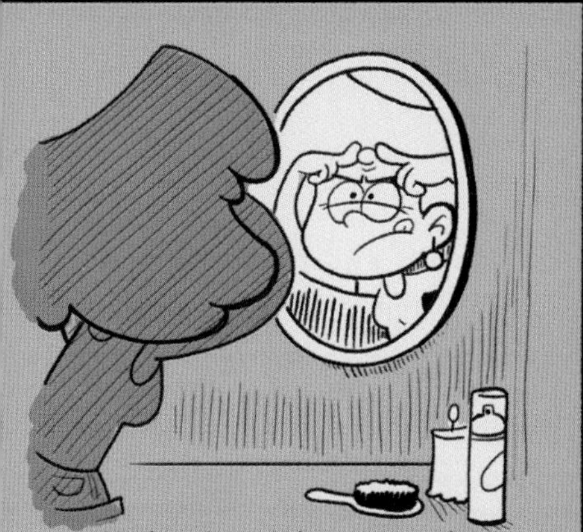

M is for Mirror and
the horrors it's seen.

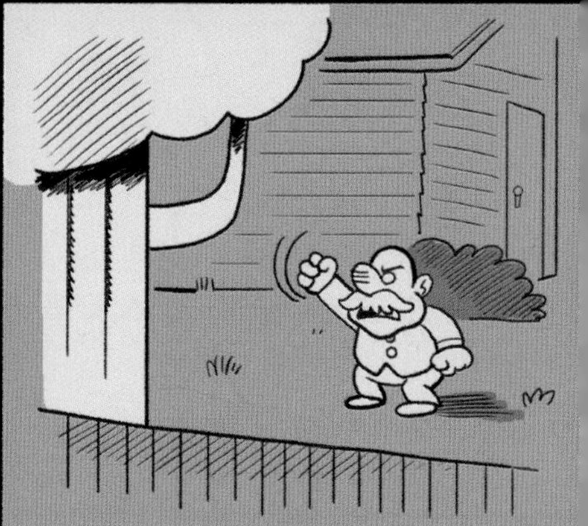

N is for Next-door neighbors
who're totally mean.

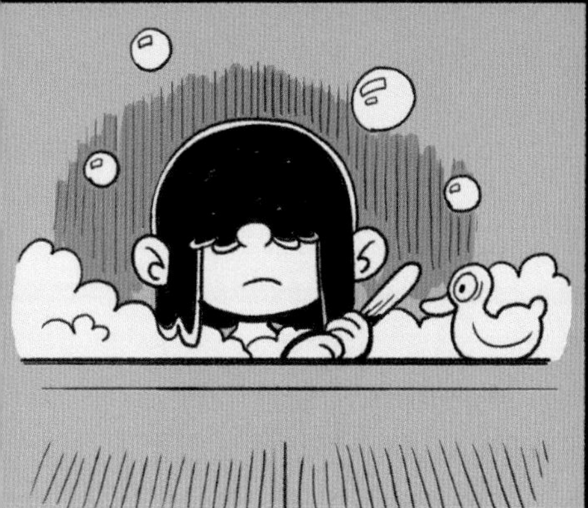

O is for Omens, which I
see in my bubble brew.

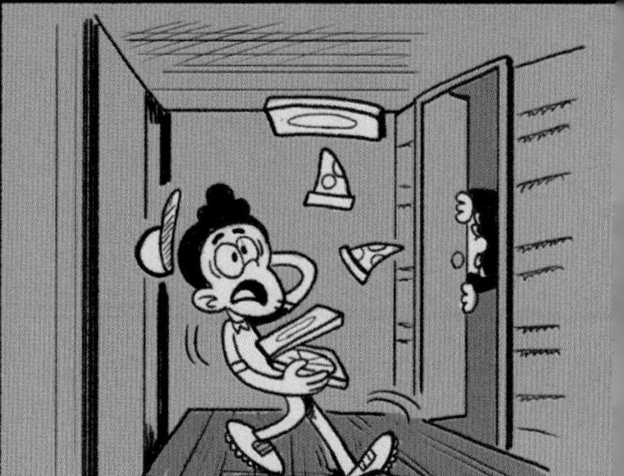

P is for Porch boards,
rotted right through.

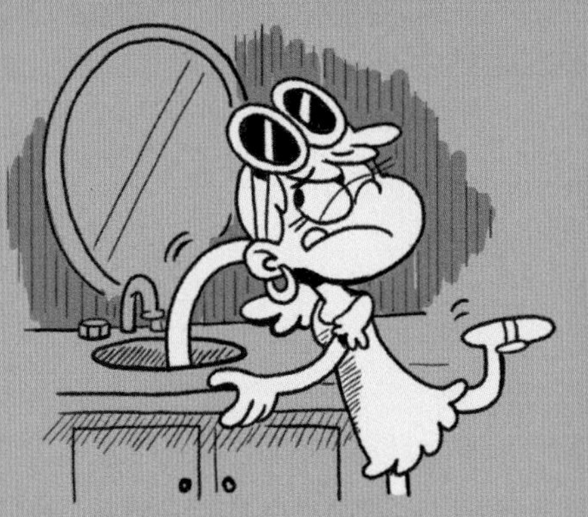

Q is for Quarters
lost down the drain.

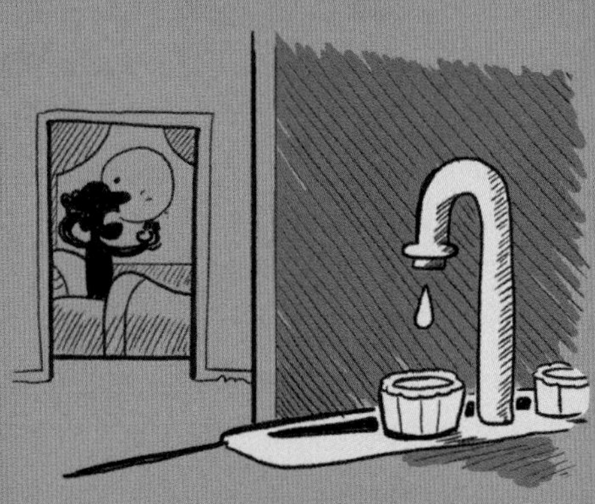

R is for Runny faucet-
it drives Dad insane!

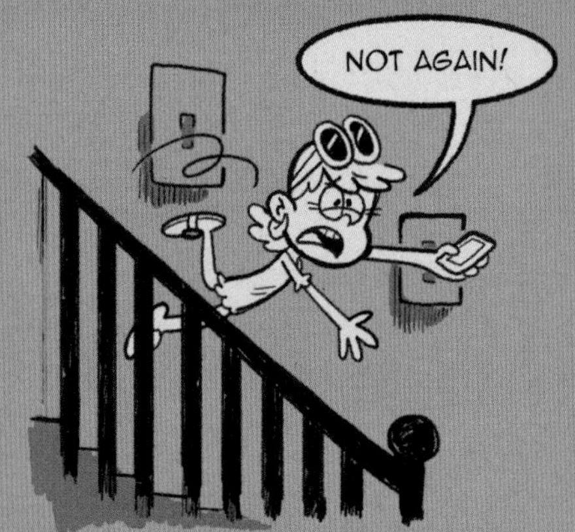
NOT AGAIN!

S is for Staircase,
where Leni pratfalls.

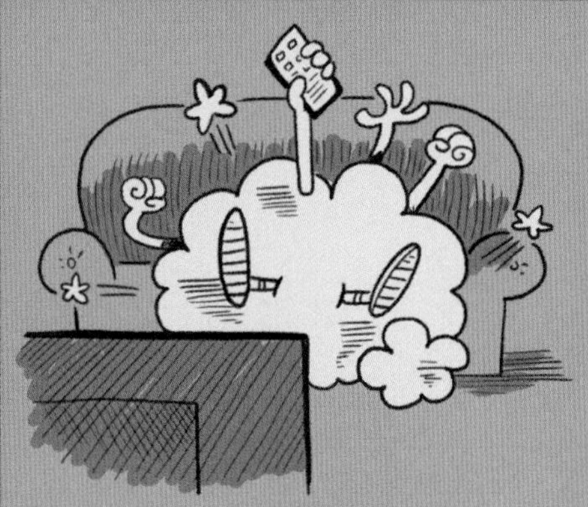

T is for TV remote,
which causes brawls.

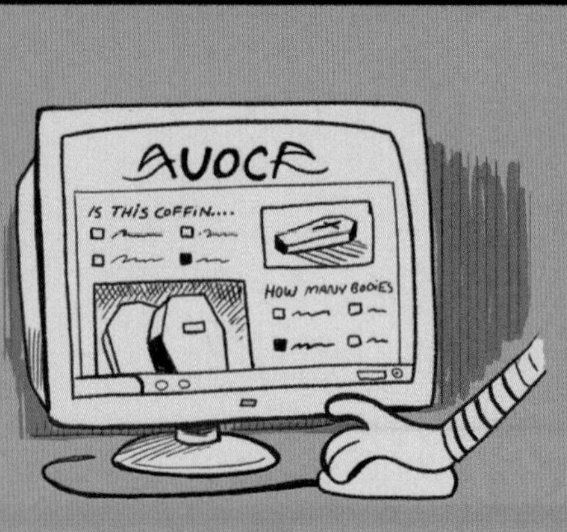
AUOCF
IS THIS COFFIN....
HOW MANY BODIES

U is for Undertaker's
online course...

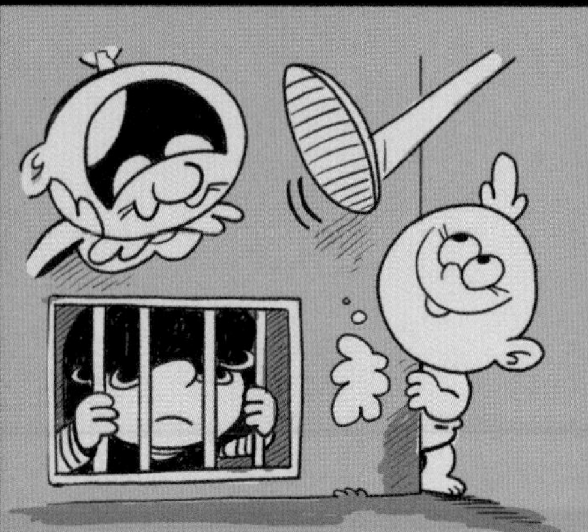

V is for Vents, when
chaos is in full force.

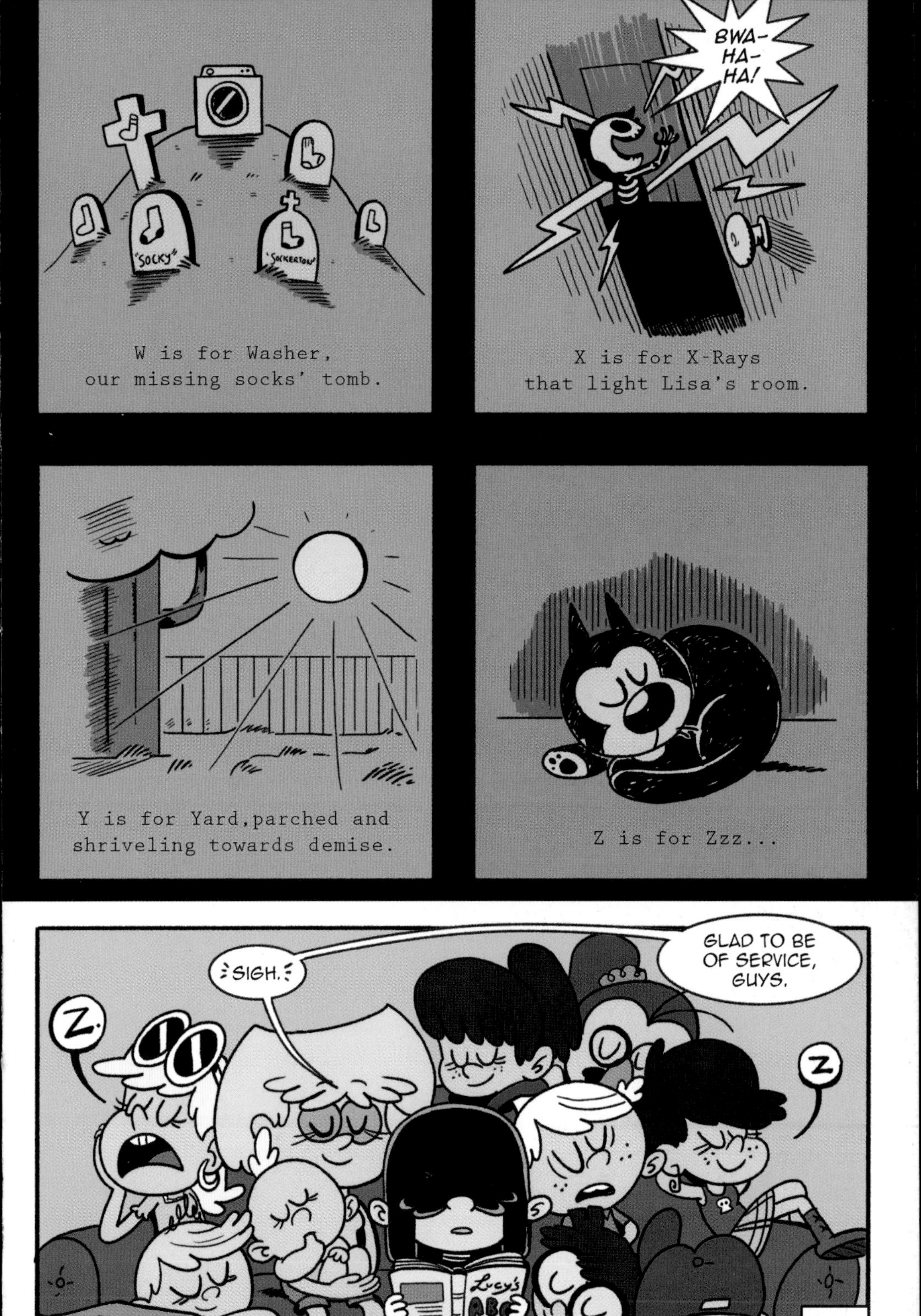
"SOCKY"
"SOCKERTON"
W is for Washer,
our missing socks' tomb.
BWA-HA-HA!
X is for X-Rays
that light Lisa's room.
Y is for Yard,parched and
shriveling towards demise.
Z is for Zzz...
Z
SIGH.
GLAD TO BE OF SERVICE, GUYS.
Z
Lucy's ABC
END

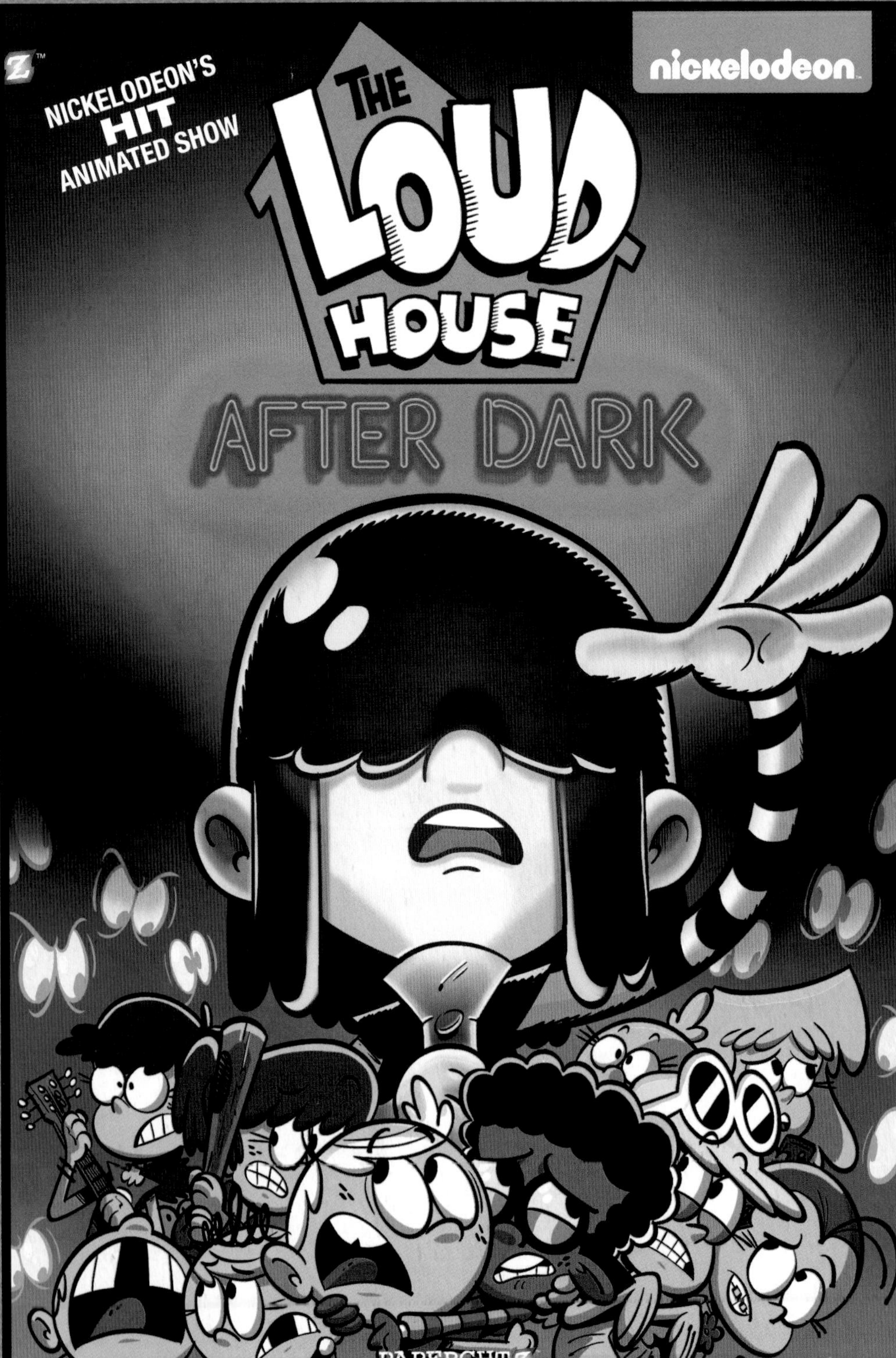
NICKELODEON'S
HIT
ANIMATED SHOW
nickelodeon
THE LOUD HOUSE
AFTER DARK
PAPERCUTZ

THE LOUD HOUSE #5 Cover Art by Jared Morgan

"10:55 PM: GHOST OF THE TOWN"

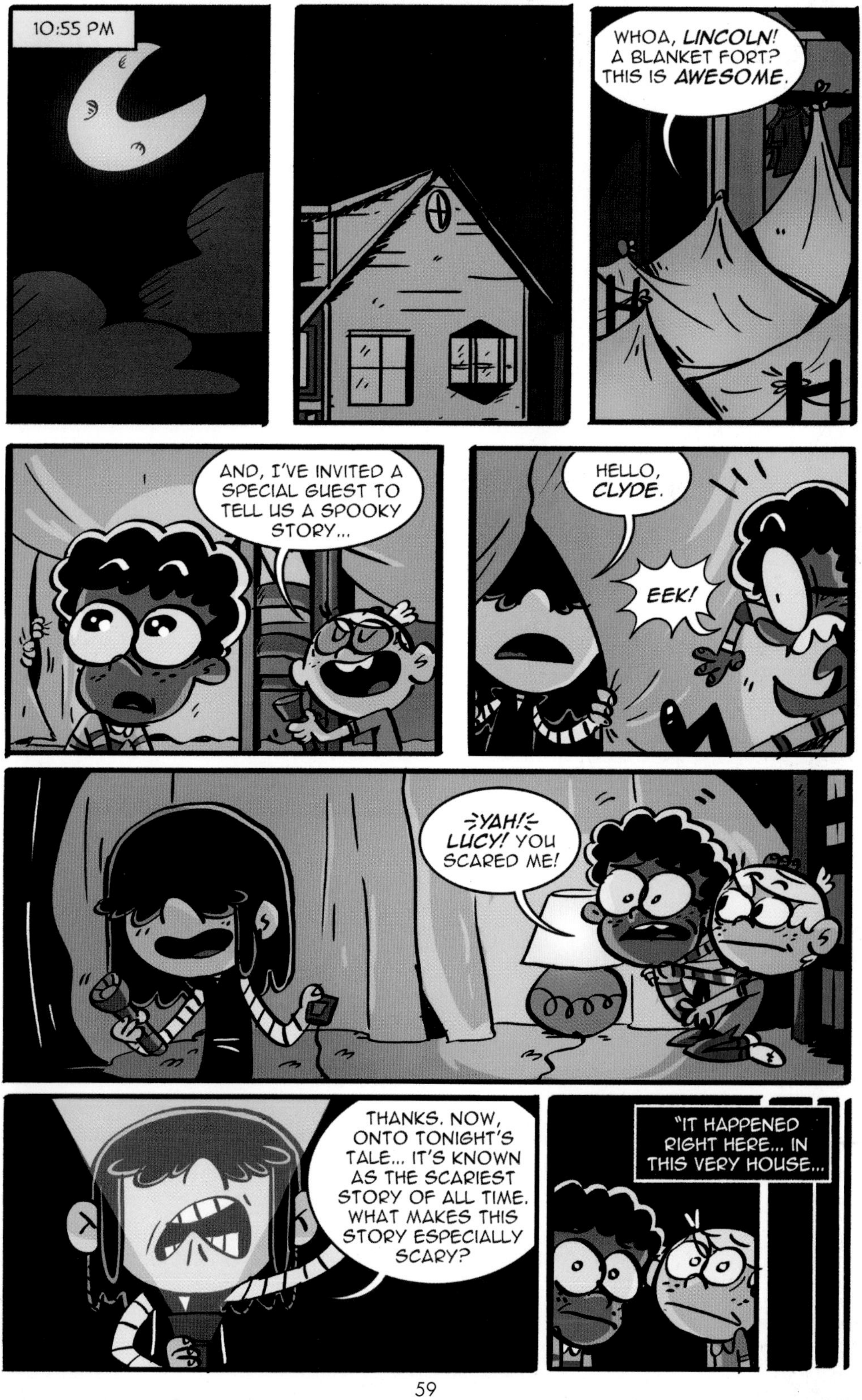
10:55 PM
WHOA, LINCOLN! A BLANKET FORT? THIS IS AWESOME.
AND, I'VE INVITED A SPECIAL GUEST TO TELL US A SPOOKY STORY...
HELLO, CLYDE.
EEK!
YAH! LUCY! YOU SCARED ME!
THANKS. NOW, ONTO TONIGHT'S TALE... IT'S KNOWN AS THE SCARIEST STORY OF ALL TIME. WHAT MAKES THIS STORY ESPECIALLY SCARY?
"IT HAPPENED RIGHT HERE... IN THIS VERY HOUSE...

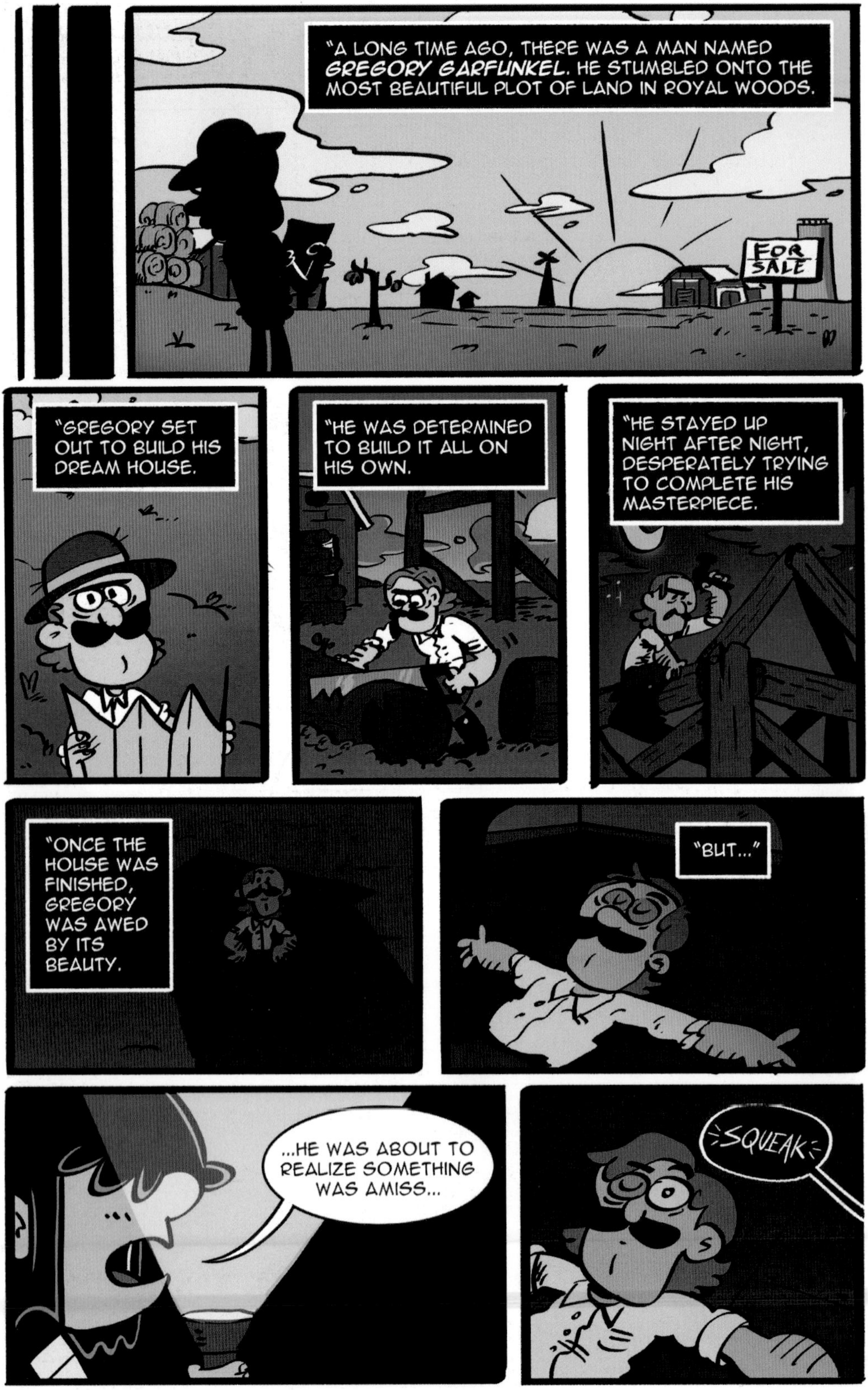
"A LONG TIME AGO, THERE WAS A MAN NAMED ***GREGORY GARFUNKEL***. HE STUMBLED ONTO THE MOST BEAUTIFUL PLOT OF LAND IN ROYAL WOODS.
FOR SALE
"GREGORY SET OUT TO BUILD HIS DREAM HOUSE.
"HE WAS DETERMINED TO BUILD IT ALL ON HIS OWN.
"HE STAYED UP NIGHT AFTER NIGHT, DESPERATELY TRYING TO COMPLETE HIS MASTERPIECE.
"ONCE THE HOUSE WAS FINISHED, GREGORY WAS AWED BY ITS BEAUTY.
"BUT..."
...HE WAS ABOUT TO REALIZE SOMETHING WAS AMISS...
SQUEAK

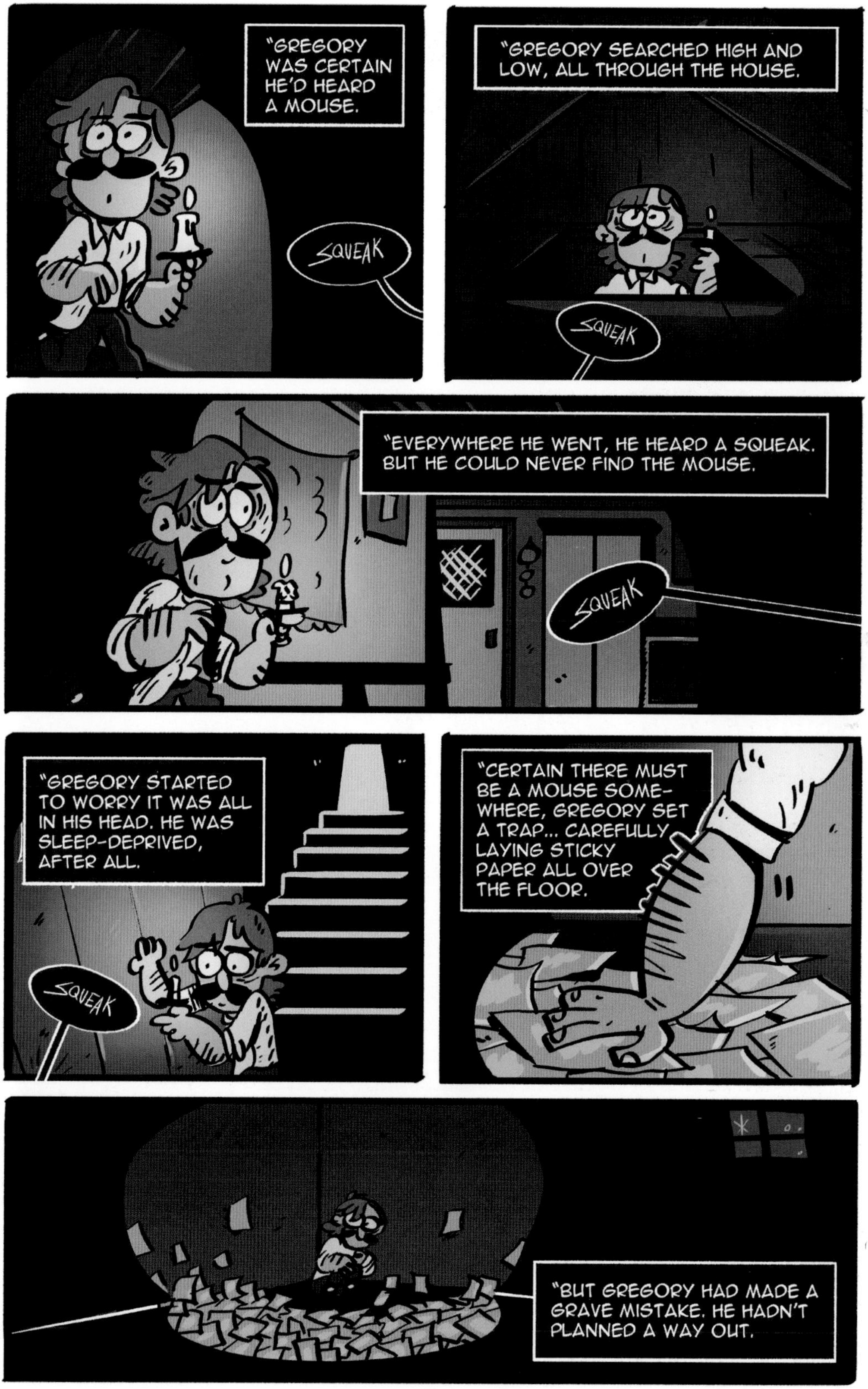
"GREGORY WAS CERTAIN HE'D HEARD A MOUSE.
SQUEAK
"GREGORY SEARCHED HIGH AND LOW, ALL THROUGH THE HOUSE.
SQUEAK
"EVERYWHERE HE WENT, HE HEARD A SQUEAK. BUT HE COULD NEVER FIND THE MOUSE.
SQUEAK
"GREGORY STARTED TO WORRY IT WAS ALL IN HIS HEAD. HE WAS SLEEP-DEPRIVED, AFTER ALL.
SQUEAK
"CERTAIN THERE MUST BE A MOUSE SOME-WHERE, GREGORY SET A TRAP... CAREFULLY LAYING STICKY PAPER ALL OVER THE FLOOR.
"BUT GREGORY HAD MADE A GRAVE MISTAKE. HE HADN'T PLANNED A WAY OUT.

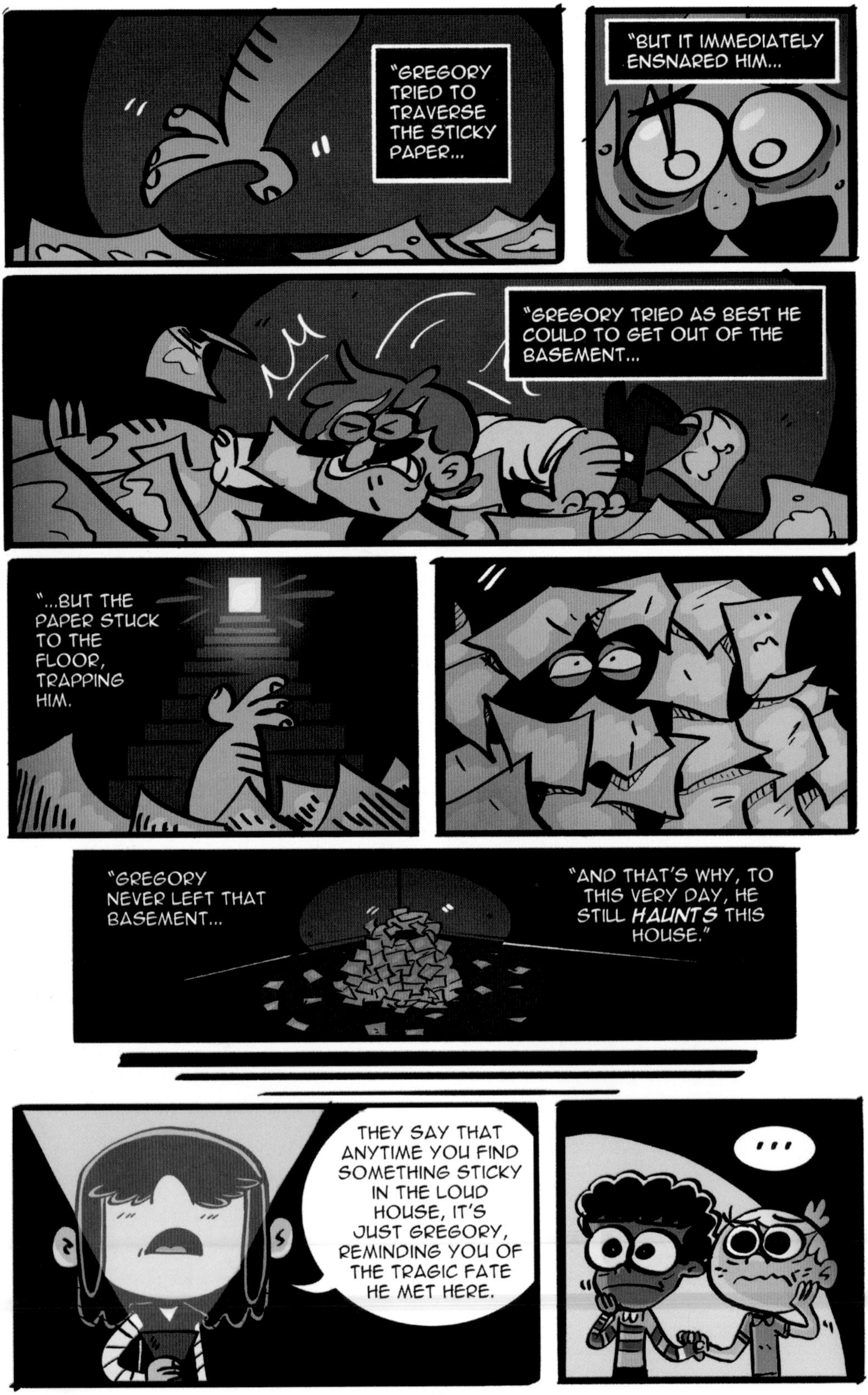
"GREGORY TRIED TO TRAVERSE THE STICKY PAPER...
"BUT IT IMMEDIATELY ENSNARED HIM...
"GREGORY TRIED AS BEST HE COULD TO GET OUT OF THE BASEMENT...
"...BUT THE PAPER STUCK TO THE FLOOR, TRAPPING HIM.
"GREGORY NEVER LEFT THAT BASEMENT...
"AND THAT'S WHY, TO THIS VERY DAY, HE STILL HAUNTS THIS HOUSE."
THEY SAY THAT ANYTIME YOU FIND SOMETHING STICKY IN THE LOUD HOUSE, IT'S JUST GREGORY, REMINDING YOU OF THE TRAGIC FATE HE MET HERE.
...

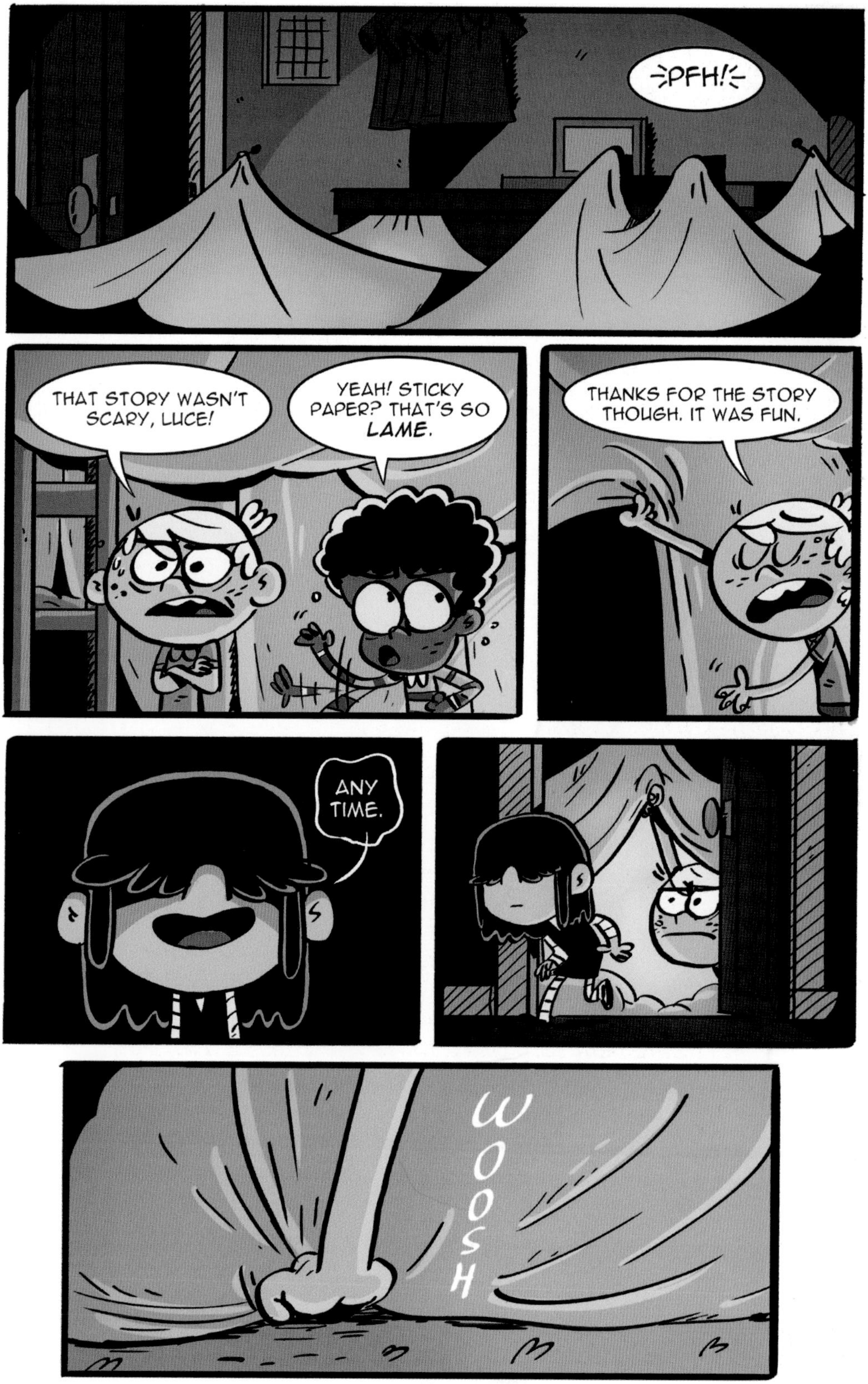
PFH!
THAT STORY WASN'T SCARY, LUCE!
YEAH! STICKY PAPER? THAT'S SO **LAME**.
THANKS FOR THE STORY THOUGH. IT WAS FUN.
ANY TIME.
WOOOSH

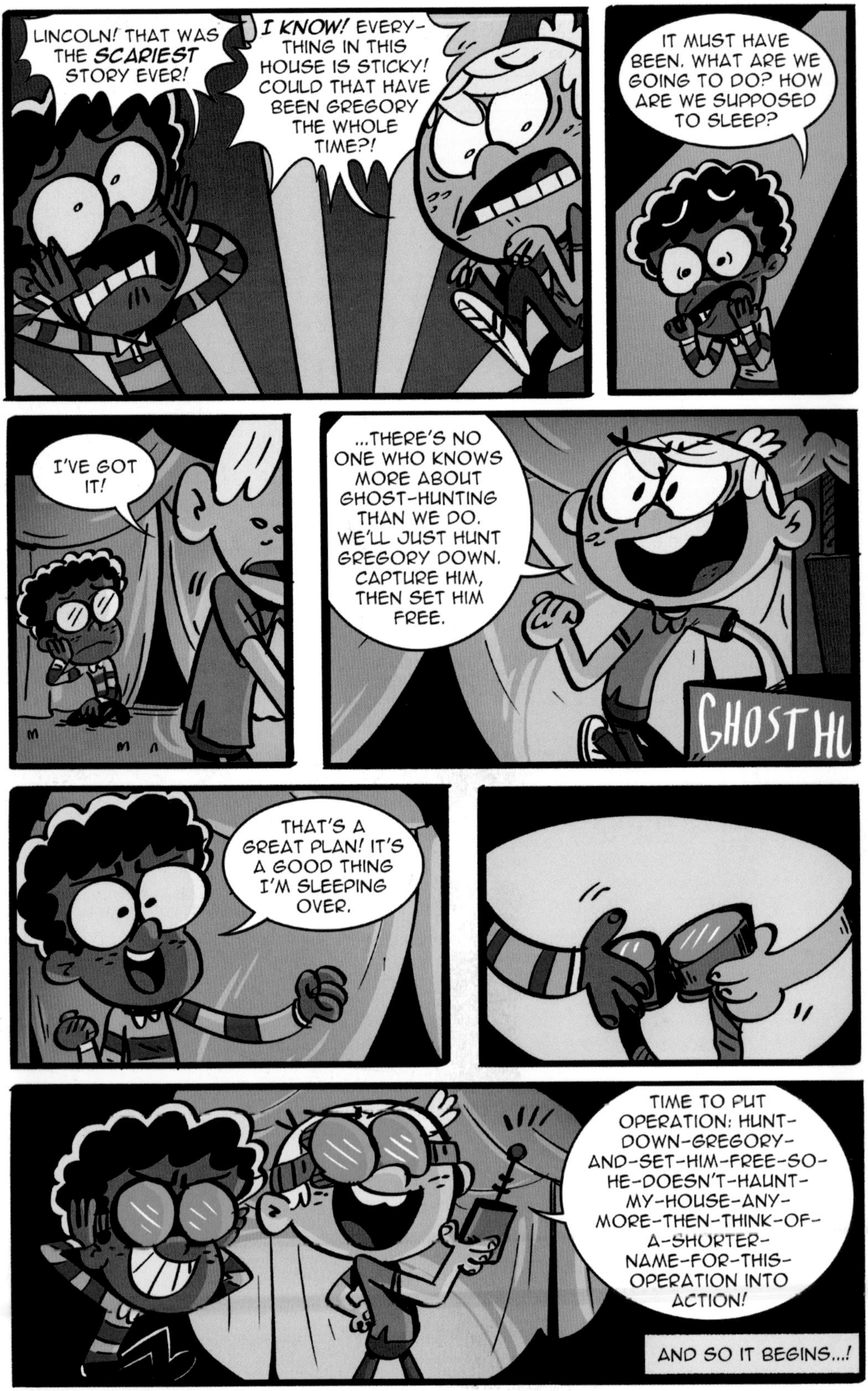
LINCOLN! THAT WAS THE SCARIEST STORY EVER!
I KNOW! EVERY-THING IN THIS HOUSE IS STICKY! COULD THAT HAVE BEEN GREGORY THE WHOLE TIME?!
IT MUST HAVE BEEN. WHAT ARE WE GOING TO DO? HOW ARE WE SUPPOSED TO SLEEP?
I'VE GOT IT!
...THERE'S NO ONE WHO KNOWS MORE ABOUT GHOST-HUNTING THAN WE DO. WE'LL JUST HUNT GREGORY DOWN. CAPTURE HIM, THEN SET HIM FREE.
GHOST HU
THAT'S A GREAT PLAN! IT'S A GOOD THING I'M SLEEPING OVER.
TIME TO PUT OPERATION: HUNT-DOWN-GREGORY-AND-SET-HIM-FREE-SO-HE-DOESN'T-HAUNT-MY-HOUSE-ANY-MORE-THEN-THINK-OF-A-SHORTER-NAME-FOR-THIS-OPERATION INTO ACTION!
AND SO IT BEGINS...!

"11:00 PM: DRAWING A PRANK"

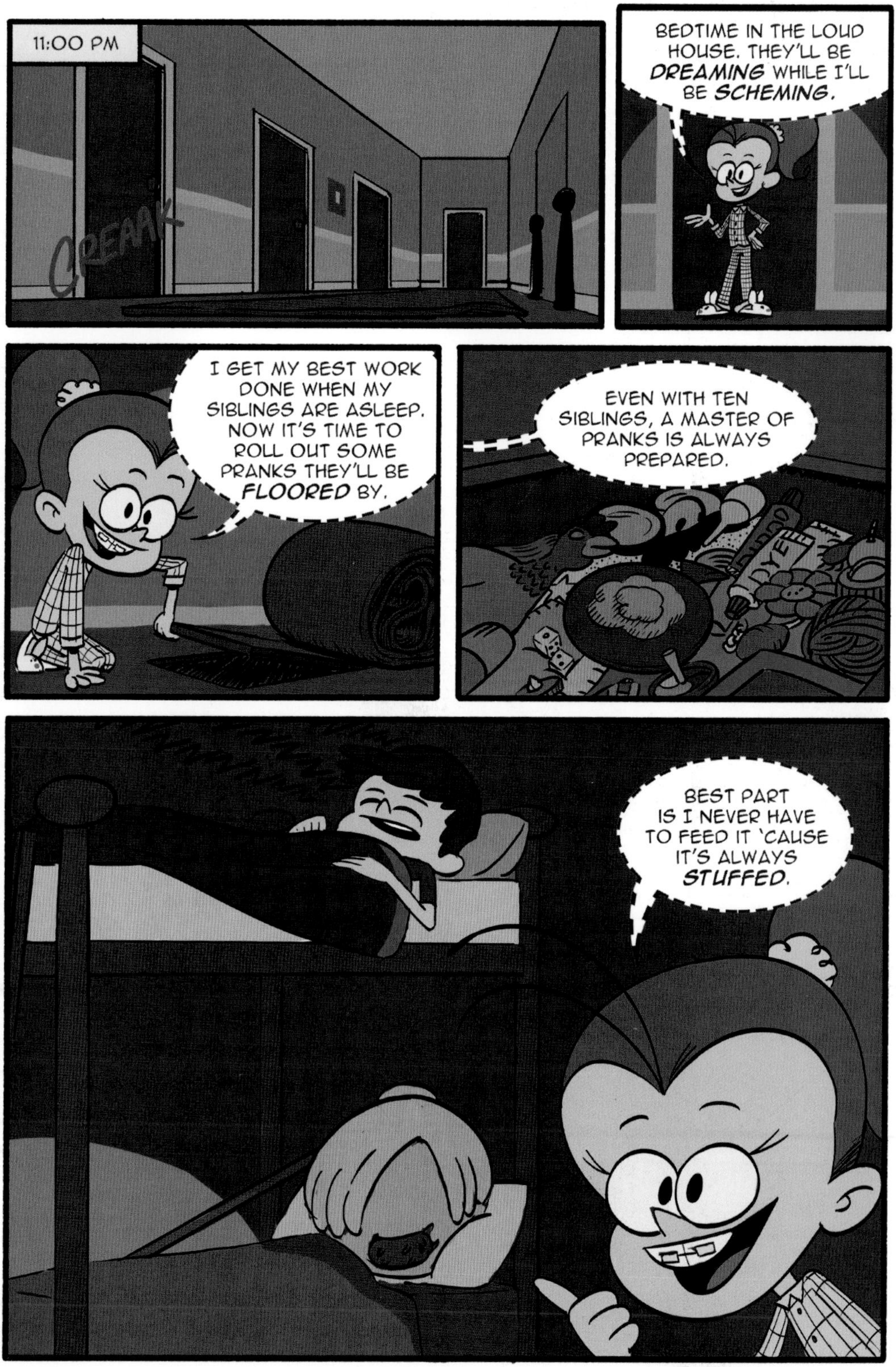
11:00 PM
CREAAK
BEDTIME IN THE LOUD HOUSE. THEY'LL BE DREAMING WHILE I'LL BE SCHEMING.
I GET MY BEST WORK DONE WHEN MY SIBLINGS ARE ASLEEP. NOW IT'S TIME TO ROLL OUT SOME PRANKS THEY'LL BE FLOORED BY.
EVEN WITH TEN SIBLINGS, A MASTER OF PRANKS IS ALWAYS PREPARED.
DYE
BEST PART IS I NEVER HAVE TO FEED IT 'CAUSE IT'S ALWAYS STUFFED.

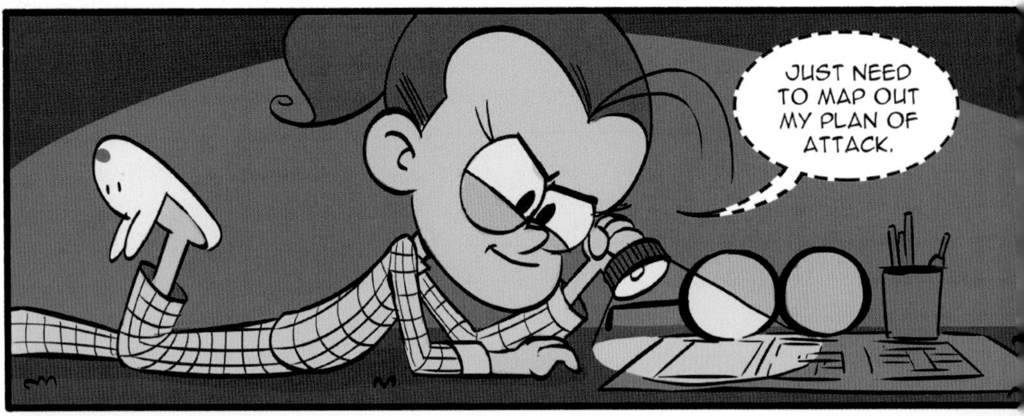
JUST NEED TO MAP OUT MY PLAN OF ATTACK.

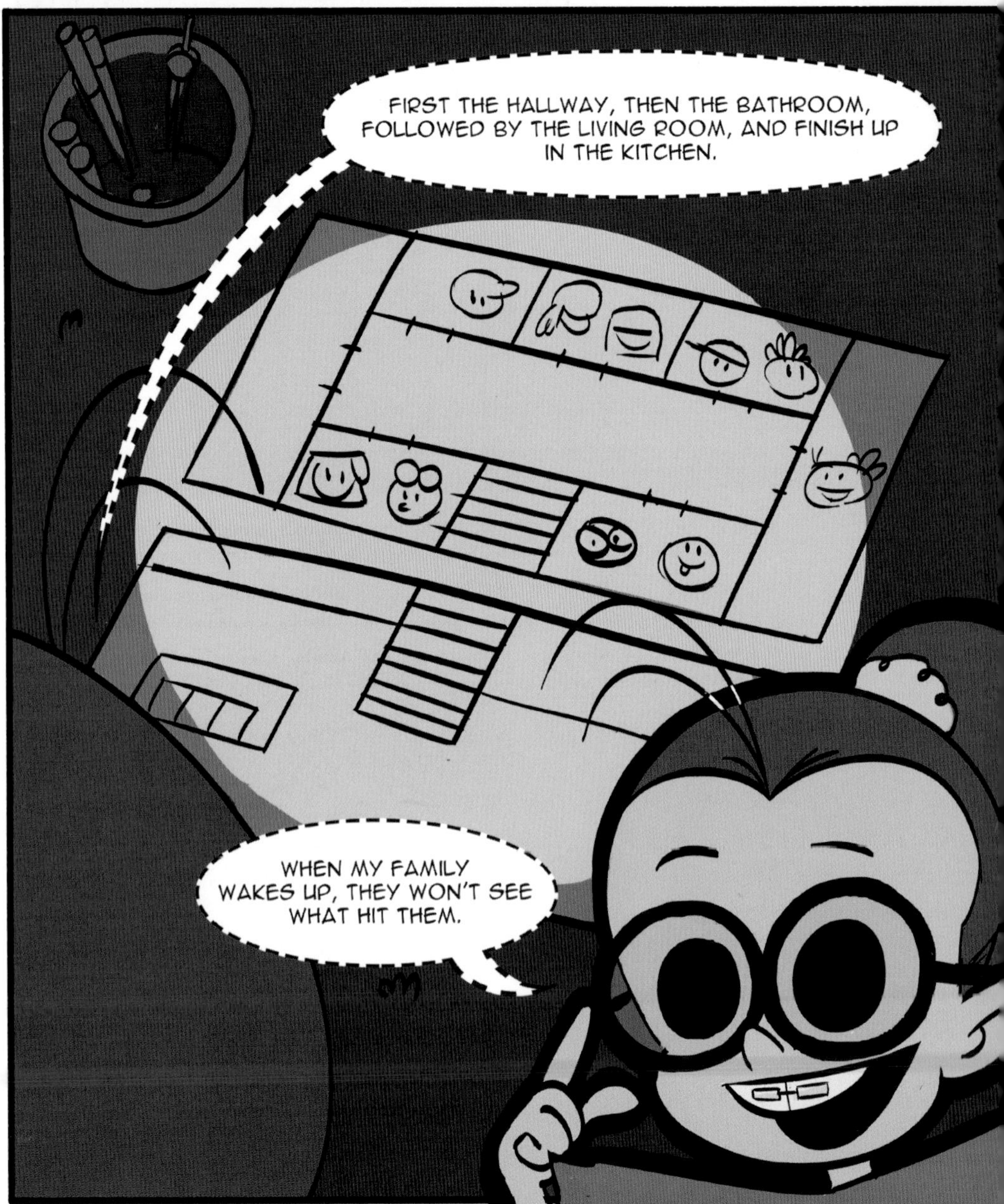
FIRST THE HALLWAY, THEN THE BATHROOM, FOLLOWED BY THE LIVING ROOM, AND FINISH UP IN THE KITCHEN.
WHEN MY FAMILY WAKES UP, THEY WON'T SEE WHAT HIT THEM.

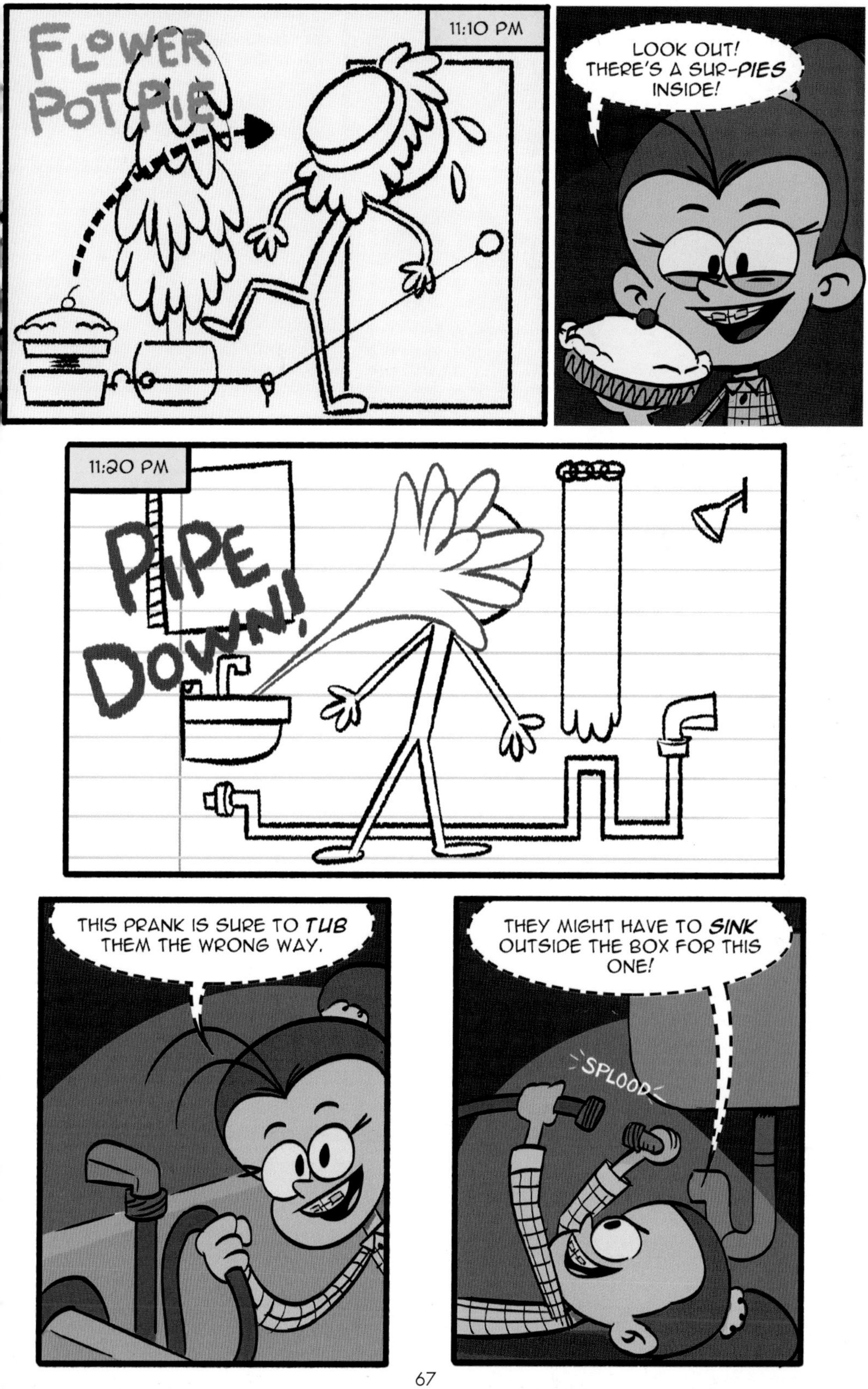
11:10 PM
FLOWER POT PIE
LOOK OUT! THERE'S A SUR-PIES INSIDE!
11:20 PM
PIPE DOWN!
THIS PRANK IS SURE TO TUB THEM THE WRONG WAY.
THEY MIGHT HAVE TO SINK OUTSIDE THE BOX FOR THIS ONE!
SPLOOP

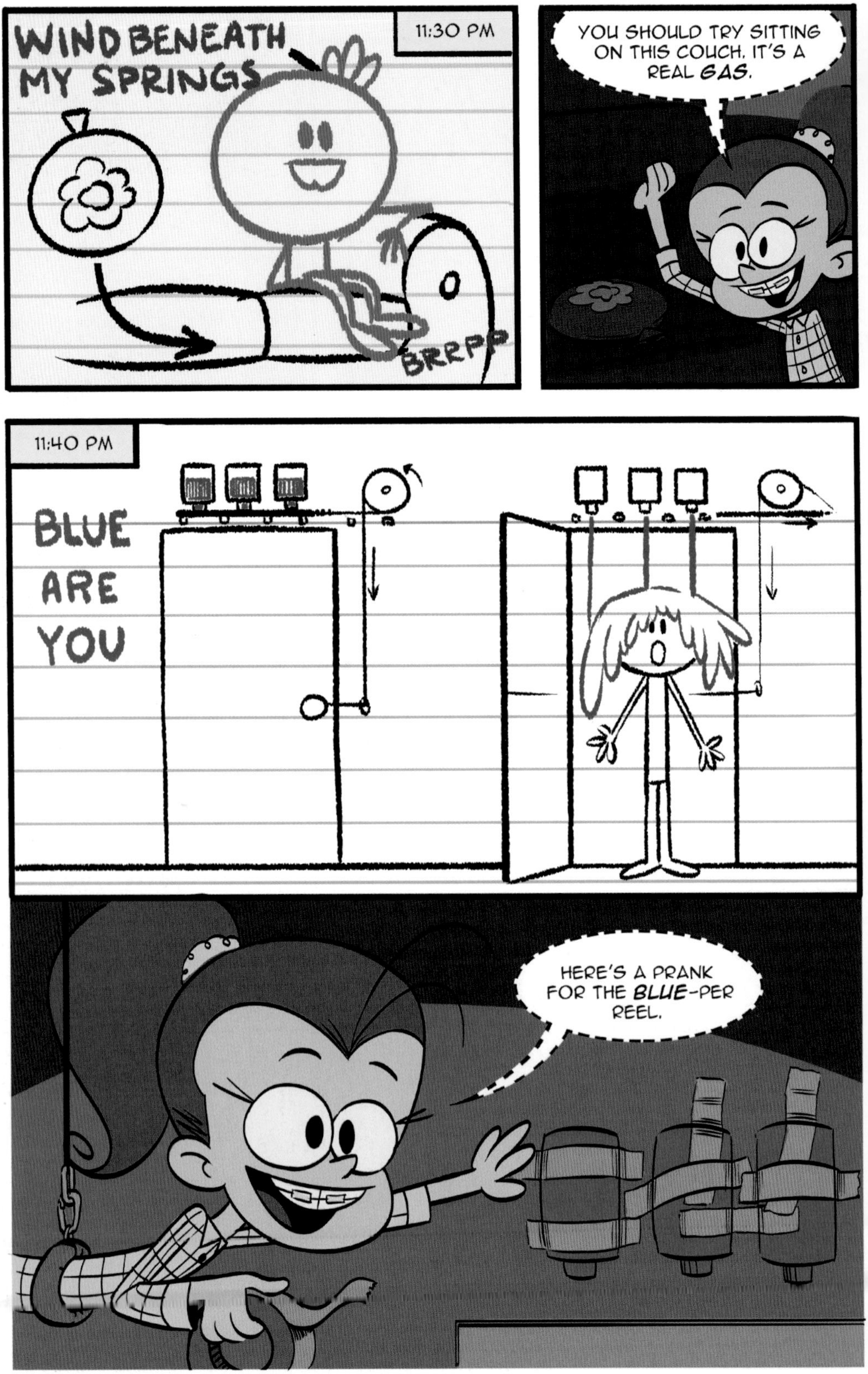
WIND BENEATH MY SPRINGS
11:30 PM
BRRPP
YOU SHOULD TRY SITTING ON THIS COUCH. IT'S A REAL GAS.
11:40 PM
BLUE ARE YOU
HERE'S A PRANK FOR THE BLUE-PER REEL.

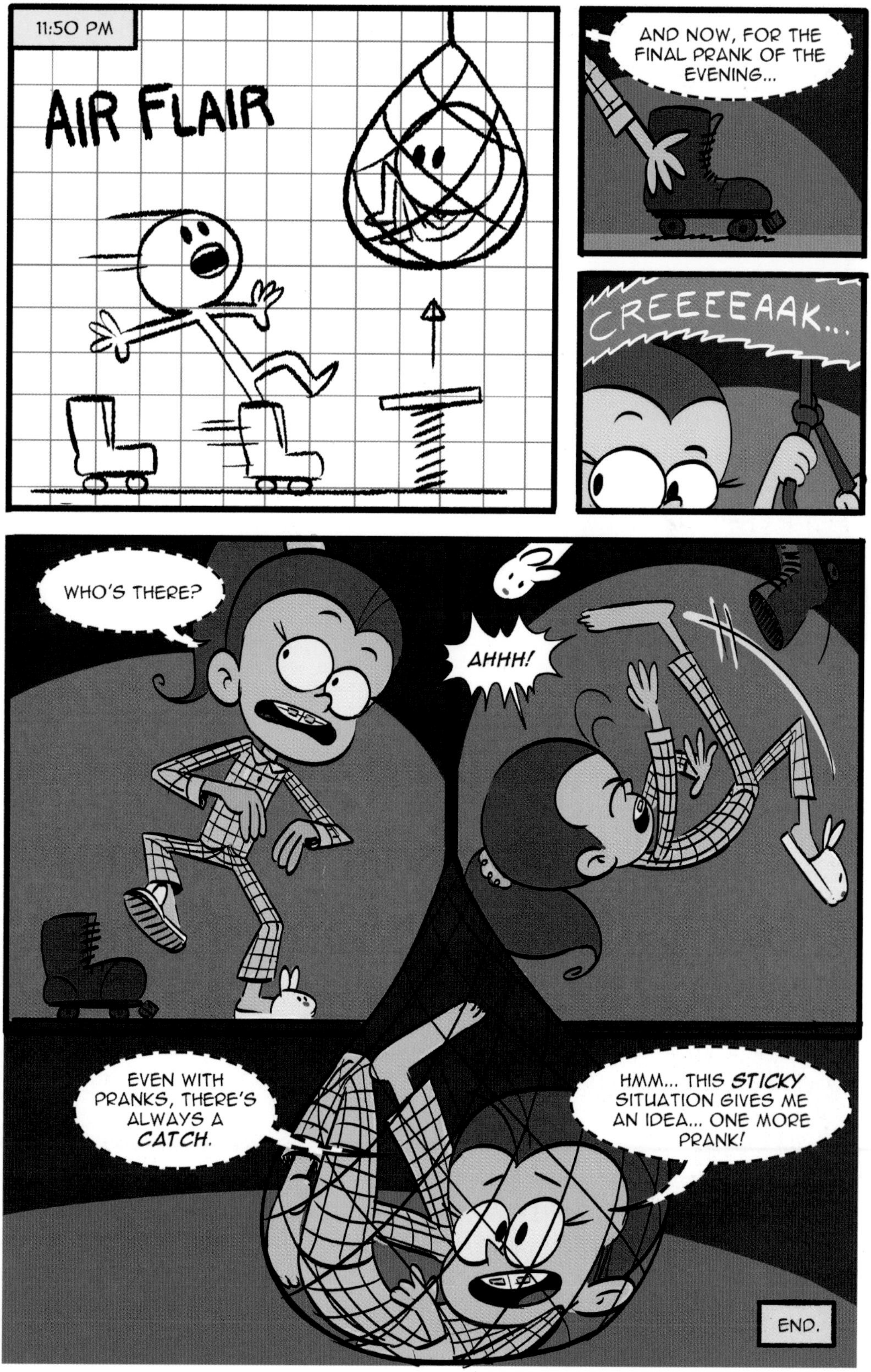
11:50 PM
AIR FLAIR
AND NOW, FOR THE FINAL PRANK OF THE EVENING...
CREEEEEAAK...
WHO'S THERE?
AHHH!
EVEN WITH PRANKS, THERE'S ALWAYS A *CATCH*.
HMM... THIS *STICKY* SITUATION GIVES ME AN IDEA... ONE MORE PRANK!
END.

"12:00 AM: MIDNIGHT MELODY"

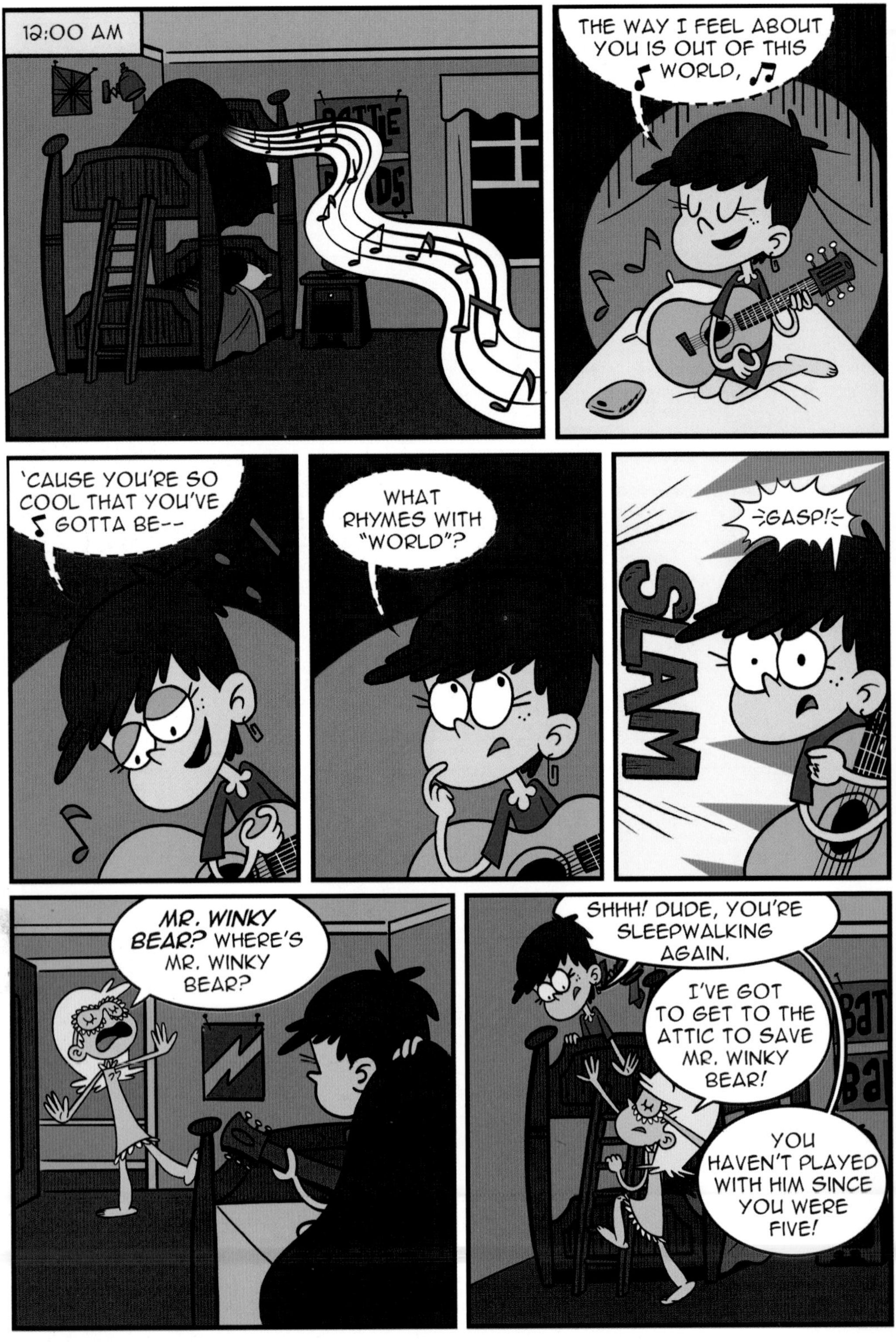

12:00 AM
THE WAY I FEEL ABOUT YOU IS OUT OF THIS WORLD,
'CAUSE YOU'RE SO COOL THAT YOU'VE GOTTA BE--
WHAT RHYMES WITH "WORLD"?
SLAM
GASP!
MR. WINKY BEAR? WHERE'S MR. WINKY BEAR?
SHHH! DUDE, YOU'RE SLEEPWALKING AGAIN.
I'VE GOT TO GET TO THE ATTIC TO SAVE MR. WINKY BEAR!
YOU HAVEN'T PLAYED WITH HIM SINCE YOU WERE FIVE!

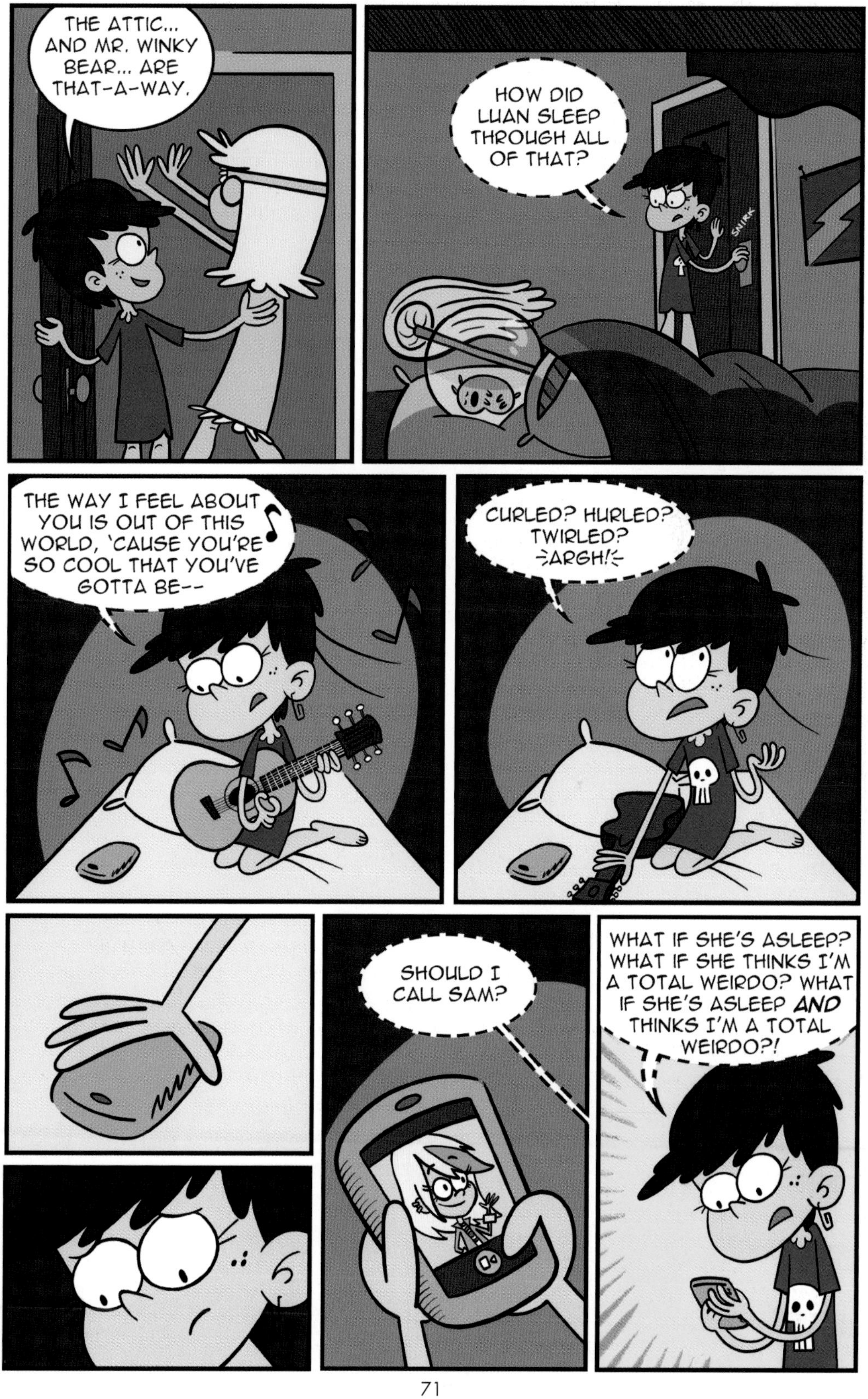
THE ATTIC... AND MR. WINKY BEAR... ARE THAT-A-WAY.
HOW DID LUAN SLEEP THROUGH ALL OF THAT?
SNIRK
THE WAY I FEEL ABOUT YOU IS OUT OF THIS WORLD, 'CAUSE YOU'RE SO COOL THAT YOU'VE GOTTA BE--
CURLED? HURLED? TWIRLED? ARGH!
SHOULD I CALL SAM?
WHAT IF SHE'S ASLEEP? WHAT IF SHE THINKS I'M A TOTAL WEIRDO? WHAT IF SHE'S ASLEEP *AND* THINKS I'M A TOTAL WEIRDO?!

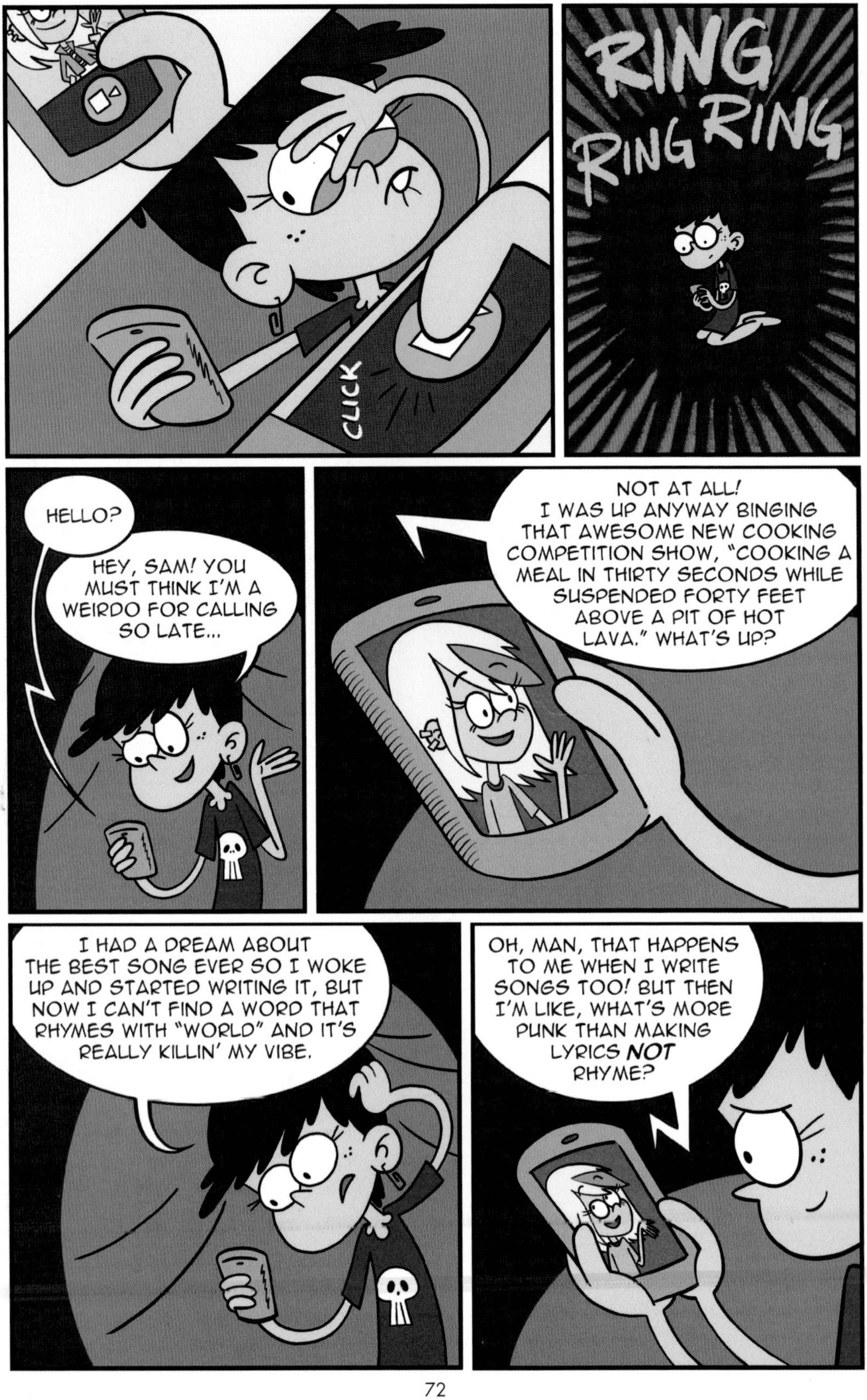
CLICK
RING
RING RING
HELLO?
HEY, SAM! YOU MUST THINK I'M A WEIRDO FOR CALLING SO LATE...
NOT AT ALL! I WAS UP ANYWAY BINGING THAT AWESOME NEW COOKING COMPETITION SHOW, "COOKING A MEAL IN THIRTY SECONDS WHILE SUSPENDED FORTY FEET ABOVE A PIT OF HOT LAVA." WHAT'S UP?
I HAD A DREAM ABOUT THE BEST SONG EVER SO I WOKE UP AND STARTED WRITING IT, BUT NOW I CAN'T FIND A WORD THAT RHYMES WITH "WORLD" AND IT'S REALLY KILLIN' MY VIBE.
OH, MAN, THAT HAPPENS TO ME WHEN I WRITE SONGS TOO! BUT THEN I'M LIKE, WHAT'S MORE PUNK THAN MAKING LYRICS ***NOT*** RHYME?

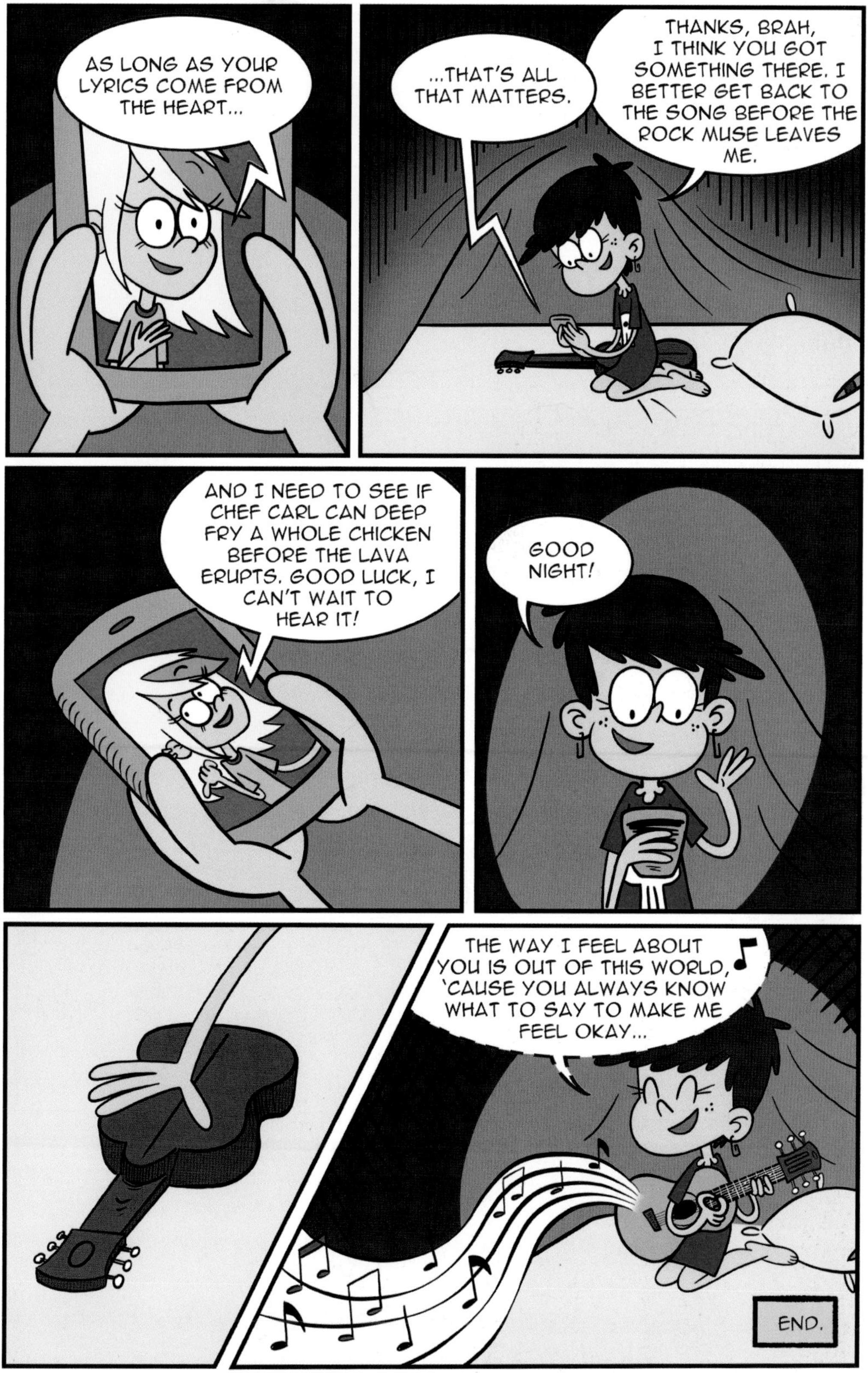
AS LONG AS YOUR LYRICS COME FROM THE HEART...
...THAT'S ALL THAT MATTERS.
THANKS, BRAH, I THINK YOU GOT SOMETHING THERE. I BETTER GET BACK TO THE SONG BEFORE THE ROCK MUSE LEAVES ME.
AND I NEED TO SEE IF CHEF CARL CAN DEEP FRY A WHOLE CHICKEN BEFORE THE LAVA ERUPTS. GOOD LUCK, I CAN'T WAIT TO HEAR IT!
GOOD NIGHT!
THE WAY I FEEL ABOUT YOU IS OUT OF THIS WORLD, 'CAUSE YOU ALWAYS KNOW WHAT TO SAY TO MAKE ME FEEL OKAY...
END.

"1:00 AM: GOAL-ORIENTED"

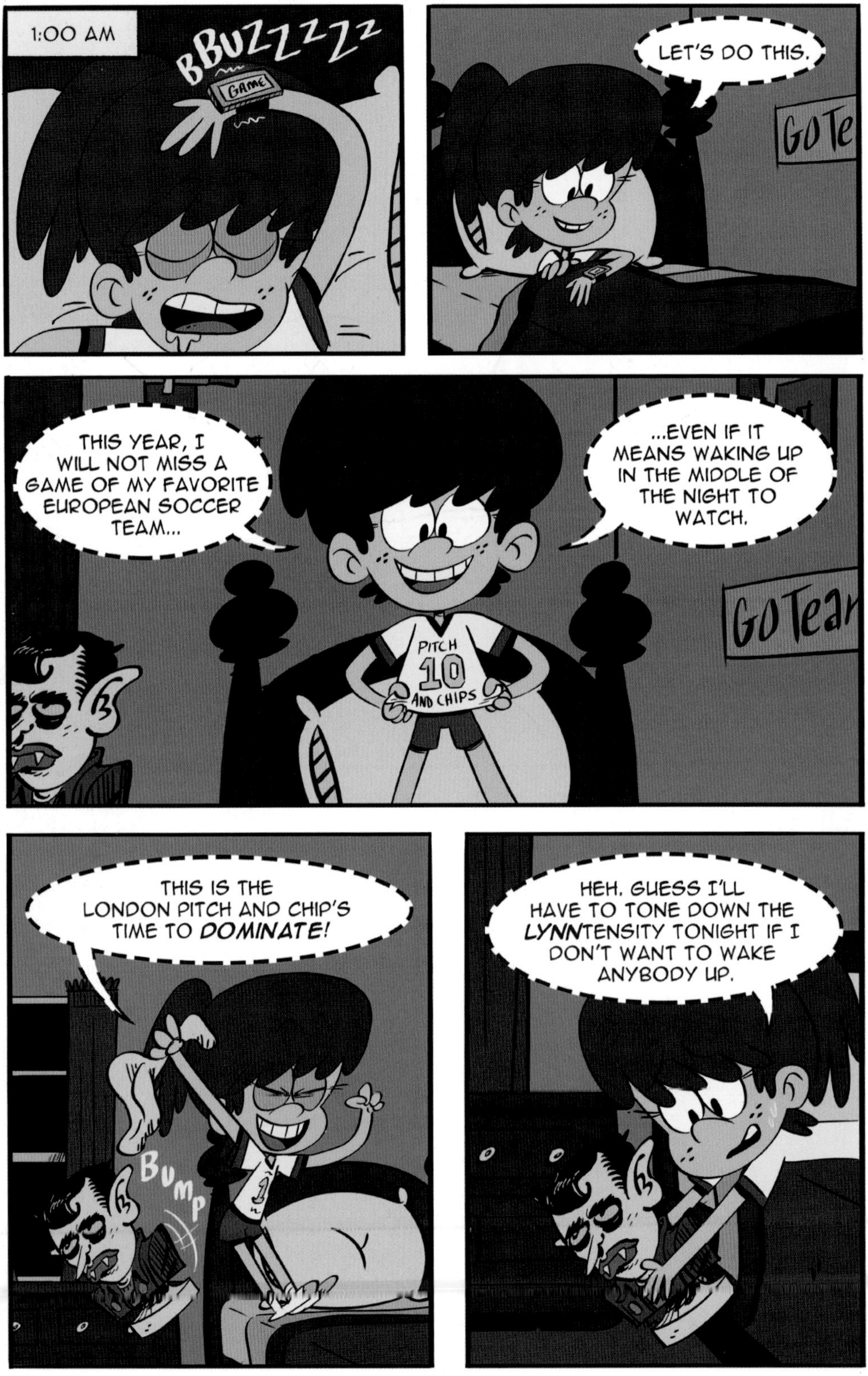

1:00 AM
BBUZZZZZ
GAME
LET'S DO THIS.
GO Te
THIS YEAR, I WILL NOT MISS A GAME OF MY FAVORITE EUROPEAN SOCCER TEAM...
...EVEN IF IT MEANS WAKING UP IN THE MIDDLE OF THE NIGHT TO WATCH.
GO Tea
PITCH 10 AND CHIPS
THIS IS THE LONDON PITCH AND CHIP'S TIME TO *DOMINATE*!
BUMP
HEH. GUESS I'LL HAVE TO TONE DOWN THE *LYNN*TENSITY TONIGHT IF I DON'T WANT TO WAKE ANYBODY UP.

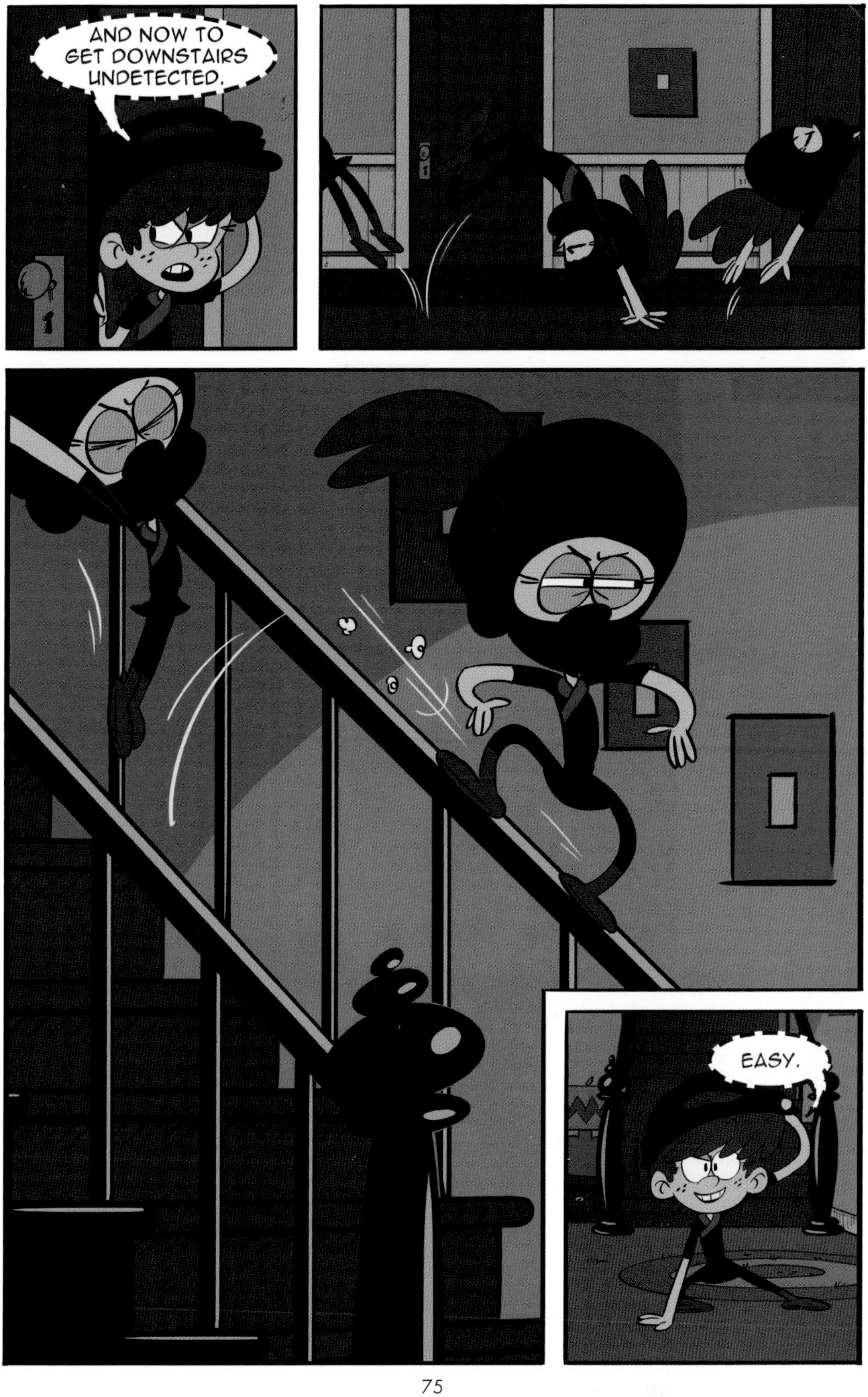
AND NOW TO GET DOWNSTAIRS UNDETECTED.
EASY.

HERE WE GO. NOT TOO LOUD.

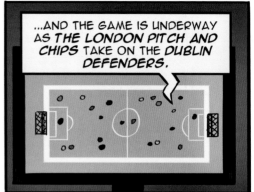

...AND THE GAME IS UNDERWAY AS *THE LONDON PITCH AND CHIPS* TAKE ON THE *DUBLIN DEFENDERS.*

1:10 AM

OH! THAT WAS A CLOSE ONE!

1:20 AM

THOSE AT HOME MUST BE *SCREAMING* WITH EXCITEMENT!

1:30 AM

AND THAT'S HALF! OUR TWO TEAMS ARE SCORELESS.

≈MMMF!≈

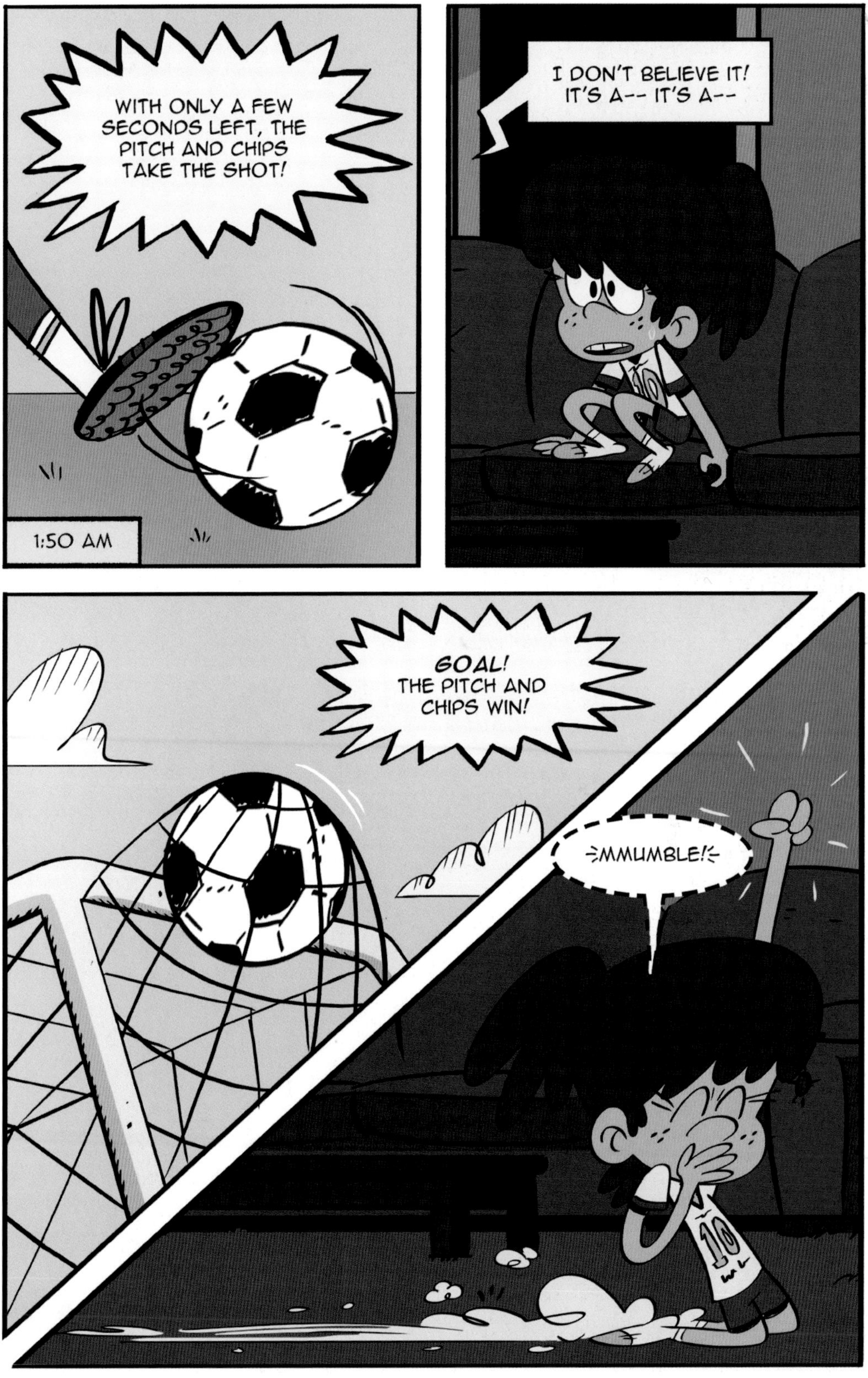
WITH ONLY A FEW SECONDS LEFT, THE PITCH AND CHIPS TAKE THE SHOT!
1:50 AM
I DON'T BELIEVE IT! IT'S A-- IT'S A--
GOAL! THE PITCH AND CHIPS WIN!
MMUMBLE!

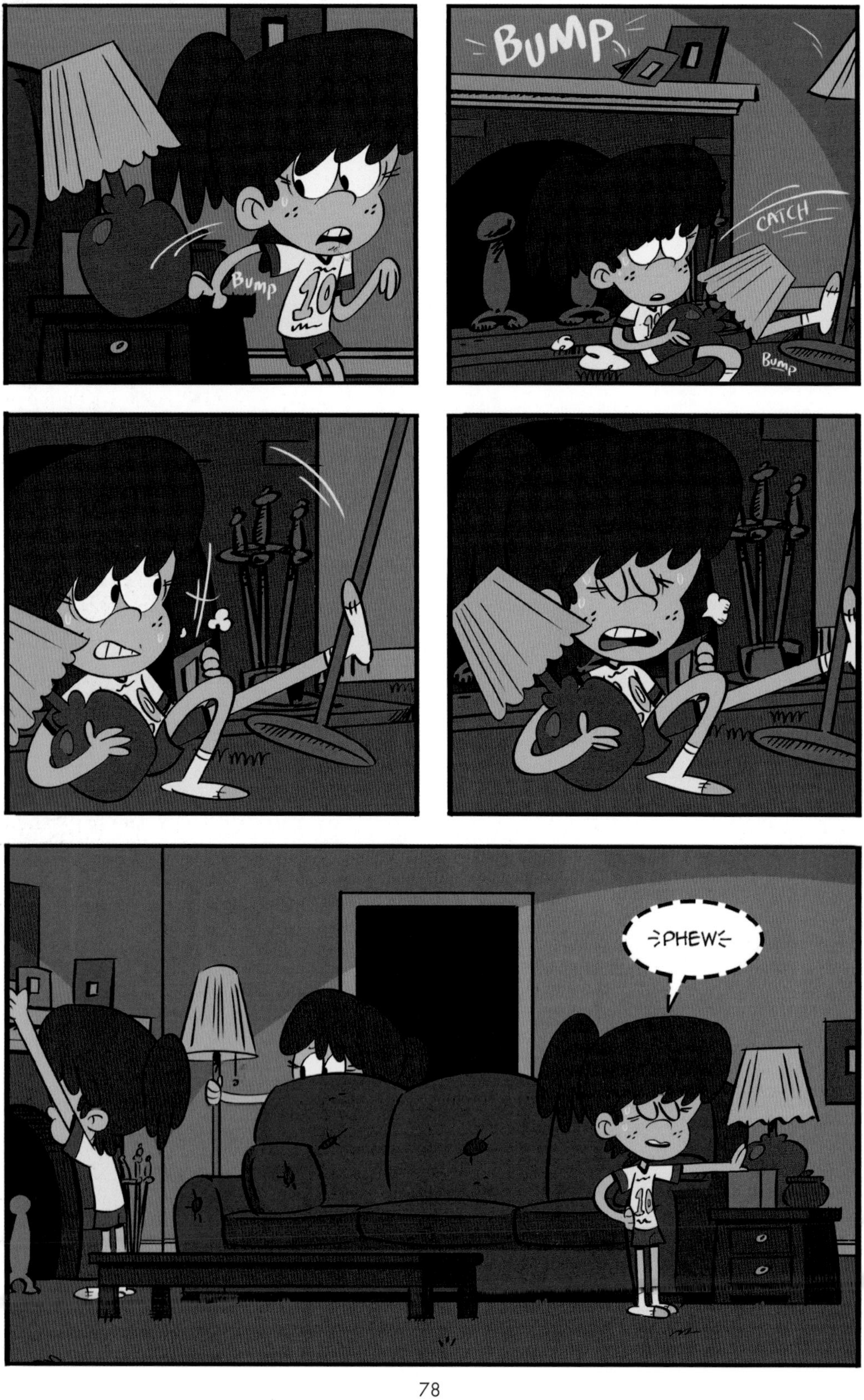
Bump
BUMP
CATCH
Bump
PHEW

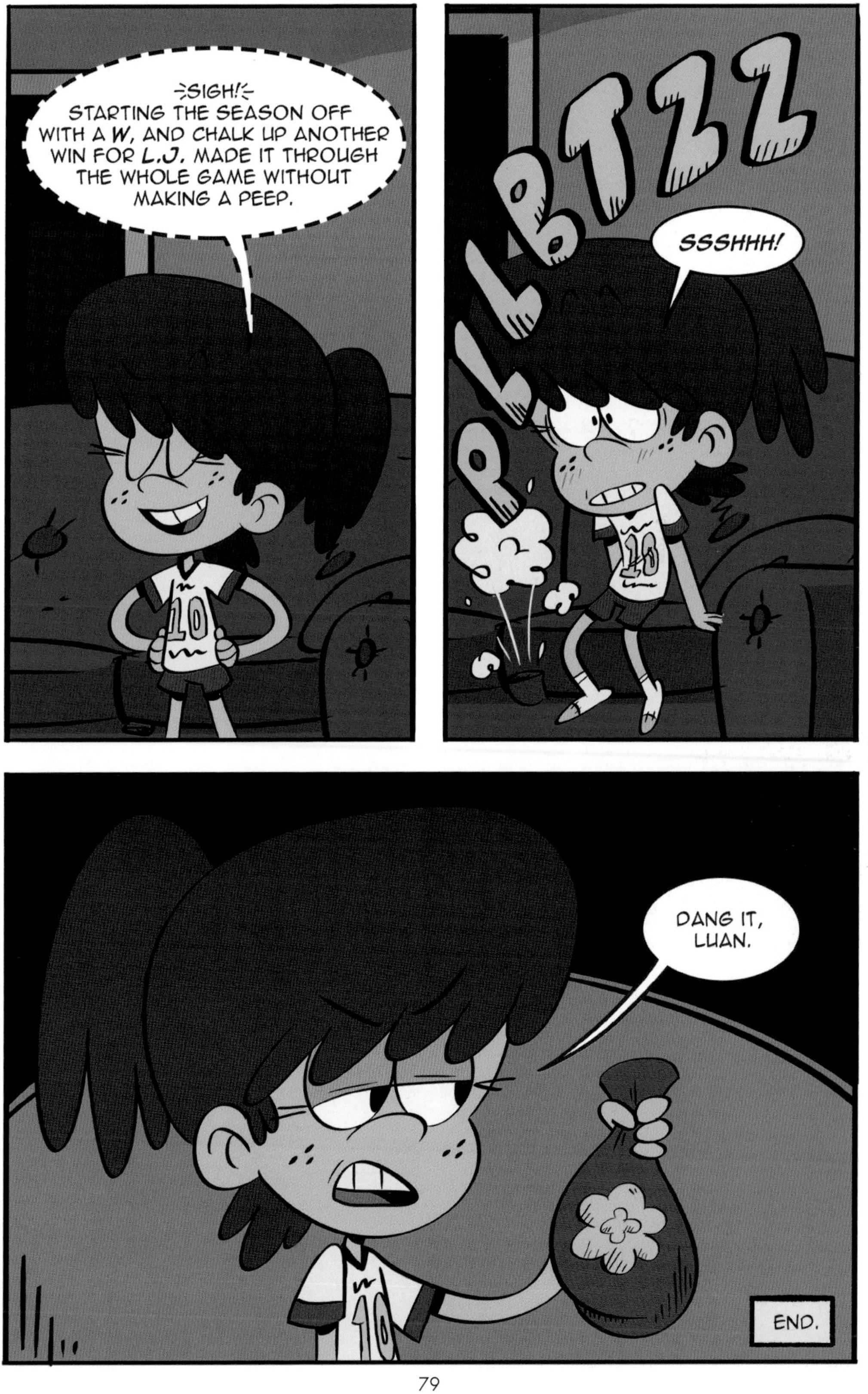

-SIGH!- STARTING THE SEASON OFF WITH A W, AND CHALK UP ANOTHER WIN FOR L.J. MADE IT THROUGH THE WHOLE GAME WITHOUT MAKING A PEEP.
PLLBTZZZ
SSSHHH!
DANG IT, LUAN.
END.

"1:55 AM: GHOST IN THE BASEMENT"

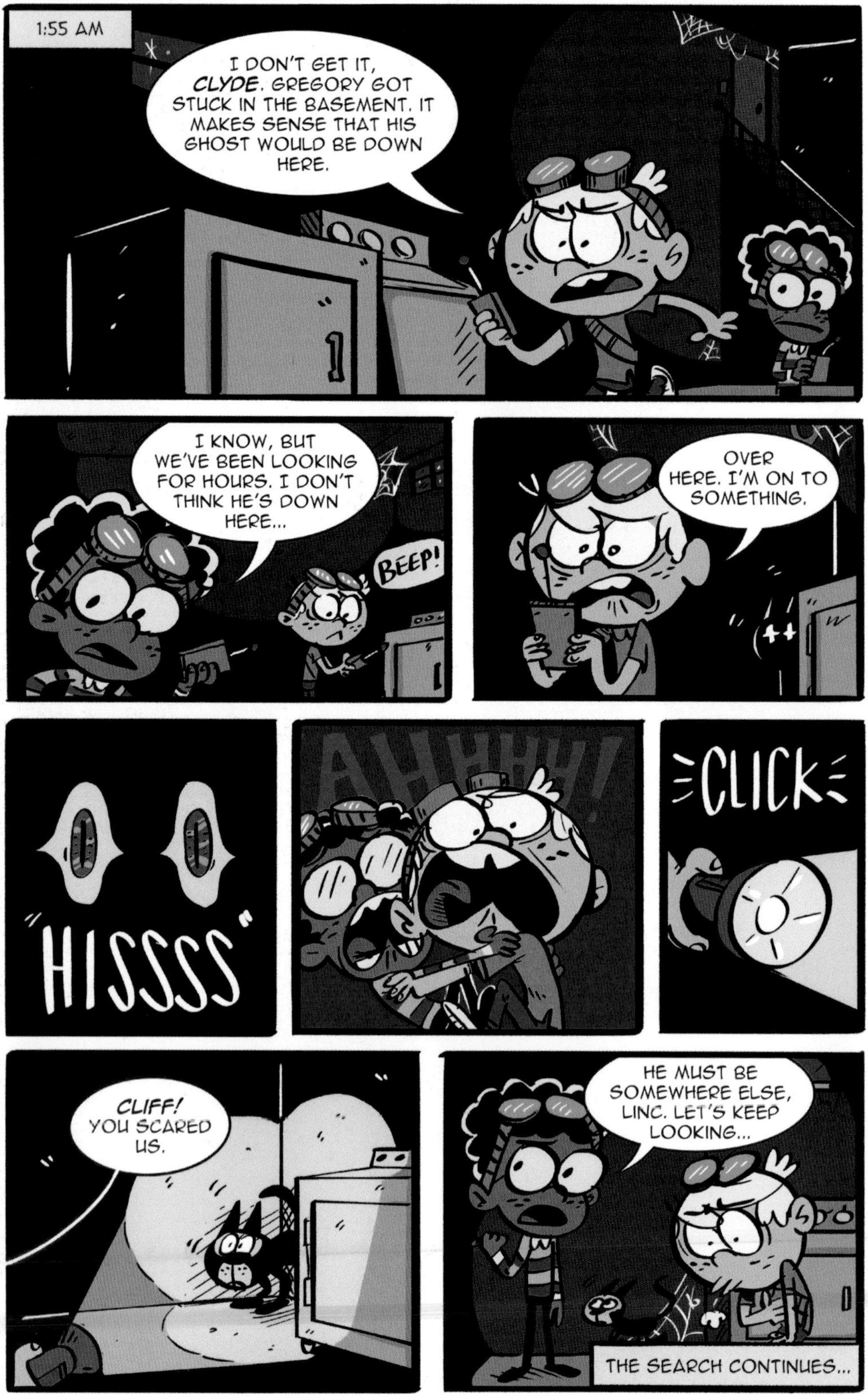

1:55 AM
I DON'T GET IT, *CLYDE*. GREGORY GOT STUCK IN THE BASEMENT. IT MAKES SENSE THAT HIS GHOST WOULD BE DOWN HERE.
I KNOW, BUT WE'VE BEEN LOOKING FOR HOURS. I DON'T THINK HE'S DOWN HERE...
BEEP!
OVER HERE. I'M ON TO SOMETHING.
HISSSS
CLICK
CLIFF! YOU SCARED US.
HE MUST BE SOMEWHERE ELSE, LINC. LET'S KEEP LOOKING...
THE SEARCH CONTINUES...

"2:00 AM: THE EARLY BIRDS AND THE WORMS"

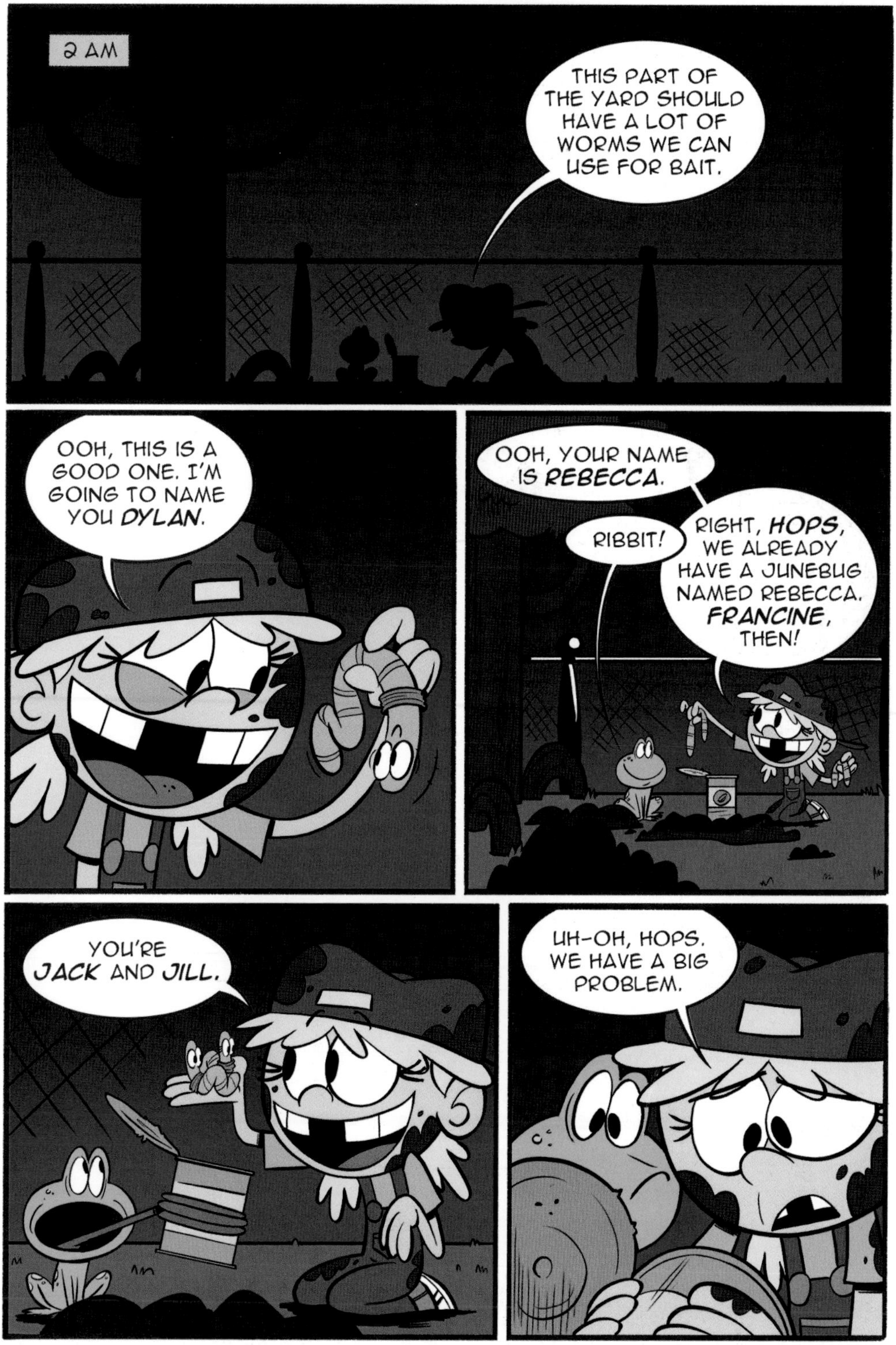
2 AM
THIS PART OF THE YARD SHOULD HAVE A LOT OF WORMS WE CAN USE FOR BAIT.
OOH, THIS IS A GOOD ONE. I'M GOING TO NAME YOU *DYLAN*.
OOH, YOUR NAME IS *REBECCA*.
RIBBIT!
RIGHT, ***HOPS***, WE ALREADY HAVE A JUNEBUG NAMED REBECCA. ***FRANCINE***, THEN!
YOU'RE ***JACK*** AND ***JILL***.
UH-OH, HOPS. WE HAVE A BIG PROBLEM.

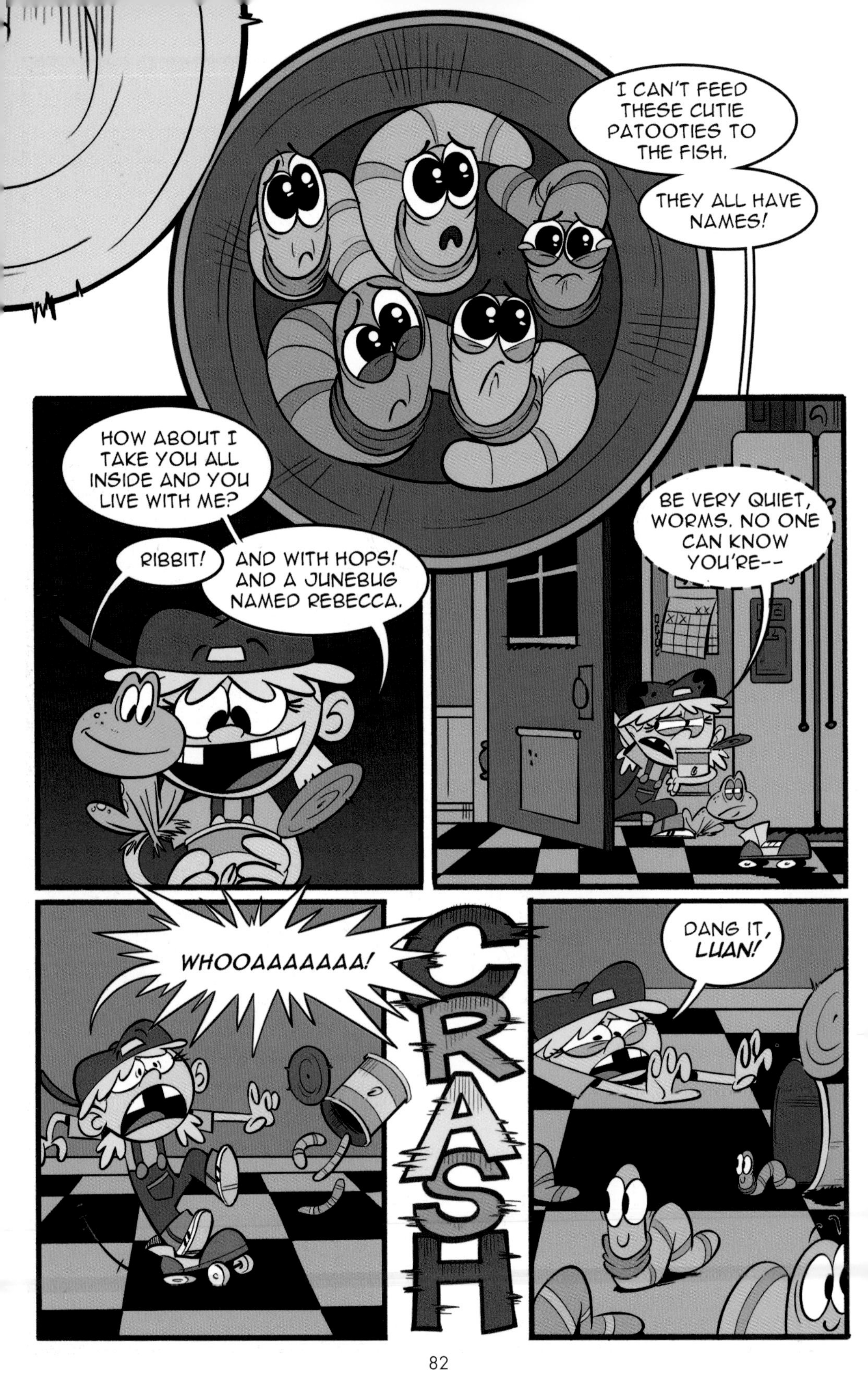

I CAN'T FEED THESE CUTIE PATOOTIES TO THE FISH.
THEY ALL HAVE NAMES!
HOW ABOUT I TAKE YOU ALL INSIDE AND YOU LIVE WITH ME?
RIBBIT!
AND WITH HOPS! AND A JUNEBUG NAMED REBECCA.
BE VERY QUIET, WORMS. NO ONE CAN KNOW YOU'RE--
WHOOAAAAAAAA!
CRASH
DANG IT, LUAN!

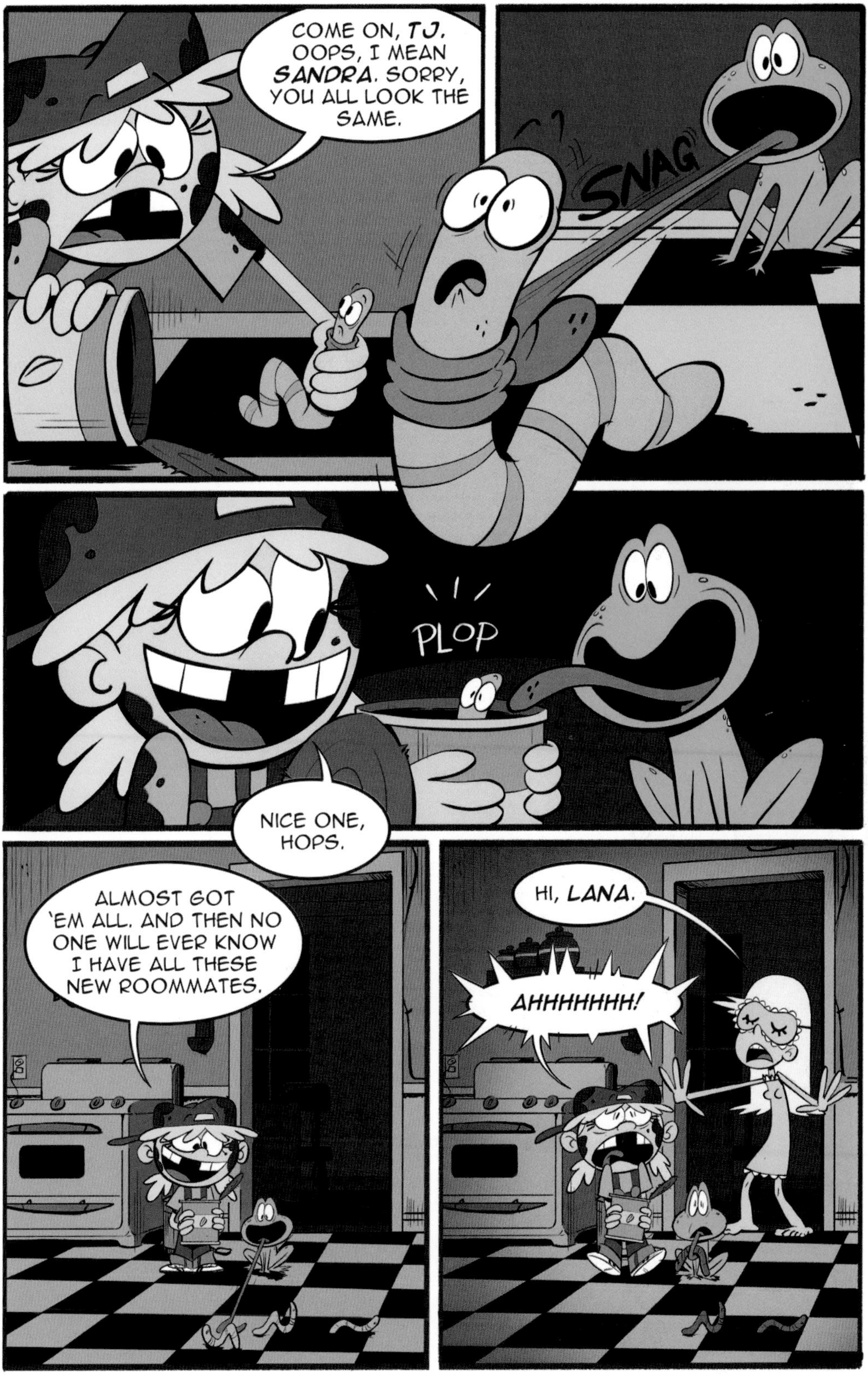
COME ON, TJ. OOPS, I MEAN SANDRA. SORRY, YOU ALL LOOK THE SAME.
SNAG
PLOP
NICE ONE, HOPS.
ALMOST GOT 'EM ALL. AND THEN NO ONE WILL EVER KNOW I HAVE ALL THESE NEW ROOMMATES.
HI, LANA.
AHHHHHHH!

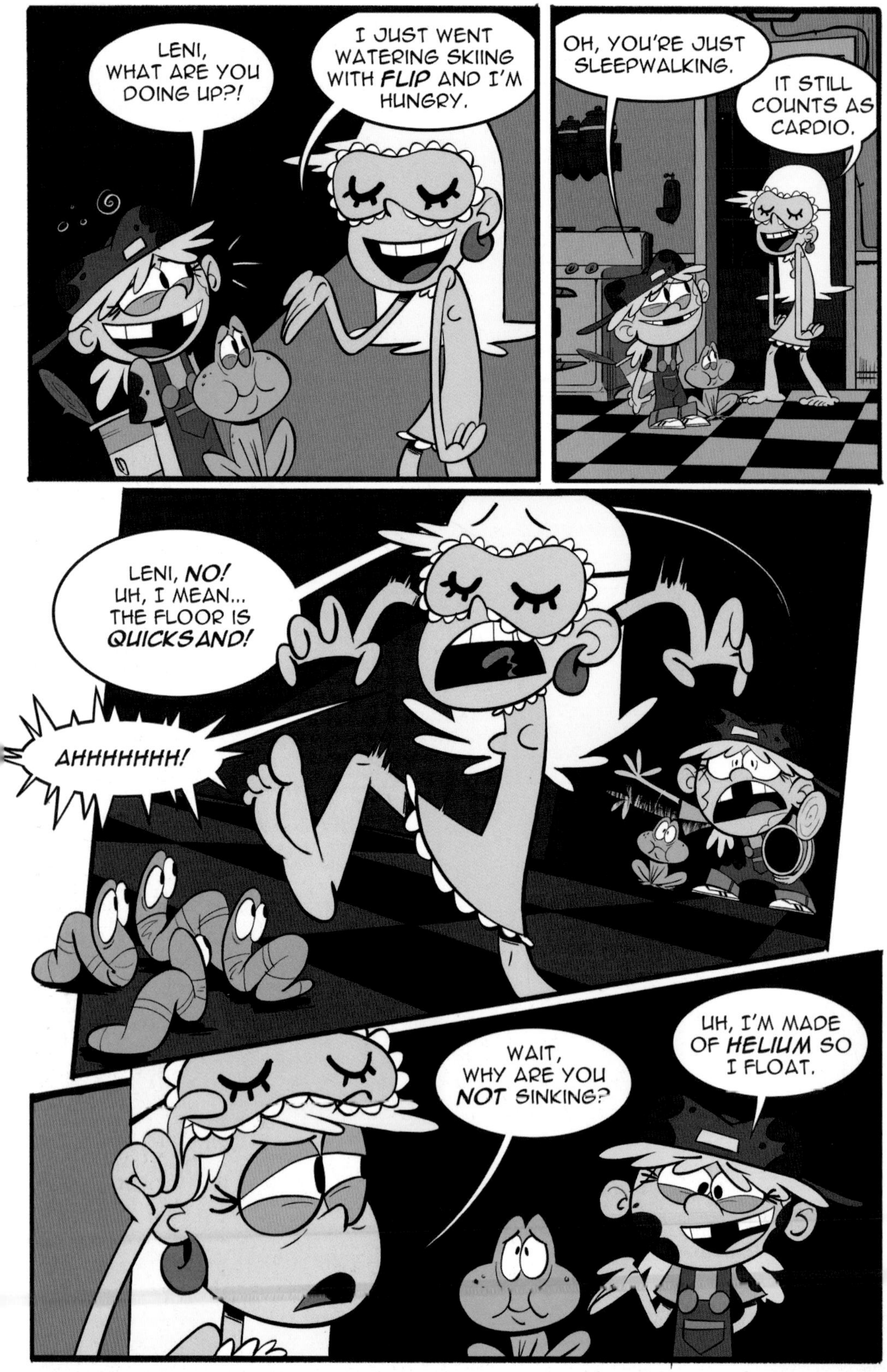
LENI, WHAT ARE YOU DOING UP?!
I JUST WENT WATERING SKIING WITH FLIP AND I'M HUNGRY.
OH, YOU'RE JUST SLEEPWALKING.
IT STILL COUNTS AS CARDIO.
LENI, NO! UH, I MEAN... THE FLOOR IS QUICKSAND!
AHHHHHHH!
WAIT, WHY ARE YOU NOT SINKING?
UH, I'M MADE OF HELIUM SO I FLOAT.

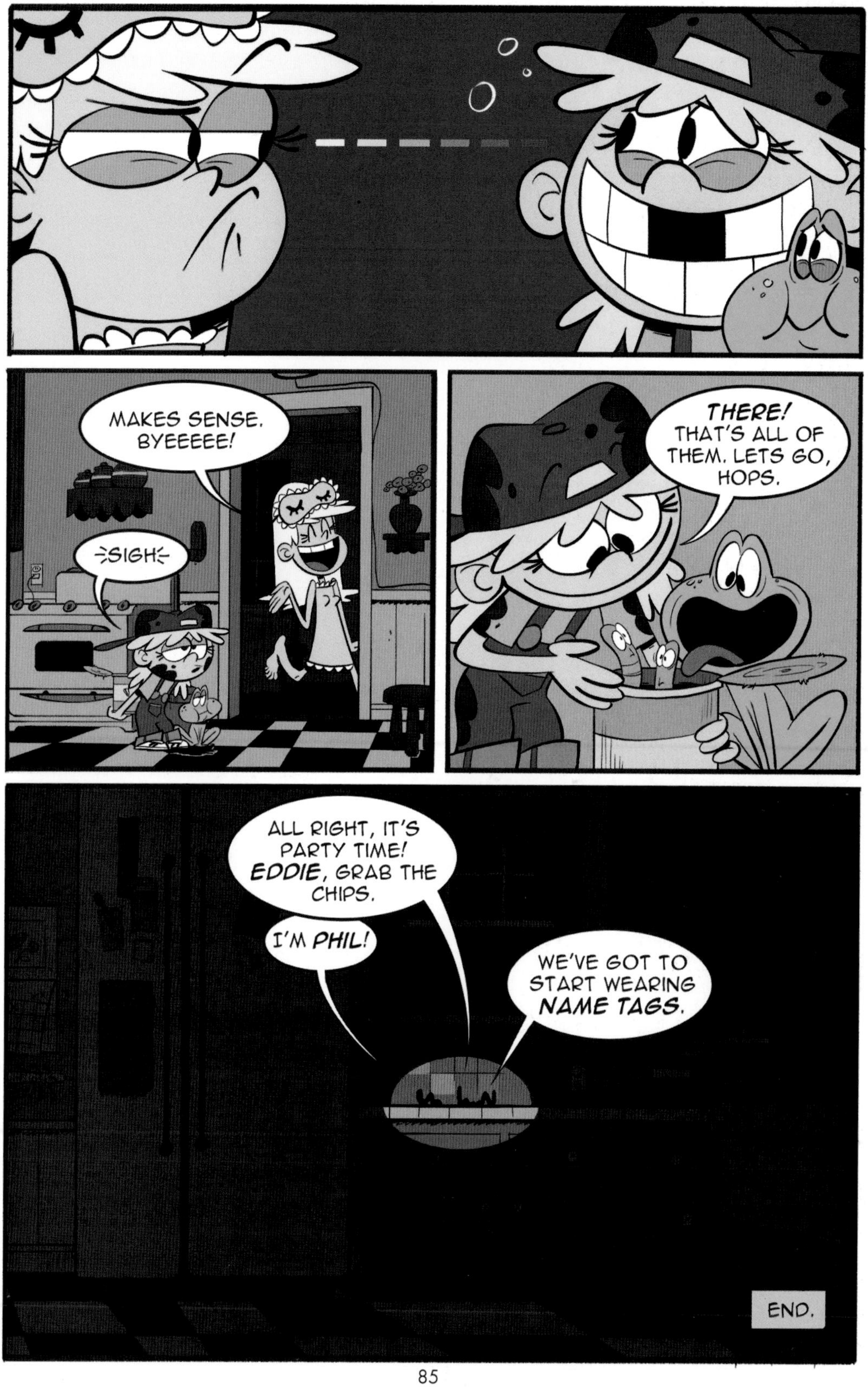
MAKES SENSE. BYEEEEE!
SIGH
THERE! THAT'S ALL OF THEM. LETS GO, HOPS.
ALL RIGHT, IT'S PARTY TIME! EDDIE, GRAB THE CHIPS.
I'M PHIL!
WE'VE GOT TO START WEARING NAME TAGS.
END.

"3:00AM: SHIPS IN THE NIGHT"

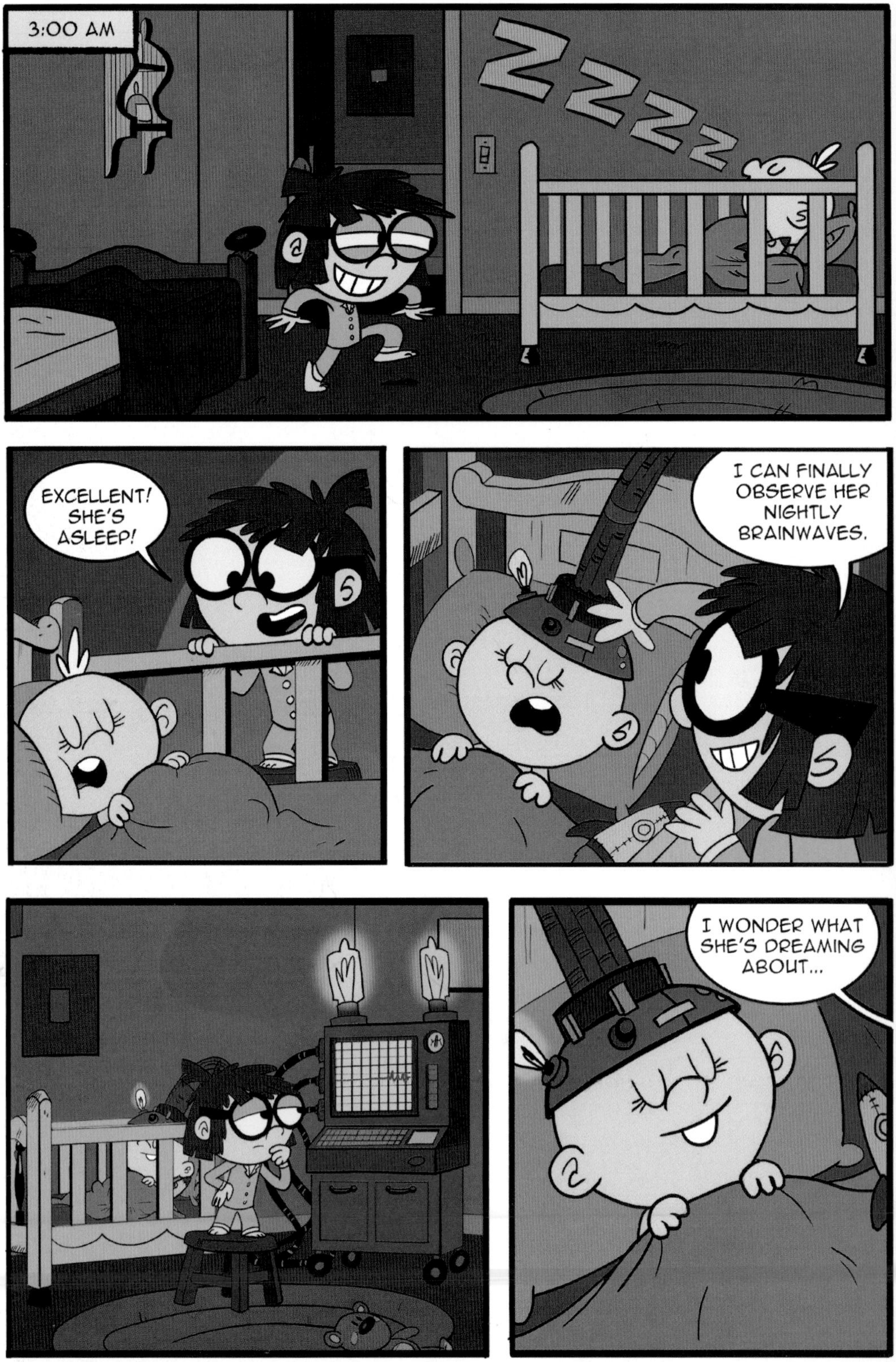
3:00 AM
ZZZZZ
EXCELLENT! SHE'S ASLEEP!
I CAN FINALLY OBSERVE HER NIGHTLY BRAINWAVES.
I WONDER WHAT SHE'S DREAMING ABOUT...

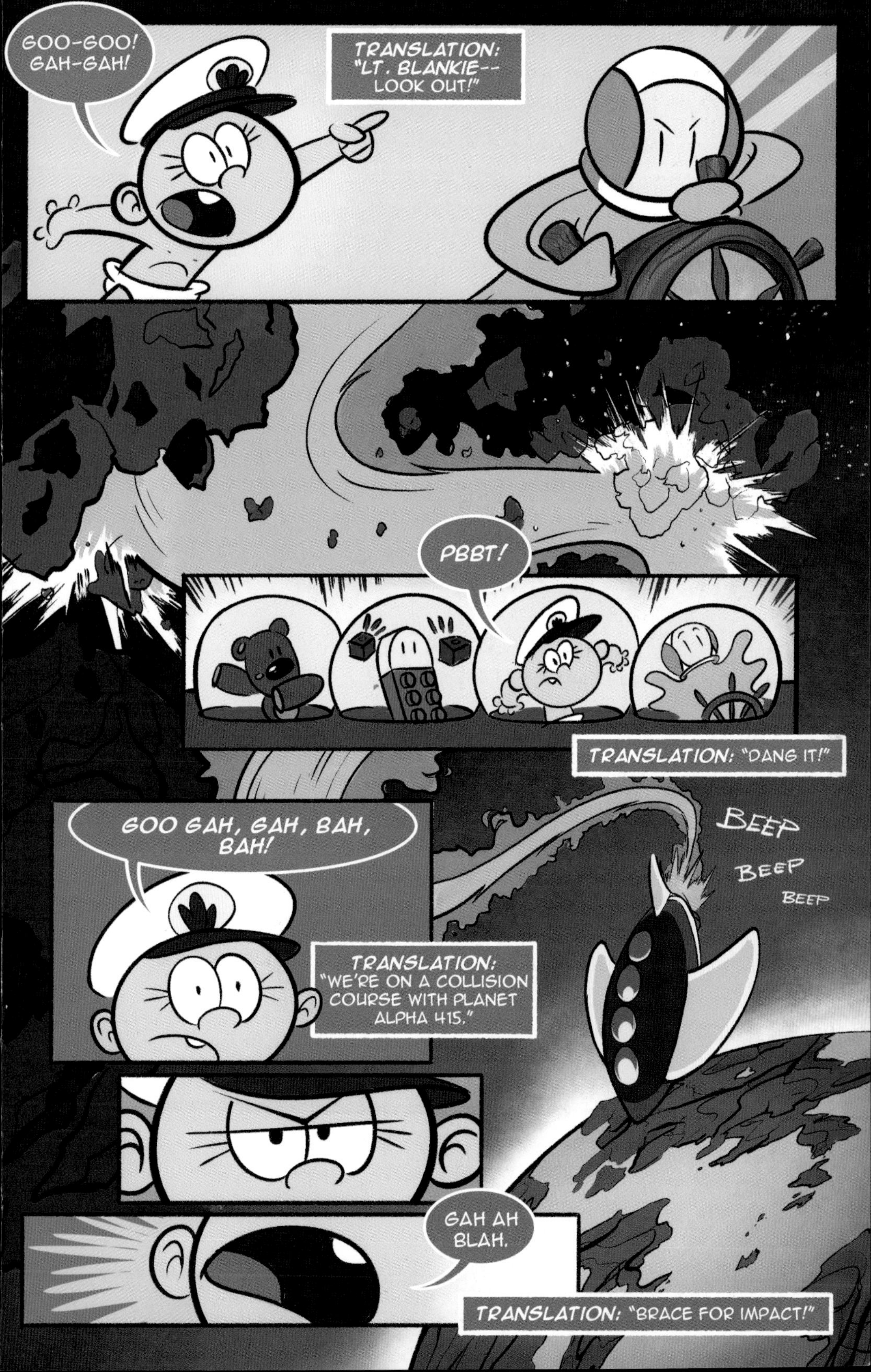
GOO-GOO! GAH-GAH!
TRANSLATION: "LT. BLANKIE-- LOOK OUT!"
PBBT!
TRANSLATION: "DANG IT!"
GOO GAH, GAH, BAH, BAH!
TRANSLATION: "WE'RE ON A COLLISION COURSE WITH PLANET ALPHA 415."
BEEP
BEEP
BEEP
GAH AH BLAH.
TRANSLATION: "BRACE FOR IMPACT!"

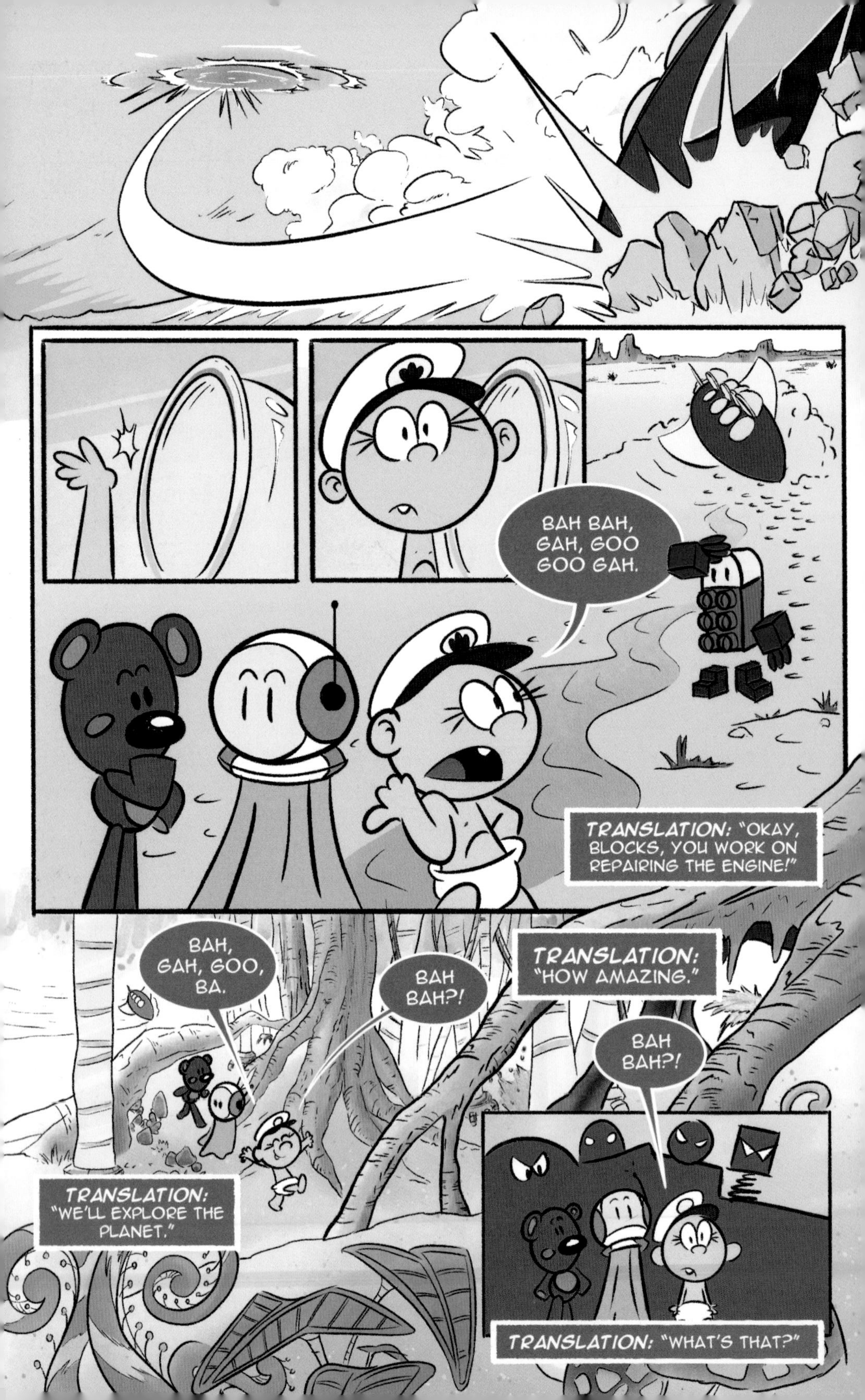
BAH BAH, GAH, GOO GOO GAH.
TRANSLATION: "OKAY, BLOCKS, YOU WORK ON REPAIRING THE ENGINE!"
BAH, GAH, GOO, BA.
TRANSLATION: "WE'LL EXPLORE THE PLANET."
BAH BAH?!
TRANSLATION: "HOW AMAZING."
BAH BAH?!
TRANSLATION: "WHAT'S THAT?"

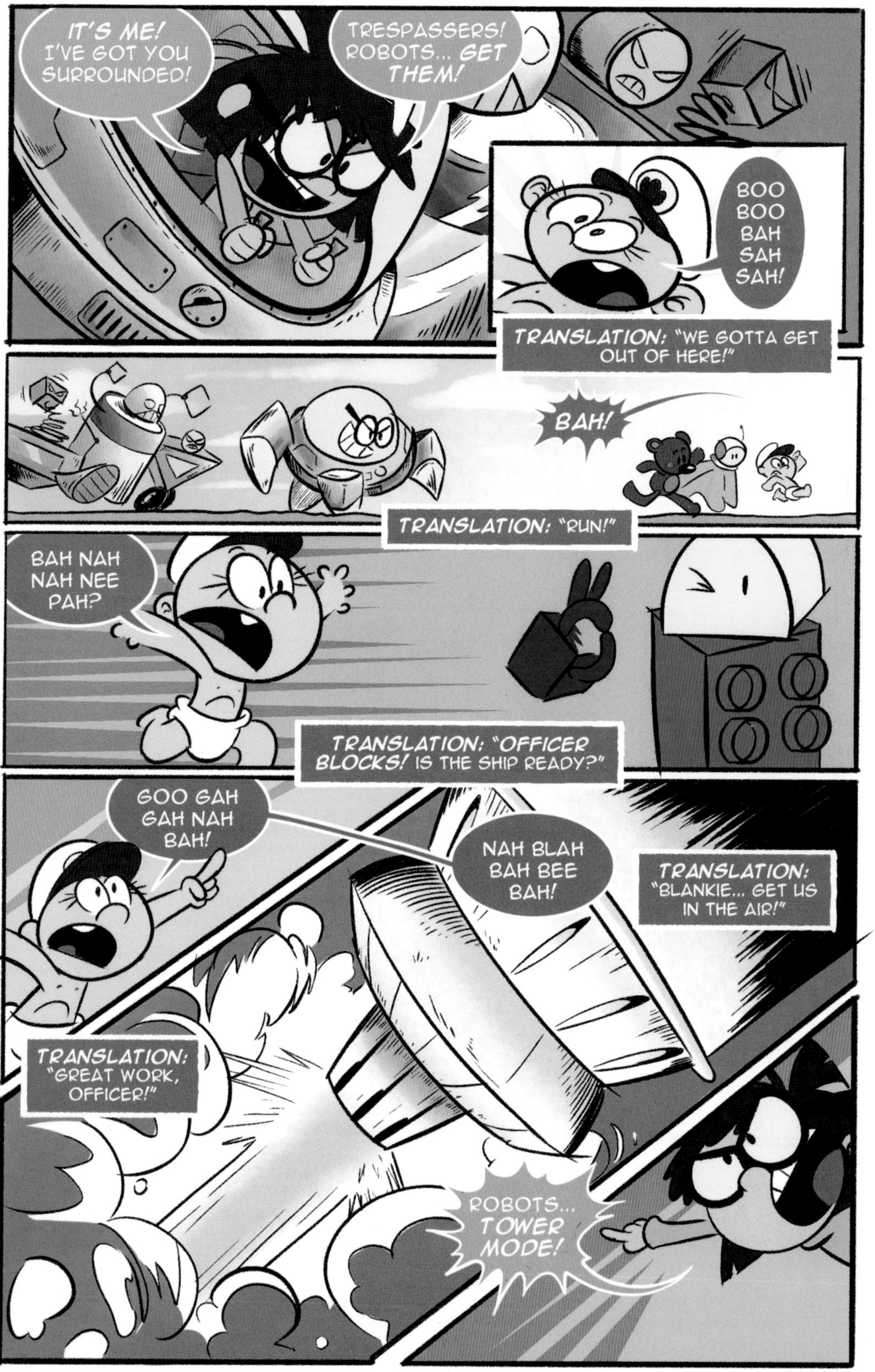
IT'S ME! I'VE GOT YOU SURROUNDED!
TRESPASSERS! ROBOTS... GET THEM!
BOO BOO BAH SAH SAH!
TRANSLATION: "WE GOTTA GET OUT OF HERE!"
BAH!
TRANSLATION: "RUN!"
BAH NAH NAH NEE PAH?
TRANSLATION: "OFFICER BLOCKS! IS THE SHIP READY?"
GOO GAH GAH NAH BAH!
TRANSLATION: "GREAT WORK, OFFICER!"
NAH BLAH BAH BEE BAH!
TRANSLATION: "BLANKIE... GET US IN THE AIR!"
ROBOTS... TOWER MODE!

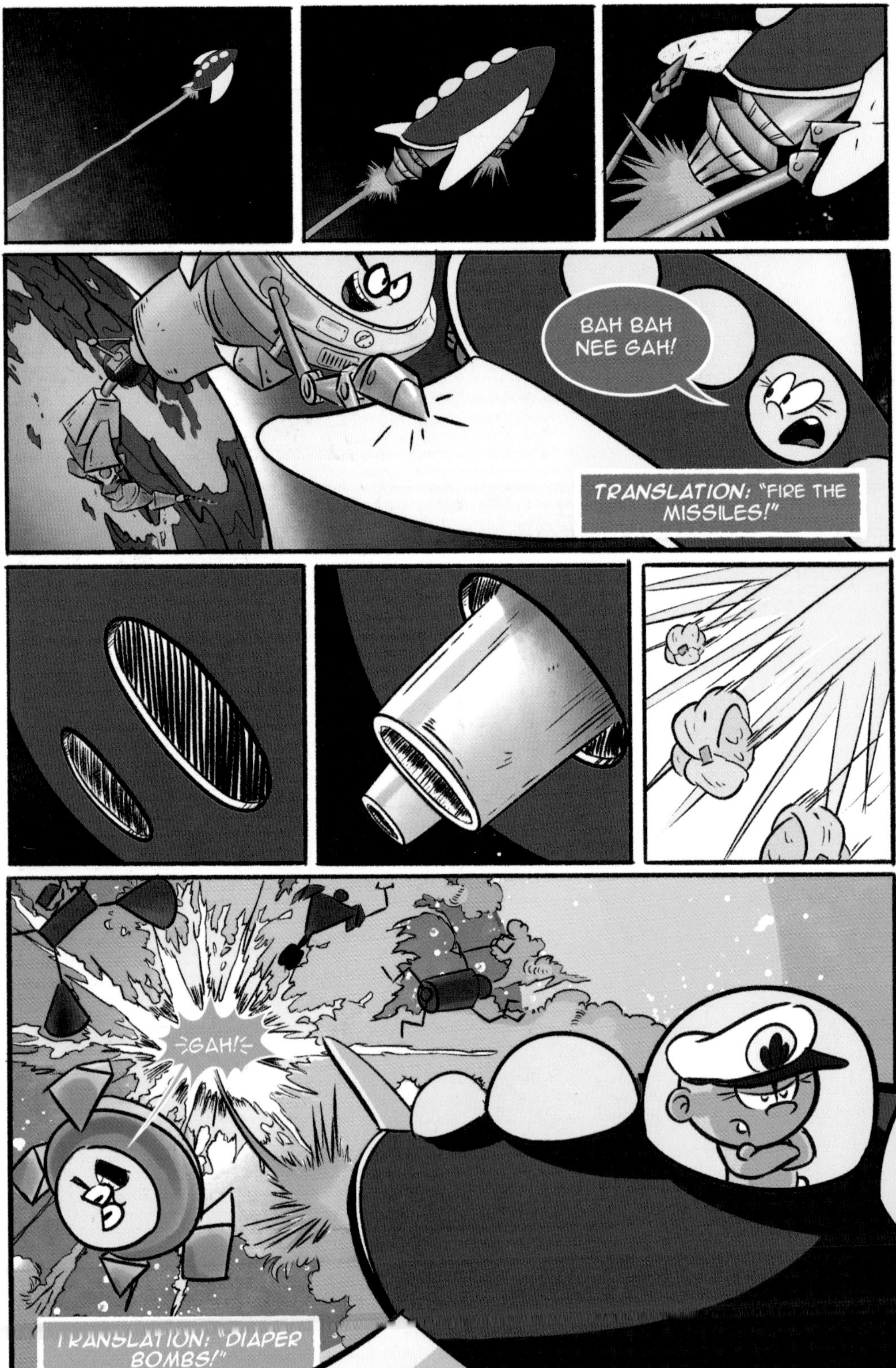
BAH BAH NEE GAH!
TRANSLATION: "FIRE THE MISSILES!"
GAH!
TRANSLATION: "DIAPER BOMBS!"

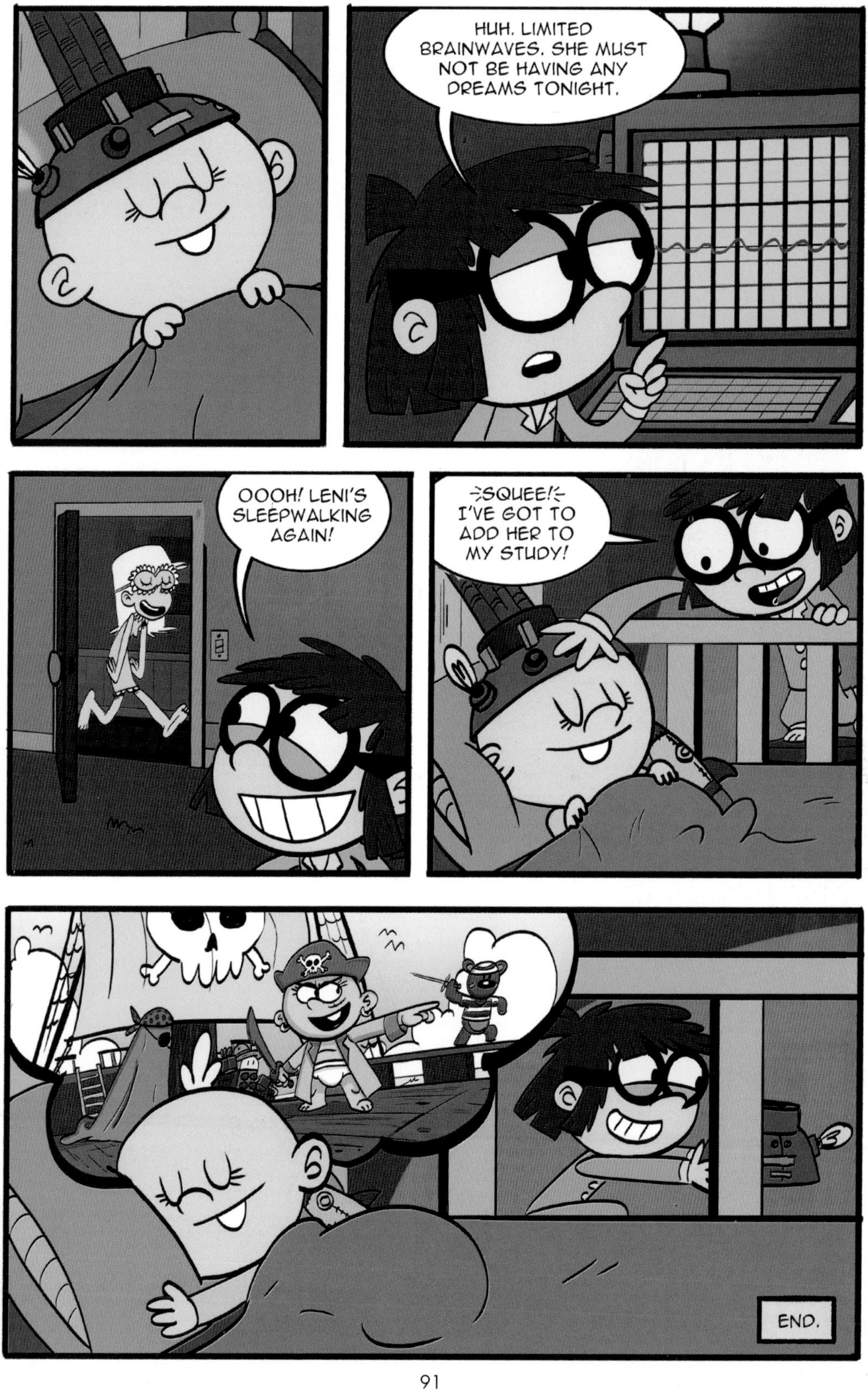
HUH. LIMITED BRAINWAVES. SHE MUST NOT BE HAVING ANY DREAMS TONIGHT.
OOOH! LENI'S SLEEPWALKING AGAIN!
SQUEE! I'VE GOT TO ADD HER TO MY STUDY!
END.

"3:55 AM: BUSTED"

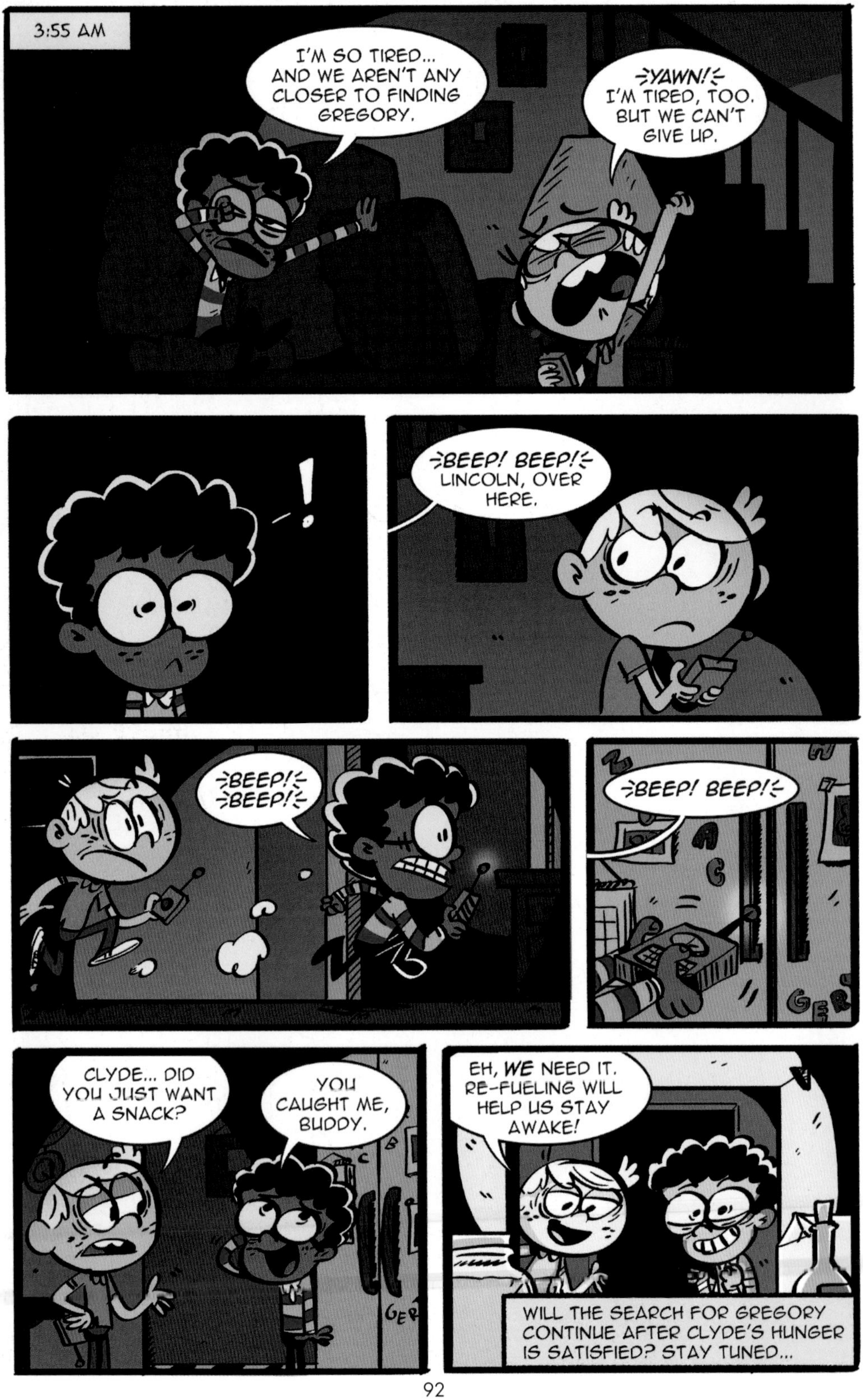
3:55 AM
I'M SO TIRED... AND WE AREN'T ANY CLOSER TO FINDING GREGORY.
YAWN! I'M TIRED, TOO. BUT WE CAN'T GIVE UP.
!
BEEP! BEEP! LINCOLN, OVER HERE.
BEEP! BEEP!
BEEP! BEEP!
CLYDE... DID YOU JUST WANT A SNACK?
YOU CAUGHT ME, BUDDY.
EH, WE NEED IT. RE-FUELING WILL HELP US STAY AWAKE!
WILL THE SEARCH FOR GREGORY CONTINUE AFTER CLYDE'S HUNGER IS SATISFIED? STAY TUNED...

'4:00 AM: THE PRINCESS AND THE PLEA'

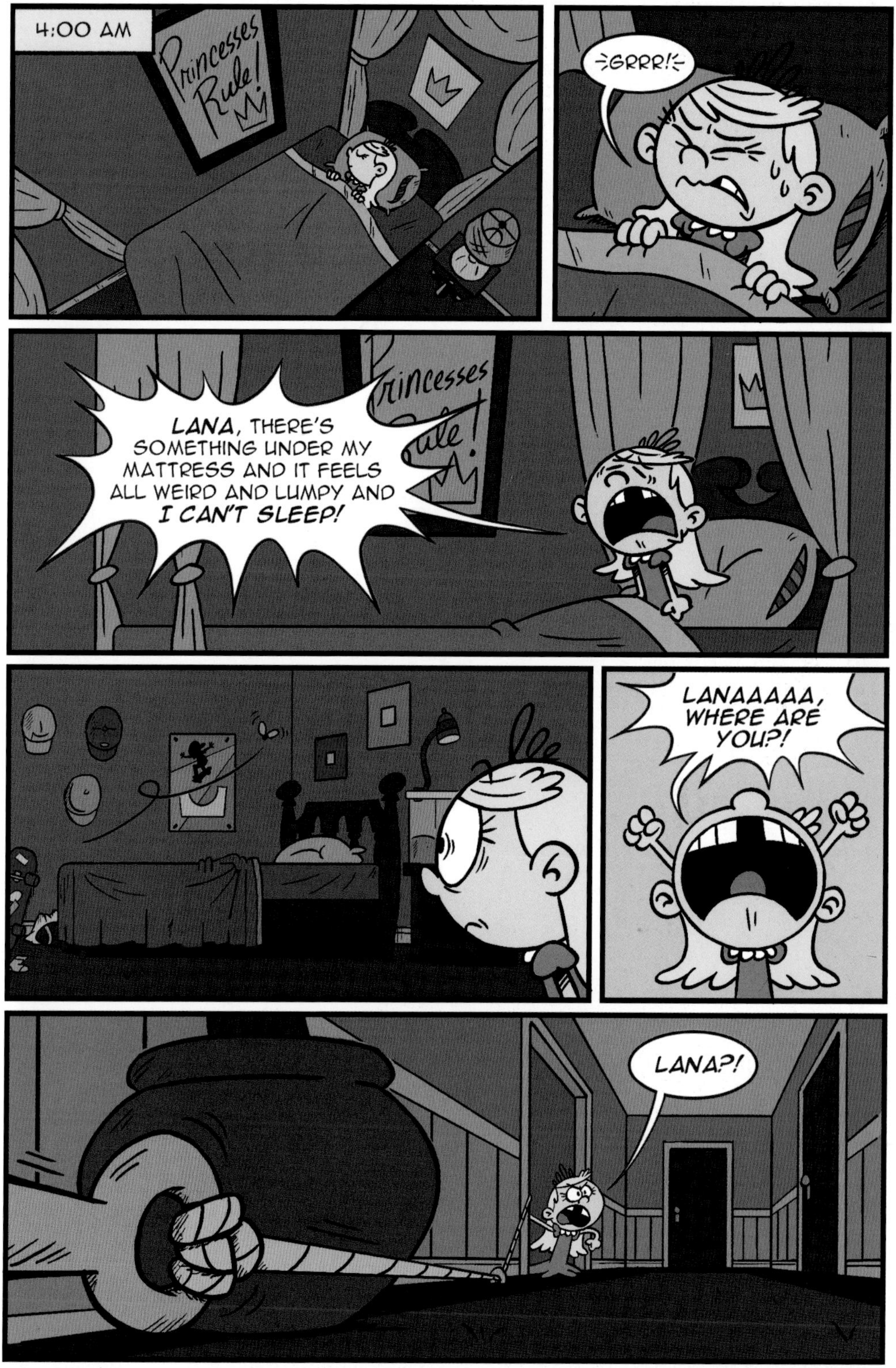
4:00 AM
Princesses Rule!
GRRR!
Princesses Rule!
LANA, THERE'S SOMETHING UNDER MY MATTRESS AND IT FEELS ALL WEIRD AND LUMPY AND I CAN'T SLEEP!
LANAAAAA, WHERE ARE YOU?!
LANA?!

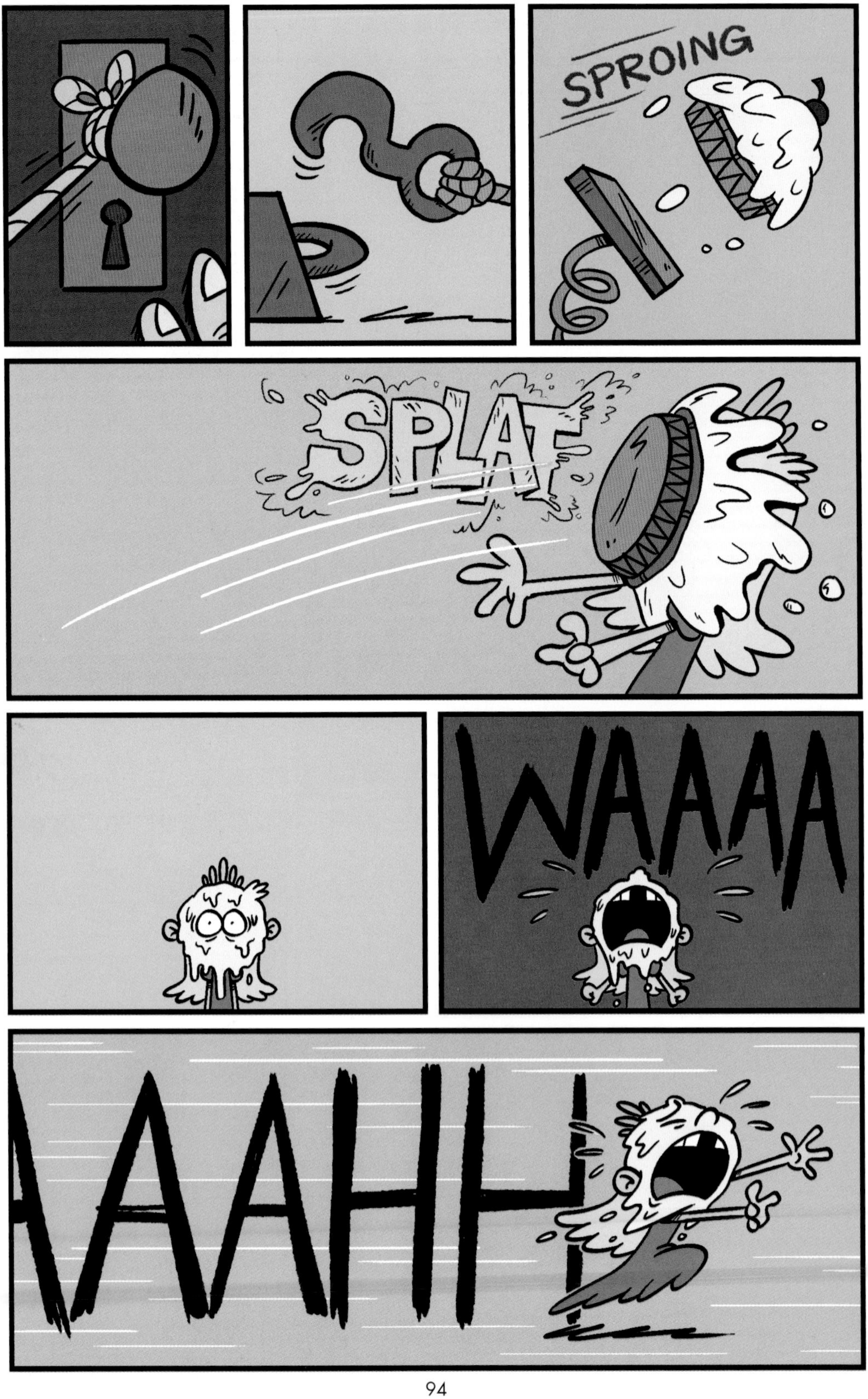
SPROING
SPLAT
WAAAA
AAHH!

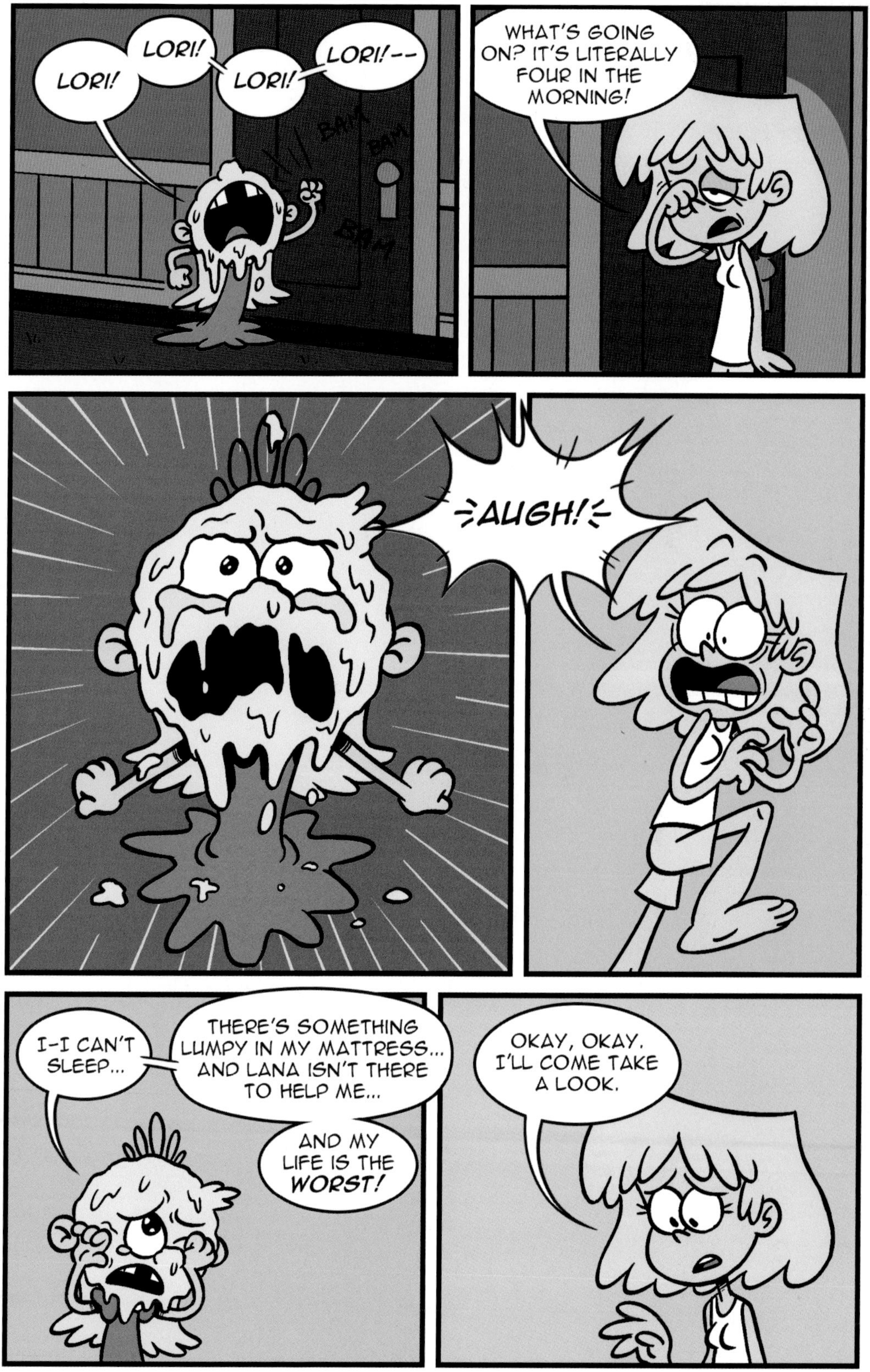
LORI!
LORI!
LORI!
LORI!--
BAM
BAM
BAM
WHAT'S GOING ON? IT'S LITERALLY FOUR IN THE MORNING!
AUGH!
I-I CAN'T SLEEP...
THERE'S SOMETHING LUMPY IN MY MATTRESS... AND LANA ISN'T THERE TO HELP ME...
AND MY LIFE IS THE WORST!
OKAY, OKAY. I'LL COME TAKE A LOOK.

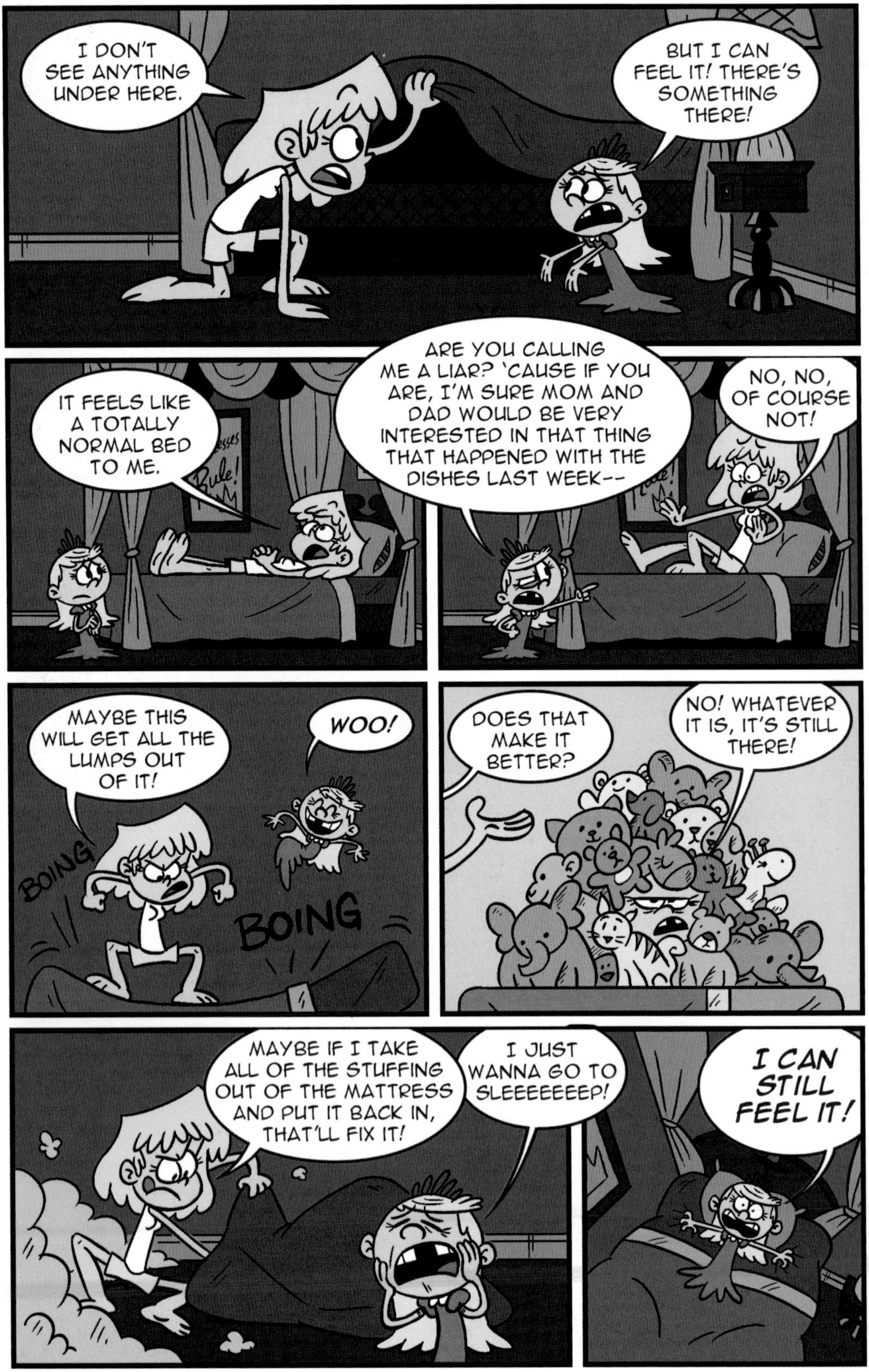
I DON'T SEE ANYTHING UNDER HERE.
BUT I CAN FEEL IT! THERE'S SOMETHING THERE!
IT FEELS LIKE A TOTALLY NORMAL BED TO ME.
ARE YOU CALLING ME A LIAR? 'CAUSE IF YOU ARE, I'M SURE MOM AND DAD WOULD BE VERY INTERESTED IN THAT THING THAT HAPPENED WITH THE DISHES LAST WEEK--
NO, NO, OF COURSE NOT!
MAYBE THIS WILL GET ALL THE LUMPS OUT OF IT!
WOO!
BOING
BOING
DOES THAT MAKE IT BETTER?
NO! WHATEVER IT IS, IT'S STILL THERE!
MAYBE IF I TAKE ALL OF THE STUFFING OUT OF THE MATTRESS AND PUT IT BACK IN, THAT'LL FIX IT!
I JUST WANNA GO TO SLEEEEEEEP!
I CAN STILL FEEL IT!

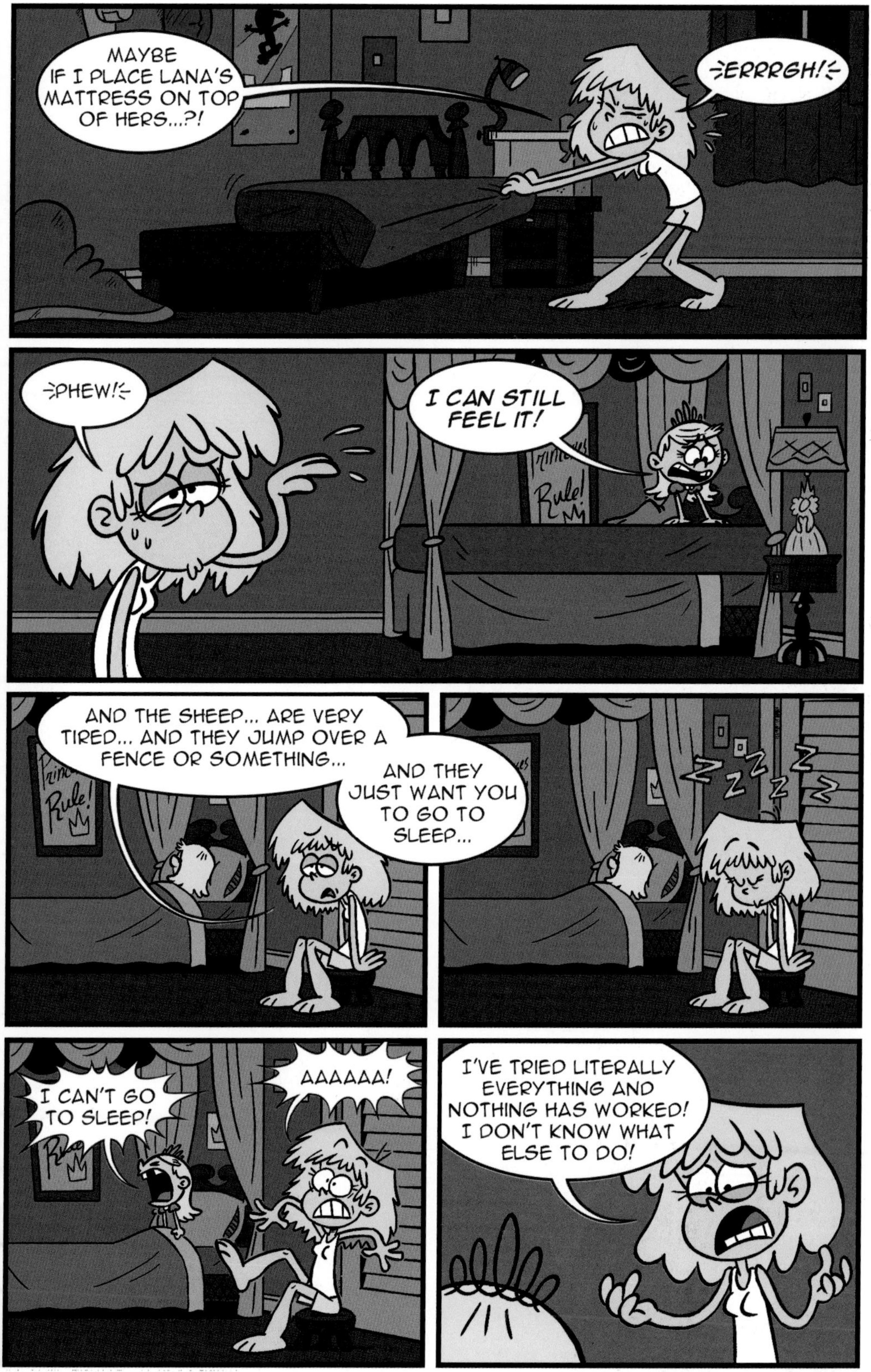
MAYBE IF I PLACE LANA'S MATTRESS ON TOP OF HERS...?!
ERRRGH!
PHEW!
I CAN STILL FEEL IT!
AND THE SHEEP... ARE VERY TIRED... AND THEY JUMP OVER A FENCE OR SOMETHING...
AND THEY JUST WANT YOU TO GO TO SLEEP...
Princesses Rule!
ZZZZZZZ
I CAN'T GO TO SLEEP!
AAAAAA!
I'VE TRIED LITERALLY EVERYTHING AND NOTHING HAS WORKED! I DON'T KNOW WHAT ELSE TO DO!

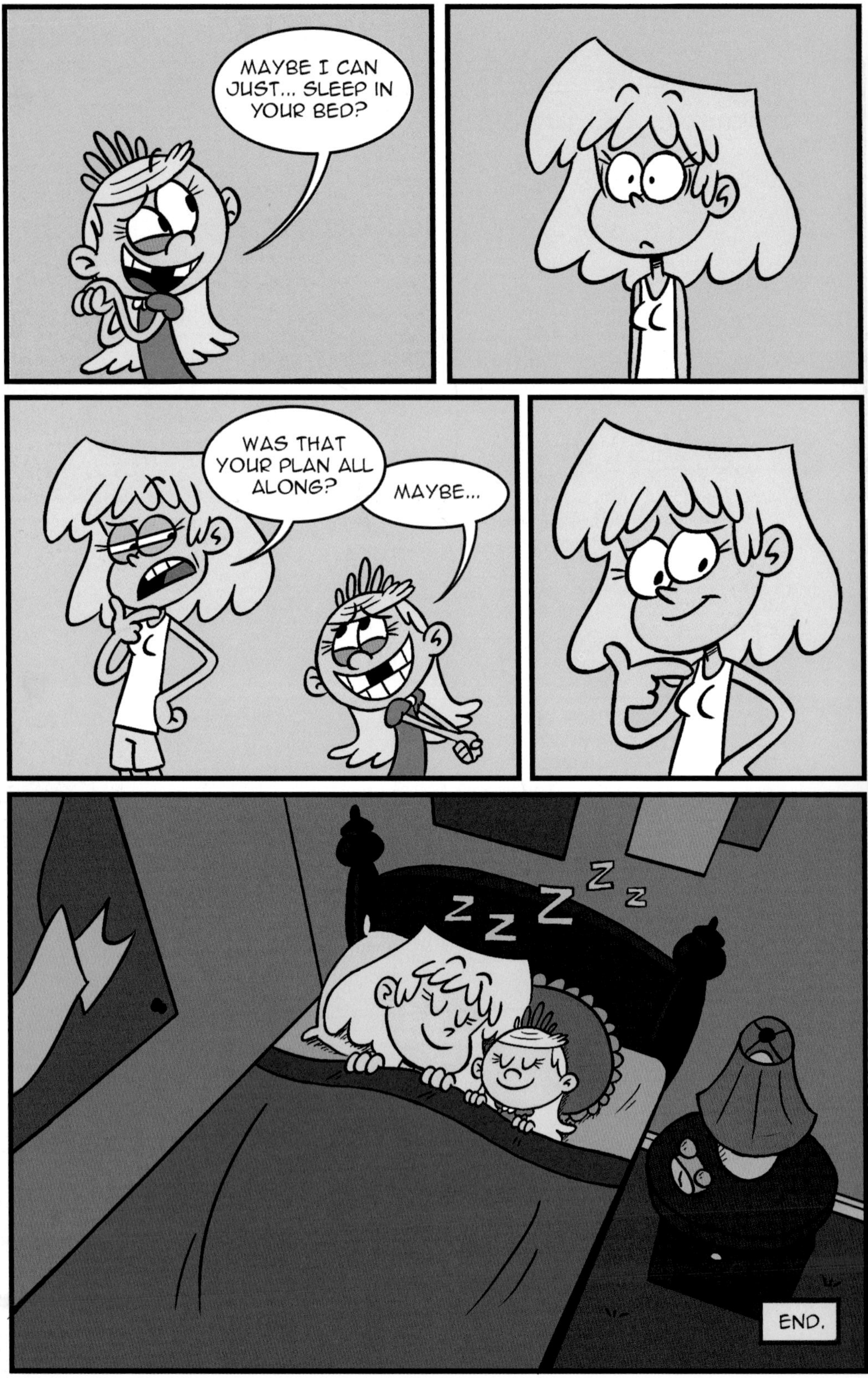
MAYBE I CAN JUST... SLEEP IN YOUR BED?
WAS THAT YOUR PLAN ALL ALONG?
MAYBE...
Z Z Z Z Z
END.

"5:00 AM: TUB TIME"

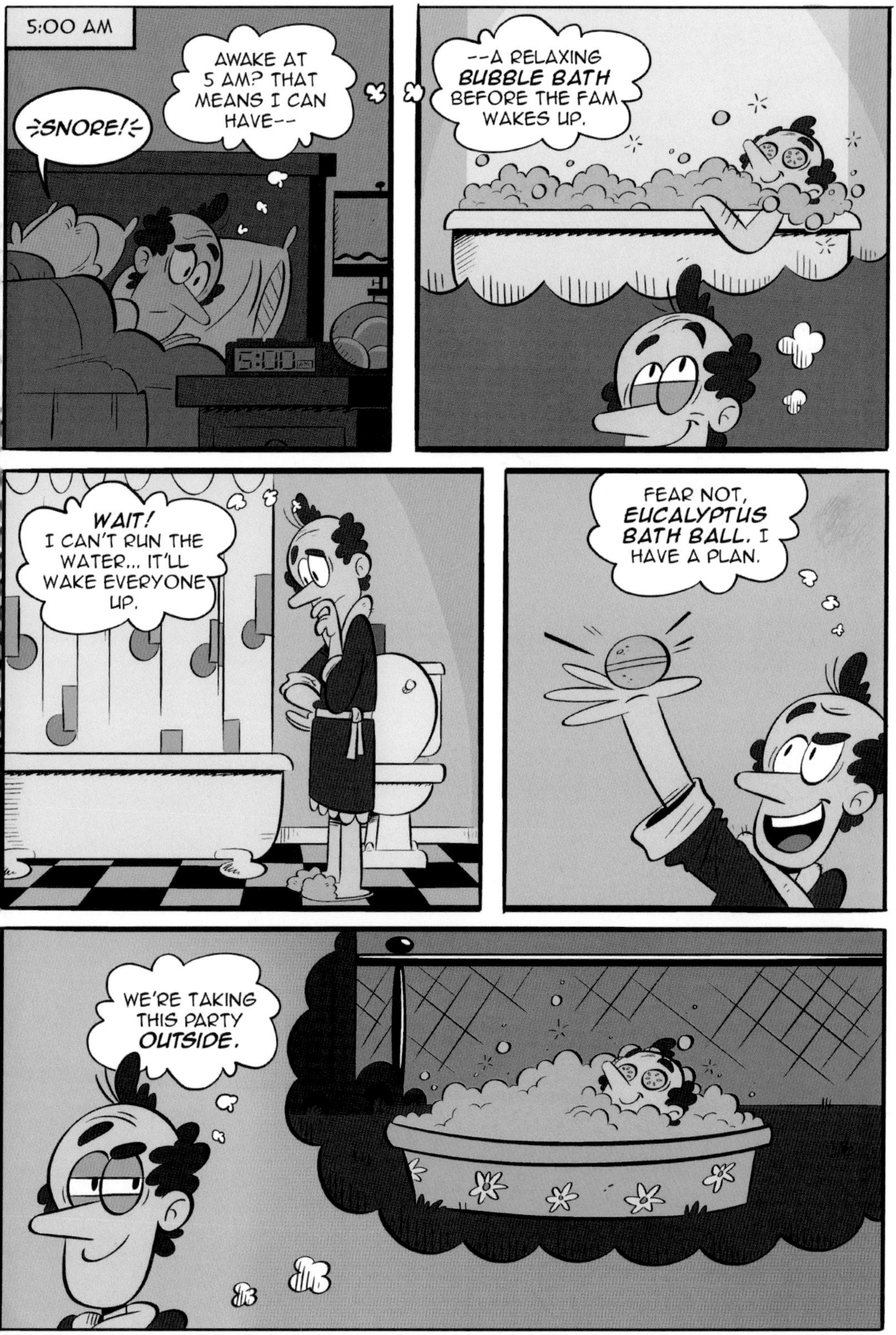
5:00 AM
AWAKE AT 5 AM? THAT MEANS I CAN HAVE--
≈SNORE!≈
--A RELAXING BUBBLE BATH BEFORE THE FAM WAKES UP.
WAIT! I CAN'T RUN THE WATER... IT'LL WAKE EVERYONE UP.
FEAR NOT, EUCALYPTUS BATH BALL. I HAVE A PLAN.
WE'RE TAKING THIS PARTY OUTSIDE.

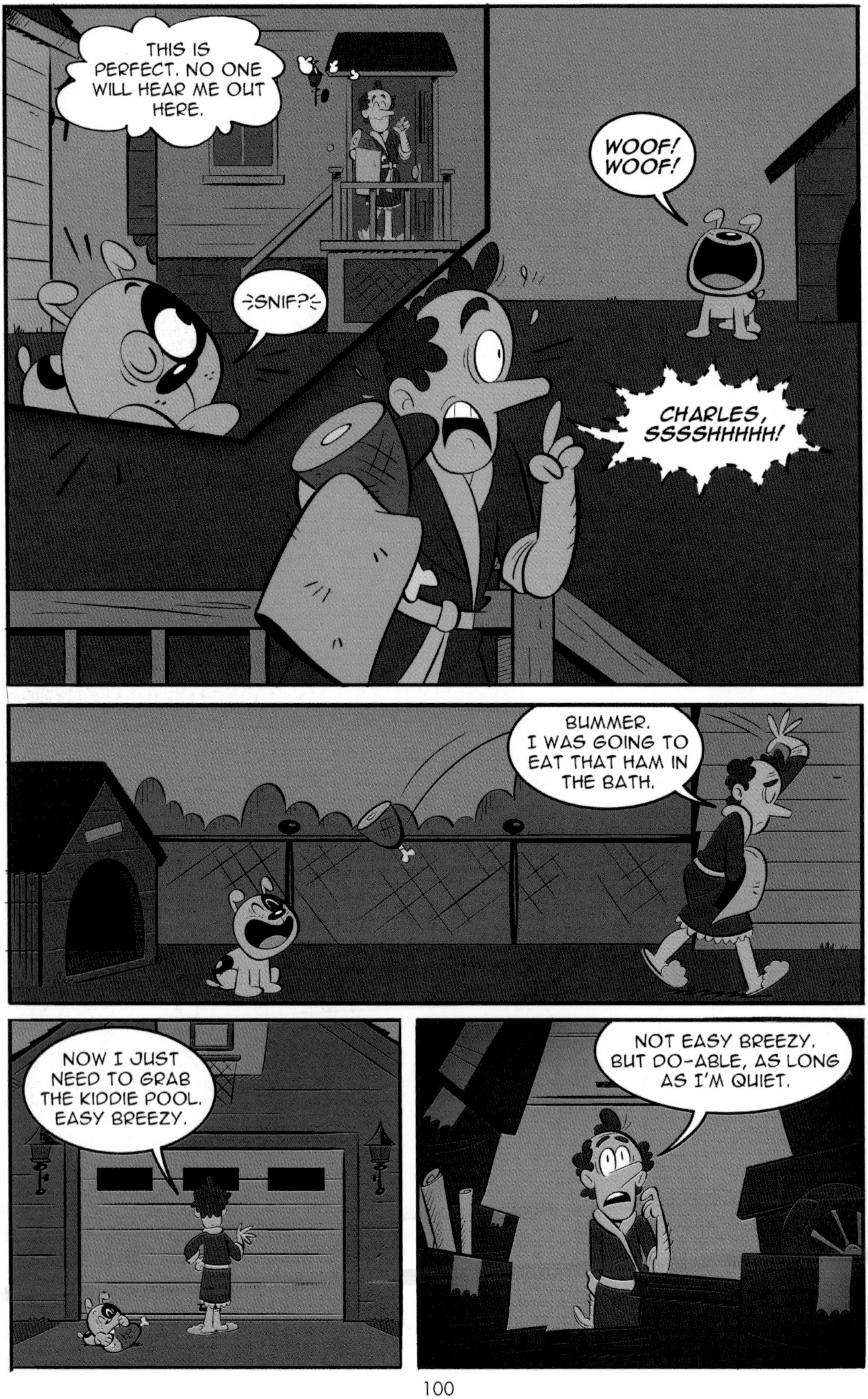
THIS IS PERFECT. NO ONE WILL HEAR ME OUT HERE.
SNIF?
WOOF! WOOF!
CHARLES, SSSSHHHHH!
BUMMER. I WAS GOING TO EAT THAT HAM IN THE BATH.
NOW I JUST NEED TO GRAB THE KIDDIE POOL. EASY BREEZY.
NOT EASY BREEZY. BUT DO-ABLE, AS LONG AS I'M QUIET.

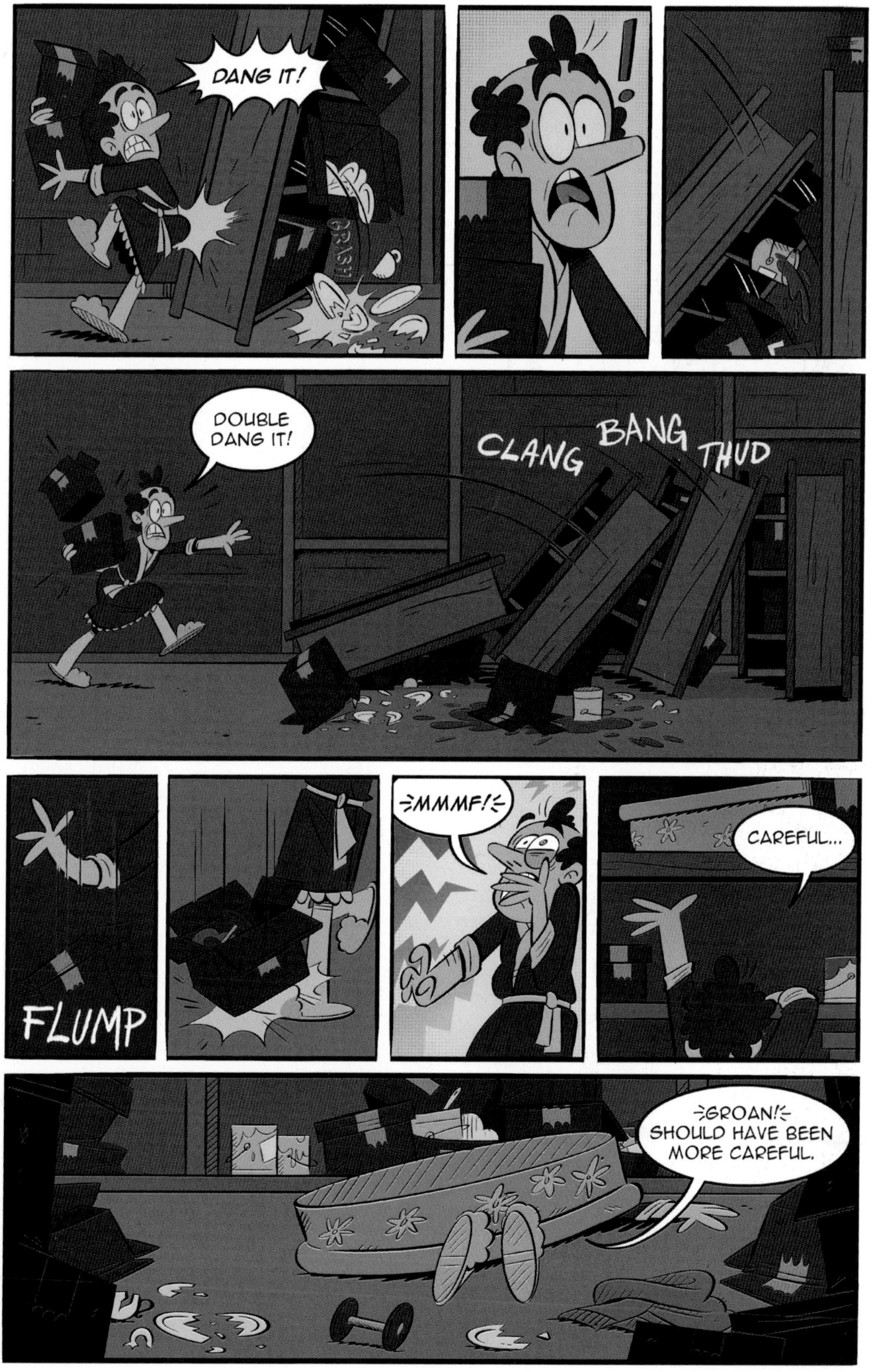
DANG IT!
CRASH
!
DOUBLE DANG IT!
CLANG
BANG
THUD
FLUMP
MMMF!
CAREFUL...
GROAN! SHOULD HAVE BEEN MORE CAREFUL.

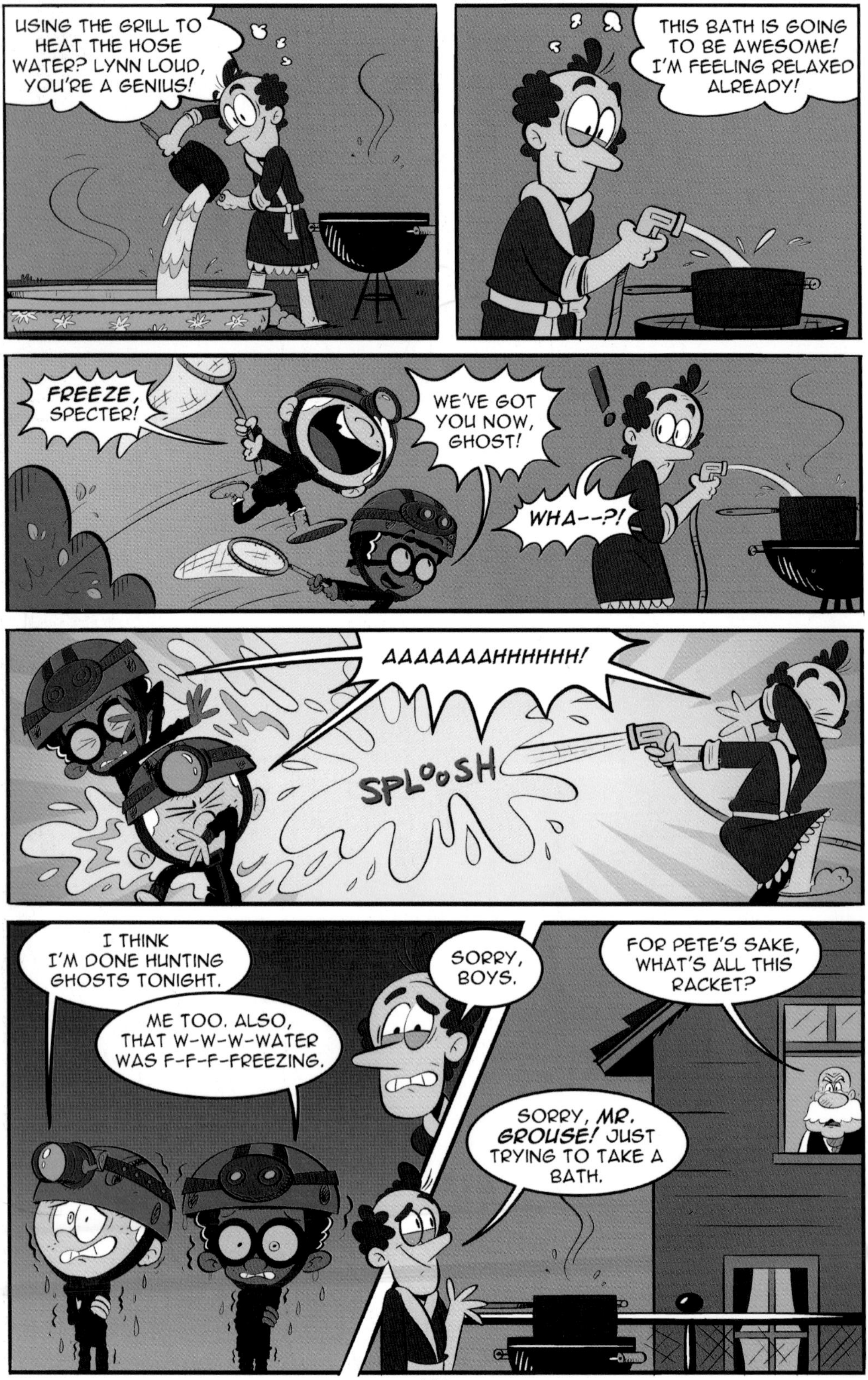
USING THE GRILL TO HEAT THE HOSE WATER? LYNN LOUD, YOU'RE A GENIUS!
THIS BATH IS GOING TO BE AWESOME! I'M FEELING RELAXED ALREADY!
FREEZE, SPECTER!
WE'VE GOT YOU NOW, GHOST!
!
WHA--?!
AAAAAAAHHHHHH!
SPLOOSH
I THINK I'M DONE HUNTING GHOSTS TONIGHT.
ME TOO. ALSO, THAT W-W-W-WATER WAS F-F-F-FREEZING.
SORRY, BOYS.
FOR PETE'S SAKE, WHAT'S ALL THIS RACKET?
SORRY, MR. GROUSE! JUST TRYING TO TAKE A BATH.

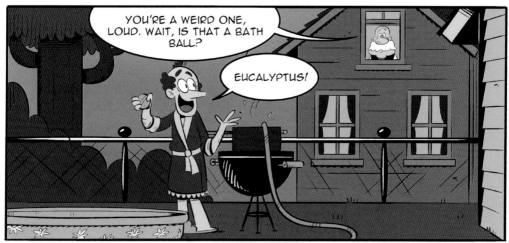

YOU'RE A WEIRD ONE, LOUD. WAIT, IS THAT A BATH BALL?

EUCALYPTUS!

WELL, I DO APPRECIATE A GOOD BATH BALL. TELL YA WHAT, LOUD...

YOU CAN USE MY TUB. ON THREE CONDITIONS.

ONE, BE QUIET ALREADY.

TWO, GET ME ONE OF THOSE BATH BALLS...

AND THREE, MAKE ME A LASAGNA.

DEAL!

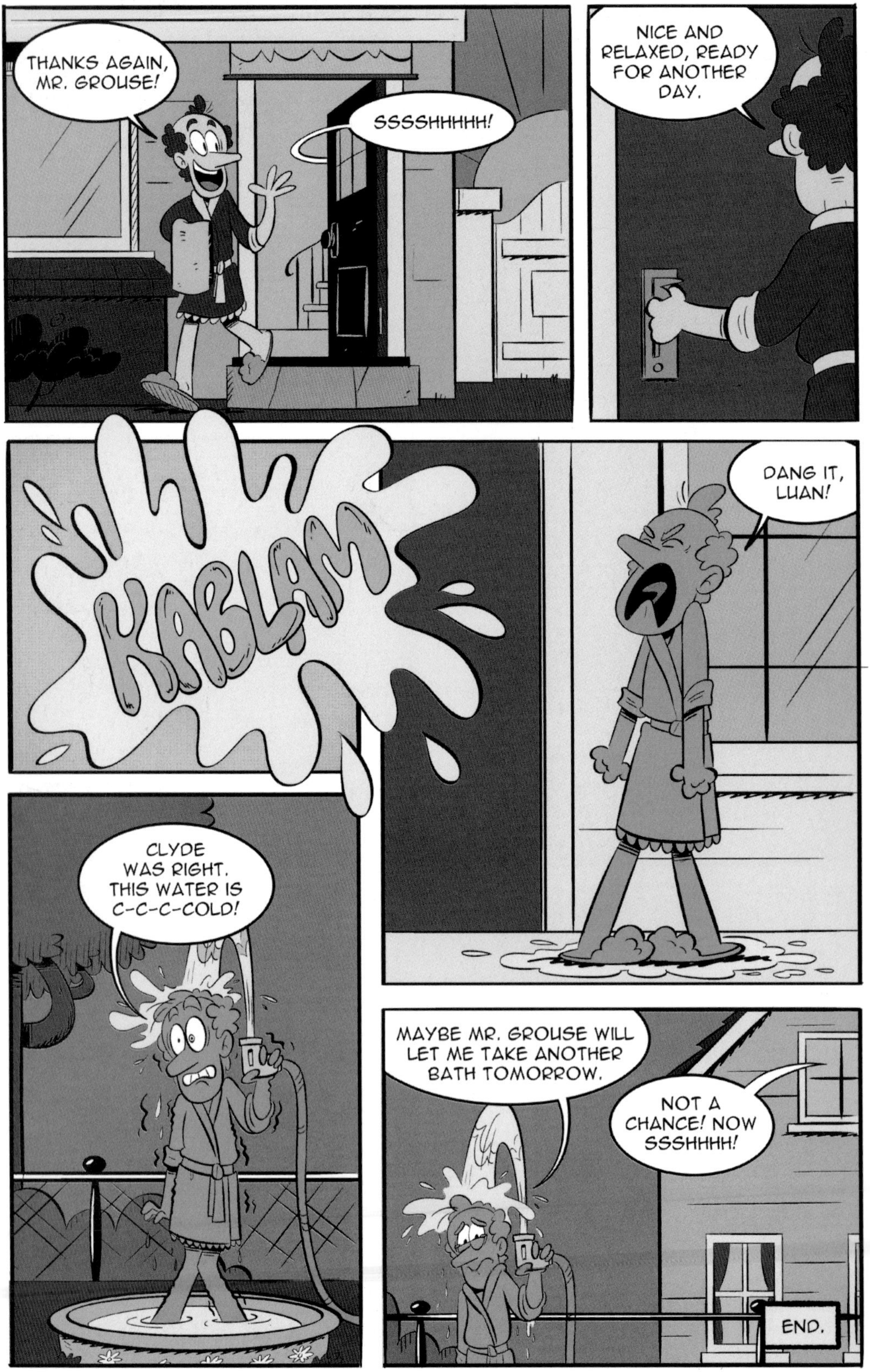
THANKS AGAIN, MR. GROUSE!
SSSSHHHHH!
NICE AND RELAXED, READY FOR ANOTHER DAY.
KABLAM
DANG IT, LUAN!
CLYDE WAS RIGHT. THIS WATER IS C-C-C-COLD!
MAYBE MR. GROUSE WILL LET ME TAKE ANOTHER BATH TOMORROW.
NOT A CHANCE! NOW SSSHHHH!
END.

"5:55 AM BOYS IN THE ATTIC"

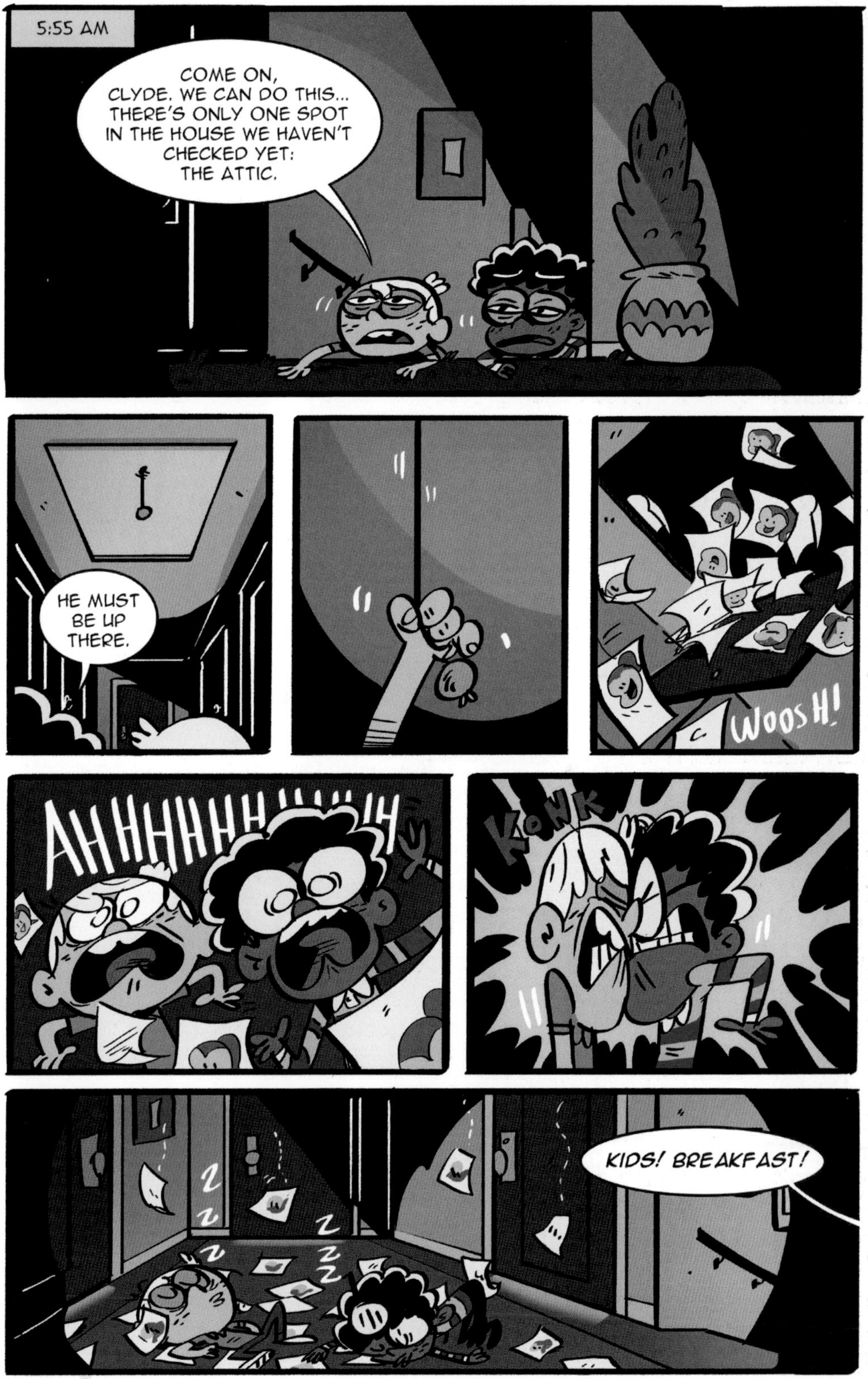
5:55 AM
COME ON, CLYDE. WE CAN DO THIS... THERE'S ONLY ONE SPOT IN THE HOUSE WE HAVEN'T CHECKED YET: THE ATTIC.
HE MUST BE UP THERE.
WOOSH!
KONK
KIDS! BREAKFAST!

"6:00 AM: BREAKFAST IS READY!"

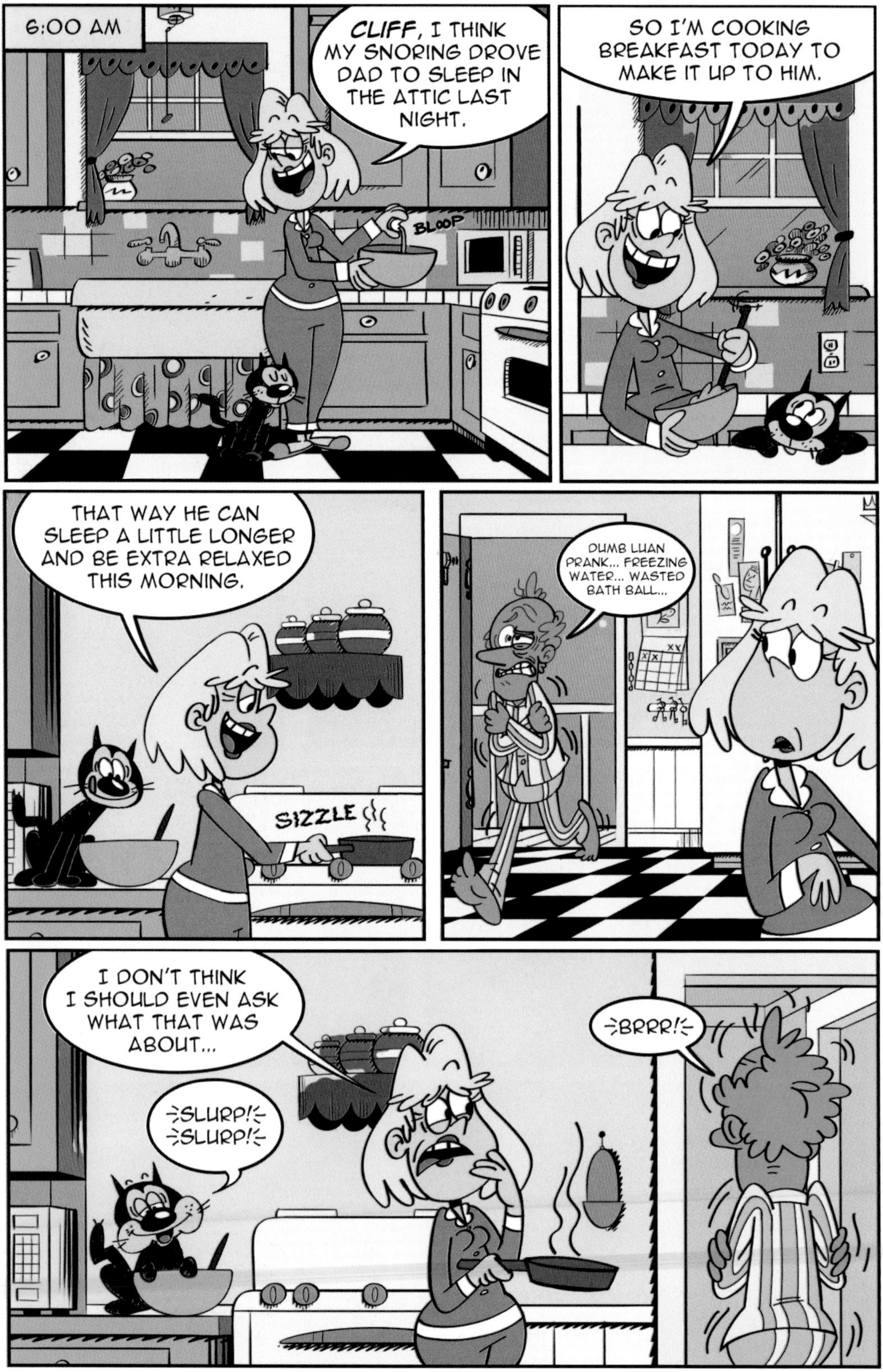
6:00 AM
CLIFF, I THINK MY SNORING DROVE DAD TO SLEEP IN THE ATTIC LAST NIGHT.
BLOOP
SO I'M COOKING BREAKFAST TODAY TO MAKE IT UP TO HIM.
THAT WAY HE CAN SLEEP A LITTLE LONGER AND BE EXTRA RELAXED THIS MORNING.
SIZZLE
DUMB LUAN PRANK... FREEZING WATER... WASTED BATH BALL...
I DON'T THINK I SHOULD EVEN ASK WHAT THAT WAS ABOUT...
SLURP! SLURP!
BRRR!

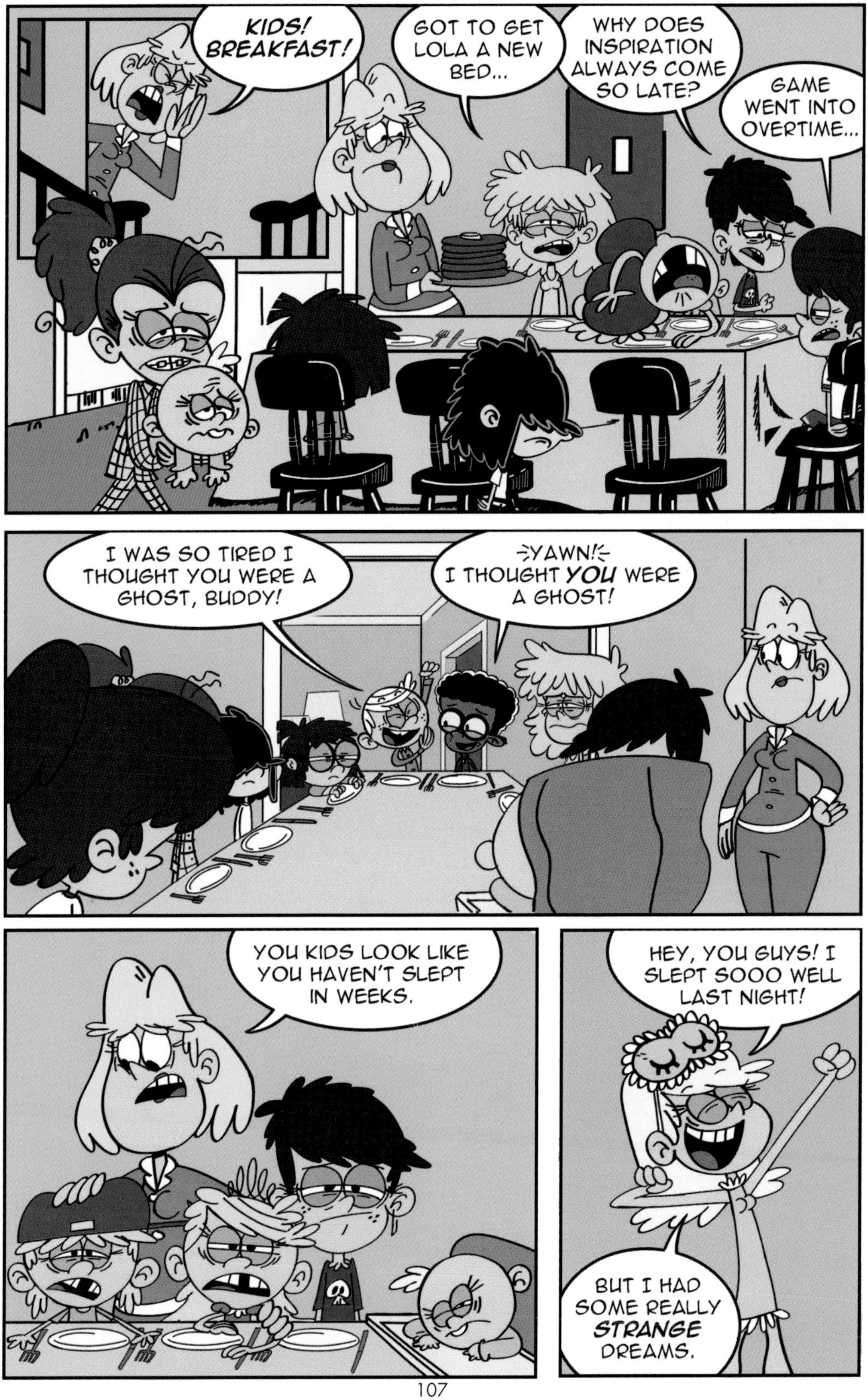
KIDS! BREAKFAST!
GOT TO GET LOLA A NEW BED...
WHY DOES INSPIRATION ALWAYS COME SO LATE?
GAME WENT INTO OVERTIME...
I WAS SO TIRED I THOUGHT YOU WERE A GHOST, BUDDY!
YAWN! I THOUGHT *YOU* WERE A GHOST!
YOU KIDS LOOK LIKE YOU HAVEN'T SLEPT IN WEEKS.
HEY, YOU GUYS! I SLEPT SOOO WELL LAST NIGHT!
BUT I HAD SOME REALLY *STRANGE* DREAMS.

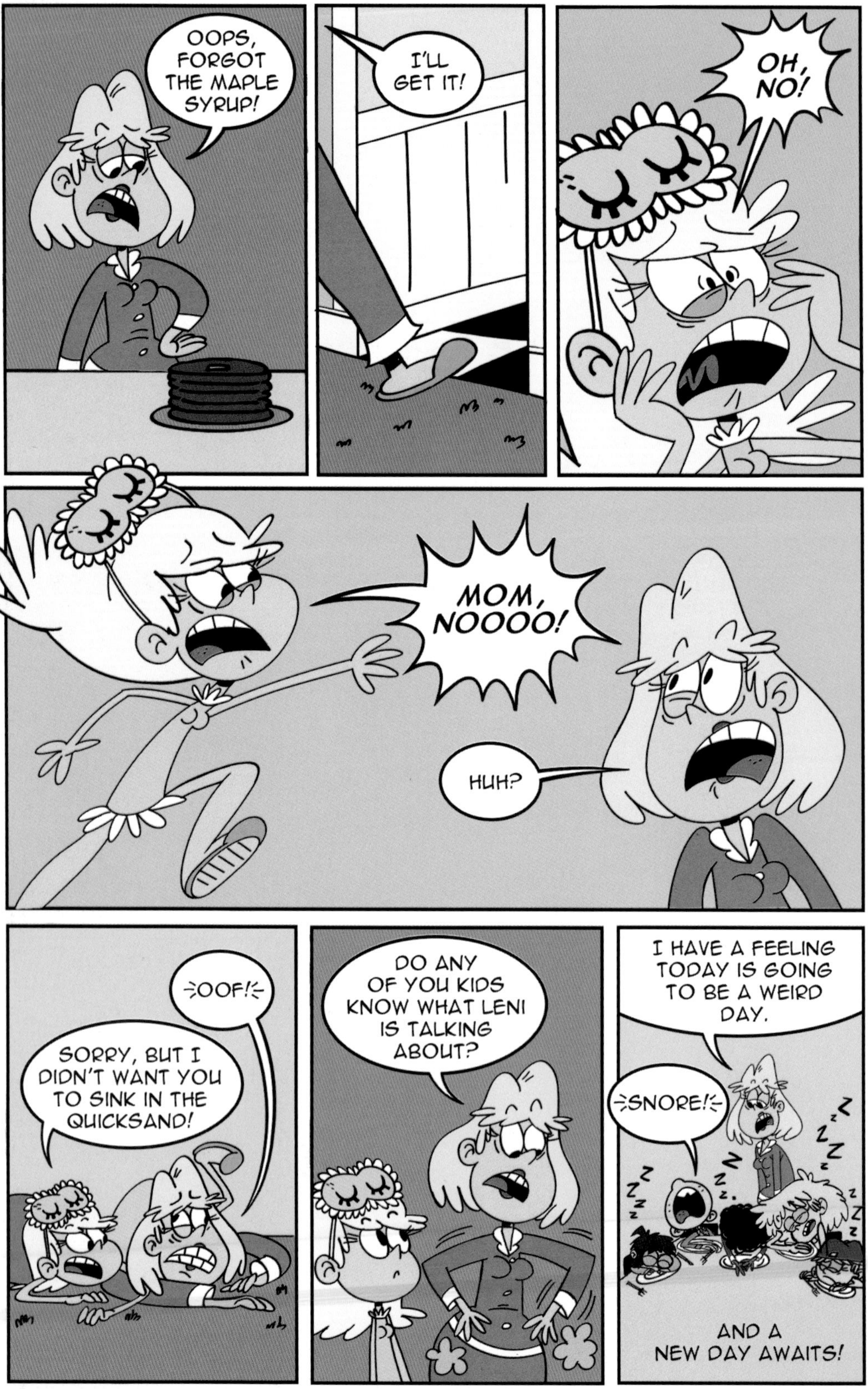
OOPS, FORGOT THE MAPLE SYRUP!
I'LL GET IT!
OH, NO!
MOM, NOOOO!
HUH?
OOF!
SORRY, BUT I DIDN'T WANT YOU TO SINK IN THE QUICKSAND!
DO ANY OF YOU KIDS KNOW WHAT LENI IS TALKING ABOUT?
I HAVE A FEELING TODAY IS GOING TO BE A WEIRD DAY.
SNORE!
AND A NEW DAY AWAITS!

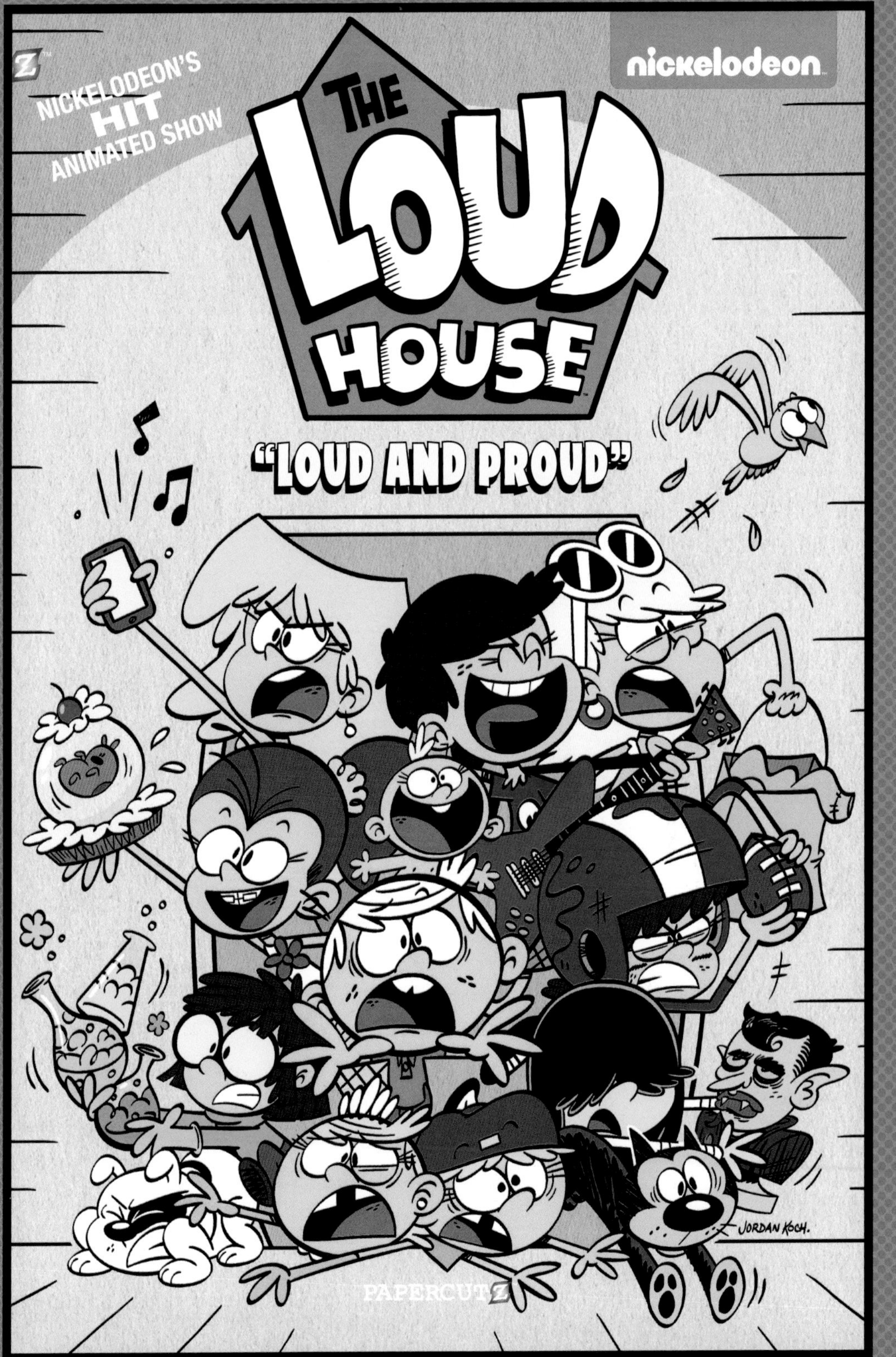
NICKELODEON'S HIT ANIMATED SHOW
nickelodeon
THE LOUD HOUSE
"LOUD AND PROUD"
JORDAN KOCH.
PAPERCUTZ
THE LOUD HOUSE #6 Cover Art by Jordan Koch

"BUCKLE UP"

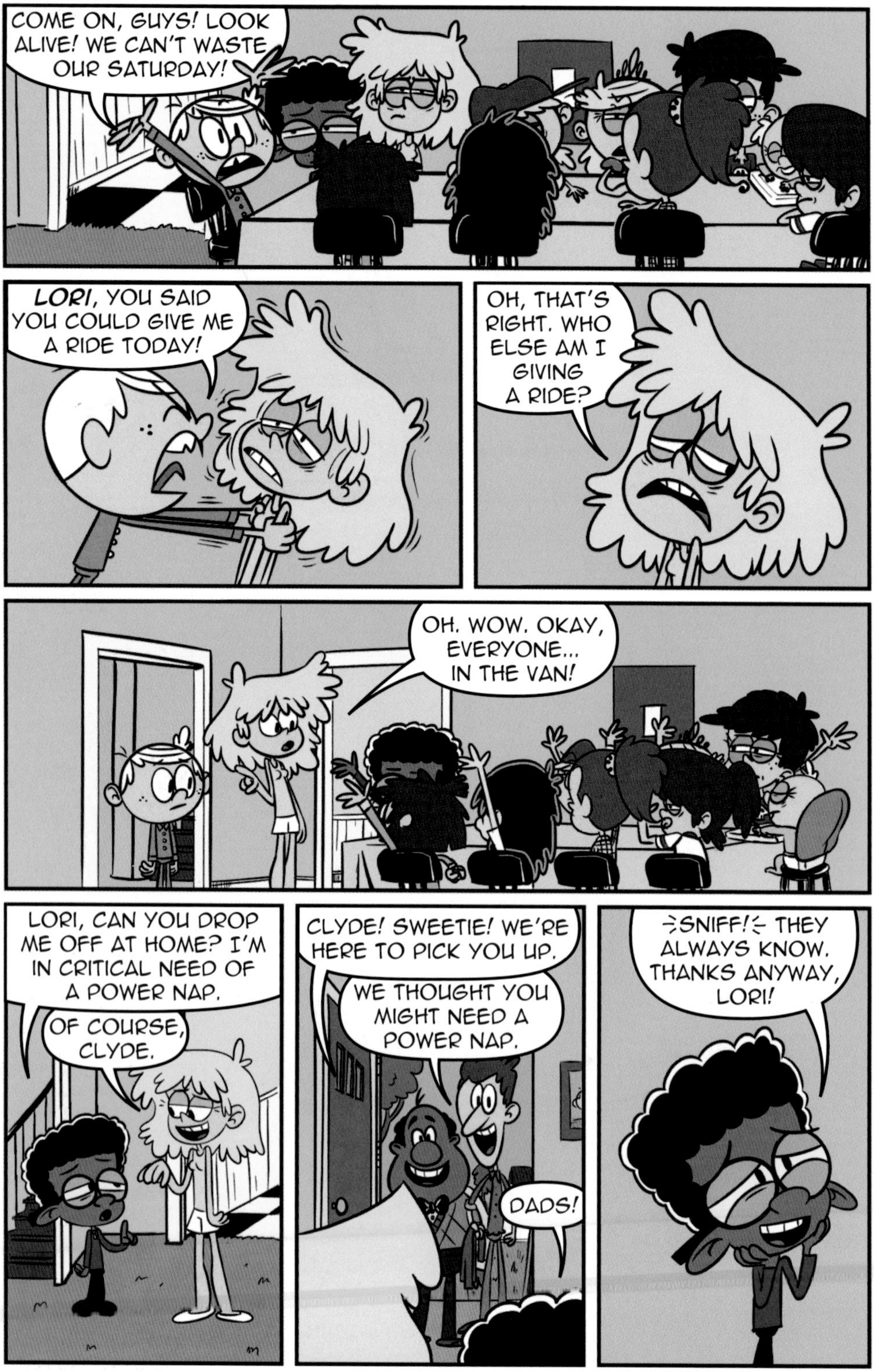

COME ON, GUYS! LOOK ALIVE! WE CAN'T WASTE OUR SATURDAY!
LORI, YOU SAID YOU COULD GIVE ME A RIDE TODAY!
OH, THAT'S RIGHT. WHO ELSE AM I GIVING A RIDE?
OH. WOW. OKAY, EVERYONE... IN THE VAN!
LORI, CAN YOU DROP ME OFF AT HOME? I'M IN CRITICAL NEED OF A POWER NAP.
OF COURSE, CLYDE.
CLYDE! SWEETIE! WE'RE HERE TO PICK YOU UP.
WE THOUGHT YOU MIGHT NEED A POWER NAP.
DADS!
SNIFF! THEY ALWAYS KNOW. THANKS ANYWAY, LORI!

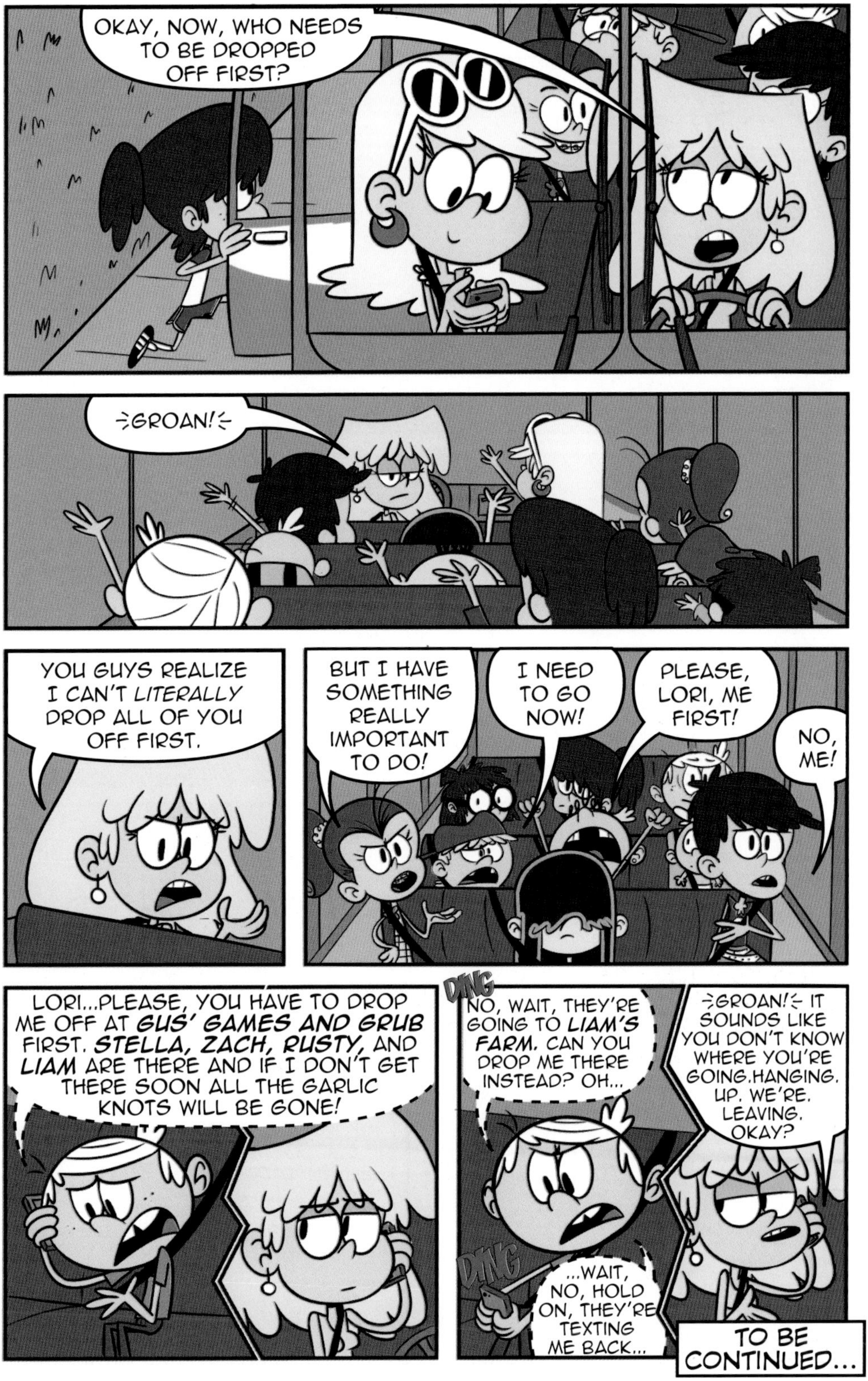
OKAY, NOW, WHO NEEDS TO BE DROPPED OFF FIRST?
GROAN!
YOU GUYS REALIZE I CAN'T *LITERALLY* DROP ALL OF YOU OFF FIRST.
BUT I HAVE SOMETHING REALLY IMPORTANT TO DO!
I NEED TO GO NOW!
PLEASE, LORI, ME FIRST!
NO, ME!
LORI...PLEASE, YOU HAVE TO DROP ME OFF AT **GUS' GAMES AND GRUB** FIRST. **STELLA, ZACH, RUSTY,** AND **LIAM** ARE THERE AND IF I DON'T GET THERE SOON ALL THE GARLIC KNOTS WILL BE GONE!
DING
NO, WAIT, THEY'RE GOING TO **LIAM'S FARM.** CAN YOU DROP ME THERE INSTEAD? OH...
DING
...WAIT, NO, HOLD ON, THEY'RE TEXTING ME BACK...
GROAN! IT SOUNDS LIKE YOU DON'T KNOW WHERE YOU'RE GOING.HANGING. UP. WE'RE. LEAVING. OKAY?
TO BE CONTINUED...

"MALL FLOP"

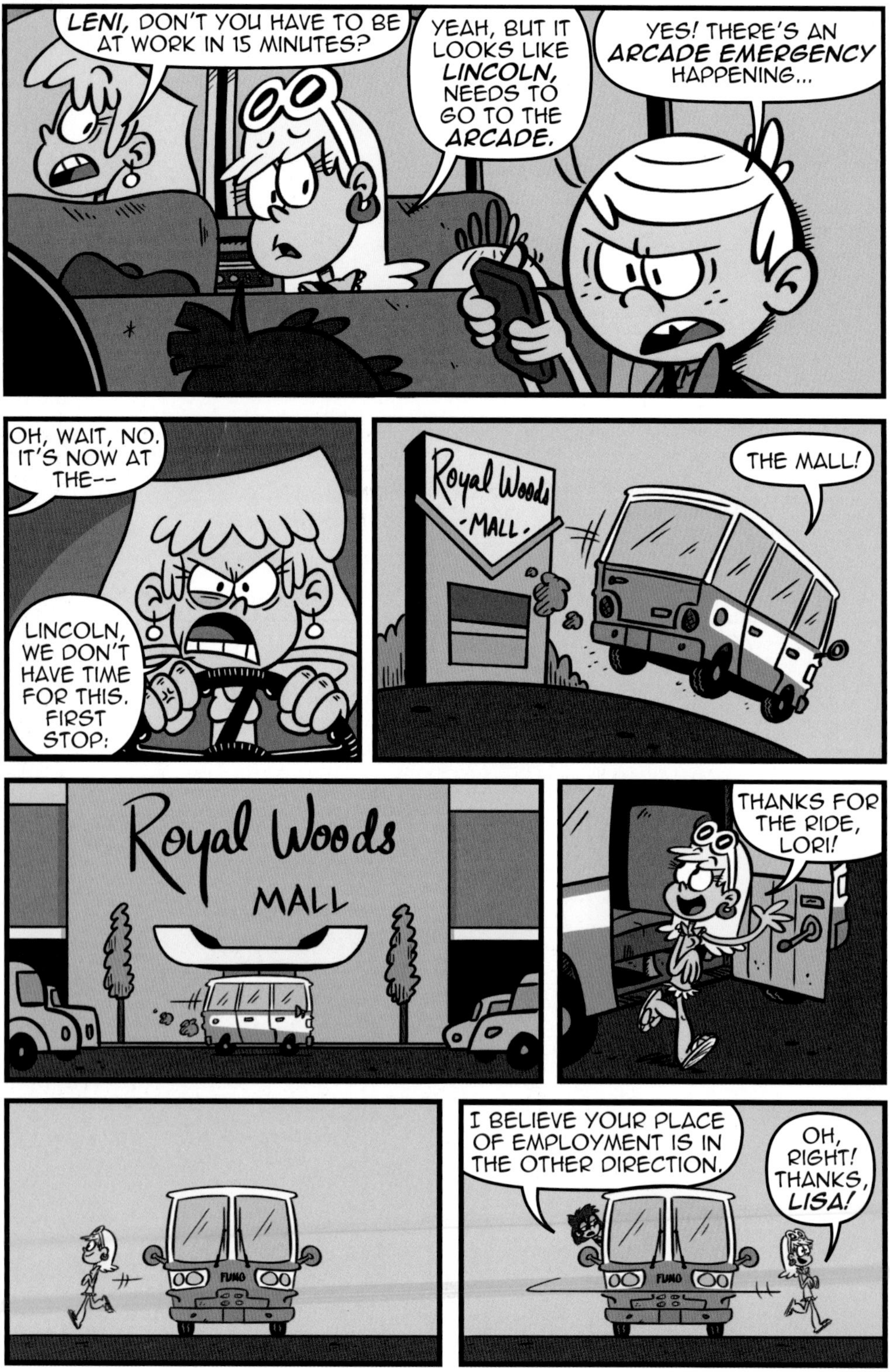

LENI, DON'T YOU HAVE TO BE AT WORK IN 15 MINUTES?
YEAH, BUT IT LOOKS LIKE LINCOLN, NEEDS TO GO TO THE ARCADE.
YES! THERE'S AN ARCADE EMERGENCY HAPPENING...
OH, WAIT, NO. IT'S NOW AT THE--
LINCOLN, WE DON'T HAVE TIME FOR THIS. FIRST STOP:
Royal Woods MALL
THE MALL!
Royal Woods MALL
THANKS FOR THE RIDE, LORI!
I BELIEVE YOUR PLACE OF EMPLOYMENT IS IN THE OTHER DIRECTION.
OH, RIGHT! THANKS, LISA!

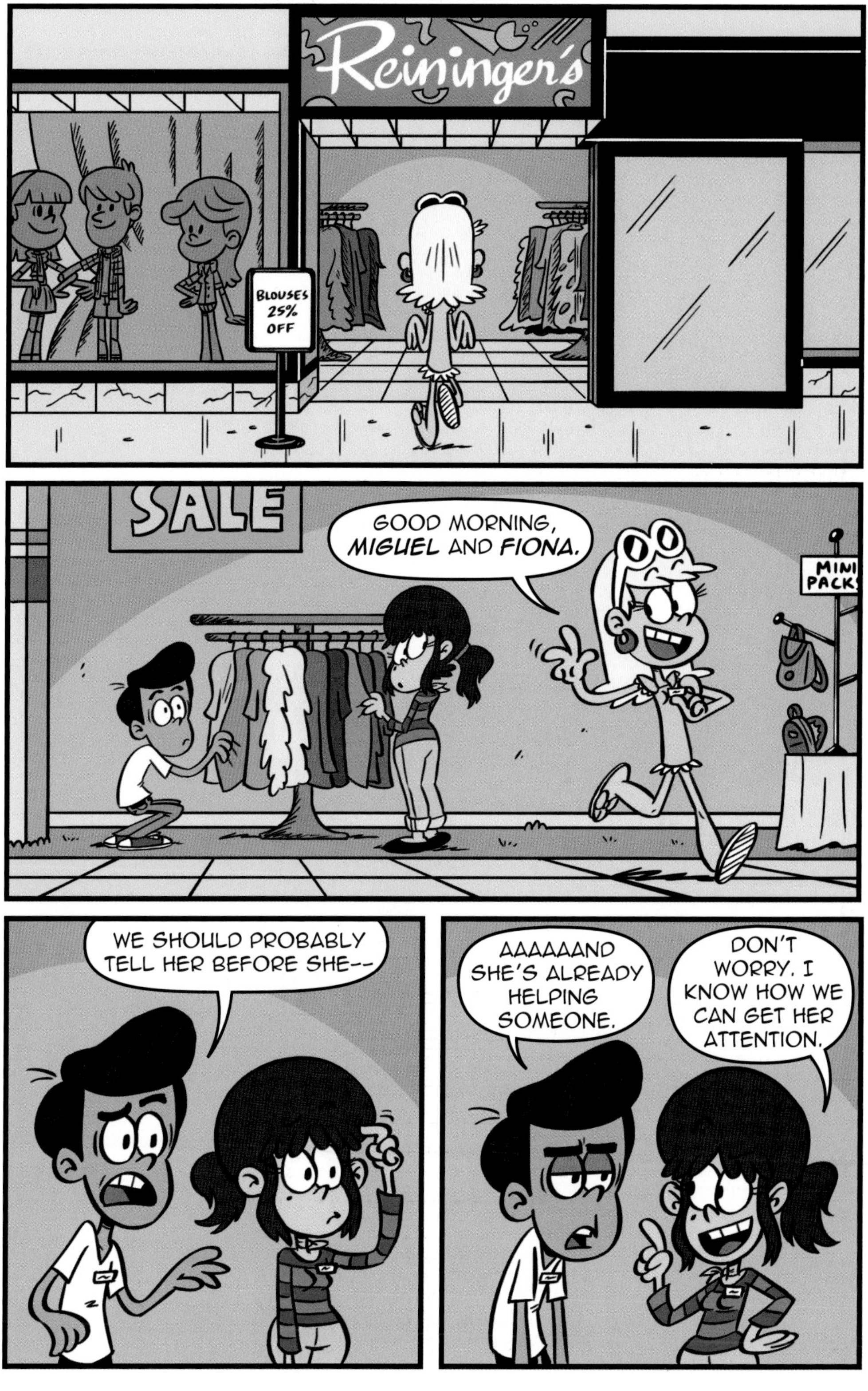
Reiningers's
BLOUSES 25% OFF
SALE
GOOD MORNING, *MIGUEL* AND *FIONA*.
MINI PACKS
WE SHOULD PROBABLY TELL HER BEFORE SHE--
AAAAAAND SHE'S ALREADY HELPING SOMEONE.
DON'T WORRY. I KNOW HOW WE CAN GET HER ATTENTION.

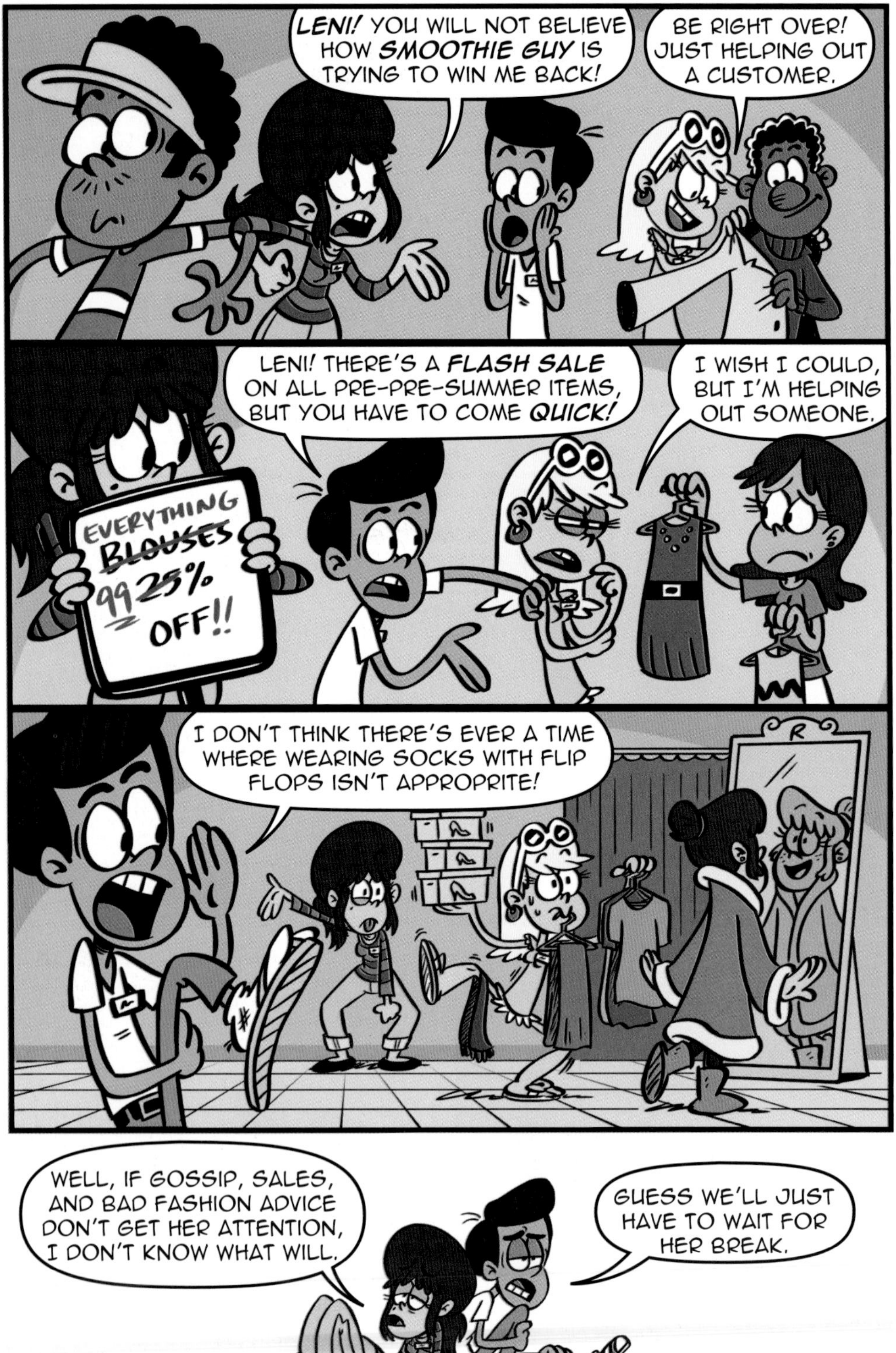
LENI! YOU WILL NOT BELIEVE HOW SMOOTHIE GUY IS TRYING TO WIN ME BACK!
BE RIGHT OVER! JUST HELPING OUT A CUSTOMER.
LENI! THERE'S A FLASH SALE ON ALL PRE-PRE-SUMMER ITEMS, BUT YOU HAVE TO COME QUICK!
EVERYTHING BLOUSES 99 25% OFF!!
I WISH I COULD, BUT I'M HELPING OUT SOMEONE.
I DON'T THINK THERE'S EVER A TIME WHERE WEARING SOCKS WITH FLIP FLOPS ISN'T APPROPRITE!
WELL, IF GOSSIP, SALES, AND BAD FASHION ADVICE DON'T GET HER ATTENTION, I DON'T KNOW WHAT WILL.
GUESS WE'LL JUST HAVE TO WAIT FOR HER BREAK.

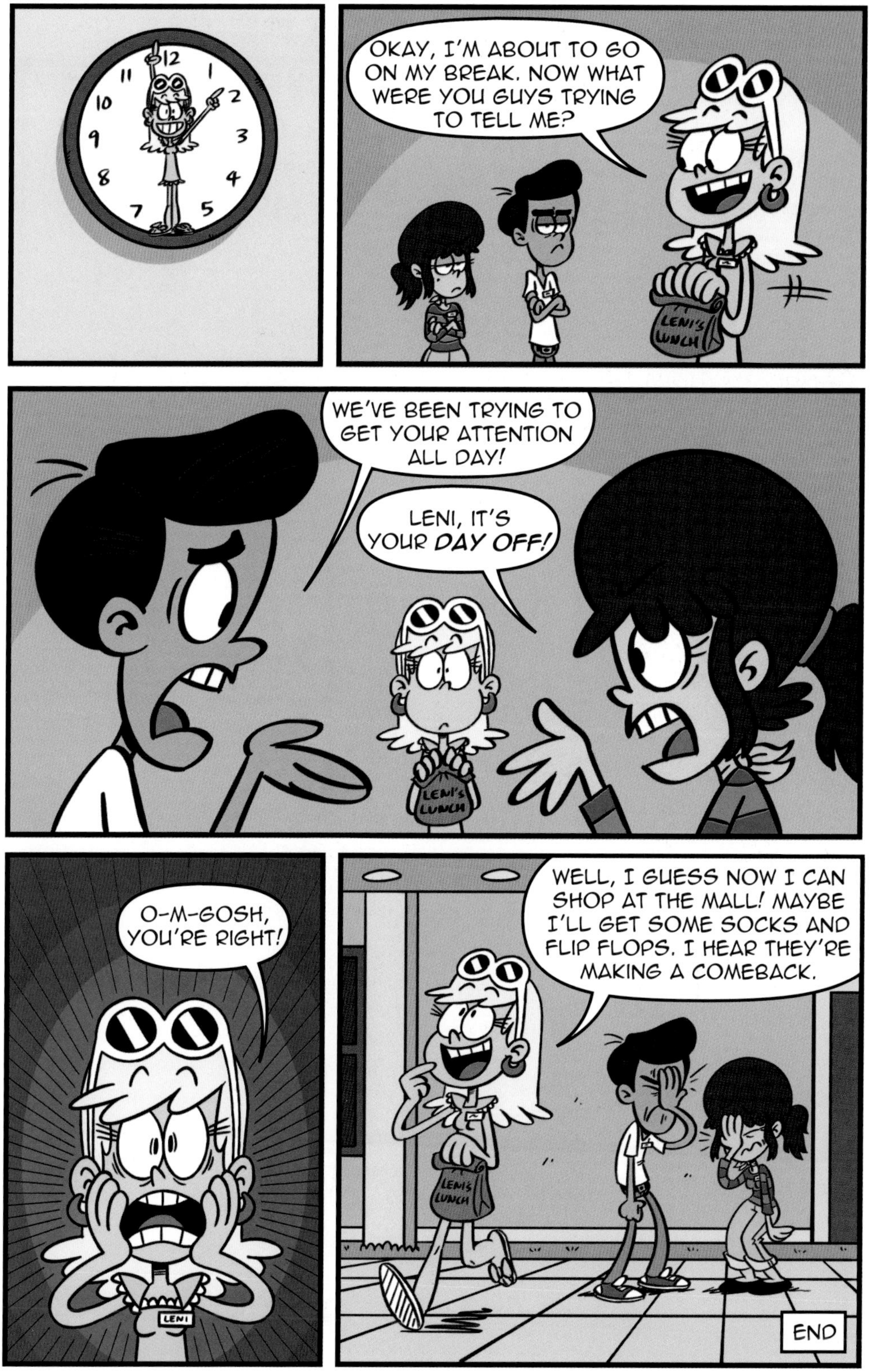
12
11
1
10
2
9
3
8
4
7
5
OKAY, I'M ABOUT TO GO ON MY BREAK. NOW WHAT WERE YOU GUYS TRYING TO TELL ME?
LENI'S LUNCH
WE'VE BEEN TRYING TO GET YOUR ATTENTION ALL DAY!
LENI, IT'S YOUR *DAY OFF!*
LENI'S LUNCH
O-M-GOSH, YOU'RE RIGHT!
LENI
WELL, I GUESS NOW I CAN SHOP AT THE MALL! MAYBE I'LL GET SOME SOCKS AND FLIP FLOPS. I HEAR THEY'RE MAKING A COMEBACK.
LENI'S LUNCH
END

"BANDS ON THE RUN"

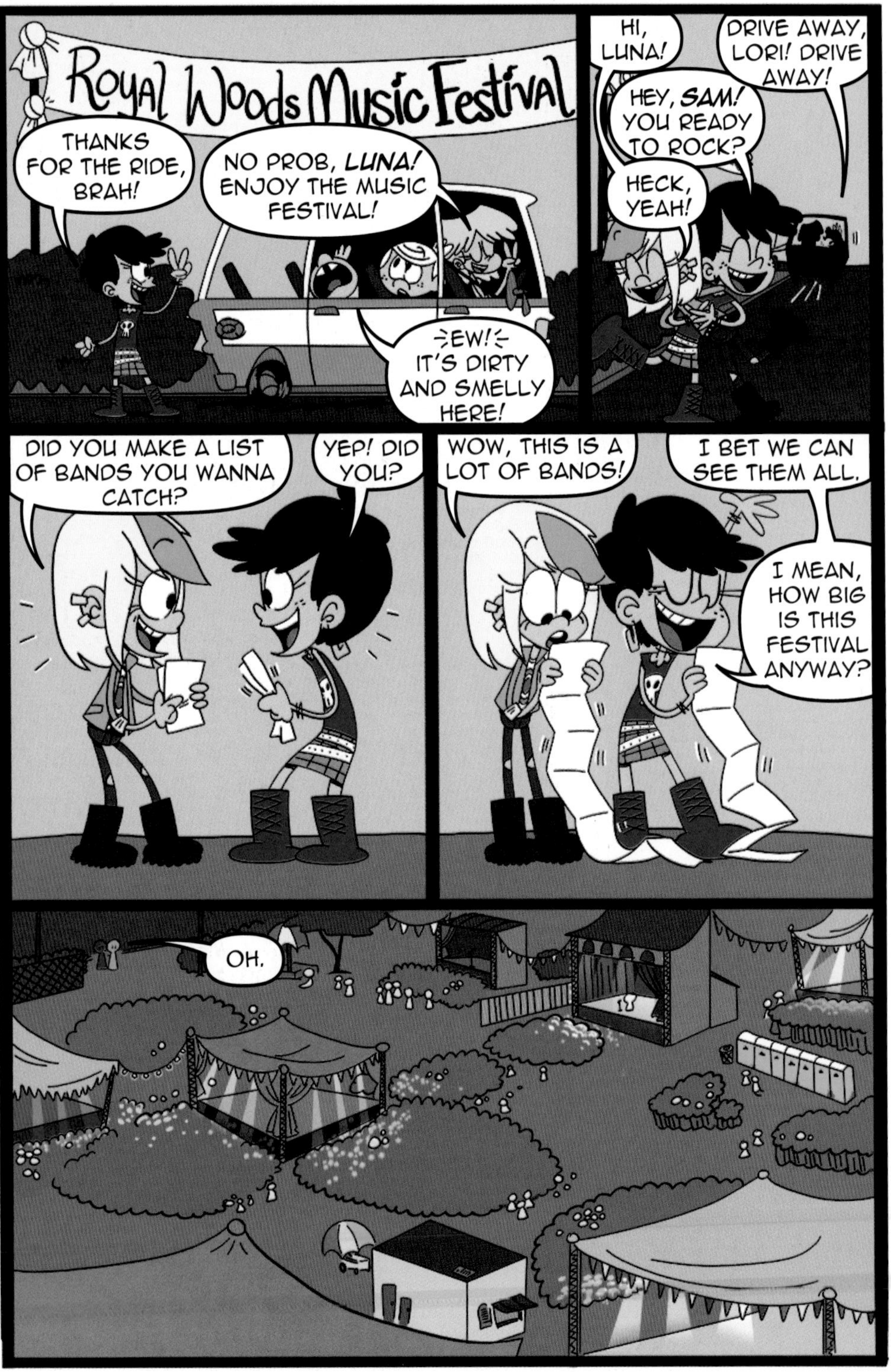
Royal Woods Music Festival
THANKS FOR THE RIDE, BRAH!
NO PROB, LUNA! ENJOY THE MUSIC FESTIVAL!
EW! IT'S DIRTY AND SMELLY HERE!
HI, LUNA!
DRIVE AWAY, LORI! DRIVE AWAY!
HEY, SAM! YOU READY TO ROCK?
HECK, YEAH!
DID YOU MAKE A LIST OF BANDS YOU WANNA CATCH?
YEP! DID YOU?
WOW, THIS IS A LOT OF BANDS!
I BET WE CAN SEE THEM ALL.
I MEAN, HOW BIG IS THIS FESTIVAL ANYWAY?
OH.

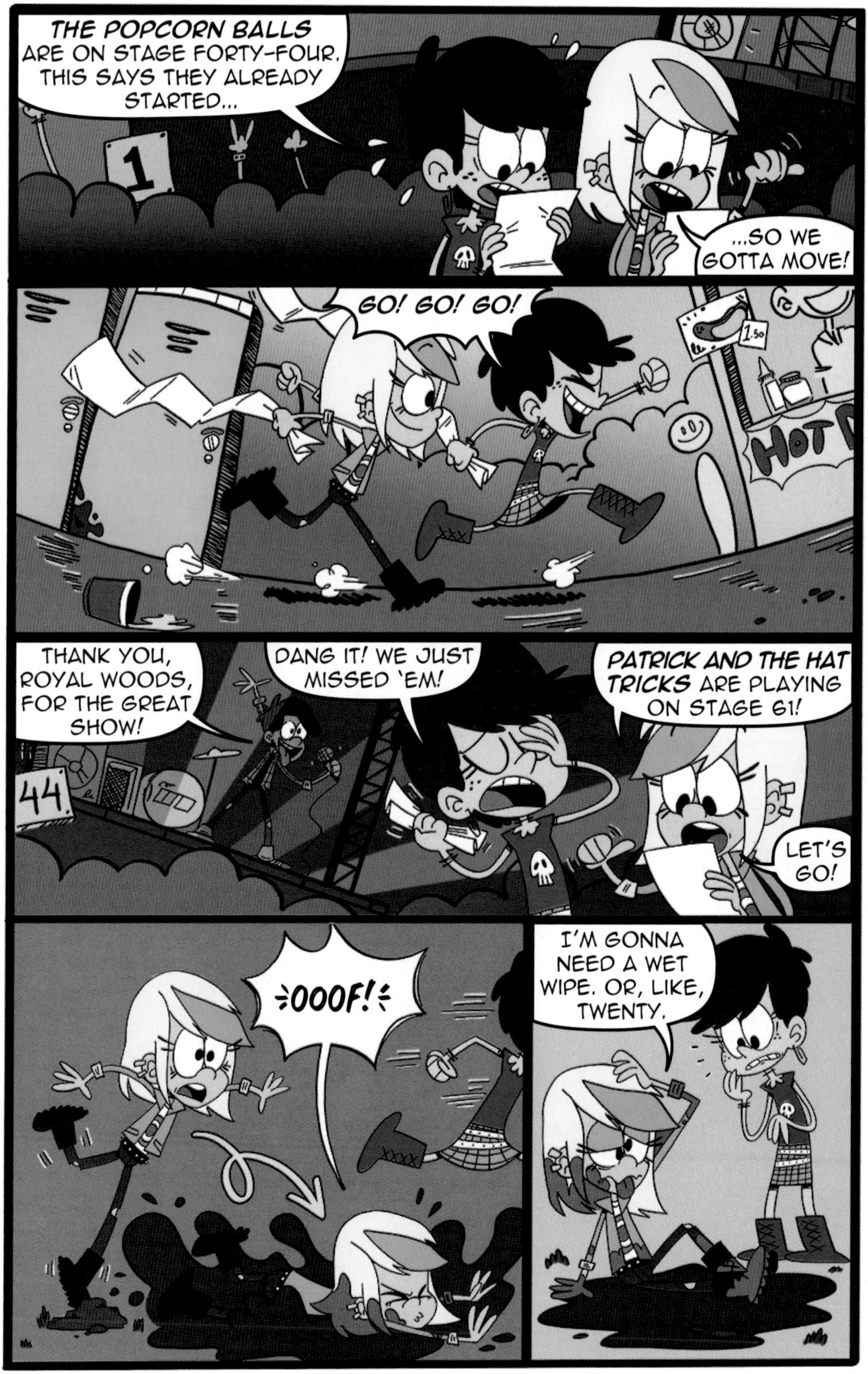
THE POPCORN BALLS ARE ON STAGE FORTY-FOUR. THIS SAYS THEY ALREADY STARTED...
...SO WE GOTTA MOVE!
GO! GO! GO!
HOT D
1.50
THANK YOU, ROYAL WOODS, FOR THE GREAT SHOW!
DANG IT! WE JUST MISSED 'EM!
PATRICK AND THE HAT TRICKS ARE PLAYING ON STAGE 61!
LET'S GO!
44
OOOF!
I'M GONNA NEED A WET WIPE. OR, LIKE, TWENTY.

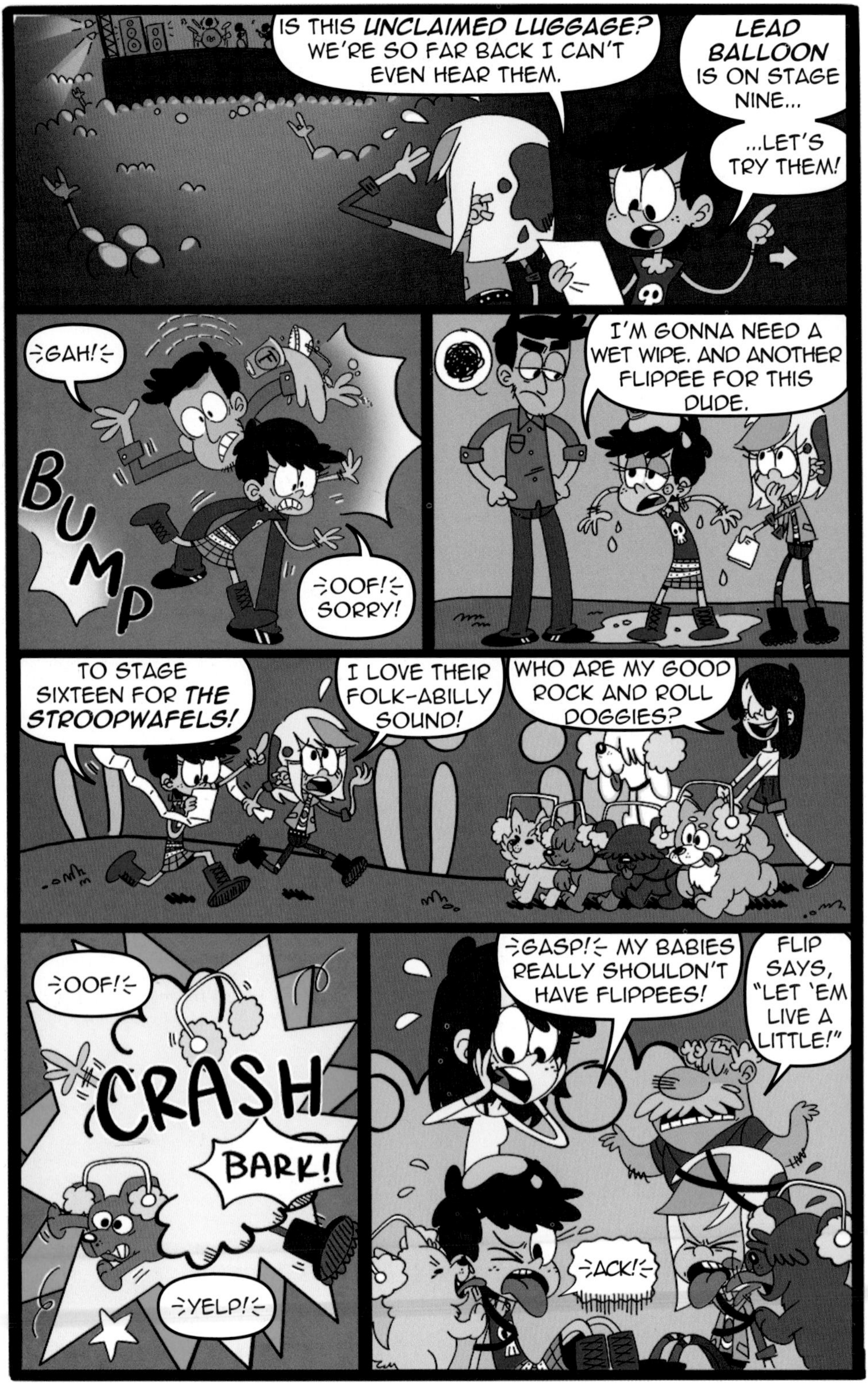
IS THIS UNCLAIMED LUGGAGE? WE'RE SO FAR BACK I CAN'T EVEN HEAR THEM.
LEAD BALLOON IS ON STAGE NINE...
...LET'S TRY THEM!
GAH!
BUMP
OOF! SORRY!
I'M GONNA NEED A WET WIPE. AND ANOTHER FLIPPEE FOR THIS DUDE.
TO STAGE SIXTEEN FOR THE STROOPWAFELS!
I LOVE THEIR FOLK-ABILLY SOUND!
WHO ARE MY GOOD ROCK AND ROLL DOGGIES?
OOF!
CRASH
BARK!
YELP!
GASP! MY BABIES REALLY SHOULDN'T HAVE FLIPPEES!
FLIP SAYS, "LET 'EM LIVE A LITTLE!"
ACK!

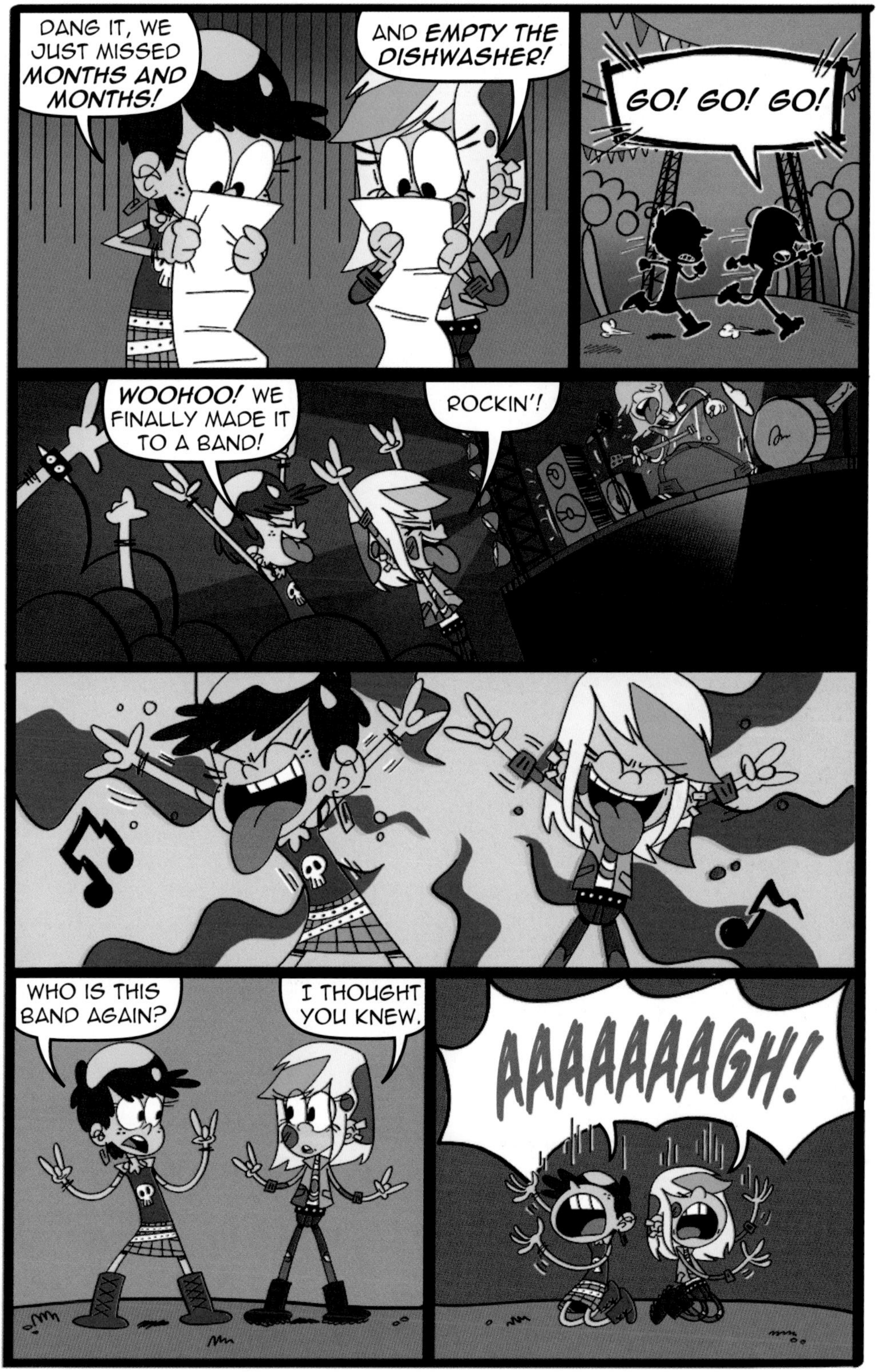
DANG IT, WE JUST MISSED MONTHS AND MONTHS!
AND EMPTY THE DISHWASHER!
GO! GO! GO!
WOOHOO! WE FINALLY MADE IT TO A BAND!
ROCKIN'!
WHO IS THIS BAND AGAIN?
I THOUGHT YOU KNEW.
AAAAAAAGH!

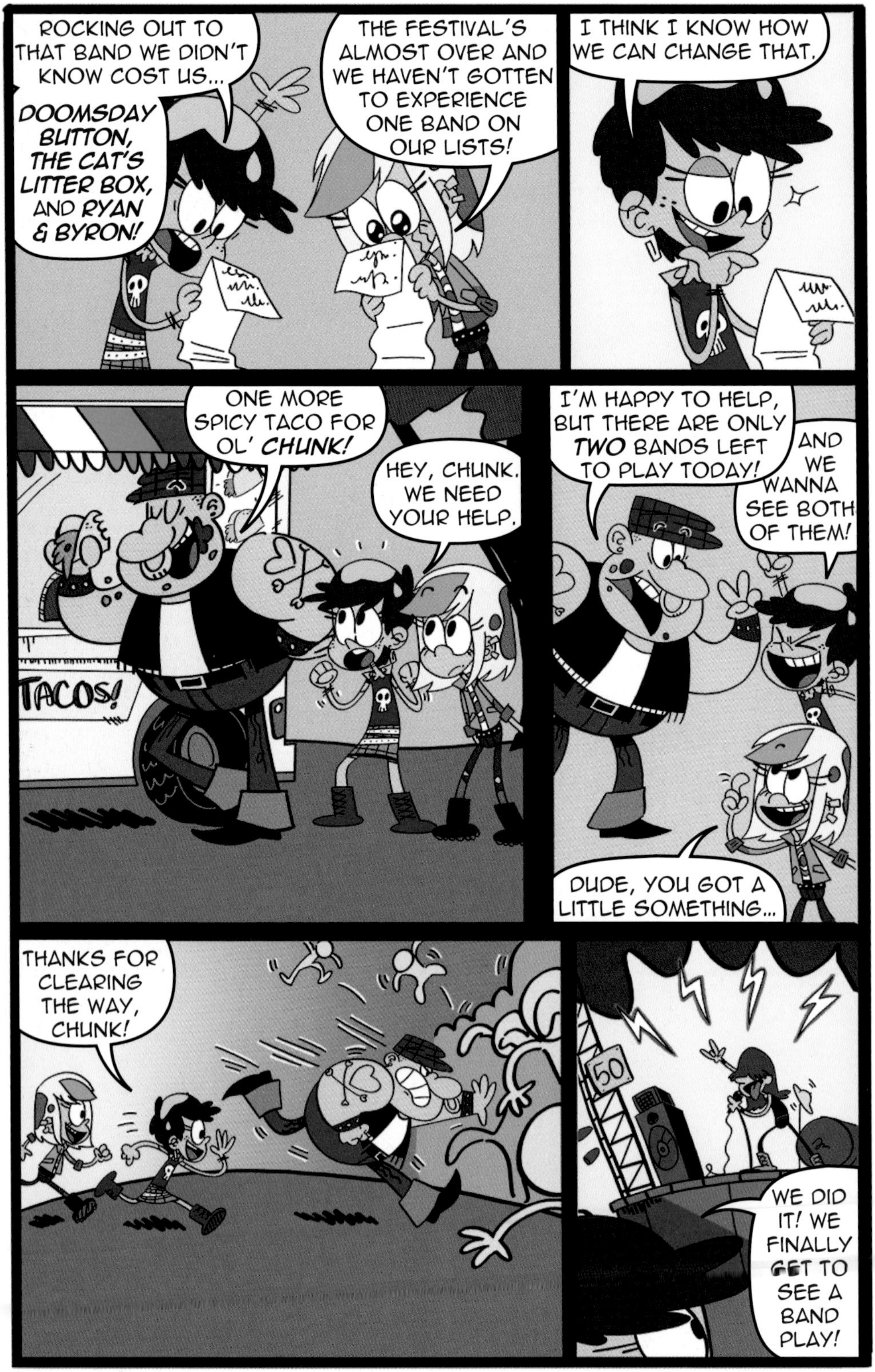

ROCKING OUT TO THAT BAND WE DIDN'T KNOW COST US...
DOOMSDAY BUTTON, THE CAT'S LITTER BOX, AND RYAN & BYRON!
THE FESTIVAL'S ALMOST OVER AND WE HAVEN'T GOTTEN TO EXPERIENCE ONE BAND ON OUR LISTS!
I THINK I KNOW HOW WE CAN CHANGE THAT.
ONE MORE SPICY TACO FOR OL' CHUNK!
TACOS!
HEY, CHUNK. WE NEED YOUR HELP.
I'M HAPPY TO HELP, BUT THERE ARE ONLY TWO BANDS LEFT TO PLAY TODAY!
AND WE WANNA SEE BOTH OF THEM!
DUDE, YOU GOT A LITTLE SOMETHING...
THANKS FOR CLEARING THE WAY, CHUNK!
50
WE DID IT! WE FINALLY GET TO SEE A BAND PLAY!

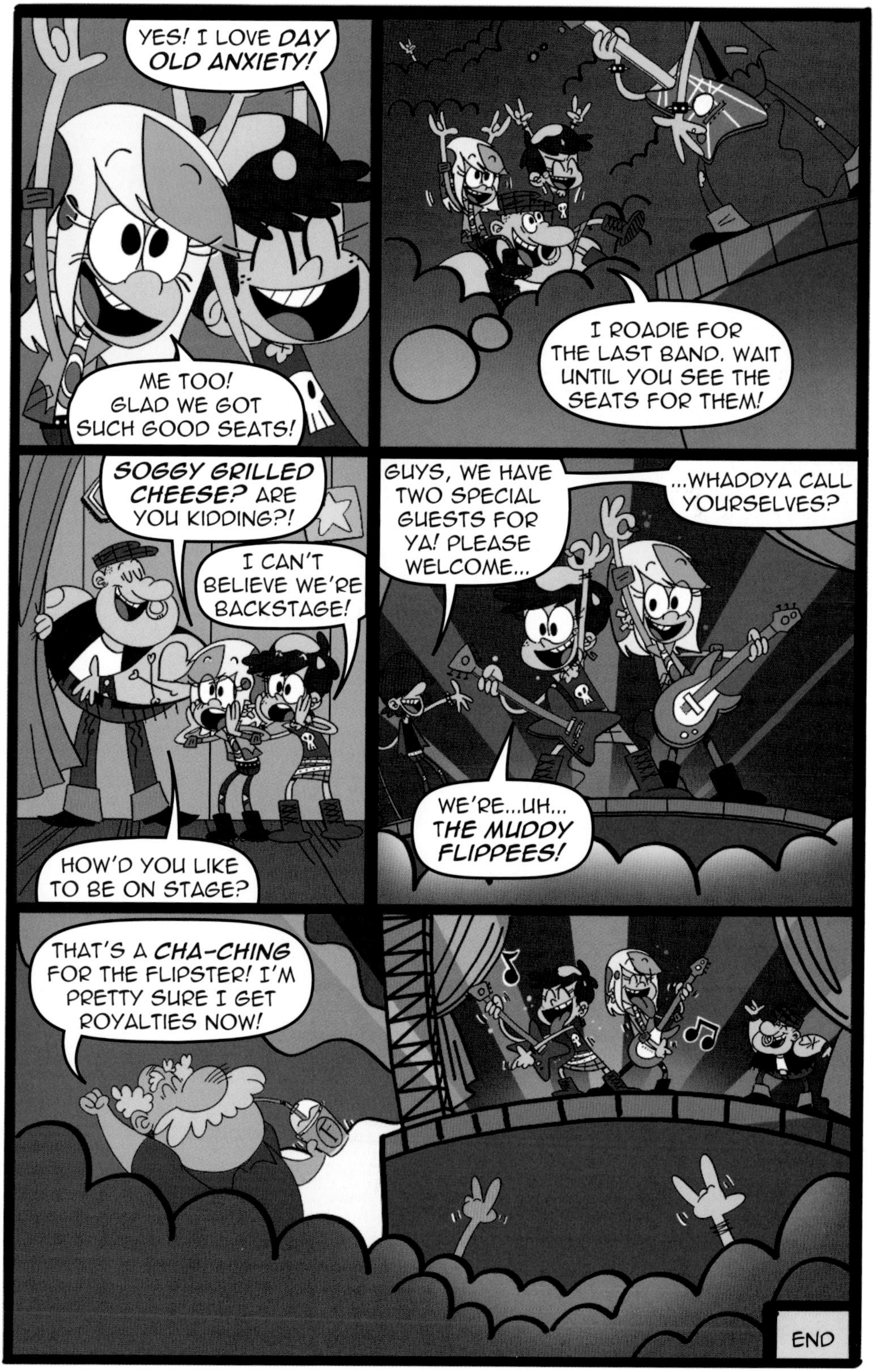
YES! I LOVE DAY OLD ANXIETY!
ME TOO! GLAD WE GOT SUCH GOOD SEATS!
I ROADIE FOR THE LAST BAND. WAIT UNTIL YOU SEE THE SEATS FOR THEM!
SOGGY GRILLED CHEESE? ARE YOU KIDDING?!
I CAN'T BELIEVE WE'RE BACKSTAGE!
HOW'D YOU LIKE TO BE ON STAGE?
GUYS, WE HAVE TWO SPECIAL GUESTS FOR YA! PLEASE WELCOME...
...WHADDYA CALL YOURSELVES?
WE'RE...UH... THE MUDDY FLIPPEES!
THAT'S A CHA-CHING FOR THE FLIPSTER! I'M PRETTY SURE I GET ROYALTIES NOW!
END

"THE PAGEANT TRAP"

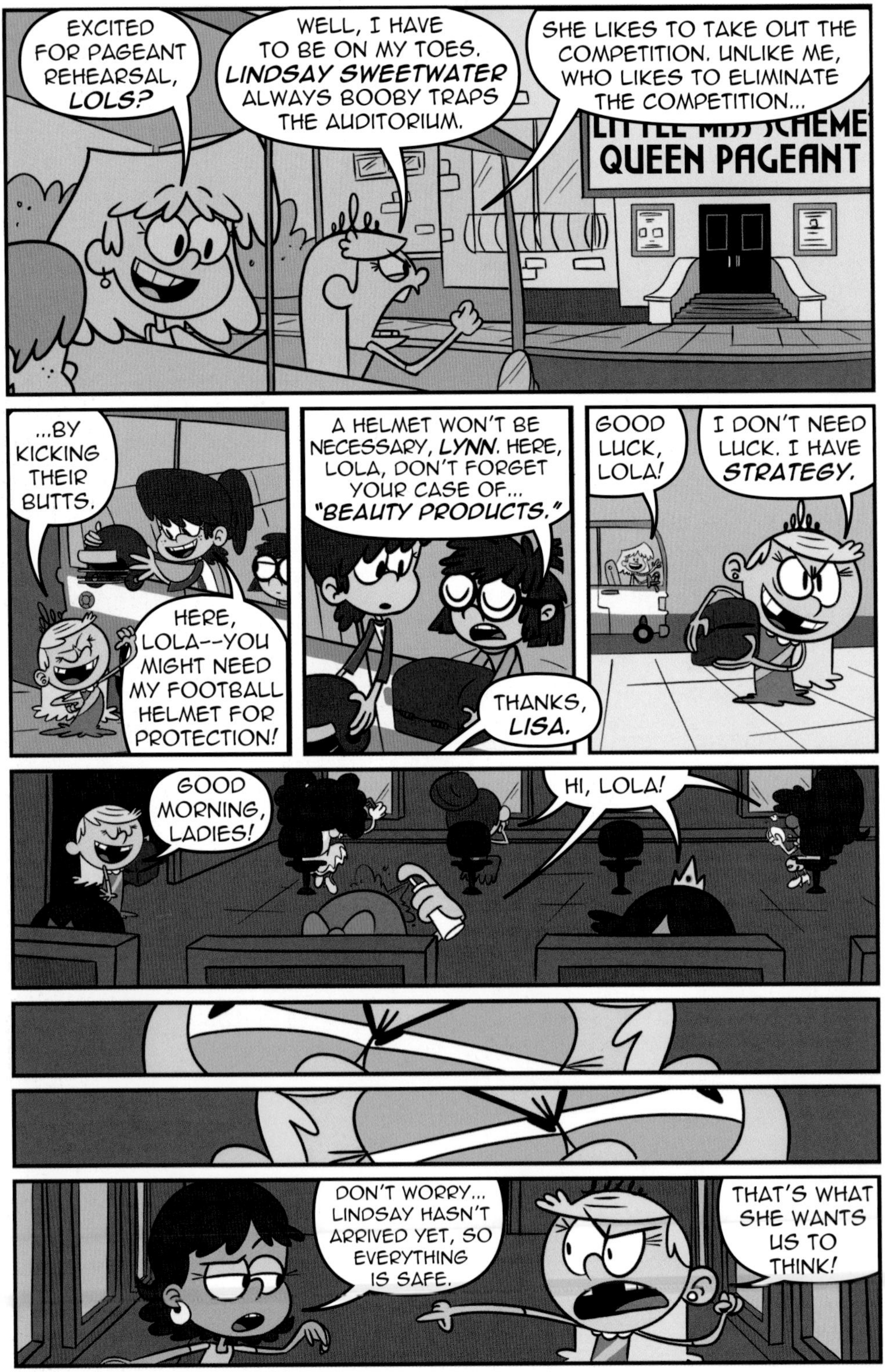

EXCITED FOR PAGEANT REHEARSAL, LOLS?
WELL, I HAVE TO BE ON MY TOES. LINDSAY SWEETWATER ALWAYS BOOBY TRAPS THE AUDITORIUM.
SHE LIKES TO TAKE OUT THE COMPETITION. UNLIKE ME, WHO LIKES TO ELIMINATE THE COMPETITION...
QUEEN PAGEANT
...BY KICKING THEIR BUTTS.
HERE, LOLA--YOU MIGHT NEED MY FOOTBALL HELMET FOR PROTECTION!
A HELMET WON'T BE NECESSARY, LYNN. HERE, LOLA, DON'T FORGET YOUR CASE OF... "BEAUTY PRODUCTS."
THANKS, LISA.
GOOD LUCK, LOLA!
I DON'T NEED LUCK. I HAVE STRATEGY.
GOOD MORNING, LADIES!
HI, LOLA!
DON'T WORRY... LINDSAY HASN'T ARRIVED YET, SO EVERYTHING IS SAFE.
THAT'S WHAT SHE WANTS US TO THINK!

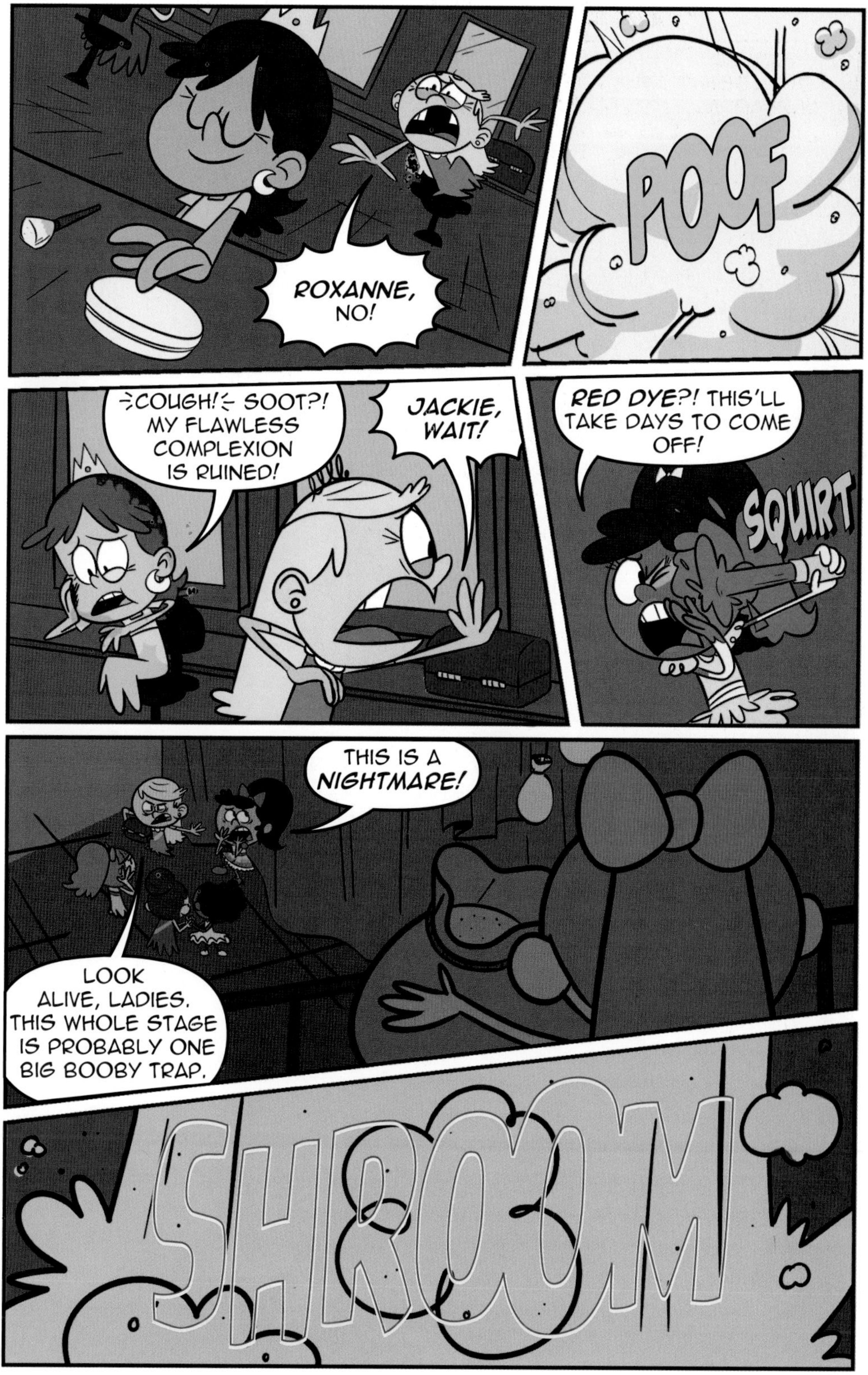
ROXANNE, NO!
POOF
=COUGH!= SOOT?! MY FLAWLESS COMPLEXION IS RUINED!
JACKIE, WAIT!
RED DYE?! THIS'LL TAKE DAYS TO COME OFF!
SQUIRT
THIS IS A NIGHTMARE!
LOOK ALIVE, LADIES. THIS WHOLE STAGE IS PROBABLY ONE BIG BOOBY TRAP.
SHROOM

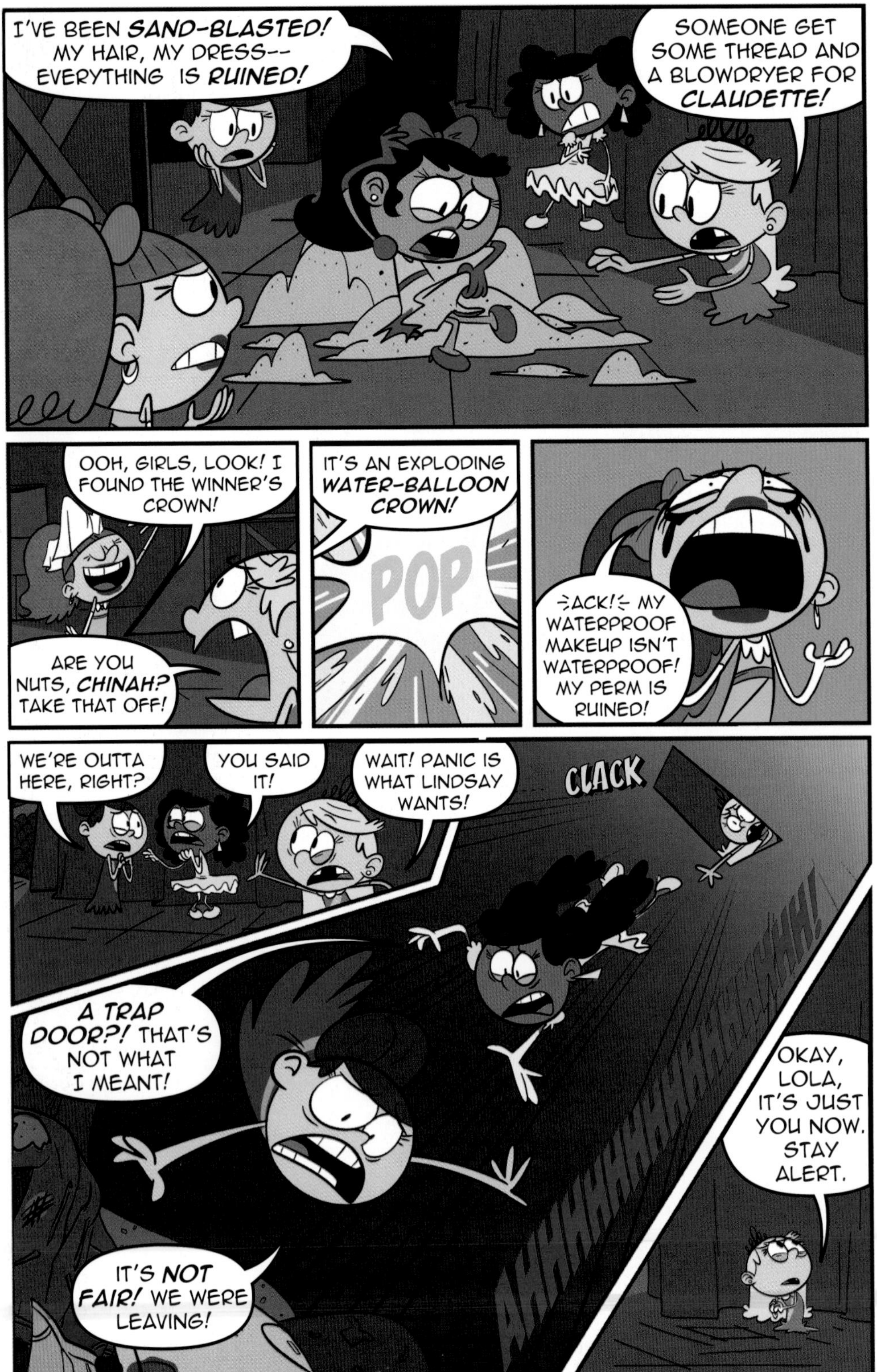
I'VE BEEN SAND-BLASTED! MY HAIR, MY DRESS-- EVERYTHING IS RUINED!
SOMEONE GET SOME THREAD AND A BLOWDRYER FOR CLAUDETTE!
OOH, GIRLS, LOOK! I FOUND THE WINNER'S CROWN!
ARE YOU NUTS, CHINAH? TAKE THAT OFF!
IT'S AN EXPLODING WATER-BALLOON CROWN!
POP
ACK! MY WATERPROOF MAKEUP ISN'T WATERPROOF! MY PERM IS RUINED!
WE'RE OUTTA HERE, RIGHT?
YOU SAID IT!
WAIT! PANIC IS WHAT LINDSAY WANTS!
CLACK
A TRAP DOOR?! THAT'S NOT WHAT I MEANT!
IT'S NOT FAIR! WE WERE LEAVING!
OKAY, LOLA, IT'S JUST YOU NOW. STAY ALERT.

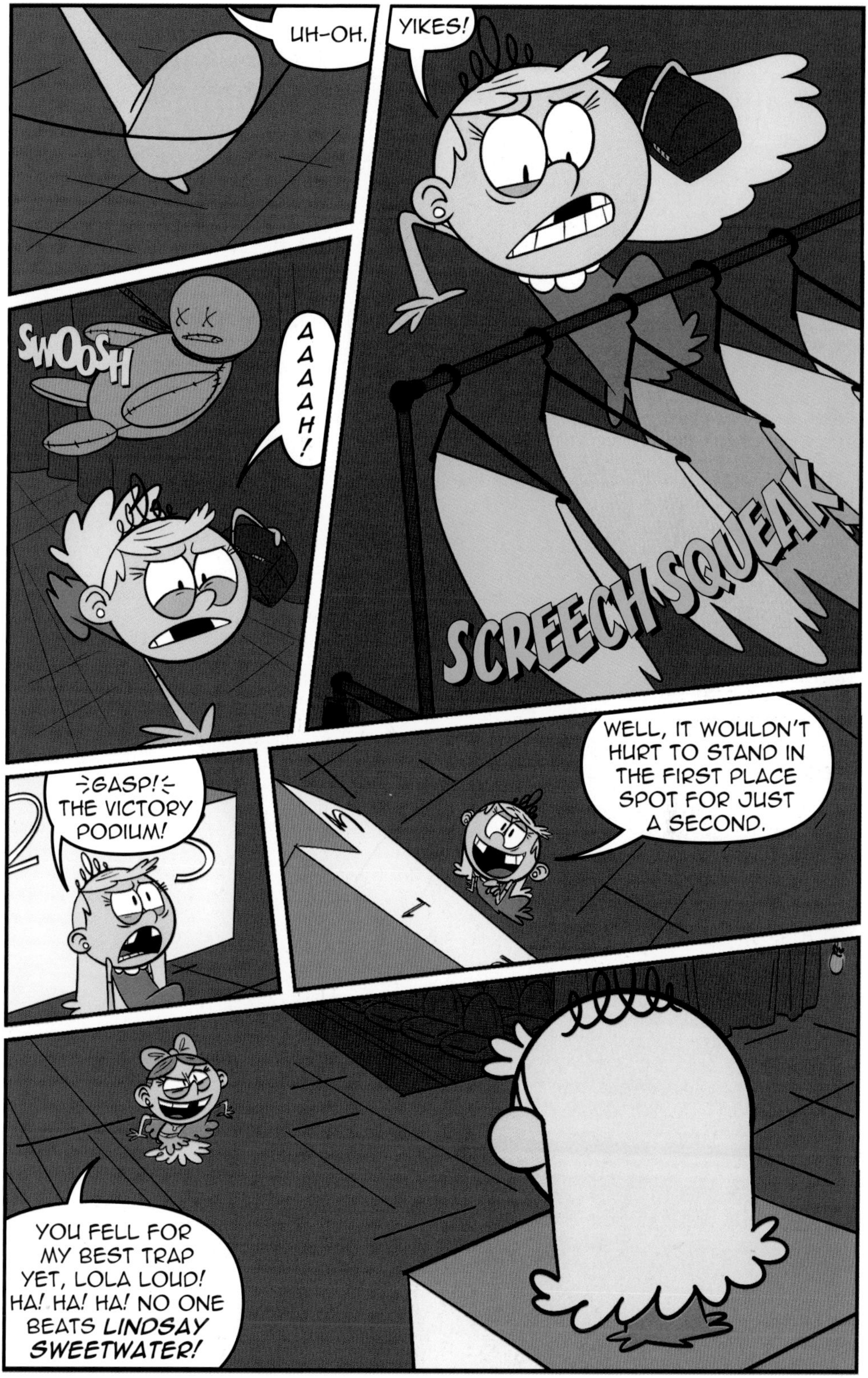
UH-OH.
YIKES!
SWOOSH
AAAAAH!
SCREECH SQUEAK
GASP! THE VICTORY PODIUM!
WELL, IT WOULDN'T HURT TO STAND IN THE FIRST PLACE SPOT FOR JUST A SECOND.
YOU FELL FOR MY BEST TRAP YET, LOLA LOUD! HA! HA! HA! NO ONE BEATS LINDSAY SWEETWATER!

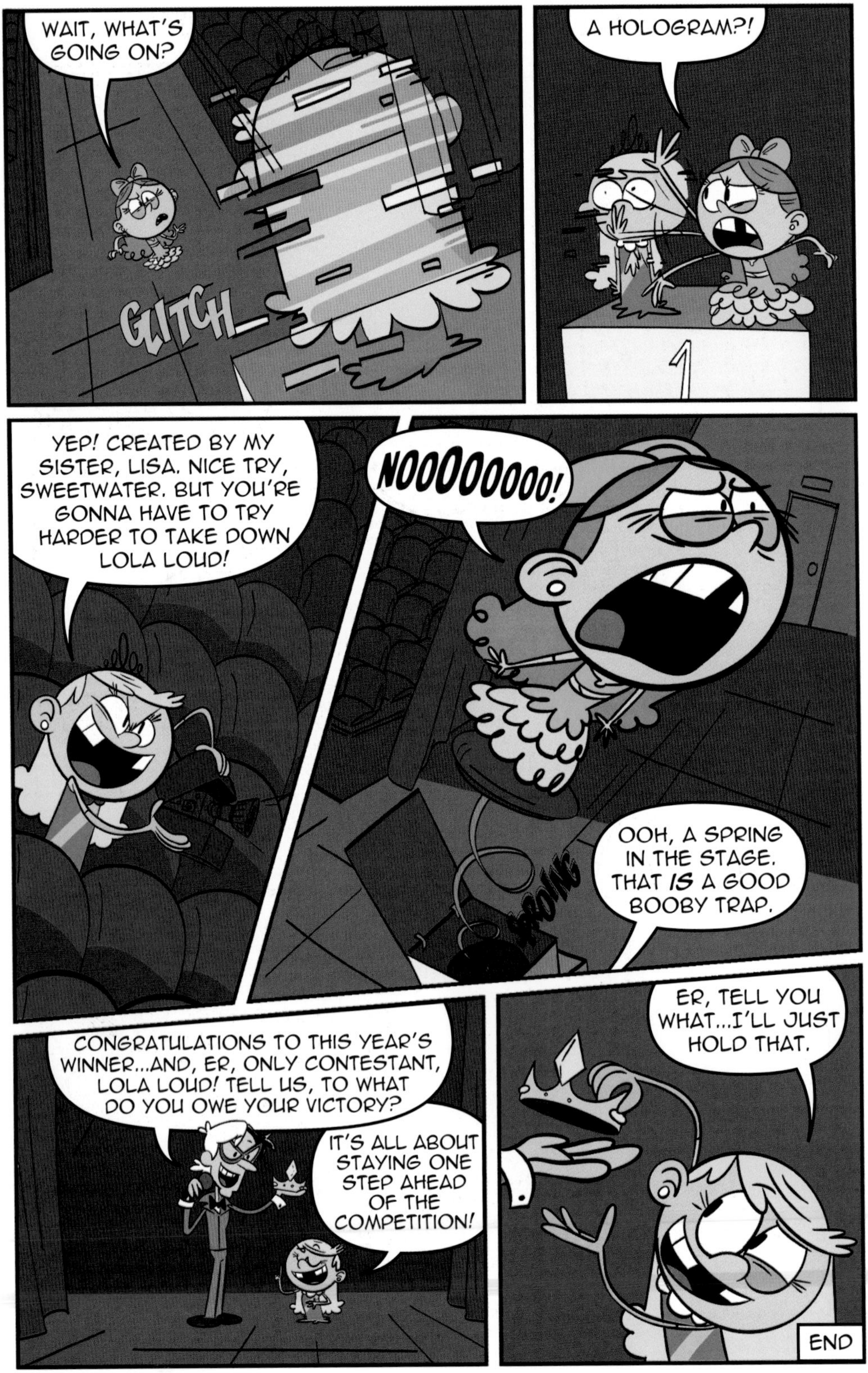
WAIT, WHAT'S GOING ON?
GLITCH
A HOLOGRAM?!
YEP! CREATED BY MY SISTER, LISA. NICE TRY, SWEETWATER. BUT YOU'RE GONNA HAVE TO TRY HARDER TO TAKE DOWN LOLA LOUD!
NOOOOOOOO!
SPROING
OOH, A SPRING IN THE STAGE. THAT *IS* A GOOD BOOBY TRAP.
CONGRATULATIONS TO THIS YEAR'S WINNER...AND, ER, ONLY CONTESTANT, LOLA LOUD! TELL US, TO WHAT DO YOU OWE YOUR VICTORY?
IT'S ALL ABOUT STAYING ONE STEP AHEAD OF THE COMPETITION!
ER, TELL YOU WHAT...I'LL JUST HOLD THAT.
END

"HURRY UP AND WAIT"

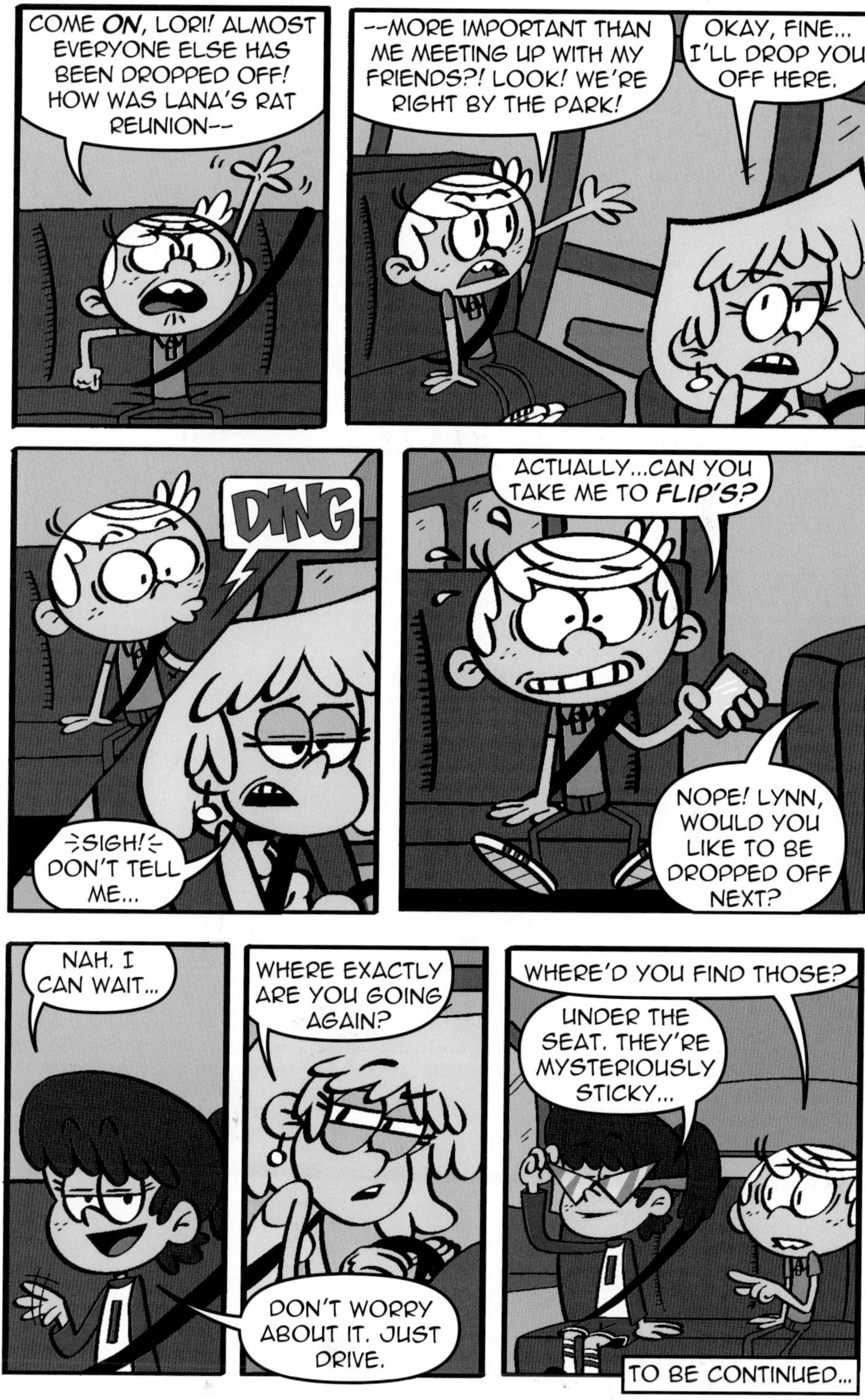
COME ON, LORI! ALMOST EVERYONE ELSE HAS BEEN DROPPED OFF! HOW WAS LANA'S RAT REUNION--
--MORE IMPORTANT THAN ME MEETING UP WITH MY FRIENDS?! LOOK! WE'RE RIGHT BY THE PARK!
OKAY, FINE... I'LL DROP YOU OFF HERE.
DING
SIGH! DON'T TELL ME...
ACTUALLY...CAN YOU TAKE ME TO FLIP'S?
NOPE! LYNN, WOULD YOU LIKE TO BE DROPPED OFF NEXT?
NAH. I CAN WAIT...
WHERE EXACTLY ARE YOU GOING AGAIN?
DON'T WORRY ABOUT IT. JUST DRIVE.
WHERE'D YOU FIND THOSE?
UNDER THE SEAT. THEY'RE MYSTERIOUSLY STICKY...
TO BE CONTINUED...

"STAGE FRIGHT"

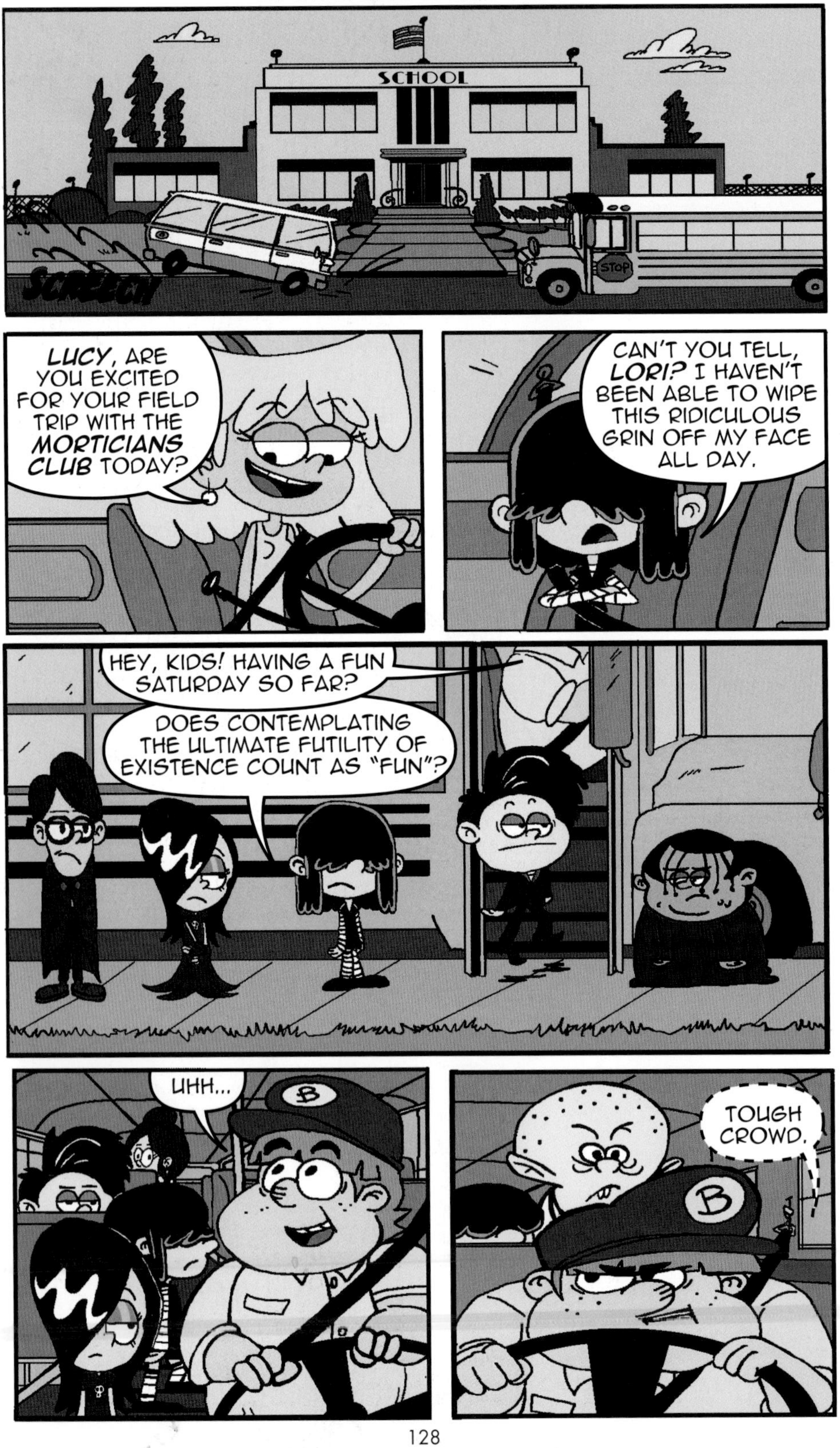
SCHOOL
STOP
SCREECH
LUCY, ARE YOU EXCITED FOR YOUR FIELD TRIP WITH THE MORTICIANS CLUB TODAY?
CAN'T YOU TELL, LORI? I HAVEN'T BEEN ABLE TO WIPE THIS RIDICULOUS GRIN OFF MY FACE ALL DAY.
HEY, KIDS! HAVING A FUN SATURDAY SO FAR?
DOES CONTEMPLATING THE ULTIMATE FUTILITY OF EXISTENCE COUNT AS "FUN"?
UHH...
TOUGH CROWD.

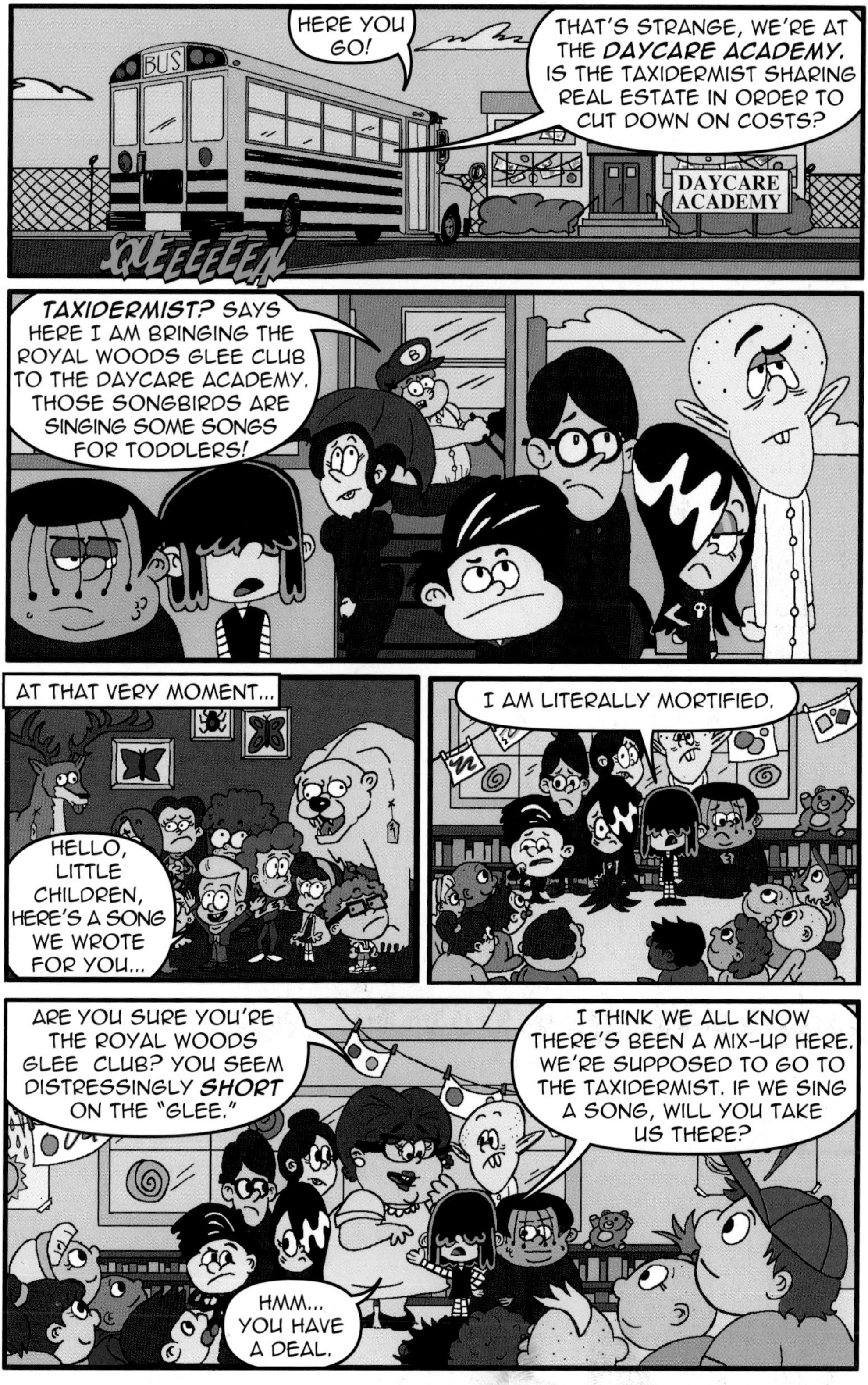
HERE YOU GO!
THAT'S STRANGE, WE'RE AT THE *DAYCARE ACADEMY.* IS THE TAXIDERMIST SHARING REAL ESTATE IN ORDER TO CUT DOWN ON COSTS?
BUS
DAYCARE ACADEMY
SQUEEEEEEEN
TAXIDERMIST? SAYS HERE I AM BRINGING THE ROYAL WOODS GLEE CLUB TO THE DAYCARE ACADEMY. THOSE SONGBIRDS ARE SINGING SOME SONGS FOR TODDLERS!
AT THAT VERY MOMENT...
HELLO, LITTLE CHILDREN, HERE'S A SONG WE WROTE FOR YOU...
I AM LITERALLY MORTIFIED.
ARE YOU SURE YOU'RE THE ROYAL WOODS GLEE CLUB? YOU SEEM DISTRESSINGLY *SHORT* ON THE "GLEE."
I THINK WE ALL KNOW THERE'S BEEN A MIX-UP HERE. WE'RE SUPPOSED TO GO TO THE TAXIDERMIST. IF WE SING A SONG, WILL YOU TAKE US THERE?
HMM... YOU HAVE A DEAL.

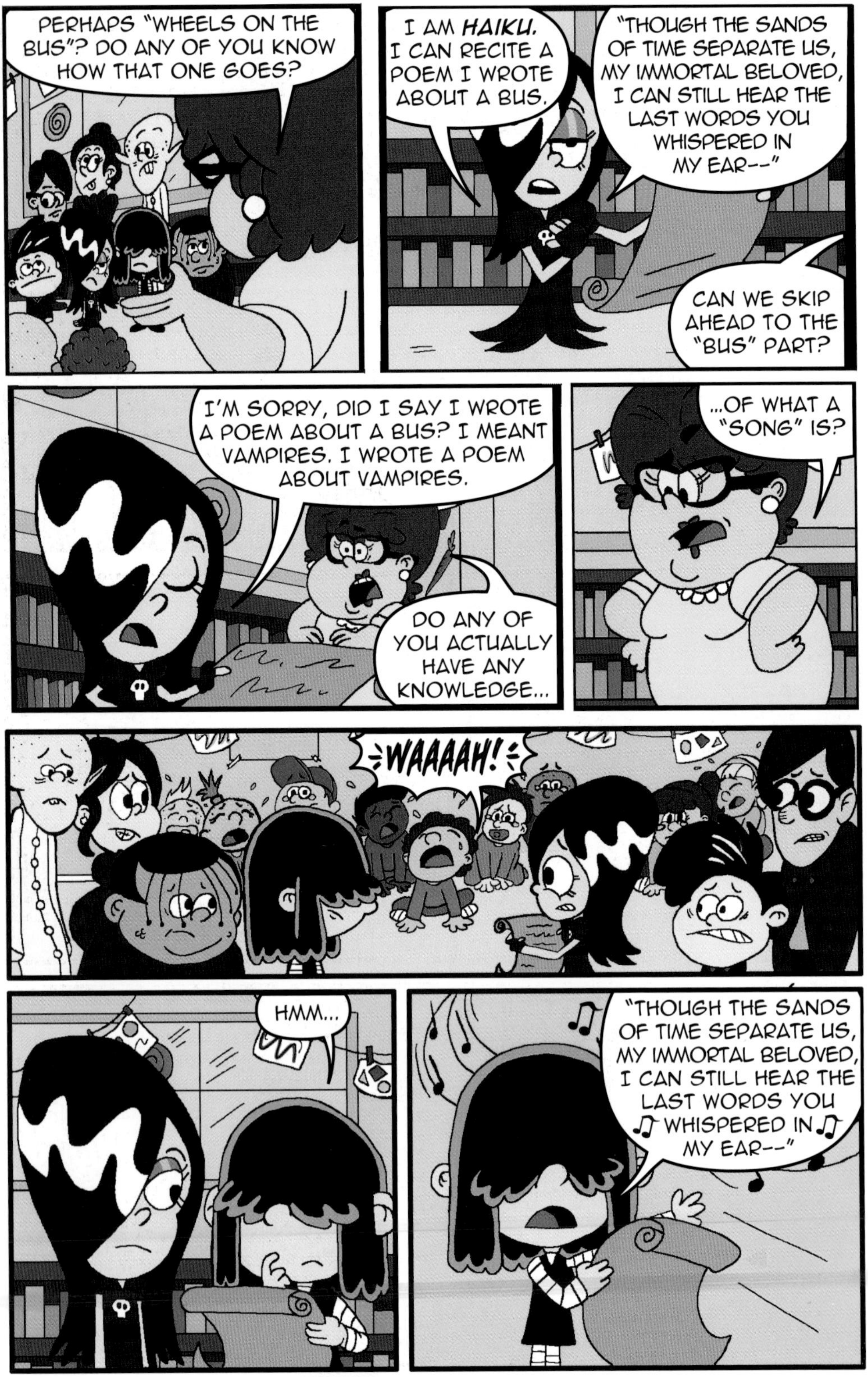
PERHAPS "WHEELS ON THE BUS"? DO ANY OF YOU KNOW HOW THAT ONE GOES?
I AM HAIKU. I CAN RECITE A POEM I WROTE ABOUT A BUS.
"THOUGH THE SANDS OF TIME SEPARATE US, MY IMMORTAL BELOVED, I CAN STILL HEAR THE LAST WORDS YOU WHISPERED IN MY EAR--"
CAN WE SKIP AHEAD TO THE "BUS" PART?
I'M SORRY, DID I SAY I WROTE A POEM ABOUT A BUS? I MEANT VAMPIRES. I WROTE A POEM ABOUT VAMPIRES.
DO ANY OF YOU ACTUALLY HAVE ANY KNOWLEDGE...
...OF WHAT A "SONG" IS?
WAAAAH!
HMM...
"THOUGH THE SANDS OF TIME SEPARATE US, MY IMMORTAL BELOVED, I CAN STILL HEAR THE LAST WORDS YOU WHISPERED IN MY EAR--"

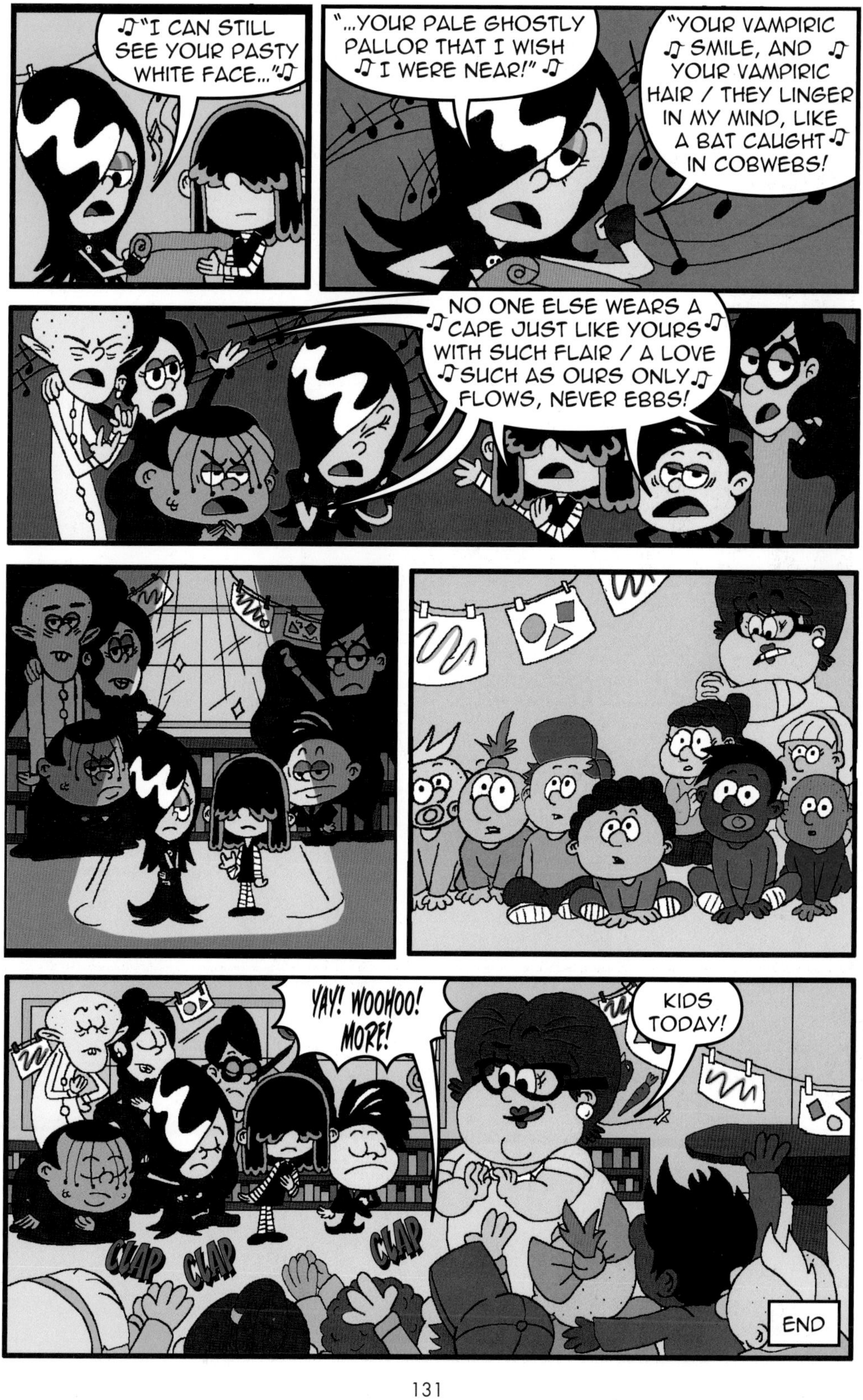
♫"I CAN STILL SEE YOUR PASTY WHITE FACE..."♫
"...YOUR PALE GHOSTLY PALLOR THAT I WISH ♫ I WERE NEAR!" ♫
"YOUR VAMPIRIC ♫ SMILE, AND ♫ YOUR VAMPIRIC HAIR / THEY LINGER IN MY MIND, LIKE A BAT CAUGHT ♫ IN COBWEBS!
NO ONE ELSE WEARS A ♫ CAPE JUST LIKE YOURS ♫ WITH SUCH FLAIR / A LOVE ♫ SUCH AS OURS ONLY ♫ FLOWS, NEVER EBBS!
YAY! WOOHOO! MORE!
KIDS TODAY!
CLAP
CLAP
CLAP
END

"DOWN IN THE DUMPS"

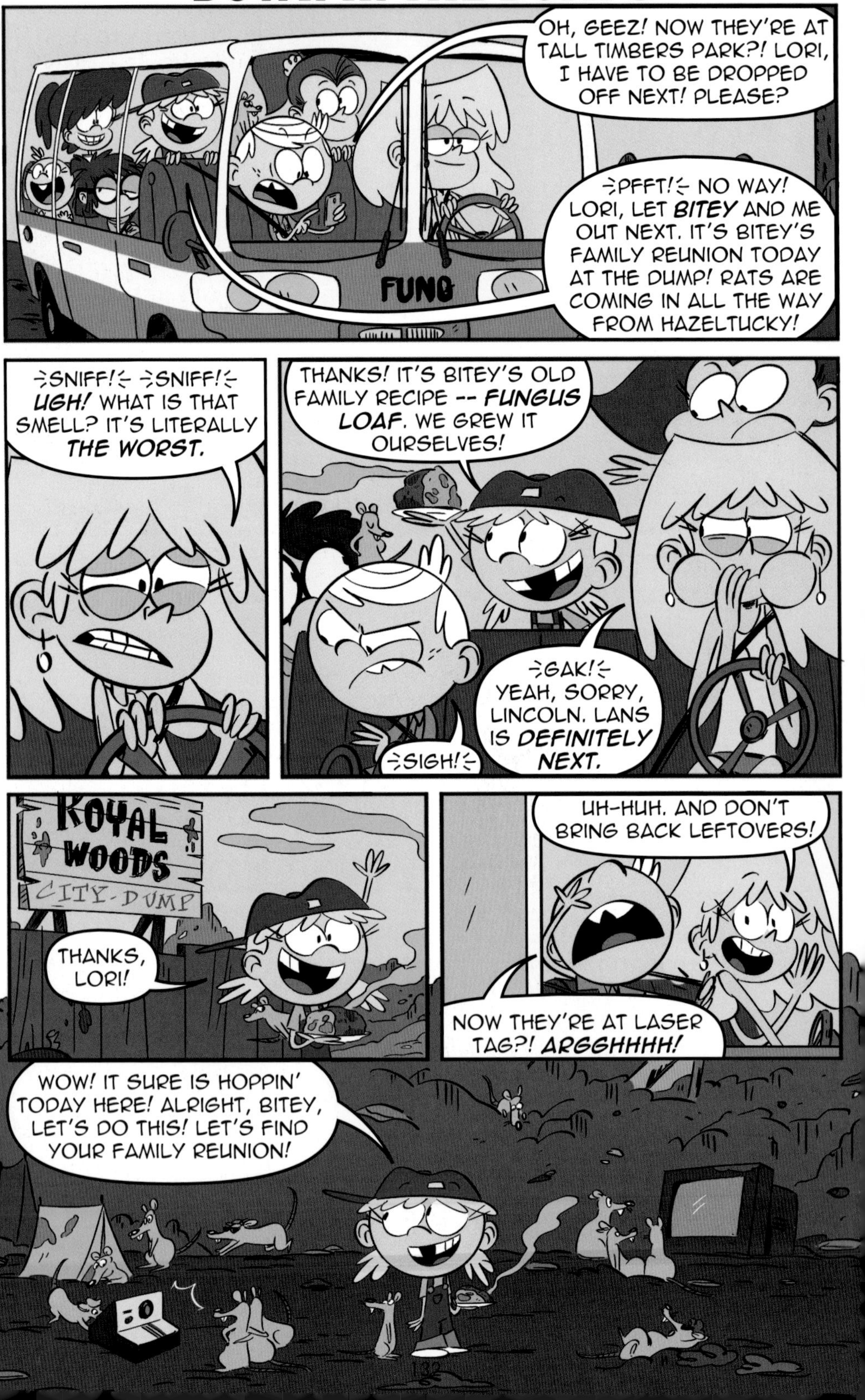
OH, GEEZ! NOW THEY'RE AT TALL TIMBERS PARK?! LORI, I HAVE TO BE DROPPED OFF NEXT! PLEASE?
FUNG
=PFFT!= NO WAY! LORI, LET BITEY AND ME OUT NEXT. IT'S BITEY'S FAMILY REUNION TODAY AT THE DUMP! RATS ARE COMING IN ALL THE WAY FROM HAZELTUCKY!
=SNIFF!= =SNIFF!= UGH! WHAT IS THAT SMELL? IT'S LITERALLY THE WORST.
THANKS! IT'S BITEY'S OLD FAMILY RECIPE -- FUNGUS LOAF. WE GREW IT OURSELVES!
=GAK!= YEAH, SORRY, LINCOLN. LANS IS DEFINITELY NEXT.
=SIGH!=
ROYAL WOODS CITY DUMP
THANKS, LORI!
UH-HUH. AND DON'T BRING BACK LEFTOVERS!
NOW THEY'RE AT LASER TAG?! ARGGHHHH!
WOW! IT SURE IS HOPPIN' TODAY HERE! ALRIGHT, BITEY, LET'S DO THIS! LET'S FIND YOUR FAMILY REUNION!

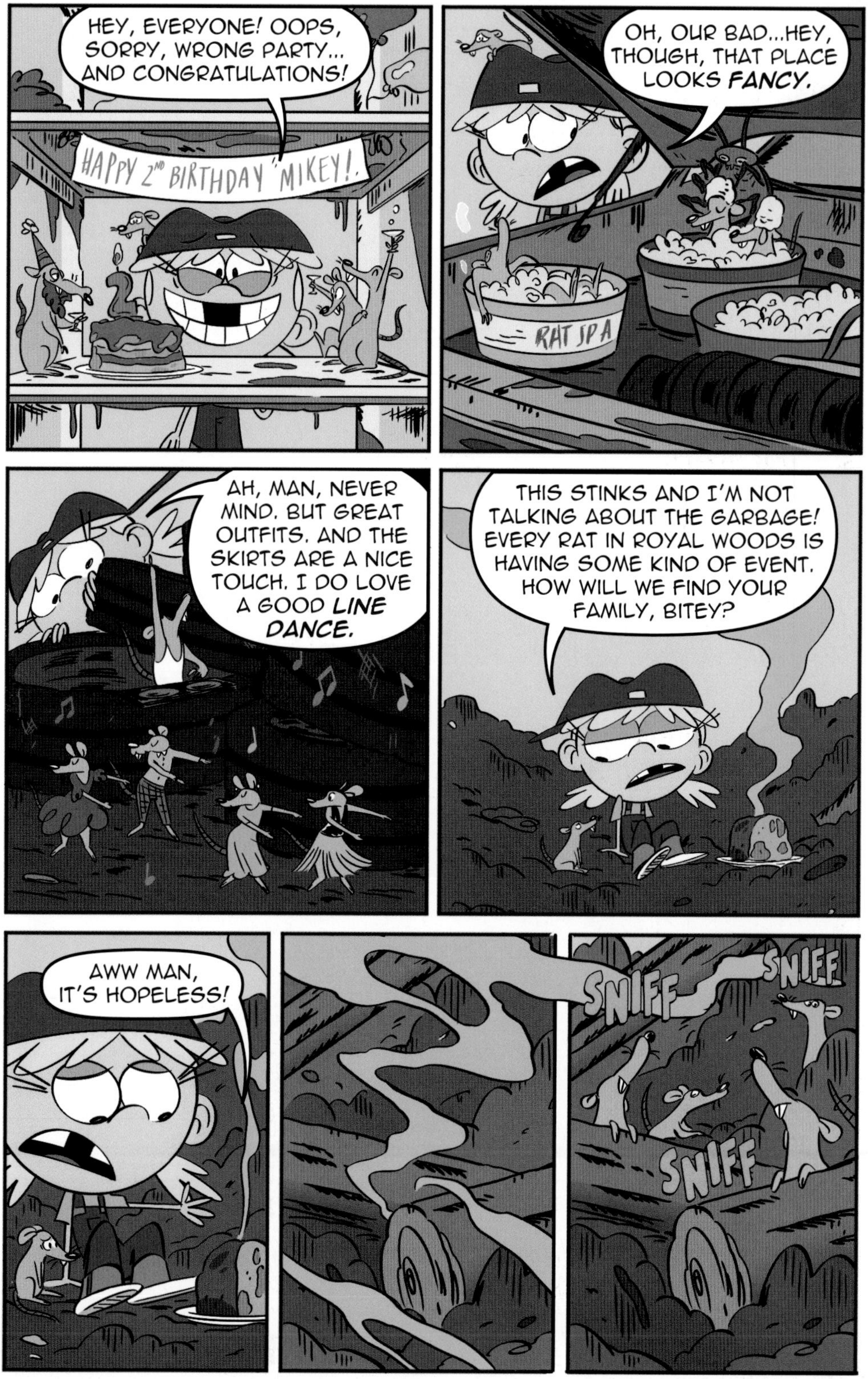
HEY, EVERYONE! OOPS, SORRY, WRONG PARTY... AND CONGRATULATIONS!
HAPPY 2ND BIRTHDAY MIKEY!
OH, OUR BAD...HEY, THOUGH, THAT PLACE LOOKS FANCY.
RAT SPA
AH, MAN, NEVER MIND. BUT GREAT OUTFITS. AND THE SKIRTS ARE A NICE TOUCH. I DO LOVE A GOOD LINE DANCE.
THIS STINKS AND I'M NOT TALKING ABOUT THE GARBAGE! EVERY RAT IN ROYAL WOODS IS HAVING SOME KIND OF EVENT. HOW WILL WE FIND YOUR FAMILY, BITEY?
AWW MAN, IT'S HOPELESS!
SNIFF
SNIFF
SNIFF

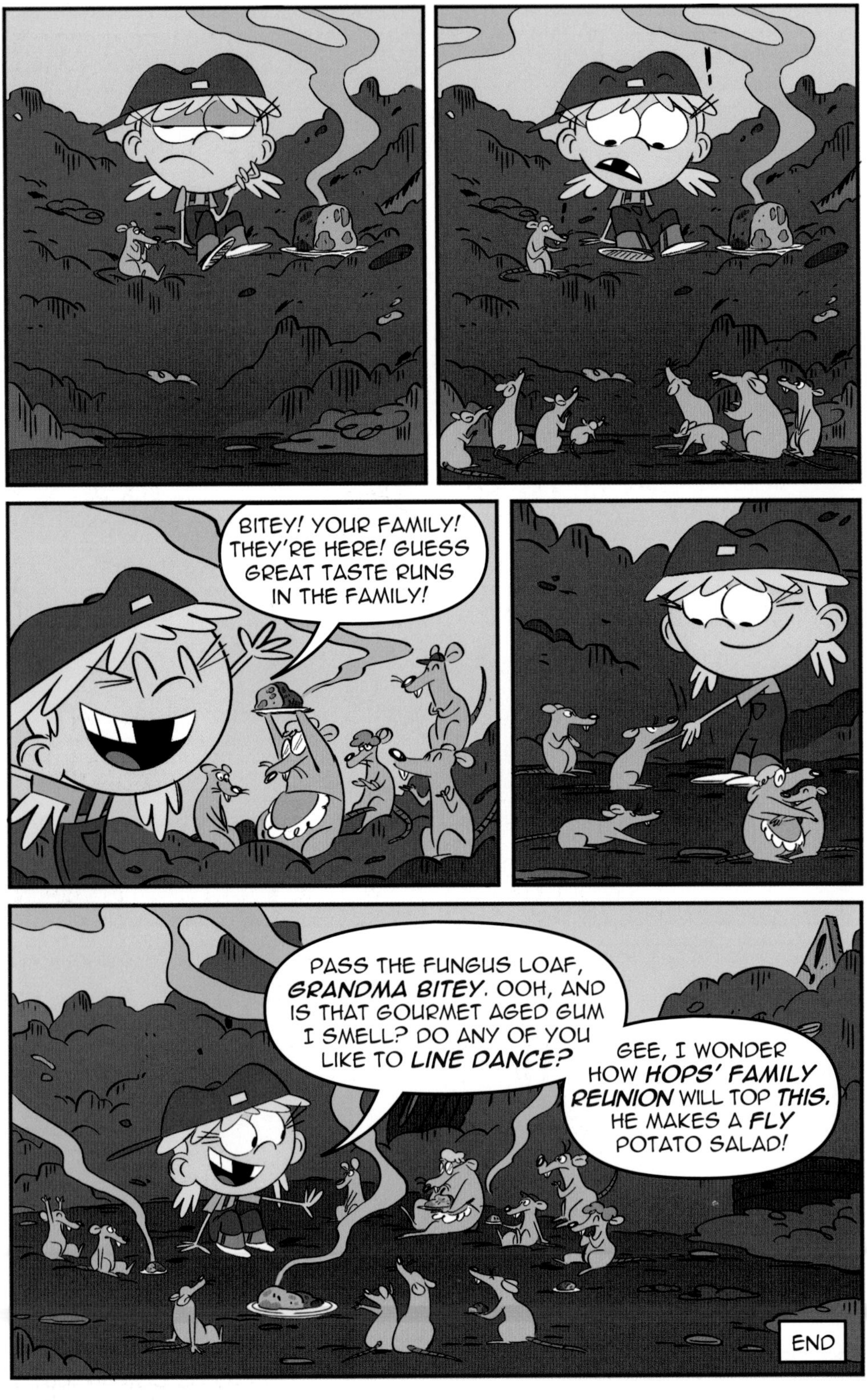
BITEY! YOUR FAMILY! THEY'RE HERE! GUESS GREAT TASTE RUNS IN THE FAMILY!
PASS THE FUNGUS LOAF, GRANDMA BITEY. OOH, AND IS THAT GOURMET AGED GUM I SMELL? DO ANY OF YOU LIKE TO LINE DANCE?
GEE, I WONDER HOW HOPS' FAMILY REUNION WILL TOP THIS. HE MAKES A FLY POTATO SALAD!
END

"VAN GO"

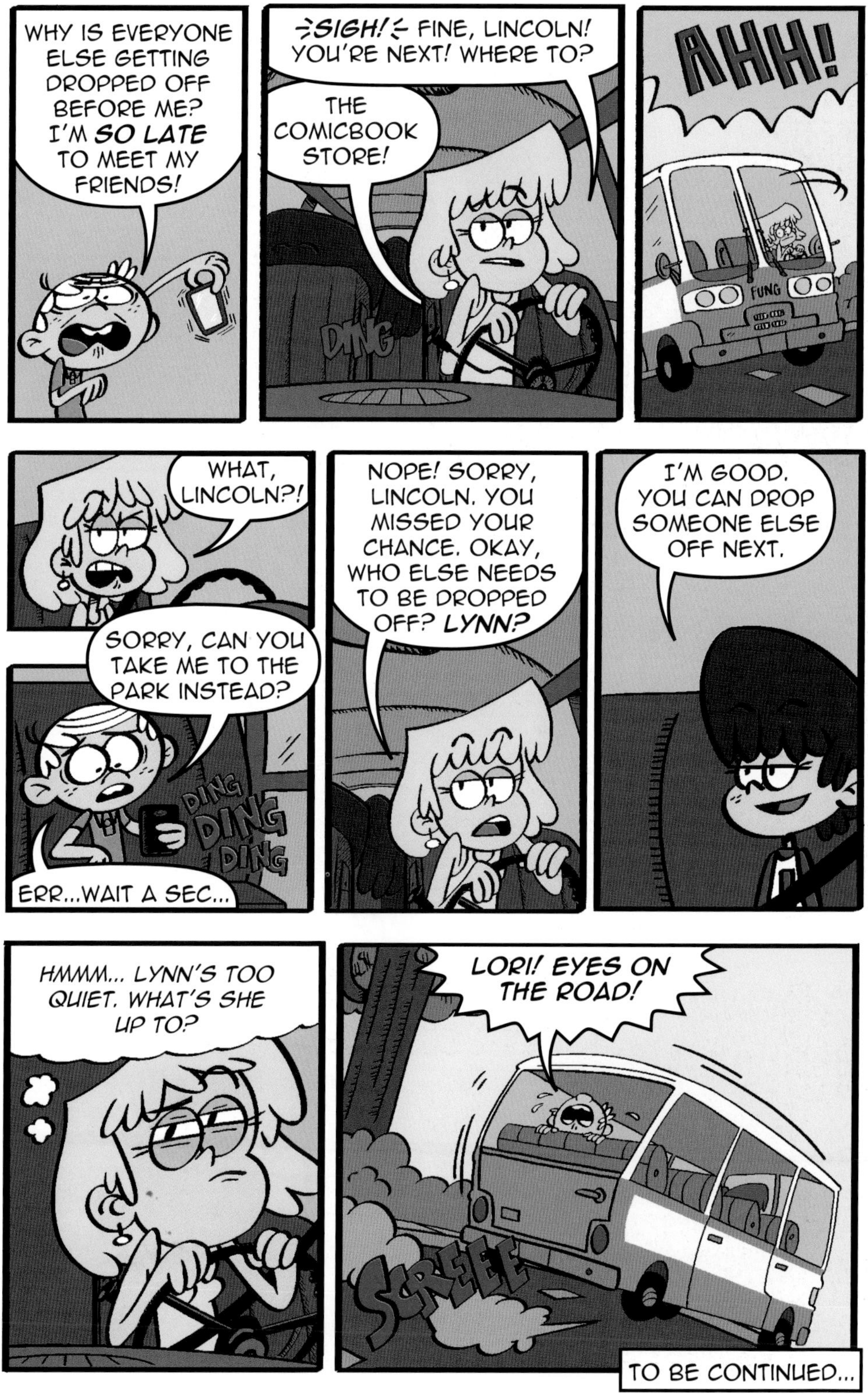
WHY IS EVERYONE ELSE GETTING DROPPED OFF BEFORE ME? I'M **SO LATE** TO MEET MY FRIENDS!
SIGH! FINE, LINCOLN! YOU'RE NEXT! WHERE TO?
THE COMICBOOK STORE!
DING
AHH!
FUNG
WHAT, LINCOLN?!
SORRY, CAN YOU TAKE ME TO THE PARK INSTEAD?
DING DING DING
ERR...WAIT A SEC...
NOPE! SORRY, LINCOLN. YOU MISSED YOUR CHANCE. OKAY, WHO ELSE NEEDS TO BE DROPPED OFF? ***LYNN?***
I'M GOOD. YOU CAN DROP SOMEONE ELSE OFF NEXT.
HMMM... LYNN'S TOO QUIET. WHAT'S SHE UP TO?
LORI! EYES ON THE ROAD!
SCREEE
TO BE CONTINUED...

"THE GOOD OLD DAYS"

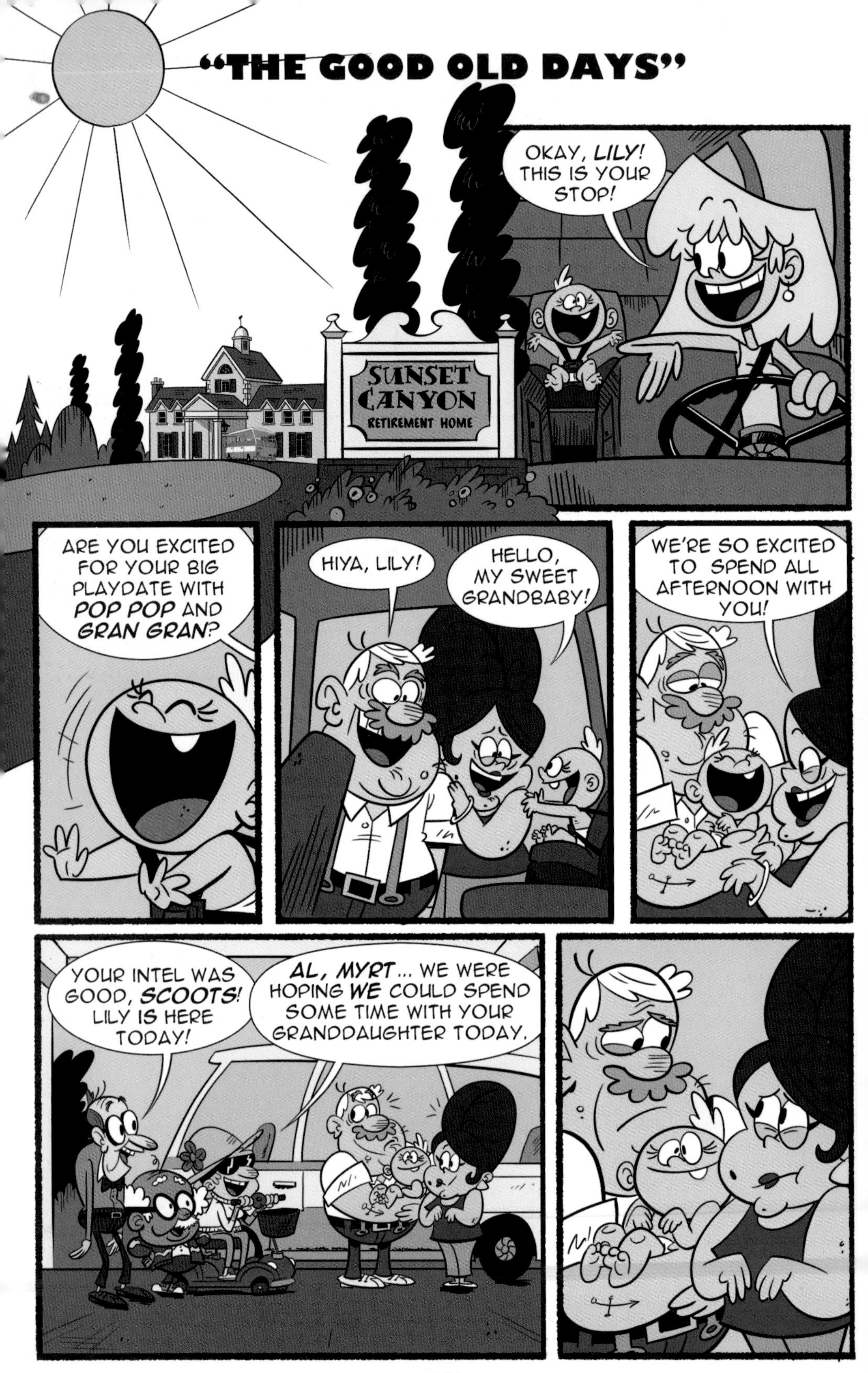
SUNSET CANYON
RETIREMENT HOME
OKAY, LILY! THIS IS YOUR STOP!
ARE YOU EXCITED FOR YOUR BIG PLAYDATE WITH POP POP AND GRAN GRAN?
HIYA, LILY!
HELLO, MY SWEET GRANDBABY!
WE'RE SO EXCITED TO SPEND ALL AFTERNOON WITH YOU!
YOUR INTEL WAS GOOD, SCOOTS! LILY IS HERE TODAY!
AL, MYRT... WE WERE HOPING WE COULD SPEND SOME TIME WITH YOUR GRANDDAUGHTER TODAY.

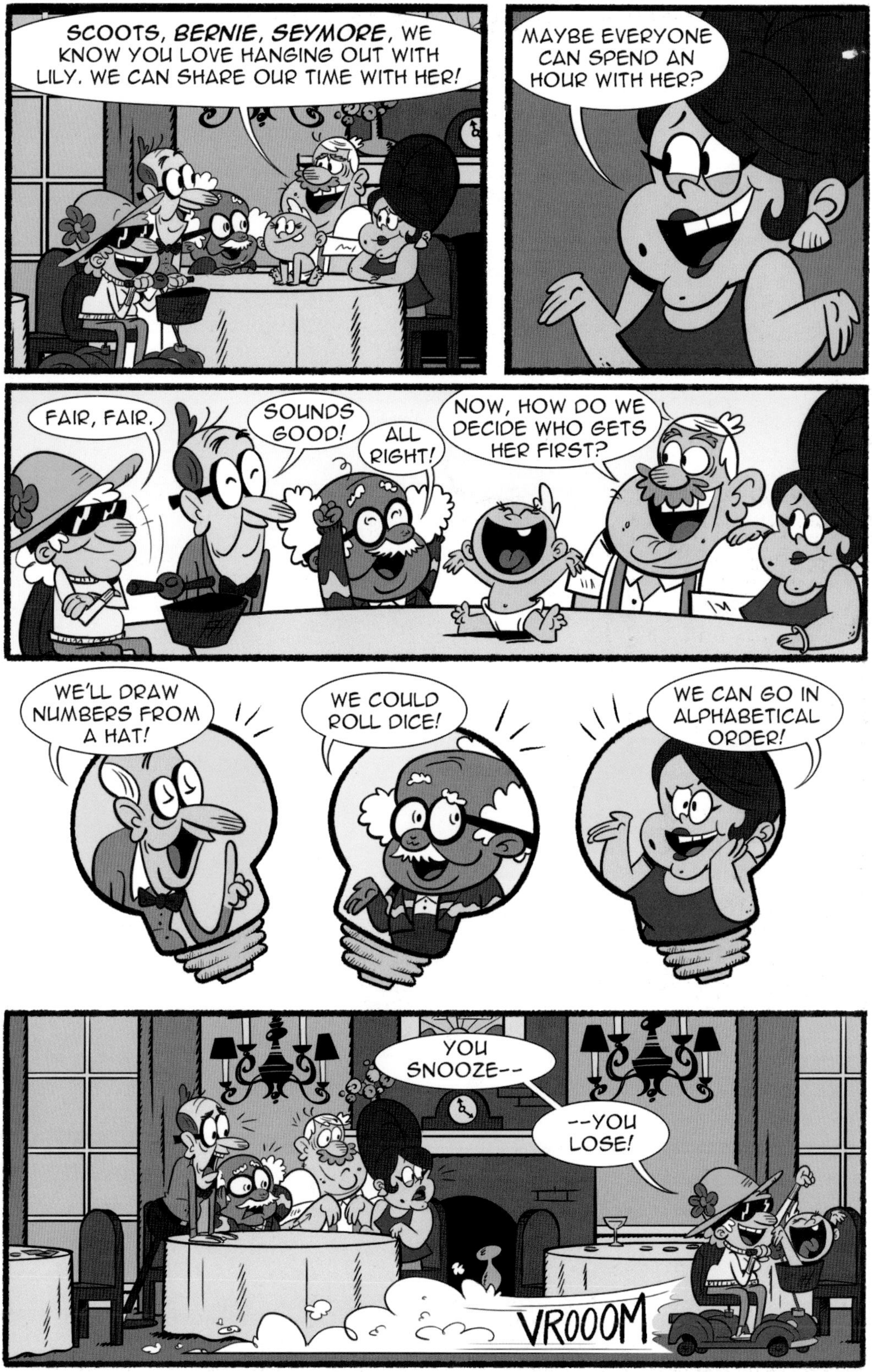
SCOOTS, BERNIE, SEYMORE, WE KNOW YOU LOVE HANGING OUT WITH LILY. WE CAN SHARE OUR TIME WITH HER!
MAYBE EVERYONE CAN SPEND AN HOUR WITH HER?
FAIR, FAIR.
SOUNDS GOOD!
ALL RIGHT!
NOW, HOW DO WE DECIDE WHO GETS HER FIRST?
WE'LL DRAW NUMBERS FROM A HAT!
WE COULD ROLL DICE!
WE CAN GO IN ALPHABETICAL ORDER!
YOU SNOOZE--
--YOU LOSE!
VROOOM

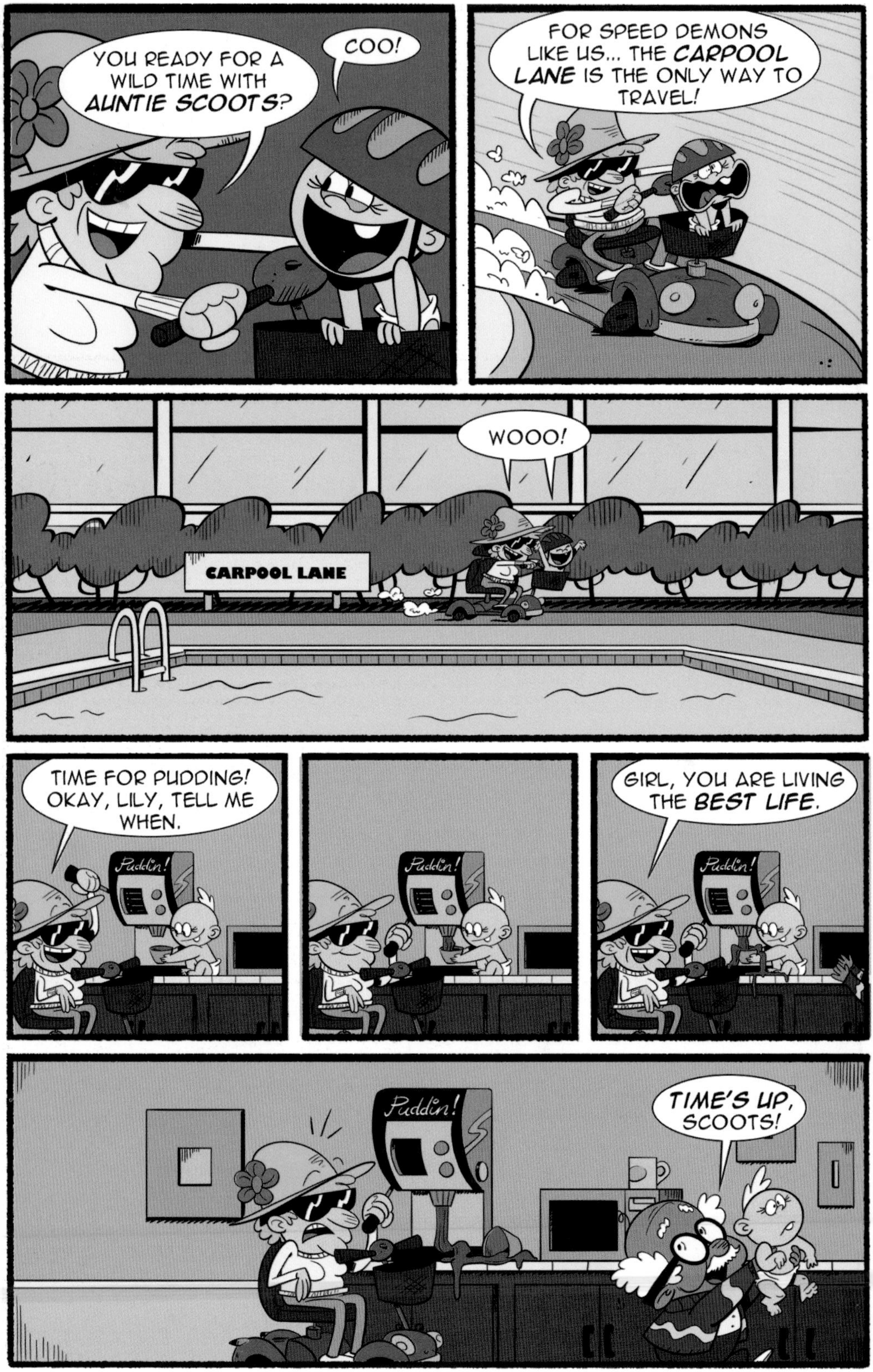
YOU READY FOR A WILD TIME WITH AUNTIE SCOOTS?
COO!
FOR SPEED DEMONS LIKE US... THE CARPOOL LANE IS THE ONLY WAY TO TRAVEL!
WOOO!
CARPOOL LANE
TIME FOR PUDDING! OKAY, LILY, TELL ME WHEN.
Puddin!
Puddin!
GIRL, YOU ARE LIVING THE BEST LIFE.
Puddin!
Puddin!
TIME'S UP, SCOOTS!

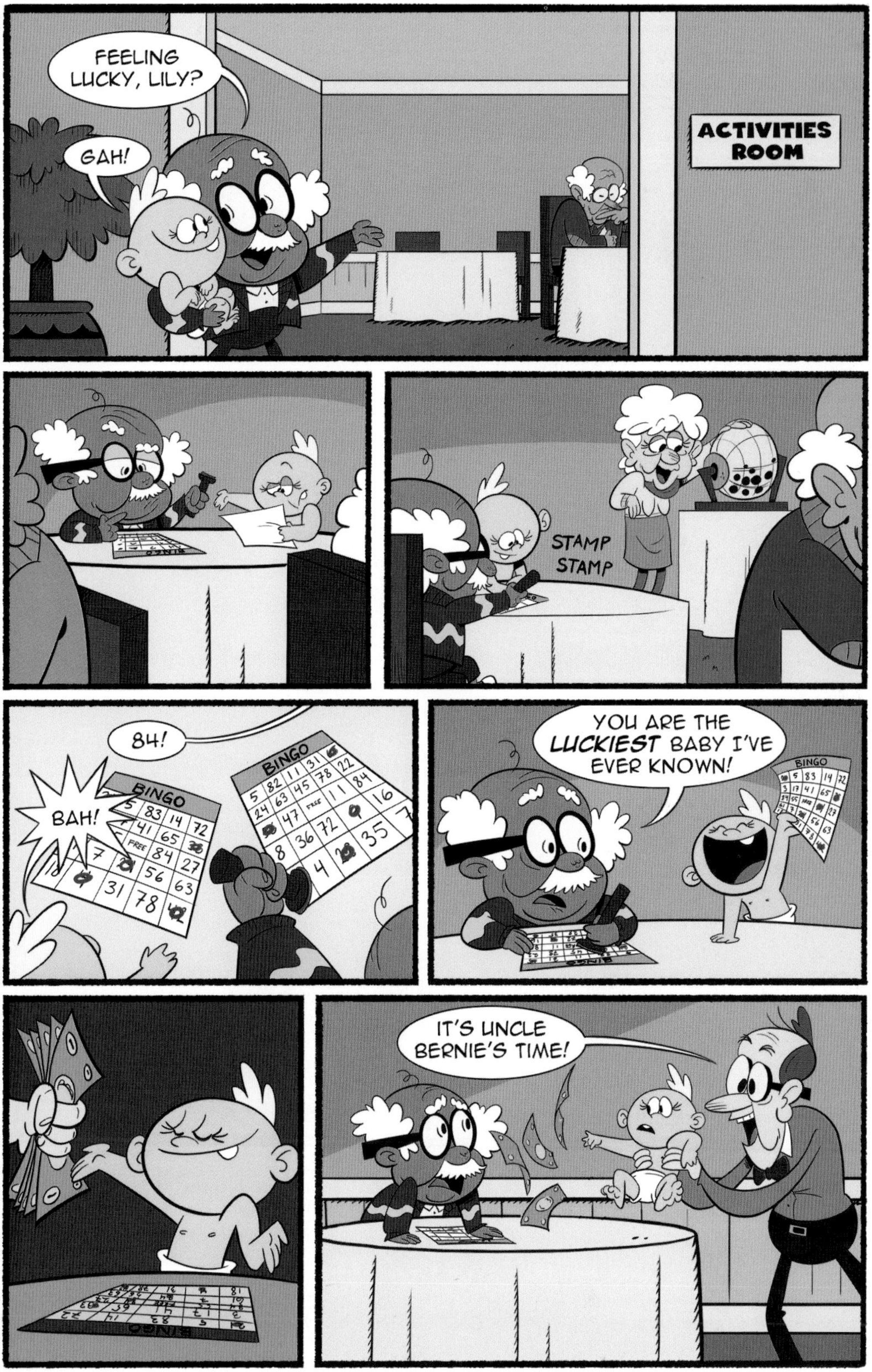
FEELING LUCKY, LILY?
GAH!
ACTIVITIES ROOM
STAMP STAMP
84!
BAH!
BINGO
YOU ARE THE LUCKIEST BABY I'VE EVER KNOWN!
IT'S UNCLE BERNIE'S TIME!

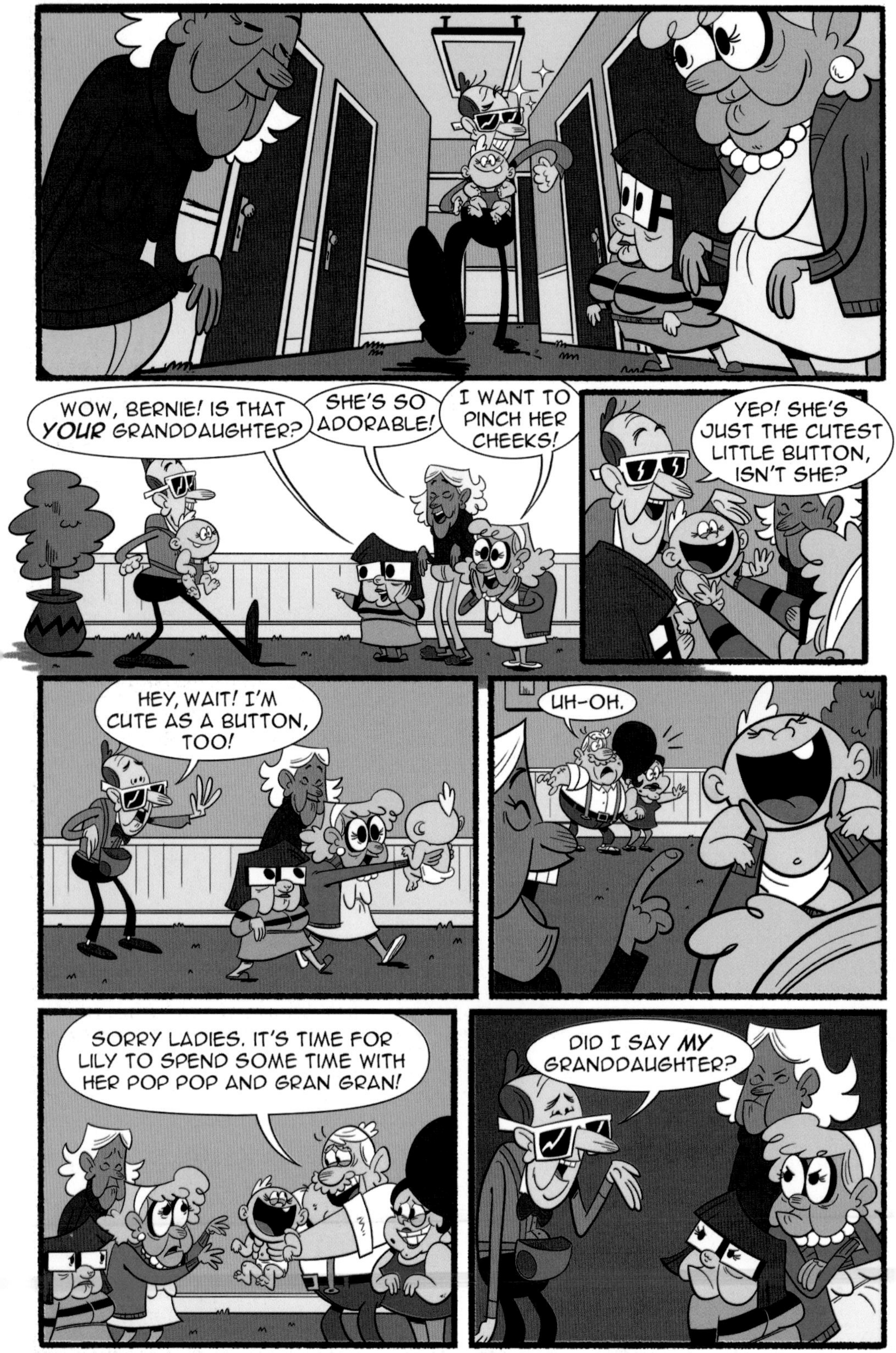
WOW, BERNIE! IS THAT YOUR GRANDDAUGHTER?
SHE'S SO ADORABLE!
I WANT TO PINCH HER CHEEKS!
YEP! SHE'S JUST THE CUTEST LITTLE BUTTON, ISN'T SHE?
HEY, WAIT! I'M CUTE AS A BUTTON, TOO!
UH-OH.
SORRY LADIES. IT'S TIME FOR LILY TO SPEND SOME TIME WITH HER POP POP AND GRAN GRAN!
DID I SAY MY GRANDDAUGHTER?

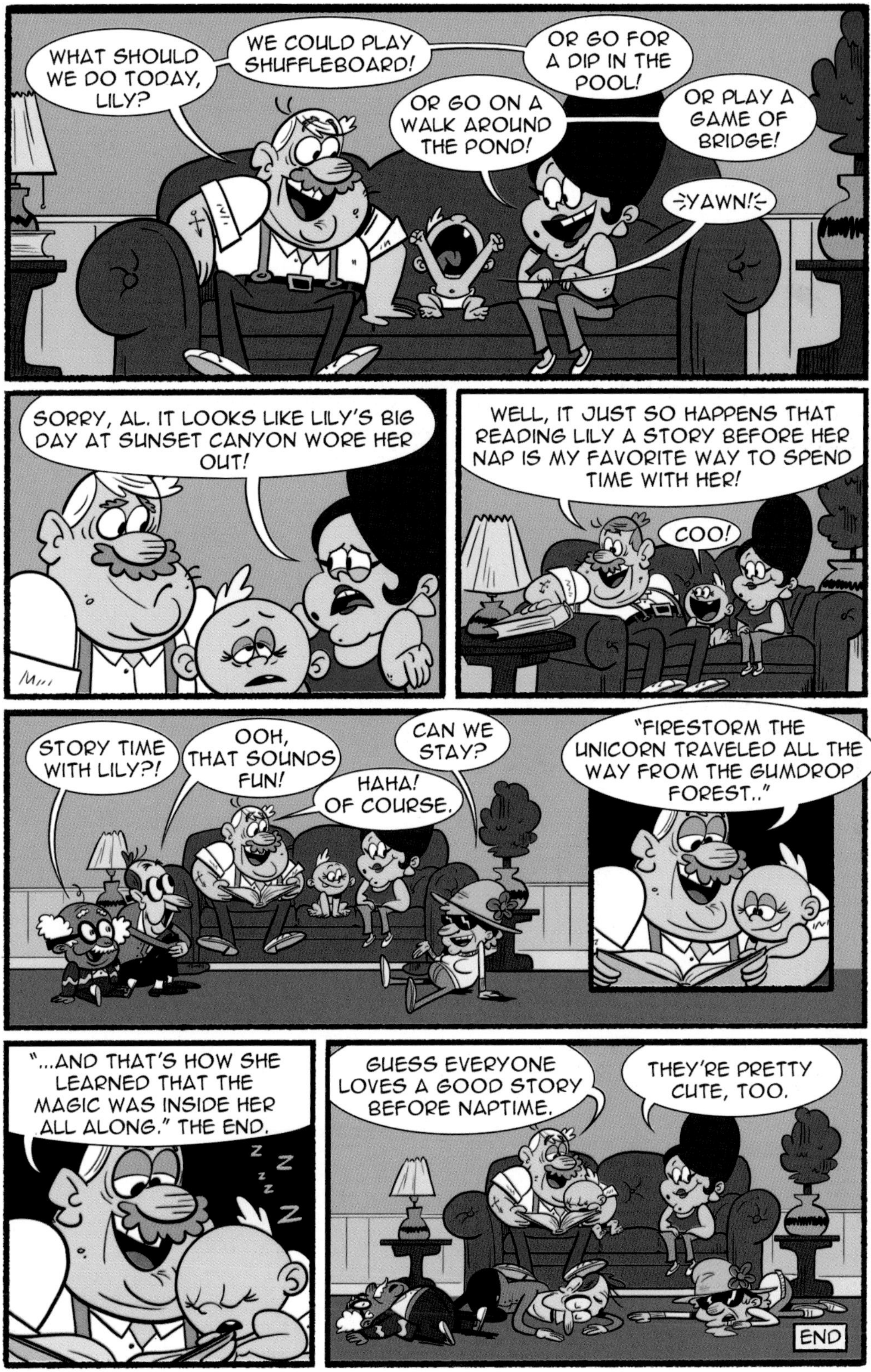
WHAT SHOULD WE DO TODAY, LILY?
WE COULD PLAY SHUFFLEBOARD!
OR GO FOR A DIP IN THE POOL!
OR GO ON A WALK AROUND THE POND!
OR PLAY A GAME OF BRIDGE!
YAWN!
SORRY, AL. IT LOOKS LIKE LILY'S BIG DAY AT SUNSET CANYON WORE HER OUT!
WELL, IT JUST SO HAPPENS THAT READING LILY A STORY BEFORE HER NAP IS MY FAVORITE WAY TO SPEND TIME WITH HER!
COO!
STORY TIME WITH LILY?!
OOH, THAT SOUNDS FUN!
CAN WE STAY?
HAHA! OF COURSE.
"FIRESTORM THE UNICORN TRAVELED ALL THE WAY FROM THE GUMDROP FOREST.."
"...AND THAT'S HOW SHE LEARNED THAT THE MAGIC WAS INSIDE HER ALL ALONG." THE END.
Z Z Z Z
GUESS EVERYONE LOVES A GOOD STORY BEFORE NAPTIME.
THEY'RE PRETTY CUTE, TOO.
END

"HATTA BOY"

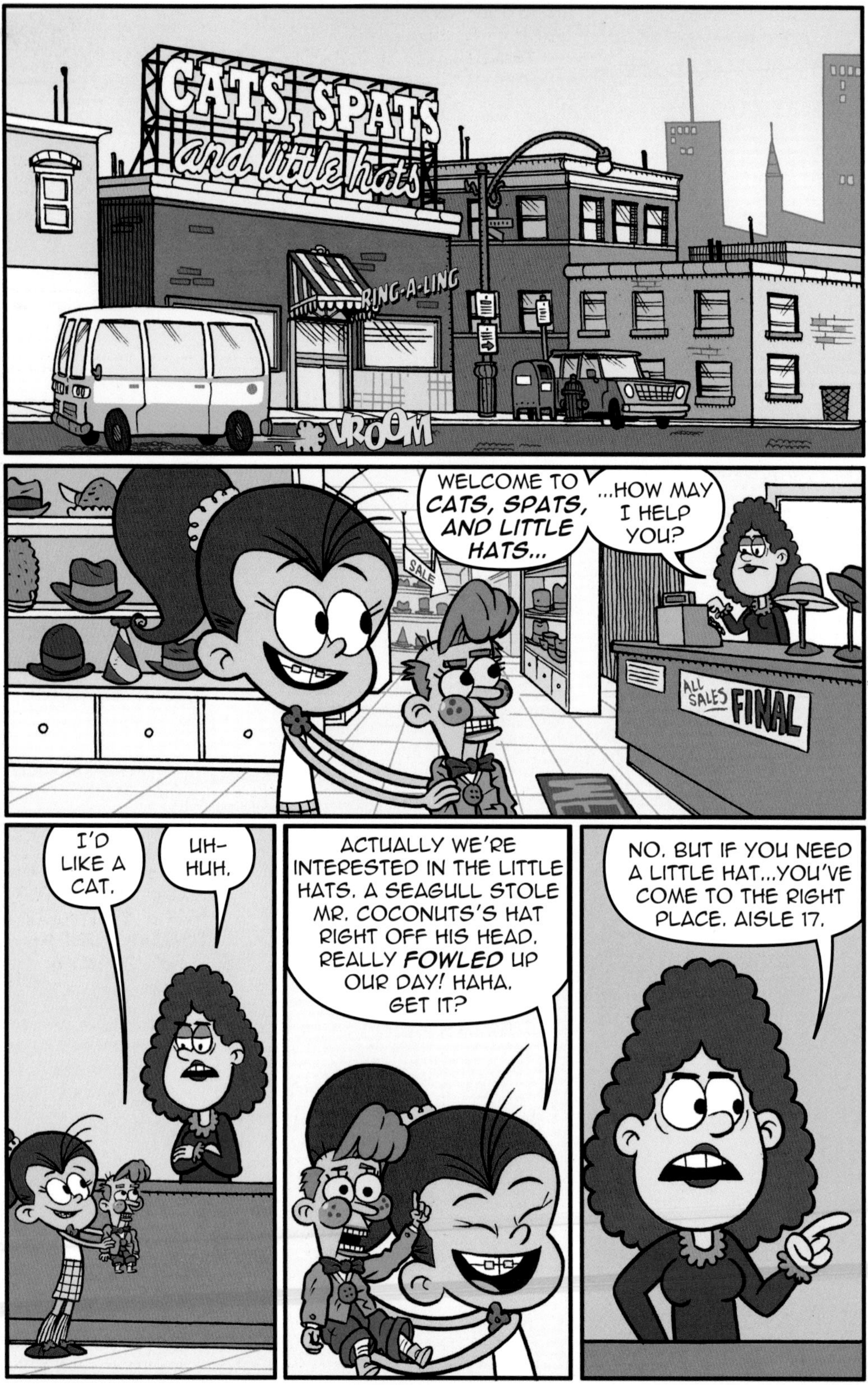
CATS, SPATS and little hats
RING-A-LING
VROOM
WELCOME TO CATS, SPATS, AND LITTLE HATS...
...HOW MAY I HELP YOU?
SALE
ALL SALES FINAL
I'D LIKE A CAT.
UH-HUH.
ACTUALLY WE'RE INTERESTED IN THE LITTLE HATS. A SEAGULL STOLE MR. COCONUTS'S HAT RIGHT OFF HIS HEAD. REALLY FOWLED UP OUR DAY! HAHA. GET IT?
NO. BUT IF YOU NEED A LITTLE HAT...YOU'VE COME TO THE RIGHT PLACE. AISLE 17.

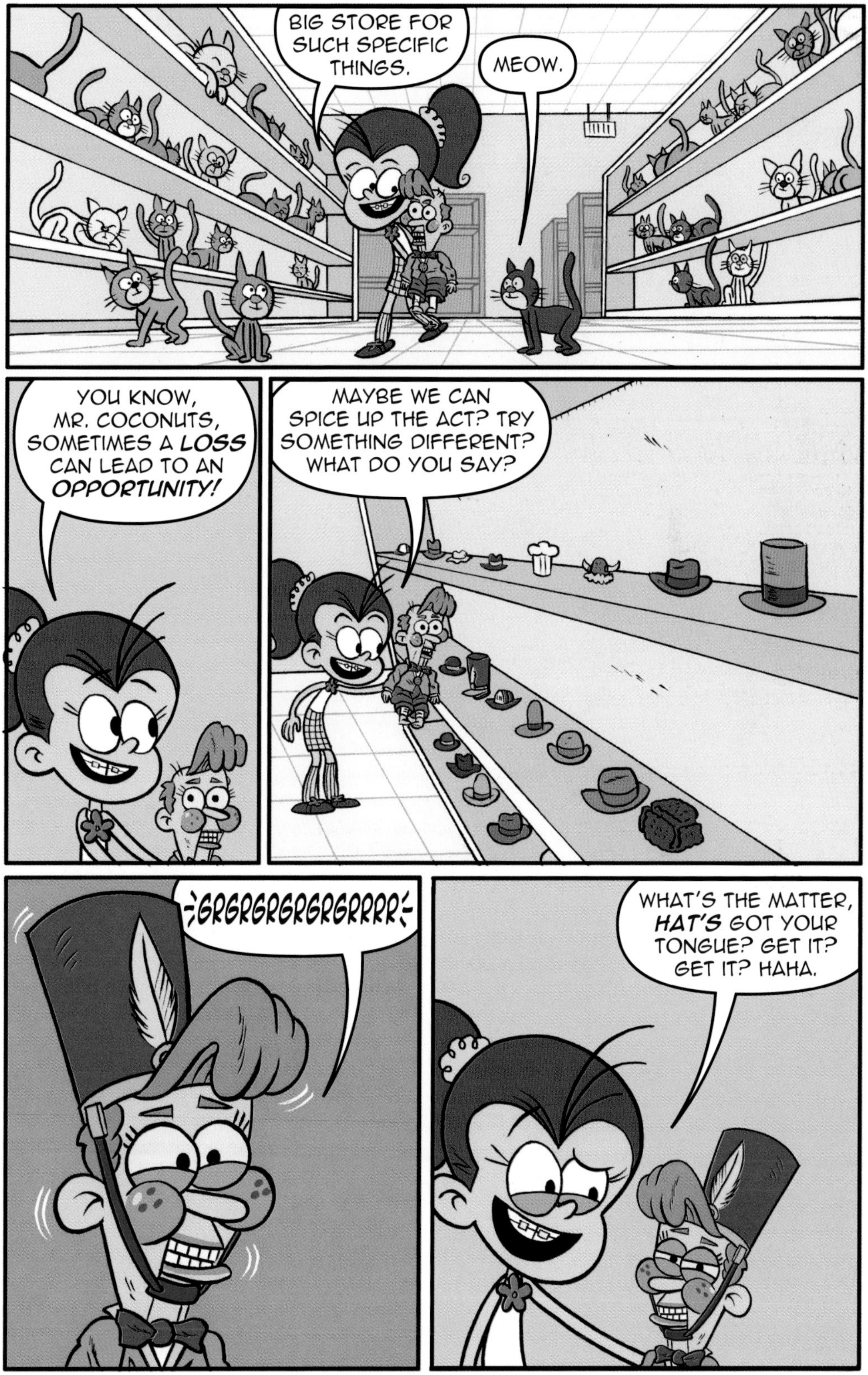
BIG STORE FOR SUCH SPECIFIC THINGS.
MEOW.
YOU KNOW, MR. COCONUTS, SOMETIMES A LOSS CAN LEAD TO AN OPPORTUNITY!
MAYBE WE CAN SPICE UP THE ACT? TRY SOMETHING DIFFERENT? WHAT DO YOU SAY?
GRGRGRGRGRGRRRR
WHAT'S THE MATTER, HAT'S GOT YOUR TONGUE? GET IT? GET IT? HAHA.

OOH, LA LA, MONSIEUR COCONUT. I LIKE THIS LOOK.

MERCI. JE N'AI PAS LE TEMPS POUR TES PETITS JEUX.

UMMMM... UMMM...I DON'T **SPEAK** FRENCH, MR. COCONUTS.

BA! C'EST TON PROBLÈME.

WELL, YOU DON'T HAVE TO BE **RUDE** ABOUT IT...!

OKAY...LETS TRY SOMETHING A LITTLE MORE **CLASSIC**.

THIS AISLE AIN'T BIG ENOUGH FOR THE TWO OF US.

MEOW?

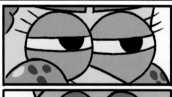

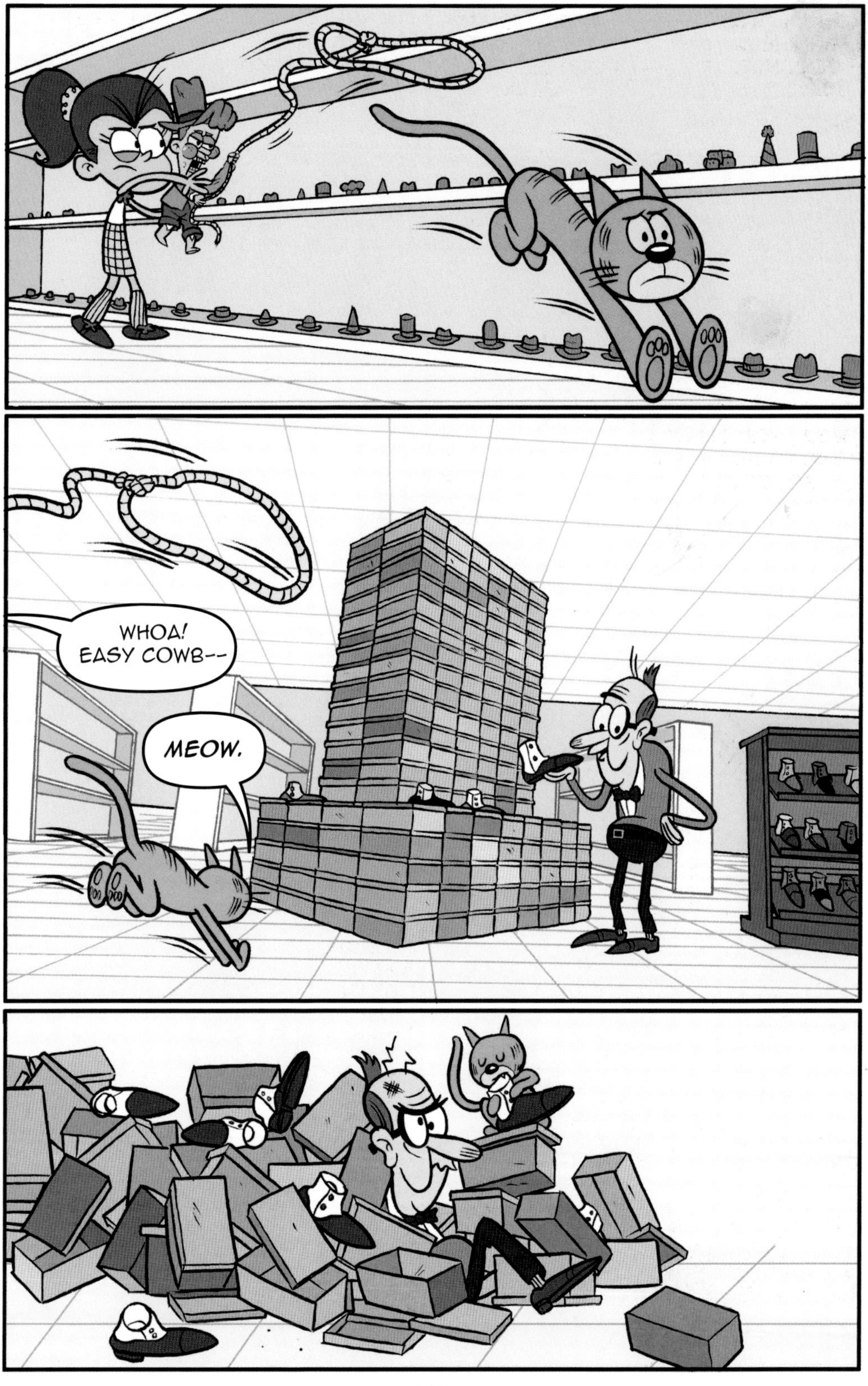
WHOA!
EASY COWB--
MEOW.

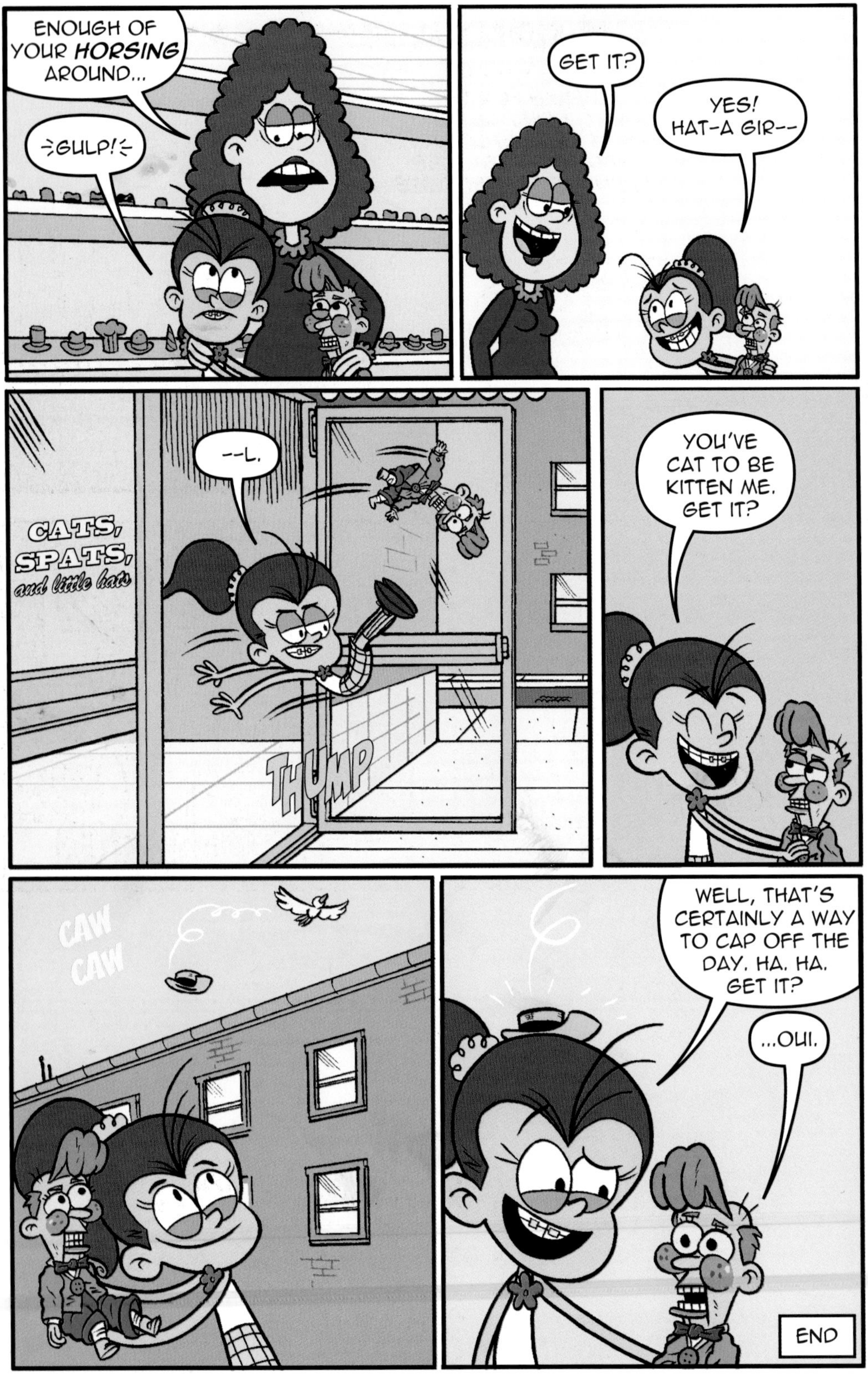

ENOUGH OF YOUR HORSING AROUND...
GULP!
GET IT?
YES! HAT-A GIR--
--L.
CATS, SPATS, and little hats
THUMP
YOU'VE CAT TO BE KITTEN ME. GET IT?
CAW CAW
WELL, THAT'S CERTAINLY A WAY TO CAP OFF THE DAY. HA. HA. GET IT?
...OUI.
END

"I'M GONNA FINE YOU"

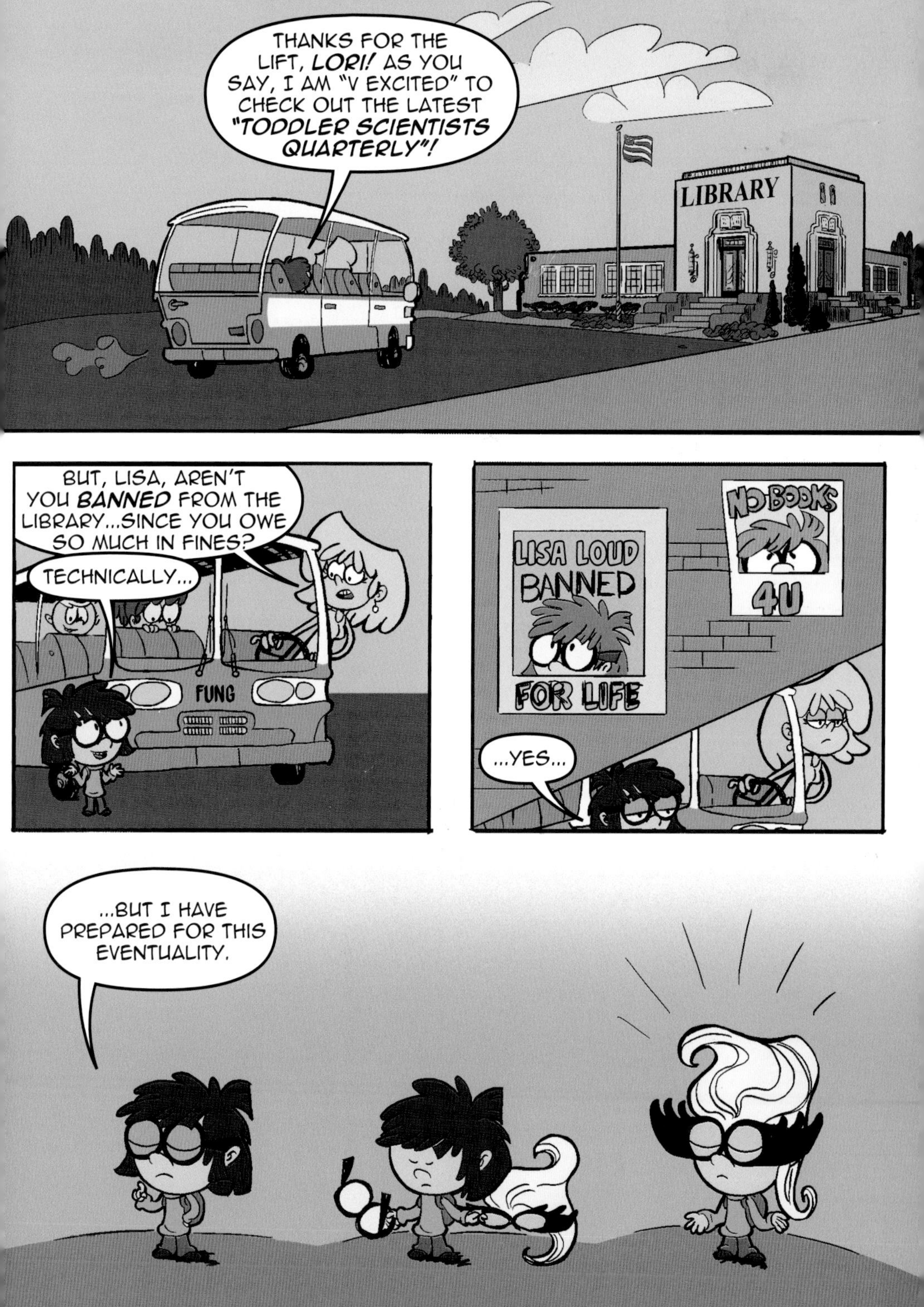
THANKS FOR THE LIFT, LORI! AS YOU SAY, I AM "V EXCITED" TO CHECK OUT THE LATEST "TODDLER SCIENTISTS QUARTERLY"!
LIBRARY
BUT, LISA, AREN'T YOU BANNED FROM THE LIBRARY...SINCE YOU OWE SO MUCH IN FINES?
TECHNICALLY...
FUNG
LISA LOUD BANNED FOR LIFE
NO BOOKS 4U
...YES...
...BUT I HAVE PREPARED FOR THIS EVENTUALITY.

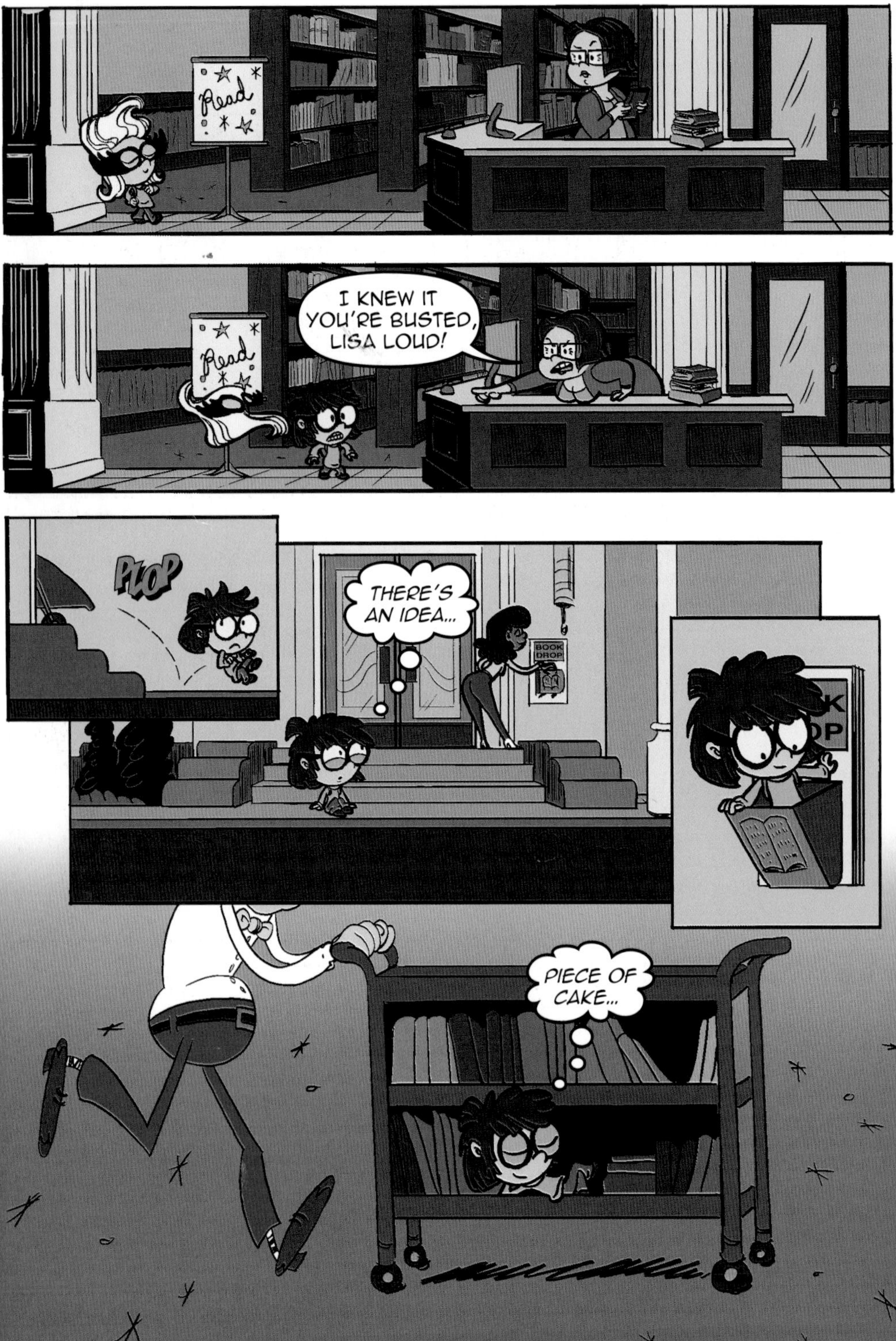
Read
Read
I KNEW IT YOU'RE BUSTED, LISA LOUD!
PLOP
THERE'S AN IDEA...
BOOK DROP
PIECE OF CAKE...

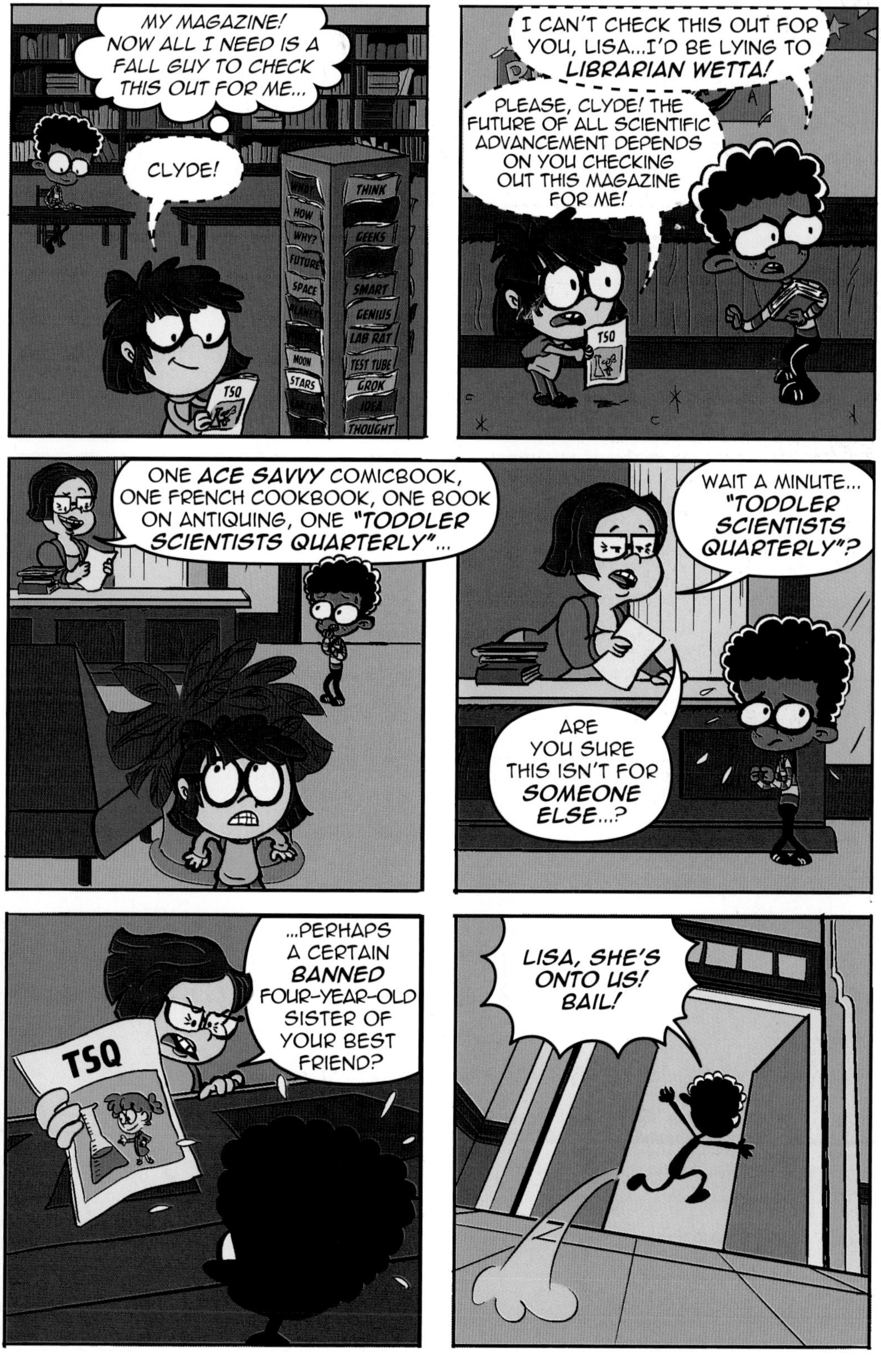
MY MAGAZINE! NOW ALL I NEED IS A FALL GUY TO CHECK THIS OUT FOR ME...
CLYDE!
WHAT
HOW
WHY?
FUTURE
SPACE
PLANETS
MOON
STARS
THINK
GEEKS
SMART
GENIUS
LAB RAT
TEST TUBE
GROK
IDEA
THOUGHT
TSQ
I CAN'T CHECK THIS OUT FOR YOU, LISA...I'D BE LYING TO LIBRARIAN WETTA!
PLEASE, CLYDE! THE FUTURE OF ALL SCIENTIFIC ADVANCEMENT DEPENDS ON YOU CHECKING OUT THIS MAGAZINE FOR ME!
TSQ
ONE ACE SAVVY COMICBOOK, ONE FRENCH COOKBOOK, ONE BOOK ON ANTIQUING, ONE "TODDLER SCIENTISTS QUARTERLY"...
WAIT A MINUTE... "TODDLER SCIENTISTS QUARTERLY"?
ARE YOU SURE THIS ISN'T FOR SOMEONE ELSE...?
...PERHAPS A CERTAIN BANNED FOUR-YEAR-OLD SISTER OF YOUR BEST FRIEND?
TSQ
LISA, SHE'S ONTO US! BAIL!

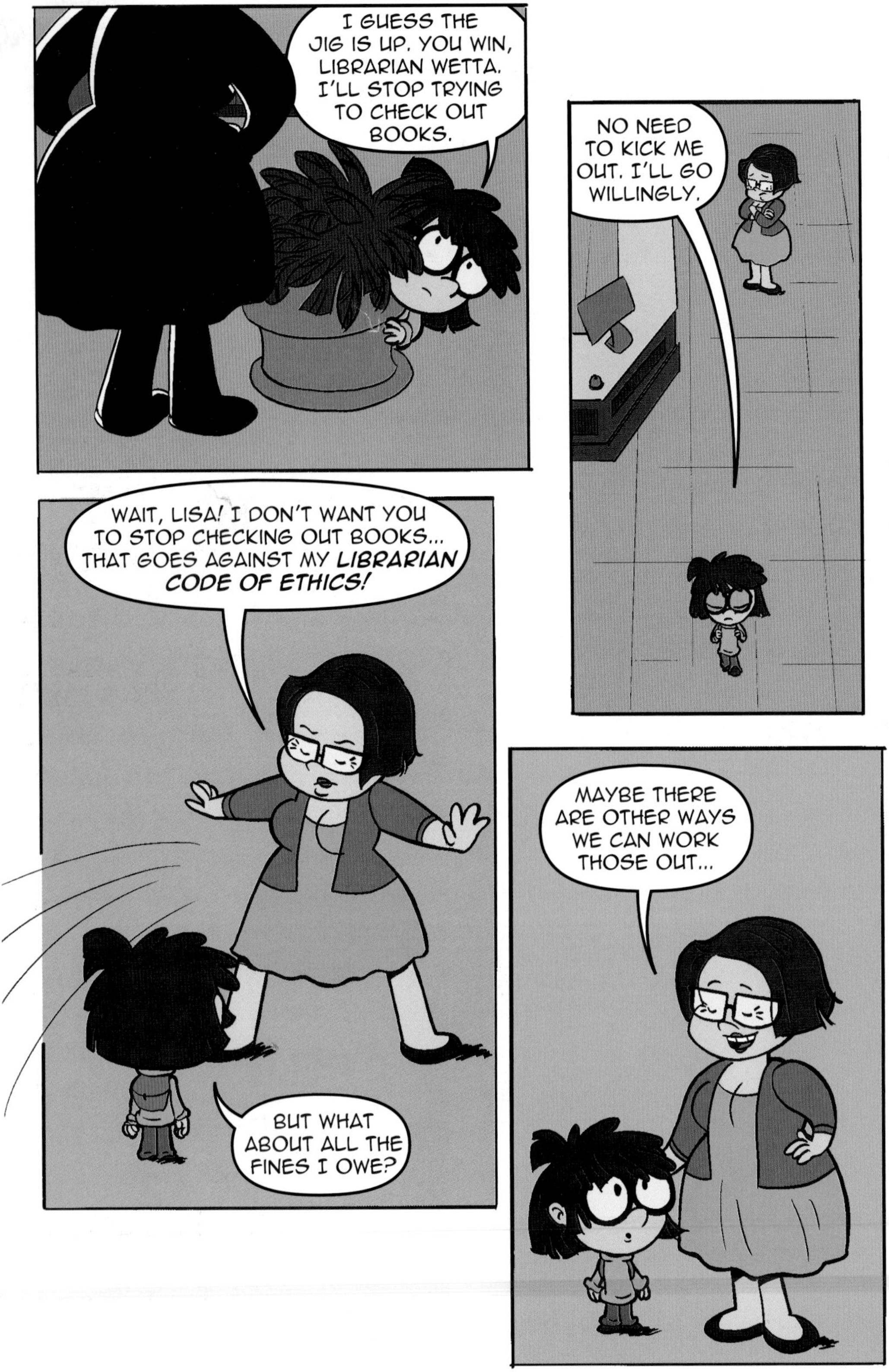
I GUESS THE JIG IS UP. YOU WIN, LIBRARIAN WETTA. I'LL STOP TRYING TO CHECK OUT BOOKS.
NO NEED TO KICK ME OUT. I'LL GO WILLINGLY.
WAIT, LISA! I DON'T WANT YOU TO STOP CHECKING OUT BOOKS... THAT GOES AGAINST MY ***LIBRARIAN CODE OF ETHICS!***
BUT WHAT ABOUT ALL THE FINES I OWE?
MAYBE THERE ARE OTHER WAYS WE CAN WORK THOSE OUT...

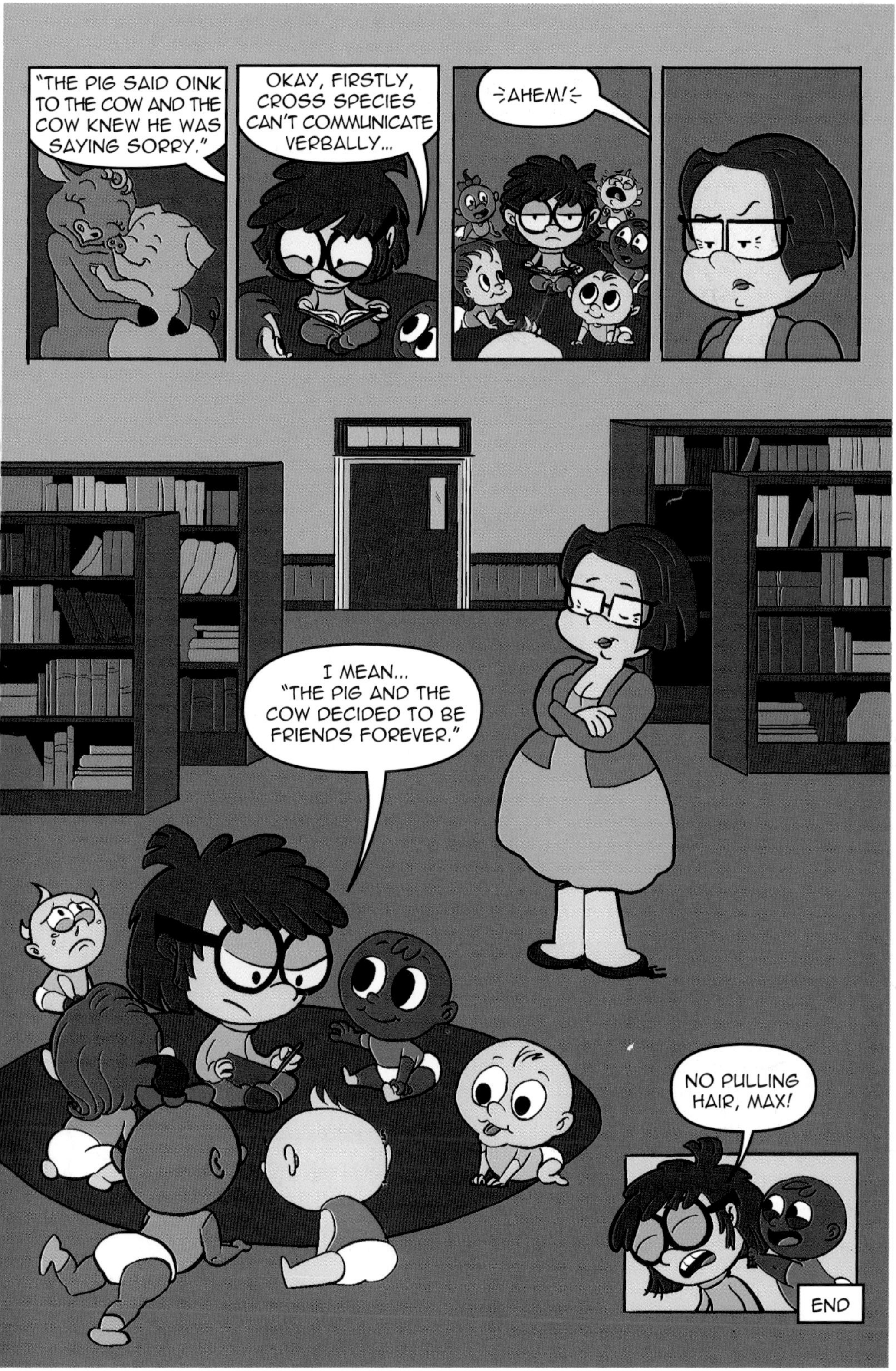
"THE PIG SAID OINK TO THE COW AND THE COW KNEW HE WAS SAYING SORRY."
OKAY, FIRSTLY, CROSS SPECIES CAN'T COMMUNICATE VERBALLY...
AHEM!
I MEAN... "THE PIG AND THE COW DECIDED TO BE FRIENDS FOREVER."
NO PULLING HAIR, MAX!
END

"AN UNEXPECTED JOURNEY"

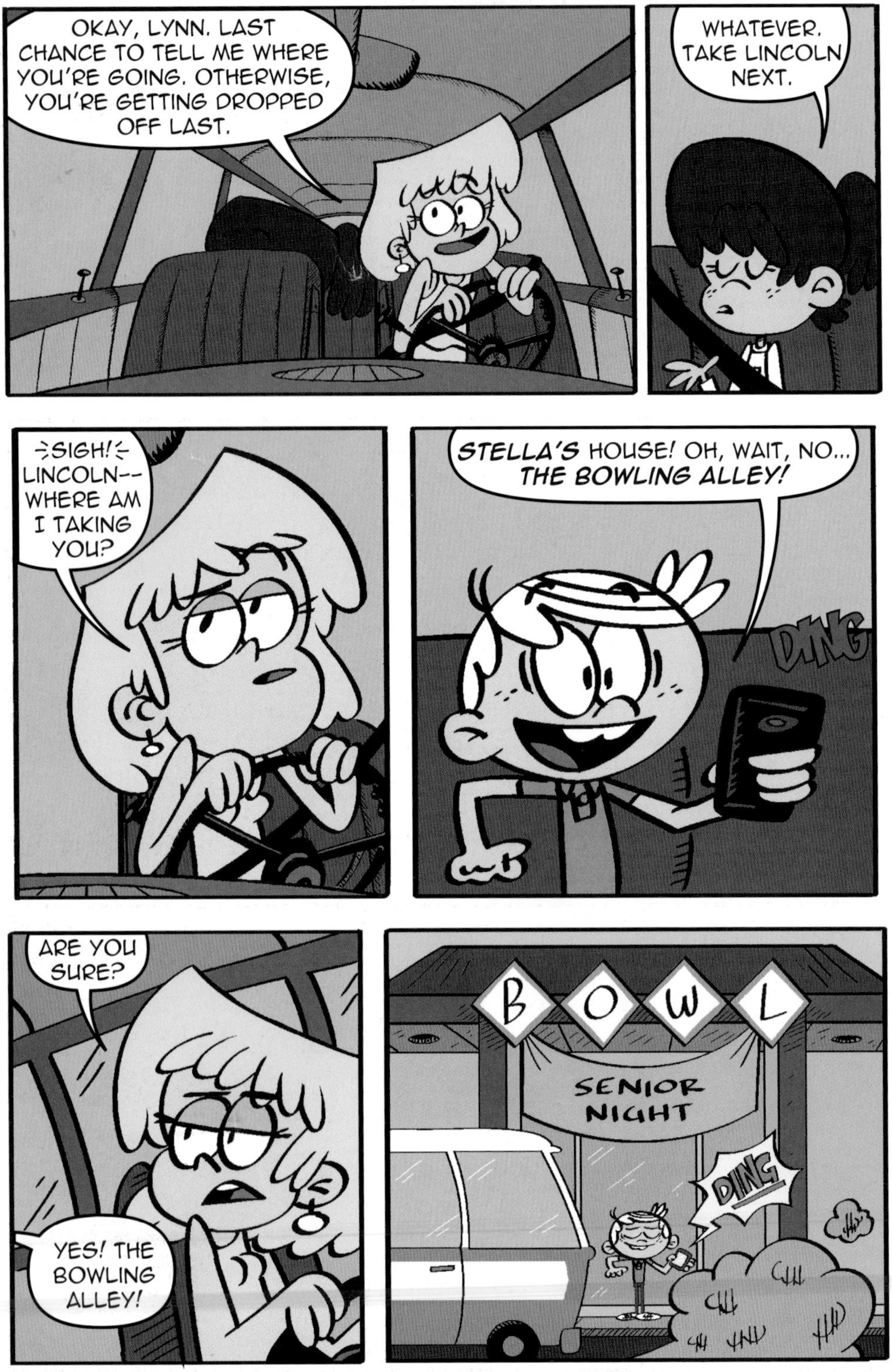

OKAY, LYNN. LAST CHANCE TO TELL ME WHERE YOU'RE GOING. OTHERWISE, YOU'RE GETTING DROPPED OFF LAST.
WHATEVER. TAKE LINCOLN NEXT.
SIGH! LINCOLN-- WHERE AM I TAKING YOU?
STELLA'S HOUSE! OH, WAIT, NO... THE BOWLING ALLEY!
DING
ARE YOU SURE?
YES! THE BOWLING ALLEY!
BOWL
SENIOR NIGHT
DING

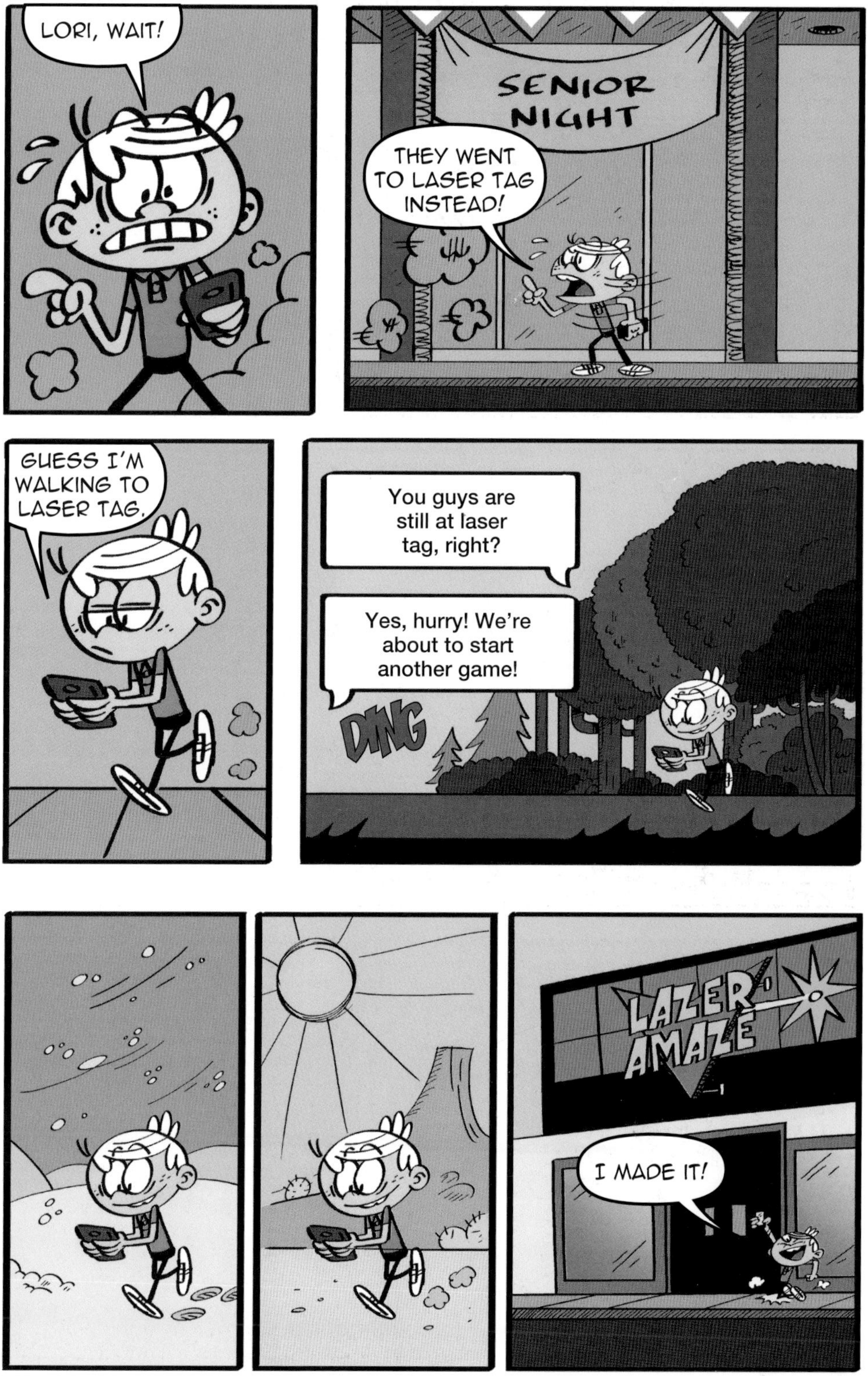
LORI, WAIT!
SENIOR NIGHT
THEY WENT TO LASER TAG INSTEAD!
GUESS I'M WALKING TO LASER TAG.
You guys are still at laser tag, right?
Yes, hurry! We're about to start another game!
DING
LAZER AMAZE
I MADE IT!

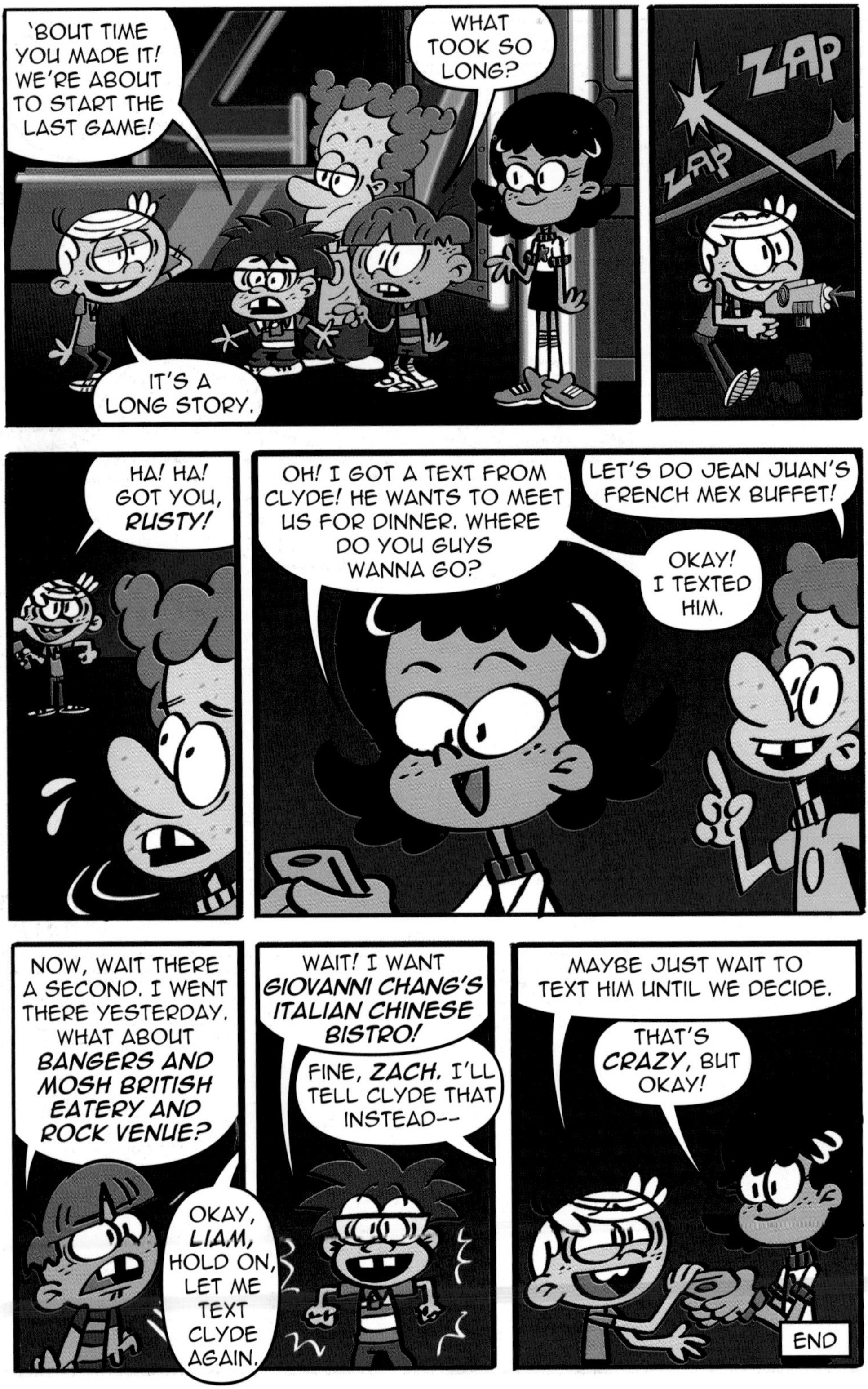
'BOUT TIME YOU MADE IT! WE'RE ABOUT TO START THE LAST GAME!
WHAT TOOK SO LONG?
IT'S A LONG STORY.
ZAP
ZAP
HA! HA! GOT YOU, RUSTY!
OH! I GOT A TEXT FROM CLYDE! HE WANTS TO MEET US FOR DINNER. WHERE DO YOU GUYS WANNA GO?
LET'S DO JEAN JUAN'S FRENCH MEX BUFFET!
OKAY! I TEXTED HIM.
NOW, WAIT THERE A SECOND. I WENT THERE YESTERDAY. WHAT ABOUT BANGERS AND MOSH BRITISH EATERY AND ROCK VENUE?
OKAY, LIAM, HOLD ON, LET ME TEXT CLYDE AGAIN.
WAIT! I WANT GIOVANNI CHANG'S ITALIAN CHINESE BISTRO!
FINE, ZACH. I'LL TELL CLYDE THAT INSTEAD--
MAYBE JUST WAIT TO TEXT HIM UNTIL WE DECIDE.
THAT'S CRAZY, BUT OKAY!
END

"BRAG RACE"

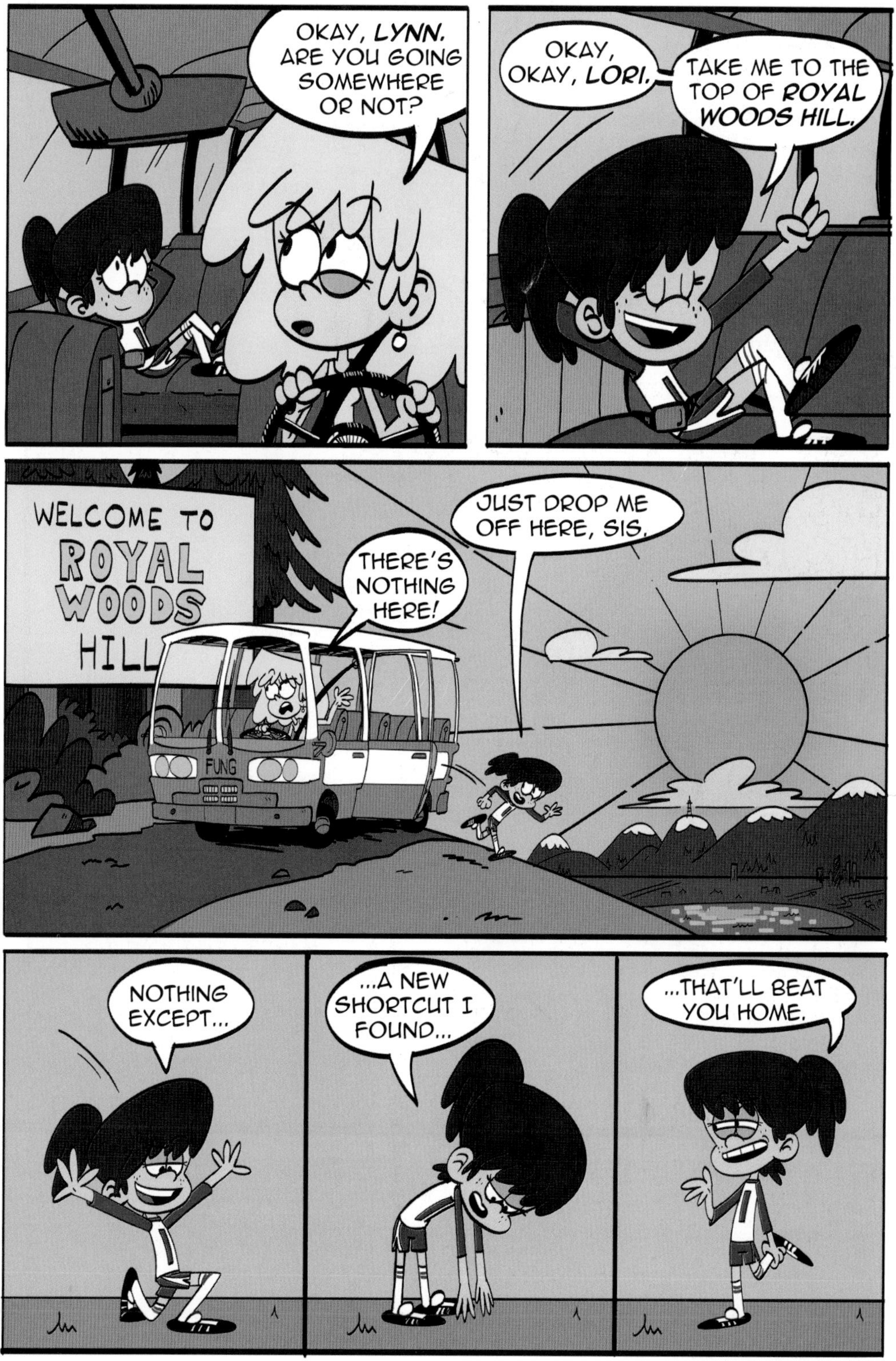
OKAY, LYNN. ARE YOU GOING SOMEWHERE OR NOT?
OKAY, OKAY, LORI.
TAKE ME TO THE TOP OF ROYAL WOODS HILL.
WELCOME TO ROYAL WOODS HILL
FUNG
JUST DROP ME OFF HERE, SIS.
THERE'S NOTHING HERE!
NOTHING EXCEPT...
...A NEW SHORTCUT I FOUND...
...THAT'LL BEAT YOU HOME.

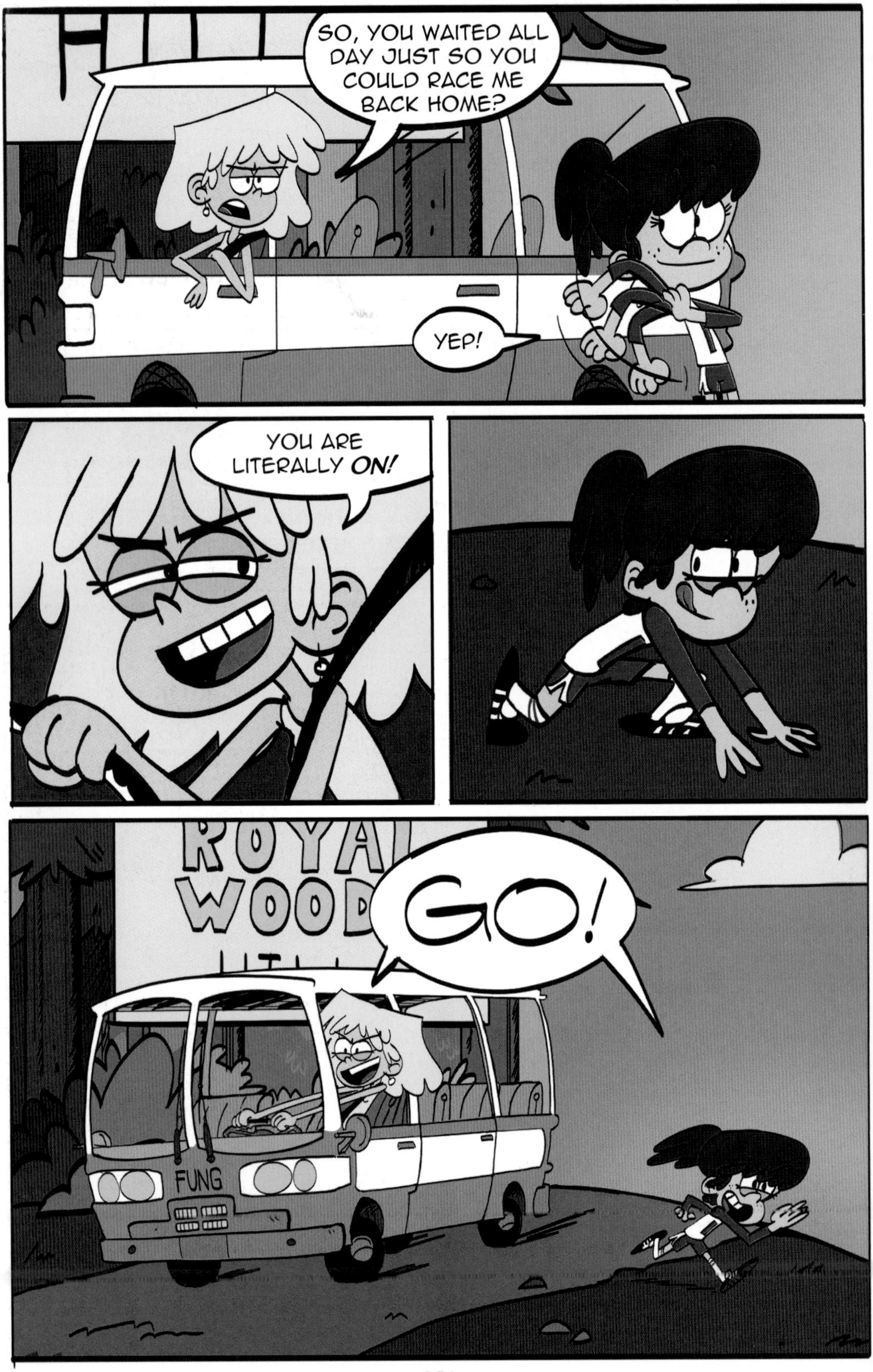
SO, YOU WAITED ALL DAY JUST SO YOU COULD RACE ME BACK HOME?
YEP!
YOU ARE LITERALLY ON!
ROYAL WOOD
GO!
FUNG

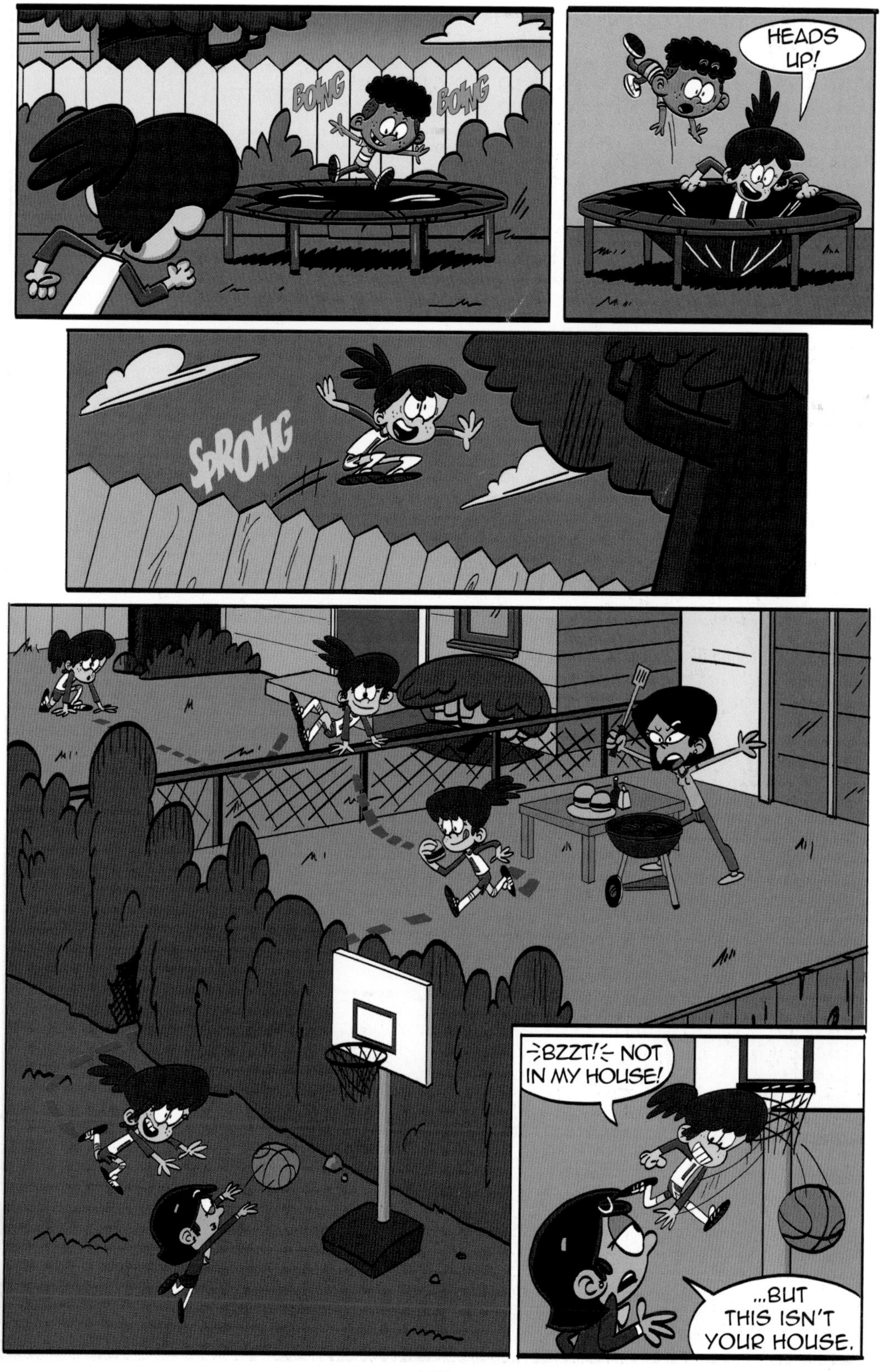
BOING
BOING
HEADS UP!
SPROING
BZZT! NOT IN MY HOUSE!
...BUT THIS ISN'T YOUR HOUSE.

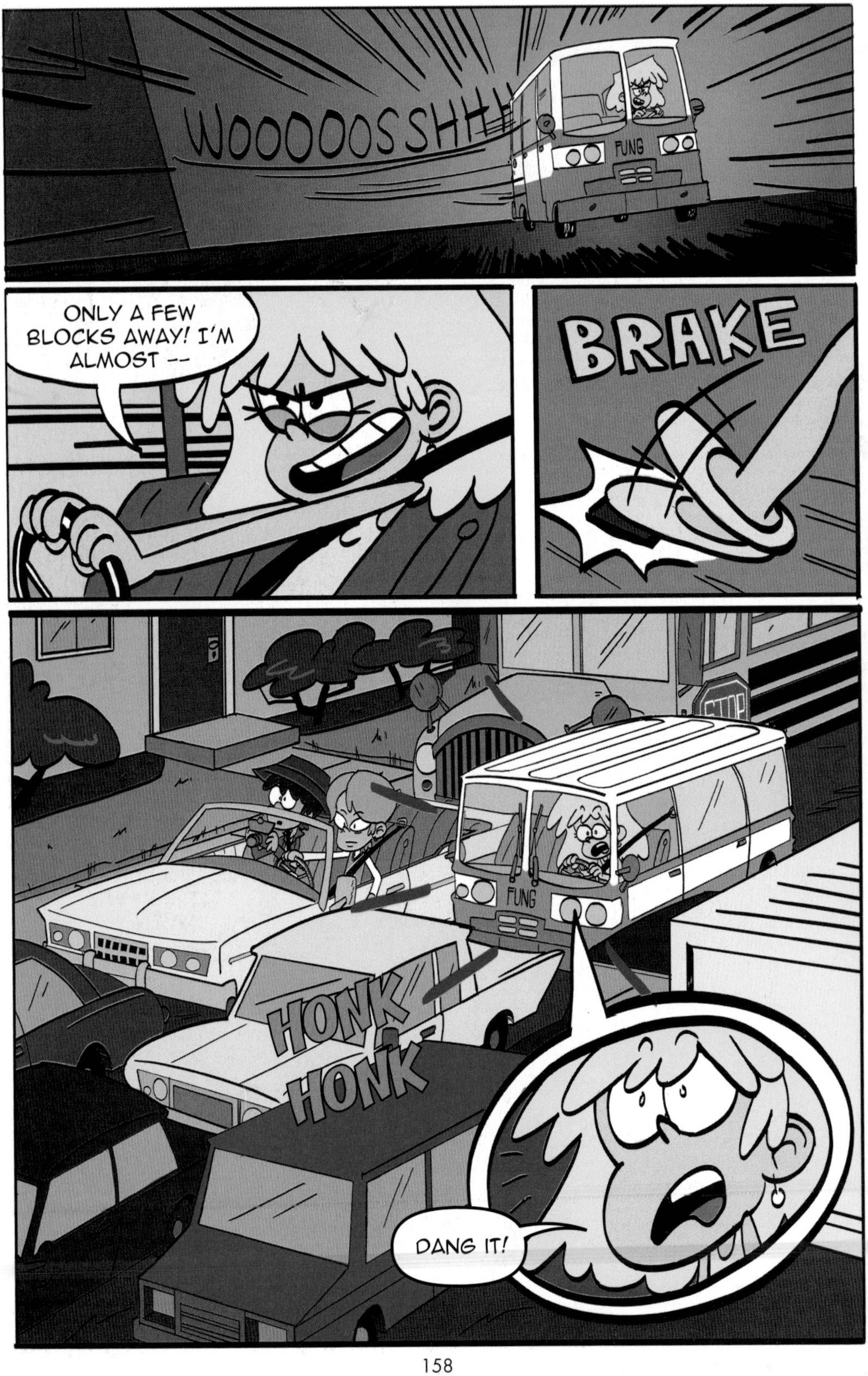
WOOOOOSSHH
FUNG
ONLY A FEW BLOCKS AWAY! I'M ALMOST --
BRAKE
FUNG
HONK
HONK
DANG IT!

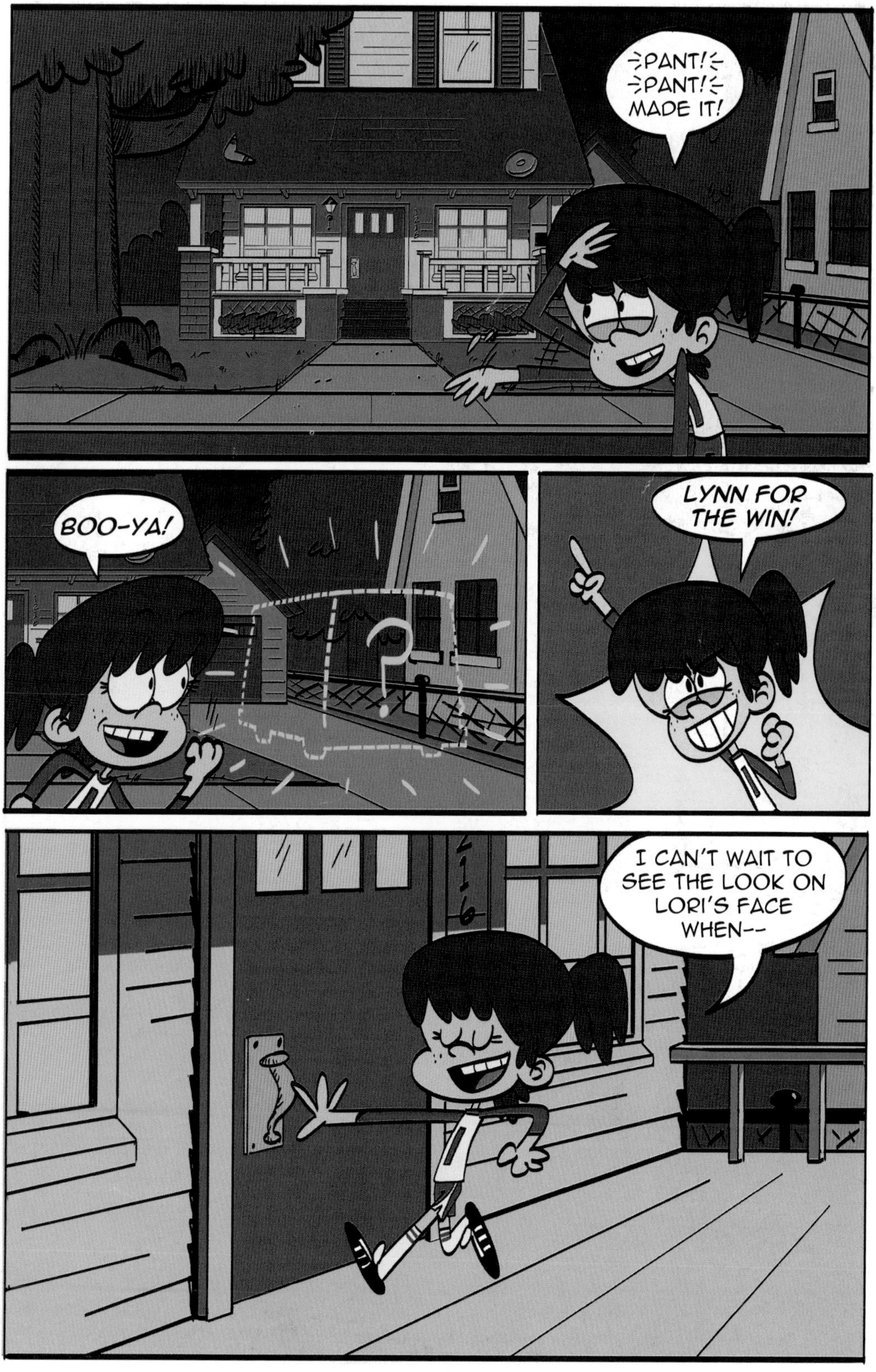
PANT! PANT! MADE IT!
BOO-YA!
LYNN FOR THE WIN!
I CAN'T WAIT TO SEE THE LOOK ON LORI'S FACE WHEN--

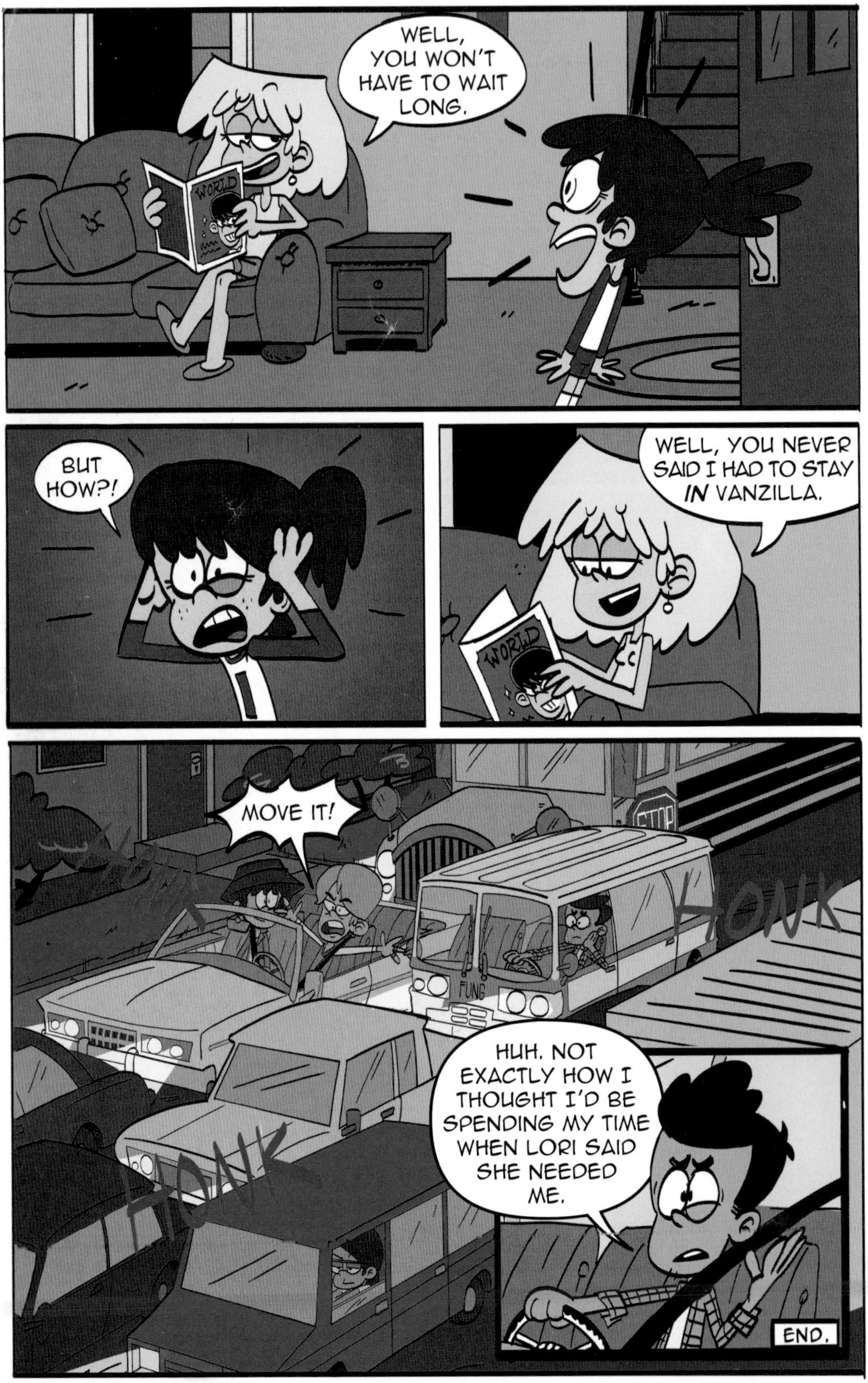
WELL, YOU WON'T HAVE TO WAIT LONG.
WORLD
BUT HOW?!
WELL, YOU NEVER SAID I HAD TO STAY *IN* VANZILLA.
WORLD
MOVE IT!
STOP
HONK
FUNG
HONK
HUH. NOT EXACTLY HOW I THOUGHT I'D BE SPENDING MY TIME WHEN LORI SAID SHE NEEDED ME.
END.